Also by Nora Johnson

Fiction

THE WORLD OF HENRY ORIENT (1958)

A STEP BEYOND INNOCENCE (1961)

LOVE LETTER IN THE DEAD-LETTER OFFICE (1966)

THE TWO OF US (1984)

TENDER OFFER (1985)

Nonfiction

PAT LOUD: A WOMAN'S STORY (1974)

FLASHBACK: NORA JOHNSON ON NUNNALLY JOHNSON (1979)

YOU CAN GO HOME AGAIN (1982)

Uncharted Places

Nora Johnson

SIMON AND SCHUSTER

New York London Toronto Sydney Tokyo

Simon and Schuster
Simon & Schuster Building
Rockefeller Center
1230 Avenue of the Americas
New York, New York 10020

Designed by Karolina Harris
Manufactured in the United States of America

1   3   5   7   9   10   8   6   4   2

Library of Congress Cataloging-in-Publication Data

Johnson, Nora.
Uncharted places / Nora Johnson.
p. cm.
I. Title.
PS3519.02833U53 1988
813'.54—dc19
88-18508 CIP

ISBN 0-671-66136-1

Uncharted Places

———

Dinah

We live on St. Petin, a tiny island in the blue Caribbean. We've been here for three months, and it's only recently that I've begun identifying with the Petinjans enough to say "we" about local matters, which implies we're here to stay. We avoid thinking very far ahead. Jason, our twelve-year-old, would never say it, and he's much more part of island life than Willy or me. We play at the word as we do about so many things. One of us drops it casually, darting a glance at the other, who pretends not to notice. Everything we do has become a sort of game as we circle each other, waiting to see what's going to happen next.

Willy wanted to live on a tropical island. The hot sun beating down, he said, the screams of tropical birds, the limpid and sparkling sea. And so when we had to make some kind of decision about the rest of our lives, it seemed, considering the choices, like the right thing to do. Now Conrad and Jessie, my stepchildren, have left to go back to college, leaving Willy, Jason, and me here to face each other.

We both swore we'd never talk about blame. But se-

cretly, under the masks we wear for the children, there's
plenty of it—though we know that the peculiar tricks of
the mind that have been our downfall can be blamed on no
one. This is harder for Willy to accept. Being a scientist,
he can't help searching for cause and effect, a scapegoat, a
source, somebody or something to point the finger at. That
there is none increases his frustration, and the disappointment comes off him almost like a smell.

Last night we were in bed reading. It was cool and lovely
the way it is after a rainstorm, and I felt peaceful lying there
between the white sheets, half dozing. But when I reached
over to touch Willy's arm holding his book, under the
brown, smooth skin and soft hair I know so well he was
tense and tight as a steel wire. And I realized that he hadn't
been reading at all, but had just been sitting like that for
half an hour without turning the page. He didn't look at
me or respond, just stared out the window as though hypnotized by the moonlight. Then, predictably, he said, "I've
got a rotten headache," and got up to get some Bufferin.
Once, a long time ago, I would have gotten it for him and
sat by him while he took it. Now, frozen, I did nothing at
all.

Before I get into what happened, which is a strange story
indeed, let me say that the way I see it, all marriages have
their problems and ours may not be any worse than the
others—which attitude is, in part, a result of life on St.
Pet's. The place has a smoothing effect, like a large steam
iron on the wrinkles of life. Nothing sticks up or down very
much. Different things become important here. The sparkle
of the sea and the day's catch. The way the beach looks first
thing in the morning, with the shadows of the sea grape
trees on the pink-white sand. The man with his cart and
horse selling breadfruit and plantains, ackee and callaloos
and pawpaws and limes, calling his two-note call. The nodding of the hibiscus against the stucco wall, the quick green
flash of a parrot fish sliding under the water. The thunder-
storms at dusk, the clickety-click of land crabs crossing the

tile floor. The sound of a boat's engine in the harbor at English Town, crossing the choppy path of the moon. The drums beating at night. These things are hypnotic. I find myself lying on the beach or the terrace for an hour doing nothing—having not read a page or thought a single thought or even moved a muscle, as still as the lizard who balloons his throat or the conch with its satiny pink lining. Then something in the air changes and I stiffen; I wait, listening, for some unannounced visitor who never arrives.

We've rented a house with a big verandah overlooking the sea, where we sit every night when Willy gets home, watching the sunset. On the beach side is a low stone balustrade, and since the beach here is used like a road, this is the way the house is usually approached. The verandah merges with the living room, extending out from the house and forming one large area comfortably furnished with wicker and canvas furniture. The primitive little kitchen is out in back. The bedrooms all open on to another verandah on the other side. Since there is no crime, people here don't close up their houses at night. So though we lock our bedroom doors, most of the house lies open day and night—a big stage facing the open sea.

The house comes with a staff of five—Winnie, Christophena, Regine, Eureka, and Lionel. It costs three hundred dollars a month. (Eureka is in charge of Charlotte, Willy's old mother.)

Before we came, I'd wondered about having all this help, which seems excessive now that the children are older. But when we got here, we found there was no way to rent a house without the four or five dusky people who came with it—unless we wanted to live in straw shacks like the Petinjans. So we've joined the colony of rootless refugees who live in the fancy villas on Yankee Beach, as our stretch of pearly sand is called, each hiding in its nest of oleander and bougainvillea and flanked by rustling coconut palms and sea grape.

So far we have only a cautious acquaintance with our

neighbors: the French family next door, the two gay British men, the American woman about my age (but oh, so different!) living with a sort of beachboy of twenty-five or so, the fiftyish woman living with, or married to, a very surly mulatto man, a scarred, mysterious older man living alone, and three women I haven't figured out—though Willy says they're Dutch. I suppose I imagined a clubby social life like the British had in India, but people here keep to themselves, hardly even smiling when we meet on the road. And yet I know we're being watched, as indeed I watch the French family walk up the road to church, and the grim scarred man leaning on his walking stick, and the two Englishmen with their collies. We all watch but don't meet —all guarding our secrets.

I thought of paying a call on the American woman with the beachboy. But I lost my nerve when I saw her sitting on her terrace without a top on and smoking a joint, jiggling around to music from headphones. Well, I'm pretty conventional.

Willy's clinic is in English Town, three miles down the road. English Town isn't particularly English but like everything else on St. Petin is a melting pot of many dregs of Western culture. Fishermen in wooden shoes speak fractured French and read *Penthouse*. Little girls in Charles and Diana T-shirts weave straw hats and sell ganja. When the cruise ships come in, motley groups of music makers appear: minstrels playing steel drums, mandolins, or harmonicas. The kids dance around in the dust and sing off-key while the tourists in white pants and alligator T-shirts stand around watching and throwing coins at their feet. Then the *Veendam* or the *QE 2* or whatever steams away, and everybody disappears and goes back to sleep.

The clinic is in a banana grove a couple of blocks inland, a stucco building deafeningly air-conditioned. The patients line up by eight o'clock with all their miseries—diarrhea, yaws, toothaches, syphilis, scorpion bites, worms and par-

asites, tumors, bleeding, blindness, madness, and now
AIDS. Willy shares the work with a one-eyed ex–Harley
Streeter named Mister Bagnold. Together they sew up
wounds, deliver babies, dole out quinine and Entero-Vi-
oform, lay on hands, comfort the dying. It's dogged, thank-
less, day-in, day-out work. But it's all right, Willy says
with a false smile. He's more essential than he used to be.
More in touch with real people. And he's still using his
hands, to push back an eyelid, to palpate an abdomen, to
lay on the head of a sick child—things he'd gotten so far
away from.

Just about a year ago, Willy was chief of his service at
New York's Episcopal Hospital. Head of the medical board,
professor and chairman of the department of surgery, author
of books and articles, and member of countless committees.
Medicine's bright star, who made a name for himself by
perfecting a technique for reconnecting severed limbs, digits, etc., with a wonderful adhesive of his own invention.
His specialty was the human hand.

I hate it when Willy lies, even when it's for my benefit.
He'd like me to think that he's happier here than he was
before in his high-powered life. But I know him too well.
He thrived on the work, the breakneck pace of hospital life,
the bizarre complexities of the medical establishment.
Nothing put him in better spirits than another intramural
shake-up; never was he better than with a new group of
dewy-eyed residents. In situations that would wilt other
men, Willy grew more alive, more potent, brave and cheerful. Power made him magnificent. His bright brown eyes,
his bristly tan hair, his tall straight body. His voice, like a
fine tenor instrument. His hands, the centers of his power:
they led him through his life like guide dogs.

The other night Willy dropped a glass. Not a big deal,
to drop your gin and tonic. Christophena came scooting out
with rags—"Oh now, do not move yourself, Mister Wakefield. I will tend to it," in her lovely singsong. But the kids

and I knew. None of us said a word, and Conrad's face had that stretched look it gets when he's miserable. And Jason, who inherited *my* klutzy hands, promptly spilled nuts all over the tile floor, where they bounced like jumping beans, Jason after them like a leggy grasshopper, leaping from squat to squat as if there weren't five people to pick up after him, as if it mattered at all.

It was the night before the older kids left. Willy said he'd heard something interesting at the clinic, that the grim scarred man across the way was an Auschwitz executioner wanted by some international tribunal for his crimes against humanity. He'd come in with a herpes infection, and Mister Bagnold, the Harley Streeter who for *his* secret reasons was no longer on Harley Street, happened to recognize him from pictures shown him by a friend who had survived Auschwitz.

This bit of gossip cheered Willy up a lot. Maybe he was starting to see a certain bizarre excitement in his present life: now he was a member of a shadowy underground of people whose pasts were more interesting than their presents. We had a spirited argument about what to do—turn him in or leave him alone. Conrad, high-strung and conscientious like his father, was for notifying the UN, Interpol, the Israeli Knesset, and the World Court. Jessie wanted to have him for drinks and "psych him out" so she could experience the mind of a murderer.

I said we should leave him alone, and Jason, after some hesitation, agreed—partly because I was purposely making sure he didn't really understand about Auschwitz. I hated the whole conversation anyway. Probably I overprotect him, but he's young and vulnerable, and it kills me to have him know about all the rotten things that go on.

Willy said, "Dinah, are you saying you wouldn't report an Auschwitz killer?"

"Maybe it's the wrong man."

"Suppose there's undeniable proof?" Willy demanded.

We looked at each other. "I'd leave him alone. He has his own nightmares."

"You have no sense of justice. You have a gap where most people have a conscience—a big white space."

"Regine," I called out, "how about some more rice? And salad?"

"Certainly, Mistress. Winnie has made a lovely pear salad for the children's last night." She meant avocado. As she spoke she looked at me with her dark lustrous eyes, giving a slight smile which Willy fortunately didn't notice. To his irritation, the Petinjans have a curious way of behaving as though they're in cahoots with me, which has been happening since the day we arrived. They're always giving me special protection: "You must not get too much sun, Mistress," and, "The woods are not safe for you at night." Jason gets some of this treatment but the others don't, which further divides our family. When I mention it they just smile and drop their eyes, as though I must know the answer already.

Jessie's fair skin was flushed as she scowled at me. "I wish you guys wouldn't argue."

"This isn't an argument, Jessie," Willy said. "Just an intellectual exchange." Conrad was staring at his plate. I wondered if it was like this with other couples. Everything means something else. Even the Auschwitz killer is a metaphor, as if he weren't metaphor enough already. Our marriage is like a big, heavy blanket that drops down and enfolds us, shutting out the children and the daylight and the world of reason. Underneath Willy and I swelter together in the dark.

To tell the truth, I was relieved when the older children left. Much as I love them (I brought them up from when they were small), they're not so easy to deal with these days. They handle their fear by picking on me. They don't approve of Jason's loose life, for instance, his evening trips to town on his dirt bike to hang out at a scummy little candy store, where one of the few TV sets on the island plays music from a Jamaican reggae station.

"Dinah, don't you know what he does down there?" Jessie complained. "He smokes dope. How can you let him?"

"Well, I can't tie him up. So he smokes a little ganja. I trust him."

"Dad's right. You're outside society." She'd had an after-dinner swim and she stood drying her mop of blond curls. Nervous about sharks, I'd watched her from the balustrade. Now she looked at me with her most high-minded expression. At seventeen she looks a lot like her mother, Liz. "He needs structure. He's going to turn into a little Petinjan."

"There are worse things."

"Then you guys will never come back." Her voice trembled.

"Of course we will." We didn't look at each other.

"Nothing's the way it used to be," Jessie said. "You used to be so, I don't know, calm and cheerful. Now you're as nervous and uptight as Dad."

Which means she doesn't trust me anymore, nor does Con—he overstayed his summer vacation by a week. Somehow what happened is my fault, and now they don't believe I'm going to take care of their father. Well, maybe they're right. My patience is running out. I'm tired of solving other people's problems and salving their hurt feelings. I'm even glad poor old Charlotte is in some world of her own.

The moon glinted on Jessie's hair. "I'm just saying this for your own good, Dinah. But ever since you got them back, you know, you've changed. And not for the better."

But I still cried at the airport the next day. How like Willy they were, she and Con, with their straight shoulders and square jaws, their brown eyes and pale curly hair. Their beautiful hands, their impossible standards, their view of life as a high-wire act. Jason is all mine. Long oval face, big hazel eyes, dark straight hair, currently long and shaggy.

Built like a scarecrow. Big feet, big toes that rise slightly. Under the suntan, a greenish complexion. Long tangly eye-lashes, big teeth. Me, turned into a young male, now rif-fling through a French girlie magazine at the newsstand. My little Petinjan.

After Air Petin's dinky toy of a plane had borne the older ones up into the blue sky, I grabbed Jason's hand and said, "Come on. It's just you and me now, kid."

"Thank God they're gone," he said as we went to the car, where Lionel was sleeping peacefully. I'd forgotten Lionel. Reveling in my new freedom, I said, "Lionel, I'll drive."

"Oh, Mistress. This car is very hard to steer."

"What's the matter with it? It's just a car."

"It has right-hand drive. You not used to."

"I'll get used to."

"Oh, but Mistress Wakefield. Not licensed for you. Only chauffeur license. If policeman see you drive, he'll give you ticket. Maybe put in jail."

"But I've seen other foreigners driving."

"Only with special license, obtainable through district court in English Town. Must have permission from con-stabulary and ombudsman, and perhaps special meeting of electoral college of third arrondissement."

"Oh, Lionel! Honestly!"

"Oh, very true, Mistress. Perhaps a meeting of Parlia-ment." His eye caught mine and he slowly shook his head, and Jason and I got into the back seat.

St. Pet's has more government bodies than all the major powers put together. Everybody wants a title, which usually means a uniform or at least a satin chest-ribbon in red or royal blue. If they don't want you to do something, forget it—you'll be old and grizzled before all the committees meet, which they only do at tax and aid time, so there's always a ton of backup agenda. If they want you to do something, however, the machinery can move with breath-taking speed. It took Willy one day to get a permit to practice medicine, because they desperately needed a doctor. His training and certification were of but mild interest, and nobody even asked about his reasons for leaving his last post.

St. Pet's doesn't want me to drive, it seems, or do anything else much, and my early resolutions to explore the island and study the local culture are fading fast. Now that Con and Jessie are gone, I sleep a lot—sometimes in one of the lounge chairs, sometimes after lunch on our bed with Willy, the white cloud of mosquito netting hanging over us in a huge floating knot. I drift off as I hear Regine washing up in the kitchen, but as soon as Willy leaves for the clinic, around three, I wake up.

Though we came here to forget, in the heat and silence of these afternoons memories crowd into my mind in such quantity that I wonder if they even fit; it seems they might spill over and get lost, and most of the time I wish they would. My life marches by like a speeded-up movie I've seen a hundred times. I look again at all my mistakes, though there's no way to change them now. Willy says our troubles come from our imperfect childhoods, which make us ill-equipped to give and receive intimacy.

But I'm tired of that facile explanation of the world's woes. It's something else, though I'm not sure what. Once I was happy, when we were first married and Jason was small; now it's irretrievably gone. Instead there's a weight on me, a force pushing me down, an obsession with long-gone events, long-dead people—even more hateful because I was spared it for so long. Now I'm hopeless, turning and twisting through endless nights full of questions. And more and more often I ask that dark question, which I never would have before: Is this all there is?

Willy

___

'm Willard Hartley Wakefield, M.D., P.C., 825 Park
Avenue, New York City 10021. Forty years old, six foot
one inch tall, 170 pounds. Attending physician at New
York's Episcopal Hospital and Medical College, professor of
the department of surgery, head of the medical board,
member of the board of trustees. Educated at Lawrenceville
School, Yale, and Harvard Medical School. Internship and
residency at New York Hospital, national and state board-
certified. Teaching fellow at Presbyterian Hospital. Surgical
specialty: the hand. Articles in *AMA Journal, International
Journal of Surgery, World Journal of Hand Surgery,* and other
distinguished professional periodicals, the most accessible
of which are "Techniques in Wrist Restringing: Tendon
Overlapping, Topping's Technique, Vein Exclusion"; "The
Nail: Some Considerations of the Cuticle"; "Analunacy
(Missing Moons)"; and "Some Thoughts on Knuckle
Matching." My book, *The Hand—Miracle of Twenty-Seven
Bones,* will be published by Basic Books in the spring.

Marriage to Elizabeth Flanders ended in divorce. Two
children: Conrad Peabody and Jessica Marie. One son, Jason
Hartley, by my present wife, Dinah Jones Wakefield. I

reside at 19 West Seventy-eighth Street, New York 10024, with my wife, three children, and mother, Charlotte Peabody Wakefield.

I started out as a general surgeon, but it wasn't long before I knew that it wasn't for me. I haven't got the stomach for it. A certain expression comes over Mac Valpey's face whenever he's operating. I notice it every time I scrub for him. Now Mac is one of the best; I'd do anything for the guy. We were residents together. But something weird comes over him. He bloats up and gets red; you can even see it over the mask. His eyes sparkle.

"I get excited," he said when I told him. "I'm just about to lift out a piece of person. I should be bored?"

Well, *chacun à son goût,* as they say! To me there's nothing more thrilling than that mighty instrument, the human hand. It hasn't been replaced yet and never will be. Microsurgery: the wonderful world of split nerve ends, tiny fractures of the phalanges, displaced capillaries, the complex implantation of the nail. It's as beautiful as a Beethoven sonata.

I chose surgery because it's so neat, quick, and complete. You make a cut and there it is. You can tell a lot about a physician from the specialty he chooses. Urology speaks for itself. So does psychiatry. The whole surgical scene suits me. I go in, the patient's draped, the instruments are sterilized and ready, the team's waiting for me to tell them what to do. I don't mind being a star!

It may look easy, but it's dependent on a fail-safe backup system. A good scrub nurse is a jewel. The anesthesiologist —there's only one at Episcopal I'll use. (Now there's a field for those hospital-investigation jokers. I know of five anesthesia deaths that have been covered up by the hospital, two because the anesthetist was high from sniffing his own stuff.) The O.R. and the equipment have to be exactly right. It all has to be choreographed. I've seen lives lost because some little detail was wrong and the surgeon went

crazy. Mac Valpey came unwound when his favorite scrub
nurse was out with cramps and they gave him another one.
It bothered him; he began making mistakes during a perfectly routine subtotal gastrectomy. The new nurse gave
him a couple of wrong instruments, and when he spoke to
her about it, she said that was the way Dr. So-and-so did it
—a guy he happens to hate. It was all downhill after that.
The patient, a sixty-two-year-old male, died on the table of
cardiac arrest. They investigated and couldn't really pin it
down, but Mac knew it had gone on too long and the man
couldn't take it. Mac still has the shadow of Mr. Morales
over him.

"You watch," he said. "It'll happen to you. You'll lose
your virginity. That's life and death out there, Willy."

"That's what we signed up for."

"Well, you and that ditsy Goldstein dance around keeping your hands clean. You're low-risk and you know it."

To Mac, being high-risk is all tied up with his macho.
And Bill Goldstein, for God's sake, is a plastic surgeon. He
has a co-op on Fifth Avenue and a farm in the Berkshires
and a condo in Florida. Ellen Goldstein is wrinkle-free and
drives around town in a Mercedes. That little clinic in the
Bahamas doesn't hurt, either. Well, I don't begrudge him
his success, except it's beclouded his brain. Once after a few
drinks he said, "Do we really need all our fingers, Willy?
Come on, admit that your digit procedure is a nicety, one
step from cosmetic surgery"—his euphemism for what he
does.

That didn't even deserve an answer, but I reminded him
that if it weren't for the opposable thumb we'd all still be
swinging from trees. The truth is they're both jealous. Wait
till Goldstein makes a mistake, an eyelid won't close or
something like that. Then we'll see who's giving the party.

The life of a successful man is a little like an operation—
it needs a perfect backup system. I've had some personal
difficulties. My first wife, Poor Liz, went psychotic when

the kids were small. She was in and out of hospitals for almost two years. I watched the person I loved disintegrate in front of me. My life was a nightmare of trying to cope with her, finding people to watch the kids and take care of the house, and keeping on top of professional obligations. I'll probably never get over it . . . and to be honest I don't think I'll ever forgive her. I know how that sounds. But it hurt too much.

After the divorce things weren't much better. Other women didn't last long; I couldn't give them enough attention. The beeper would go off just as the martinis arrived, and that would be the end of the evening, especially after I was on the hospital board. What I didn't tell my dates was that half the time it wasn't a medical emergency, it was Mother reporting some domestic catastrophe or else a call from some crazed doctor or hospital official yelling about imaginary threats to his money or power. Women are less than interested in all this.

But Dinah's different. There's no side to her; she just takes things the way they are. She's cheerful and serene. Poor Liz used to be miserable because nothing was turning out the way it was supposed to. From the day Dinah moved in, everything worked better. She absorbs tensions and anxieties like a sponge. The kids love her. For the first time in years I could relax, knowing things were being taken care of at home. My children would be safe; things would be in order. She could even handle Mother. We began entertaining and going to dinners and parties. Dinah learned how to dress and talk to people. I wouldn't call her a world-beater of a conversationalist. Nor is she a brilliant intellect. I know some compare her to Liz, who was Sparkle Plenty before she went around the bend. But I've had enough sparkle, I want some peace. Dinah provides that and more.

She's made me a happy man. Still, there's always a kvetch around. The other day that little prick Mike Portoff, who's angling for my post on the medical board, made some provocative remark about my wife's "past." (Chris Portoff and Dinah were roommates for a while, and she got me and Dinah together.) I told him any more cracks like that and I'd make sure he lost his admitting privileges. And maybe sue him for slander. Past—my butt! That's just what she *doesn't* have! What life she has I gave her, and we've agreed to forget the rest. Because Dinah doesn't remember a damn thing that happened to her before June 6, 1969, when she was—we think—twenty-three years old.

Dinah

I was born on Lexington and Fifty-ninth, in front of the
subway station across from Bloomingdale's. Willy likes
to say I was disgorged from the depths of the earth by
some gigantic IRT birth pain. But it was more that I faded
in, like a person in an old movie. First I wasn't there and
then I was!

I first saw myself in a coffee shop mirror. Could that
scarecrow be me? Cuts and bruises everywhere, a dirty yellow T-shirt and jeans, an old gray sweatshirt tied around
my waist. I looked as though I hadn't had a bath for a week.
Dark messy hair, big frightened eyes. I didn't know who I
was, where I was, how I got there. I reached into my pocket
and found a few dollars but no identification.

I never really told Willy how I was then. Cuts, gashes,
dried blood flaking into dirty old sneakers. I didn't know
what was wrong with me. My mind was gone; it didn't
work. Everything looked strange, as though seen through a
gauze. The shops on the street—a bakery, a fancy restaurant, a Chinese laundry—were veiled in dreamlike unreal-
ity. And yet it was all at the tip of my tongue, as though it
had just slipped my mind, the way a friend's name does

sometimes when you're about to introduce her. Everything was like that until the amnesia kind of settled down and jelled. But at first it drove me crazy.

I was frightened to death.

I had to find clues—a sign, a face, a street that looked familiar. A newspaper headline or magazine cover might do it. I tapped at that closed door in my mind, pried at it experimentally, pulled it, tried to kick it down. I walked past a hairdresser and a deli, an apartment building, a supermarket, a window full of bathtubs with golden swan faucets. A mountain of stuffed green plastic bags, a white truck full of plants, a man with long golden hair. I went back into the subway and got into a train, but when I saw the graffiti and those numb, staring faces I started to cry. Nobody paid any attention to me.

Willy once called me Rip Van Winkle (one of the rare times he mentions it, much less jokes), but I had no points of reference—no friends with whitened hair or a boarded-up house. He'll never understand what it was like those few days when I was born and traveled around the world, chasing my lost memory like a runaway dog, living like a tramp, because I had no place to go.

Through the Village, Chinatown, along the wharves on the river I tracked it. Sometimes I ate something from a street vendor, a hot dog here, an egg roll there. I thought a taste might open the trap, or the way something felt or smelled—the texture of brick, the smell of diesel fuel, the sun on my back as I lay in Washington Square. Or a sound —a child's cry or the flute being played by a Christ-like person nearby. History I remembered, but not my own.

I was haunted, though by what I couldn't say. Memory seems too narrow a word. I had no sense of self, no consciousness, but still felt naked and exposed, as though everyone who saw me must know. Something enormous lay behind that closed door. (But even when you remember the friend's name, and introduce her, there's a terrible feeling

of letdown, as though you'd been tapping on the door of
God's house and all you got was Mary Ann.) All along the
way were little teasing bits of false excitement. Something
about a Hasidic Jew behind his window on Orchard Street
. . . the tone of his skin, the wooden windowsill. I'd been
there before. But it slipped away. The East River at night,
the chips of light on the choppy water, made my heart beat
faster. Why did I remember it? The familiarity and frustration made me want to cry. Oh, I was always so close to
something I couldn't have!

The first night I slept in Central Park. And the second
too. I was such a mess even the rapists didn't bother with
me. The next night I stayed at a dumpy hotel on Fifty-
ninth Street. They didn't want to let me in, but I showed
them my money and the man took me to a room. When I
woke up it was barely light. I went into the bathroom and
looked at myself in the mirror—a filthy, demented-looking
witch, with puffy eyes peering out of a dirty and bruised
face. When I took my clothes off to bathe, my body
frightened me—gashes on my legs and rib cage, yellow-
green bruises on my chest and arms. But as I sat there on
the lumpy bed, slowly drying myself, I realized that *I could
remember everything that had happened since I came out of the
subway.*

It took a moment for the importance of this to sink in.
Then I sat there on the bed, laughing crazily. No wonder
newborns cried. No wonder it took weeks for them to smile!
You have to create your self, to exist in your own mind! I
had three whole days that were mine, and now I was real.

Gradually I began to grasp what was wrong with me. I
probably wasn't crazy, as I'd feared. I was untied, or uncon-
nected—an astronaut whose tether has come undone, who
floats, doomed, away from his ship. I seemed to have no
mother or father, no husband or lover or children, friends,
even a pet; no home, town, city, or continent; only three
days of experience. I knew that every hour I could remember
was strength, which was why I'd been wolfing down every-

thing around me like a starving person. Very slowly I
understood that I must have existed before, had a whole life
somewhere. But curiously enough, the more time that
passed, the less interested I was in finding it. This fresh
new life had more magic.

Late the next afternoon I was on a pretty, tree-lined street
on the East Side, staring into somebody's kitchen. It was
dusk, the lights were just going on; the place was so familiar, and so appealing, that I'd stopped to admire it—the
black stove, the copper pots and hanging plants, the cat on
the windowsill made me feel sad, almost desperate, though
whether from some lost memory or just hopeless envy, I
didn't know. Then the people inside, a woman and a child,
began making faces and shooing me away, and in a moment
a man in a brown uniform appeared and wanted to know
what I was doing. I tried to sound normal, though when he
found I didn't even know my own name, he got suspicious.

We attracted a small audience. Several people drifted
over and began listening, including a ragged old woman
with two stuffed shopping bags and a woman in blue jeans
with white hair. She noticed the charm bracelet I was wearing.

"Dinah," she said. "Your name must be Dinah." So they
all got into it. I went through my pockets again. A wadded-
up list, which looked as though it had been through the
laundry: beer, bread, orange juice, Prell, hamburger, broc-
coli, Cokes. "Call G." The stub of a Greyhound bus ticket,
origin illegible, destination New York. A message from a
fortune cookie: "A journey will bring you lifelong happiness." A couple of movie ticket stubs. A slender young man
with a dog said he thought I had amnesia. "Man, it's *Random Harvest!*"

The woman in the house, safe in the presence of the law,
called from the window, "This poor girl needs medical care.
She's in a terrible situation. Dinah, can't you remember
anything?"

"Nothing, I told you."

"Do you have any friends or any place to go?" the guard asked.

"No."

There was a rather spirited debate about what to do with me. The lady in pink said from the window that she'd take me in, except her husband might not like it, and both the dog owner and the white-haired woman offered to take me in, as though I were a stray kitten. The guard pressed his beeper.

"This is a case for the police. They'll find out where you belong fast enough."

"Oh, shit," said the shopping bag woman. "She's simple. Leave her alone. She ain't do nothin'."

"Don't you want to go home, Dinah?"

"No," I said. Why should I exchange my three precious days for a big blank?

"You've scared her," said the white-haired woman. "She's in no condition to be dragged to police headquarters and questioned like a criminal. Dinah, come with me. I'll keep you for a few days, and then we can figure out what to do next." She seemed nice enough, and her face looked younger than her hair suggested, though I wished she wouldn't stare at me so hard.

At that moment a police car turned up the street, and before they could stop me I turned and ran without looking back. I tried to run faster as I heard the car motor behind me, but my leg was hurting badly, and as I started to slow down the car screeched to a stop and a cop got out and grabbed me in a sort of flying tackle. I began to scream, and the cop said, "Hey, lady, I'm not going to hurt you. Hey, calm down, will you?" Defeated, I burst into tears. Worse, the white-haired woman arrived panting.

"Officer, give her to me. I'm her sister Sal. Dinah, come home with me and you can have a nice rest."

For all I knew it was true, but I didn't trust her. "I won't go with you. I'm all confused, and I'm afraid of *losing my*

mind!" I screamed, causing them all to fall back in alarm.
"If I go completely psycho it's your fault, all of you—*your
fault!*"

With little preliminary, the cop hustled me into the
patrol car next to his pal. "You're going to the hospital,
baby. Nobody goes psycho on me," and we drove off, leaving Sister Sal on the sidewalk. Then they had an argument
about where to take me; one said Bellevue, but the other,
Gil, said he wouldn't put a dog in that place, much less a
nice young lady like me, and anyway I didn't seem so much
crazy as scared and battered up, and it was anybody's guess
how I got that way. They brought me into some emergency
room, a very crowded, noisy place, and deposited me in a
chair.

"Just sit here, sweetheart. They'll take care of you. Then
in a few days, after you've had a little rest, you'll come
down to the nineteenth precinct and ask for Gil, okay?
Meanwhile we'll send the story out on AP and UP, okay?"
—snapping a couple of Polaroid pictures. "Now take care.
Have a good day, baby."

Fear crept up my spine. I didn't like this place at all. It
was full of dead-faced mothers, crawling, crying children,
and spavined old men. Three more policemen brought in a
handcuffed man with blood running down his face, followed
by a staggering woman in a bathrobe who kept saying,
"Coo, coo! Where are you? Help me, coo!"

A hawk-faced woman next to me said, "Christ, I'm sick
of junkies. Fucking sick of 'em." She had copper ringlets
and a purple mouth. "I've never done smack and I never
will. Now that one's full of it, I can tell."

I asked, "What's smack?"

"Smack is horse, darling. And it's slow suicide. I've seen
it again and again. I hope you never fool around with it."

"Oh, I wouldn't."

"What's wrong with you, anyway? Get beaten up?" She
was smiling through missing teeth.

I got up. "I'm leaving this place." The woman in the bathrobe had started to cry quietly, saying, "Coo, coo. You promised you'd come. Please, coo." I was afraid they'd put me in some kind of crazy ward.

"Better go home, sweetheart," said my companion. "Hospitals make you sicker."

As she began laughing, I got up and went toward the door where I'd come in. I saw Gil and Mel standing by the reception desk joking with the nurse, and I tried to get past them. What happened next is a little confused. I guess I tried to make a break for it, and Mel saw me and yelled, "Hey, where do you think you're going?"

Then I got scared and ran for the door, and a couple of guys in white clothes appeared, doctors I suppose, and I guess I got really scared and went crazy. Then somebody stuck a needle into me, and everything went blank again.

In spite of the bad beginning, I enjoyed my stay at the hospital. I didn't even mind that they poked and prodded, tapped my knees and had me play number and word games. What mattered was that I had a bed and three meals a day, and that I remembered every single thing since I'd faded in.

Dr. Portoff, who was in charge of me, explained that they didn't get their hands on a genuine amnesiac every day.

"You're reasonably intelligent," he said. "Most of the interesting psychoses turn up in inarticulate morons." He was short and fat, with a mustache, black eyes, and tiny hands and feet. He'd perch on the windowsill and cross his fat little arms and legs. He told me that since I remembered everything since I'd come to, I was capable of learning. "If you weren't, you could end up in the dippy ward, picking at your gown for the next twenty years." Besides him, there was Dr. Mood, a neurologist who scraped the soles of my

feet with a pin, and Dr. Liverwood, a psychiatrist, who
wanted me to free-associate. He talked about hypnotizing
me and giving me something called an Amytal interview to
bring back my memories—which I was more and more
determined to avoid.

I was never bored. I had plenty to think about, even if
my life was only a week long. After dinner I'd sit on the
windowsill and look out at the dark river and the city lights
through my own translucent reflection. I read newspapers
and books from the Gray Lady's cart till the snack nurse
came by with her apple juice and graham crackers. Her
name was Bonnie and she lived on Staten Island. "Listen,
Dinah, I wouldn't mind having a bop on the head myself."
Her husband had left her with two little kids and her
mother had Parkinson's disease. She talked to me because I
was the only one on the floor who wasn't terrified, dying,
in intractable pain, or drugged to incoherency. After she
went I'd lie in the dark and listen to the squeak-squeak of
the night nurses' shoes on the floor of the hallway. Sometimes I'd hear my doctors' names over the page system, like
guardian angels: "Doctor Portoff Doctor Michael Portoff
pick up please pick up Doctor Liverwood Doctor Frank
Liverwood please pick up . . . Doctor Wakefield Doctor
Willard Wakefield . . ."

I told Willy later I heard his name on the page, and I'm
almost sure I did. It was as though we passed in the night.

I shared the room with an old lady named Janet, who
told me her troubles with her children. One never phoned
her. Another was very mean and sarcastic, and the third
never brought the grandchildren for a visit. She told me
how happy life had been when they were small, how loving
and affectionate they'd been, how devoted her dead husband. When I told her what was the matter with me, she
said she envied me having nothing to remember, because it
must make the present easier to bear.

It made me really think about the whole business of

going back, which they all, the psychiatrist included, thought I should do. But the residue of my past life wasn't too appealing—a lot of cuts and bruises and some cheap clothes and a grocery list. If I wasn't actually a criminal— a murderess or thief or drug smuggler—there was the danger of being claimed by whatever husband, lover, or father had beaten me up or smashed up the car or thrown me over a cliff. At most my past life seemed dreary and charmless, my concerns centering around movies, the supermarket, and fortune cookies. I'd probably come from some dull place which paled beside what I saw out my window every night, the city lights of Manhattan piled before me like jewels. I suspected that there was a reason for all this. I'd just taken off and left that past life, and then forgotten it. Happy people didn't do things like that. The odds were that through a remarkable piece of good fortune, I'd been given a second chance.

After I'd been there a few days, the white-haired woman in blue jeans walked into my room.

"Remember me, Dinah? I'm Sister Sal."

"You're the one that chased me up the street," I said. I didn't trust her, and I stayed in bed with the covers pulled up to my chin.

"I was trying to save you from the police." She sat on the end of the bed and lit a cigarette.

"That's not the way I remember it."

She laughed. "Well, sweetie, your memory's a little, um, skewed, isn't it?"

I didn't like her sense of humor either. "I think you'd better leave."

"Just give me five minutes. I promise you won't regret it."

She was a writer, she said, and she wanted to write "my story." She would follow me around with a tape recorder and document my memory as it returned. This was a miraculous opportunity. I was Cinderella, Rip Van Winkle, the Three Faces of Eve. I was hot. I'd just have to take her word for it, she had terrific credentials. With her reputation and my story, we were talking six-figure advance plus first serial rights, paperback, and feature film, or at least a TV movie. And it was a natural for a sitcom!

"Think of what's happening to you, Dinah. You're a chrysalis!"

I didn't really understand what she was talking about, so I said no.

She scrunched out her cigarette. "So you have other plans?"

"Well, I hadn't really thought about it. I suppose I'll look for an apartment, and a job, of course. And try to meet some people."

She smiled. "Well, good luck. It isn't easy." She took out a silver pen and wrote something on a card. "In case you change your mind." Then she turned and left quickly, her short cap of silver hair shining as she walked down the hall.

I hadn't really thought much about the future. It was as big a blank as the past, but I knew I had to make some plans. *It isn't easy,* she'd said. New York, in my brief experience, had not been a friendly place. In fact there had been times when I'd been lucky to survive. I should probably find a job first. I could serve drinks at a bar or take care of somebody's children. Maybe I could be a telephone operator. I'd find a place to live, and meet people through my job. Eventually it would all fall into place.

I'd half forgotten about it when, a day or two later, Portoff came in and perched on the end of the bed, like a little Buddha.

"Well, Dinah. We've just about shot our wad here. I'm discharging you in a day or so."

I clutched the covers tighter. Now that the moment was at hand I was frightened to death. "But Dr. Portoff . . ."

He flipped through pages on his clipboard. "Positive

Babinski. Corneal cortex receding. Pathogenic clouds in the
left ocular field. Vitamin deficiency in the spinal fluid,
seizure pattern in the EEG. Rorschach, IQ, Wechsler,
MMPI. There's nothing wrong with you."

"But I have no place to go. No money. No job . . ." I
knew I sounded like a baby, but I didn't want to end up
sleeping in the park again.

"And of course you don't have your memory. These are
perfectly valid problems, Dinah. And it's crucial that you
keep going to Frank Liverwood because only he has the key.
As for the practical matters, well, what about the woman
who wants to write the book?"

"I don't like her."

At this Portoff hopped off the bed, pursed his lips, and
looked at me. "I see. Do you have something else in mind?"

"No."

"Well, there's an old saying, Beggars can't be choosers.
We can't keep you here forever; we need the bed."

He zipped off just as Sister Sal had. As soon as I said no
they raced out the door. But what else was I to do? It was a
bad evening—the worst I'd had, and I couldn't even talk
to Janet because they'd taken her to surgery and removed
half her stomach, and when they brought her back she
might as well have been dead. And not one of those shitty
children of hers turned up. I sat by Janet's bed, looking at
her poor old white face, occasionally reaching over to
smooth back her hair. Next time anybody asked something
of me, I'd better say yes.

To my untutored eye, Christine Rappaport's apartment was
dazzling. It had a white fur rug, flowered wallpaper, and
little velvet chairs that might have belonged to the Seven
Dwarfs. Little tinkly lamps with pink shades sat on mirror
tables with silver-framed pictures, including one of Portoff
in his white coat and one of Christine in a bikini. A white

love seat with a big fat rose embroidered on each pillow. A taffy-colored kitty-cat that hated me on sight, but possibly only because it had been forever consigned to wearing a lavender velvet collar with a pearly buckle.

In the bedroom, a double bed with a dozen or so ruffly pillows on it, a canopy, and a satin pouf. Nearby a velvet chaise longue and a dressing table with an organdy skirt, where Christine sat and blow-dried her tiny golden curls. A collection of little china dogs, a cute little Sony TV, which I watched in the afternoon.

And Christine herself: much smaller than me, hardly five feet, and all curvy and wiggly. Tits always half hanging out or vividly outlined. Too-short skirts that cupped her behind, and when she sat down her silky panty hose slithered audibly as she kicked off her shoes and crossed her legs. A voice like cake icing, big wet blue eyes. A way of scratching her crotch when she was thoughtful, the way some scratch their heads.

This was Portoff's girlfriend, who had bewitched him so he had to struggle to concentrate on medicine, which was why I was there at all. With her, he turned from a cartoon into a man. That she pulled back just a little spurred him on. "Oh, Michael," she'd purr. "Do you really think so? Do you really want to? Oh, honestly, Michael, I just don't know." And Portoff grew strong and purposeful. "Chrissie darling, I know I'm right. Just listen to me. I've thought it all through. It's going to work, sweetheart." And she'd say, "But Michael, what about so-and-so? I just don't know, I honestly don't. It sounds so cra-a-a-zy." He'd get manly and commanding, giving her a kiss, saying, "Just leave everything to me, my love. It's going to work out fine."

It was remarkable how many things this conversation could apply to. Any plan or suggestion could start them off, from putting onion in the tuna to getting married to moving me in. Through life's difficult passages Portoff led, persuaded, and cajoled his Christine, while she hung back, pouted, scratched her crotch.

She was only nineteen, he'd explained to me, and had led a very protected life. And never in a thousand years would her parents in Scarsdale approve of her living with somebody she wasn't married to. So she kept her apartment, which she was hardly ever in, being, of course (self-conscious laugh), with him. But her parents were beginning to think it was funny that she was never home, and that was where I came in. I could be Chrissie's roommate! I could live here for nothing for a while, because Mr. Rappaport paid the rent, and all I had to do was answer the phone and when the parents asked for Chris, say she was at the supermarket or the movies or something, then give Chris the message later.

Portoff had gotten this inspiration the day before I was to be discharged, at which point I was considering faking insanity so they'd have to keep me there. As he sat on the windowsill outlining his plan, he'd never looked so happy. It would work out perfectly for all of us. I could stay there and practice typing, or whatever I thought necessary to make myself employable. I could learn to cook, and he was sure I wouldn't mind keeping the place in order as a little repayment for this favor. Of course continue my "therapy." And hey, here was an idea. Chris would see if they needed another waitress at the place where she worked.

I said yes. I didn't even think.

At first Chris and Portoff, freed from worry, virtually disappeared. Every morning at nine thirty or so Mrs. Rappaport called.

"Who's this?"

"I'm Dinah, Chrissie's roommate." (I had to tell her every time.)

"Oh, yes, Dinah. Will she be back soon?"

"She just ran over to Bloomingdale's, Mrs. Rappaport. She should be back in an hour."

"I wonder what she went there for. They're so rude and snippy. In an hour. You wouldn't happen to know what she went there for, would you?"

"Oh, I think she said shoes. She mentioned a sale."

"I told her not to get shoes there. It's the worst place in town for shoes. Did she say what kind?"

"What kind. Let's see. I think black ones. Or maybe brown."

"She's got black ones, both leather and suede. And the old patent leather. She must have said brown."

"Well, actually, I think she did. She was in kind of a hurry."

"Oh, she was? What for?"

"I'm not sure. She might have mentioned meeting someone."

"Oh, really. Did she say whom?"

I'd hang up in a cold sweat and phone Chrissie.

"You went to Bloomingdale's for shoes, because there's a big sale going on. Then you met somebody for lunch."

"Oh, God, Dinah. If she looks in the paper and finds out there's no shoe sale, I'll have to explain. Can't you be more vague?"

"I can't help it. She pumps me. I thought I was supposed to be friendly."

Now that I think back on it, Christine treated me like a rather slow-witted servant. Not that I was aware of it. I was too inexperienced, too stunned by the world's complexity, too busy trying to understand each puzzling, frightening day. Now I had to take care of myself. I was grateful, certainly, to be taken in, and I did my best—the housework that was part of the deal, and those infernal phone conversations. But the days were long. I had no more money, and even if I had, I wouldn't have known what to do with it. I walked around the neighborhood; I watched television; I read Chrissie's magazines. I let in the exterminator, the dry cleaner, and United Parcel. At night I slept in Chrissie's bed among the lacy pillows.

She came every couple of days to change, dumping her soiled clothes in the hamper or on the floor.

"Dinah, would you mind horribly doing the wash? I mean, it would give you something to occupy your time. And do you remember how to iron?" Sometimes she sat down for a cup of tea, which I looked forward to, for I was very lonely.

"I didn't know you'd be here so little." I must have sounded pathetic.

"Oh, well, neither did I. But I'm trying to see what it's like really living with Michael. Which I wouldn't be doing if I were running over here all the time, would I?" She was sprawled on the velvet love seat in her bra and pants. "I don't suppose you know anything about men. Or living with one. I mean even if you did, you don't remember."

"No."

"Oh, well. I just wonder if it's always like this. I mean, I know he's busy. I know he's practically married to that hospital. But he's a slob, leaving things all over the place and expecting me to pick up after him." In the next breath —"Christ, I have to get to Snapper's" (the restaurant). "I'll just put these things in the sink, and you can do them later when you do the dinner dishes, okay?"

One day I brought up the money problem. My jeans and T-shirt were getting weak and threadbare from being washed so often, and my Keds were starting to split. Chrissie couldn't help. She was much smaller than me, and she didn't have much money either. Daddy paid the rent and the utilities and Bloomingdale's, inspecting the bills closely. Her earnings from the waitress job barely covered food and transportation and extras. When she gave me ten dollars one day I was touched, because I knew how little money she had.

She tried Portoff. "Michael, can't you give Dinah some money? She's sick to death of those old clothes."

Portoff looked from her to me to her again. "Dinah

doesn't want handouts. They're degrading. She wants to stand on her own feet. Don't you, Dinah?"

"Sure," I said. The conversation took place as we stood by the door, Portoff and Chrissie being on their way out to dinner. After almost two weeks there, we had never sat down to talk like three ordinary people—though I was, of course, not an ordinary person. Negotiations were always on the run, as Portoff and Chrissie were always on their way somewhere. "Of course I do, Dr. Portoff . . . Mike." I was supposed to call him Mike. "It's just that, well, I need toothpaste and stuff," I mumbled, hating the whole conversation. "If I could borrow some from you, I could pay it back after I'm working."

He gave me a baleful look, dug out two twenties, and put them on the little glass table, as though to neutralize this distasteful act.

"Mi-chael, don't be so mean to Dinah," said Christine as they went out the door. "How's she going to learn to be nice, if we don't show her?"

Then one inevitable morning Mrs. Rappaport arrived, not much bigger than Chrissie, splendid in beige linen.

"You must be Dinah. I'm Christine's mother." She came in, peeling off her gloves. Who was I again? From where? Doing what? I mumbled manufactured lies. I made myself a twenty-three-year-old (Portoff's assessment) divorcée from Colorado. Poor old Janet had come from there, and she'd told me a little about it. I had no children. I was starting again in a new place.

Over coffee, Mrs. Rapp inspected me. Though polite, she wasn't sure I was a suitable roommate for Christine. Divorcées were freer about certain things. Did I know Michael? Did Michael ever—ah—spend the night? They'd prepared me for that one.

"Oh, never, Mrs. Rappaport."

Mrs. Rapp leaned forward and dropped her voice as though the walls had ears. "Her father would be simply furious, Miss Jones, if anything like that were going on. He'd cancel the lease here and send her right back to Mount Holyoke. You understand." And, as she left, "I'll be dropping by from time to time. I'm taking a course at the Metropolitan Museum."

On the heels of this killing test in human negotiation came Daddy Rappaport, who did everything but go through the drawers. He was fiercer, and in my nervousness I made a mistake.

"She does not work on Thursdays. She told her mother she had Thursdays off. So why am I not hearing the truth?"

"To tell the truth, I don't know exactly where she is."

"You live with her and you don't know where she goes?"

"But I don't know where she is every minute, Mr. Rappaport!"

"I called the restaurant and they said she wasn't there. So why isn't she here?"

"*I don't know,*" I said, and might have burst into tears if Christine hadn't walked in at that moment.

"Daddy! What a surprise!"

"Damn right it's a surprise. There's going to be more surprises here too."

"What's wrong?" She glanced at me in frightened suspicion.

"Your father got a little upset when you weren't here, Chris."

But now Mr. Rapp had a big smile. "Disappointed, Miss Jones, is all, not to see my little girl." To Chris he said, "We have to have a little talk now, darling. If Miss Jones will leave the room."

Chrissie said to me imperiously, "Please excuse us, Dinah."

The upshot was that Mr. Rappaport was ready to break her neck, not for the first time, or else take her home to Scarsdale, threats Portoff took more seriously than Chrissie did.

"Chris, you've got to move back."

"Oh, Mi-chael, do you really think so?"

"We have no choice, darling. I'll leave my clothes at home but stay for the night. Dinah can sleep on the Hide-A-Bed."

The decision was made as usual by the front door, and they both turned and looked at me as he said it. "You won't mind, Dinah. I sleep there myself sometimes. And we'll all be perfectly private and cozy."

"Now Dinah, be sure and take down phone messages carefully," said Portoff. "Write them down so you don't forget them."

"You know where the clean sheets are," caroled Chrissie, as they slammed their way out.

There was a faint silver lining to their presence. Sometimes I worried about being dull and naive, a person without references or resonance, a flat person with no echoes. But if the conversation of these two was any example of ordinary human exchange, I had little to worry about.

"Michael, look what he did to my hair." "It looks great, sweetheart." "Great? It's ghastly. He practically gave me a crew cut. When I looked in the mirror I almost cried. God, can't you tell?" "No—er—yes. It'll grow out. Christ, I'm tired." "You're always tired. I don't think you eat right. You shouldn't eat that stuff from vending machines." "I'm tired because I work hard, Chrissie. It has nothing to do with vending machines." "Oh, but it does, sweetheart. I was reading an article in *Mademoiselle*." "I'm a doctor, Chris. I know all about the human body. And you quote from *Mademoiselle*." "If you're so smart about health, why don't you take care of yourself, then? How can you eat those chocolate doughnuts for breakfast?" "Well, because I like them, that's why. Anyway, there's never anything else around here." "That's not true, Michael. There's always fruit and bread. There's cottage cheese and eggs." "Well, I can't find it. I have ten minutes to eat and I grab the first thing I see, which yesterday happened to be a chocolate doughnut." "The only reason you have ten minutes to eat is because you sleep too late." "Well, then, set the fucking alarm earlier," etc.

But at night it was harder. From the sleep-sofa I heard them as they cuddled among the ruffles together, more than I ever asked to hear. "Oh, Mi-chael, I don't think that's a good idea." "It is, darling, you'll see. Just try it." "But I feel funny about it, Michael. It just doesn't seem right." "It's right, it's right. We love each other. And everybody else does it." "How do you know?" "I'm a doctor, darling." "Have you ever done it with anybody else?" "Of course not, Chrissie." "Then how do you know?" "Oh, sweetie. Oh God. I just know. I just know." "Mmmmm . . . are you sure?" "Chrissie darling, move your sweet little ass over here," etc.

Did I mean to hear or not? Loneliness surrounded my heart like a cold pool. Did I remember love, or was I hearing about it for the first time? And to drive out images of Portoff on his fat knees atop Chrissie, her legs bent out, her arms around his neck (I must have known it, or how would such a picture be in my mind?), I'd remember the kitchen on Sixty-fifth Street, with the woman in pink and her child, and the plants and copper pots and the cat sleeping on the windowsill, and I'd imagine myself there, wearing the pink dress, reading the child a story, with some Portoff of my own on his way home.

Whether out of loneliness, or frustration about having no money, or the half-conscious realization that I was being had, I began considering Sister Sal's offer. It would be just for a while. Then I could take the money and be on my own. Sal hadn't been so bad; probably I'd mistrusted her out of the poor judgment I'd had then. Though I had bed and board, I knew I was with the wrong people now. I could stay for months doing Chrissie's laundry, and then when they were tired of me they'd throw me out into the street. I was beginning to understand that if you wanted to make things better, you had to do it yourself, for nobody else was going to do it for you. I went back and forth; then one night I told Portoff I was leaving.

To my surprise he gave me a dark look of hurt disbelief. "Dinah, I can't believe this. I didn't think you were this sort of person."

"But Dr. . . . Mike. I don't understand. I certainly appreciate everything and—"

"Dinah. Chris is only here temporarily until the Rapps calm down, which they're already starting to do. But if you left they'd be very suspicious because they'd think Chris was clearing the decks, so to speak."

"But Mike. Now that Chris is back, I don't think it really matters that—"

"And there's another thing." He smiled from beneath his little mustache. "Let's sit down, Dinah."

I sat on the velvet love seat, Portoff on the sleep-sofa. Chris was at Snapper's. "Your . . . ah . . . anomaly is so unusual that I guess I don't always take it enough into account. I forget that you're a severely compromised person." I swallowed to keep my throat from tightening up, which it often did when he was talking. "It makes you very innocent about things the rest of us take for granted. I'm talking about the cost of your hospitalization. Do you have any idea where that came from?" I shook my head. "You arrived at the hospital as an indigent, Dinah. No name, no social security number. No insurance. By rights you should have gone to Bellevue." Bellevue—where Gil wouldn't put a dog! "But we wanted to keep you there, which we managed by some very tricky maneuvering with the hospital board. Thanks to my persistence and Dr. Liverwood's grant."

"What grant?" I wasn't going to admit I didn't know what a grant was.

"His National Institute of Mental Health grant for mem-

ory disorders paid for your room—three hundred dollars a
day—and all your tests, plus all of our time. Thousands of
dollars' worth. But that's all right"—as my eyes widened
at this phenomenal amount of money—"because you're a
very remarkable case, Dinah, and your data value alone will
pay it back ten times. We've gambled on you, Dinah; Frank
Liverwood's grant depends a great deal on his success with
you."

I'd hardly gone to Liverwood since I'd left the hospital;
it was so boring just to sit there, or lie there, and say
nothing. "Well, he'd better not gamble, because I might
never remember. In fact I've pretty well decided not to go
back, but to just go ahead with my new life."

"Dinah." Portoff sat forward, leaning his elbows on his
knees. "There are so many things you don't understand.
Responsibility. Gratitude. Obligations to others. As doctors these things are as natural to us as breathing. We live
to serve others," and on he went about the interdependence
of people and how "no man is an island." How if it hadn't
been for him I'd be on the streets, so therefore I owed him
something—which was getting my memory back so Liverwood could keep his grant. And why did he care? Because
if Liverwood kept his grant—which only I could enable
him to do by allowing him to cure my amnesia—he would
throw his weight behind Portoff for the place on the medical
board which Portoff most ardently desired, since he lusted
for power at Episcopal Hospital as much or even more than
he lusted for Chrissie.

"There's a saying, Dinah: He who forgets the past is
condemned to repeat it. You can't run away. You have to
face it sometime. Anyway, as your doctor I don't like the
idea of your running around alone. You could black out
again." He stood up on the thick-soled shoes that made him
an inch taller. "I hope you'll think very seriously about what
I said, Dinah. Your only hope lies in staying here with us
and going regularly to Frank Liverwood and trying. To put

it more clearly, you have an obligation to me, Dinah—
which if I'm correct can be legally enforced."

Slam.

What throw of the dice had delivered me to Portoff?
What forgotten thing had I done to deserve him? I might
have been better off in Washington Square, eating hot dogs,
till winter came anyway. He left me with knees shaking,
for I believed him: I was thousands of dollars in debt to
him. Nobody was going to forgive me anything just because
I couldn't remember. But then, I thought, why not pay
him back from all the money Sister Sal and I were going to
make from her best-seller? Surely I owned my own life,
including the right to examine it or ignore it, as I saw fit.

"You look much better," Sally said matter-of-factly as I got
out of the taxi. "Rested. And all those cuts and bruises are
healed. In fact, you're a different girl."

It was one of those lovely Manhattan dusks, the long end
of a summer day. The golden light was cool and remained
as a coppery haze after the sun had disappeared. (It's one of
the things I miss, those long dusks. Here in St. Pet's the
sun drops behind the horizon like a tennis ball, and in about
five minutes it's dark. But in New York the light pulls out
and extends and sweetens the world for an extra magic
hour.)

Sally lived on the ground floor of a mansion near Madison
in the sixties. I thought her apartment was strange. The
furniture was either straw or wood that looked sandpapered
and not painted. And baskets all over the place, some with
big bunches of old weeds in them. Some crude-looking
paintings: two dolls, holding hands, wearing stiff-looking
coats with lots of buttons. A quilt hung on the wall over
the sofa. On the tables were short, fat candles, and painted
vases with more weeds. Lots of enormous plants—so many
I forgot I was inside, even more so because that liquid

evening light came in through big glass doors that led out
to a small backyard where a white table was set for two.

The kitchen was small, separated from the living room
by a counter. Sal opened the oven, where a brown and
succulent duck was roasting. Sitting on the counter was a
bowl of salad greens and a loaf of bread so fresh the crust
flaked off.

I didn't know what to make of all this. Sal, in her jeans
and a silky shirt, reached into the refrigerator for a bottle of
wine and two glasses.

"Wine all right? Or would you like something else?"

"Like what?" This was my first encounter with alcohol.
Chris and Portoff hadn't offered me any, whether because I
was "mental" or because I was the maid, I didn't know.
But sometimes I had inexplicable associations. Beer came
to mind. Something called a bourbon and ginger.

"A bourbon . . . and . . . ginger." Sal put down the
wine bottle and looked me fully in the face. "Is that what
you drink?"

"I don't know," I said, embarrassed. "Look, I won't have
anything. I see you're expecting guests and I'll just—"

"Dinah." She poured two glasses of white wine. "You are
the dinner guest. You are the guest of honor."

"Me. But you shouldn't have gone to all this trouble." I
didn't like the wine. "You know, I told you on the phone I
wasn't sure if—"

"Look, sweetie. Will you just relax?" She pulled a tray
of minuscule pies out of the oven. "Let me feed you. Let me
take care of you. You'll find out where I'm coming from,
and I'll find out where you're at. We'll just enjoy ourselves."

I sat in a wicker chair in the garden, where Sal had
planted geraniums and petunias. There were ferns in hanging baskets and a parrot in a big cage. Sal put on some
music and poured more wine as I bit into one of the tiny
pies. It was a small crusty cup of cheese and onions.

Mostly she talked and I listened. She told me about her

childhood in New Jersey, and how she came to Manhattan, and her early marriage and divorce, and her rotten son whom she never saw, and her lover who was twenty-three and something called bi. She told me about the books she'd written and the articles and the television scripts, disappearing occasionally to put the potatoes on or toss the salad. When I told her I thought the wine was too sour, she put a red syrup in it that made it sweeter and called it a kir. I had a few of those, so by the time dinner appeared I was relaxed, to say the least.

She was some cook. I'd never eaten food like that, that I remembered, anyway. That dark duck, strange-looking but wonderful, with shiny crackly skin and pink tender meat, and little buttery potatoes, and that shiny, starched salad, and that fresh bread, and some kind of moldy cheese. And more wine, red this time. I kept saying "Mmm," and, "Oh, boy, is this yummy," and she said, "You poor kid, what have they been feeding you?"

"Oh, ordinary food. Macaroni . . . tuna fish (hic) . . . Cokes. But never anything like this."

"Oh, Dinah, Dinah." She leaned back and smiled. "What a big, wide world is out there for you to discover." I was beginning to like her better. She wasn't as pushy as she'd been when I first met her.

"Well, sometimes it's a little scary. I'm like a little child, I don't know anything. And I'm afraid of making mistakes."

"What kind of mistakes?" She poured more wine and offered me a cigarette, which I accepted.

"Oh, I guess mistakes with people. The things they do are so complicated. They say one thing and mean something else. And I feel so dumb, because afterwards they don't understand why I don't understand." Of course I was talking about Portoff and Chrissie, and it was a relief to tell her all about them.

"Oh, the bastard," she said, "the little rat. Oh, it's hard to believe there are really people like that." She brought coffee in a little metal pot and rolled something she called a joint, which we shared. I felt as though my head was floating away. Soon Sally and I were best friends, and she was holding my hand in the candlelight.

"Poor baby. You're so vulnerable, it's frightening. Listen, I think this could work. You're honest and you're smart enough, and I think we could go to the moon with this." Those dark brown eyes bored into me as she pressed my hand. "Dinah, don't you remember anything?"

"Well, sometimes funny things come into my head, but they might be dreams. Once I even dreamed about that dark curtain, and I was standing on the side of the stage pulling the rope, but it wouldn't open."

"Far out," said Sally, her eyes dark pools I was drowning in. "What else?"

"And every once in a while something will seem familiar, but I'm never sure whether it really is or whether it's the false flashes."

"What false flashes?" She whipped a little black box out of her pocket and put it on the table. "You don't mind if I tape, it's so fresh the way it is now."

"Well, Sally, sometimes something looks familiar and I know it isn't. I mean I know I've never been there before so . . . ." The creepy thing was, that was exactly the way the garden was beginning to look, luminous with undefined memories like an old snapshot. It made me so sad I felt like crying. What was I, where had I come from?

"But you don't know, darling," she said, "you know nothing. None of us do. What we know is the tip of the iceberg. We know nothing and everything. The fact that you know nothing probably means you know more than all of us."

Whatever that meant. I didn't really care anymore. She was holding my hand in hers and squeezing it every once in a while. It was nice. I hadn't been touched by anybody except the doctors. If anybody needed a friend, it was me.

"Well, sometimes it scares me," I said. "Thinking about what my life might have been before. It might have been rotten. I might have been lucky to get away. Now the slate's been wiped clean."

"But it hasn't, baby." She was stroking my fingers, one by one. "It's all there, it always is. It has to come out sometime. And when it does I'm going to be there to catch it." She stroked my thumb. "You have no idea how beautiful you are, do you?"

"Oh, Sally, I'm not." I was delighted. How could I not be?

"You have a face like a Modigliani. And what a smile. And that pretty dark hair." She reached out and lifted a strand of it. "Silky dark hair." Then with one finger she traced the outline of my face, while I closed my eyes. When she got to my mouth she gently poked my teeth. "Those lovely teeth."

"Oh, do you think so?" Now her hand moved down to my breasts, still in that old yellow T-shirt. Some faint alarm went off in my head. "Gee, maybe I'd better go home. I think I'm drunk."

"Don't be silly, you'll stay here. We're going to work together." Her finger was stroking my nipple, and I tried to push her hand away. "I need you, baby. Real bad. We have a lot to do together. You see, darling . . . I can't separate my work from my emotional life. It's all one living, throbbing thing. Everything feeds on everything else. Look at the karma we've got here, you and I. It's beautiful. Just put your arms up, love."

I did. Now what? Dumb. Was I dumb! Before I hardly knew what she was doing, she'd taken off my T-shirt and hung it on the parrot cage. If you think a person can't take off another person's T-shirt with hardly an objection, you've never been as drunk and stoned as I was. "Now, Sally. I don't know if—"

"Listen, darling. Before this adventure is finished I'm

going to know everything about you. Every nook and cranny. Every dark corner. We're going to open that curtain forever." She sat back and looked at me, and I at her. She had a good-looking, square face with a prominent chin, and she was probably around forty. Her voice was husky and suggestive. "Oh, baby. You're so lovely you make me want to cry. You're like a great uncharted country and I'm the mapmaker. You're unexplored—that's why you're so exciting. Till I saw you, I didn't think there was anything new left."

I don't know exactly when I was lost, when I turned the last corner—whether it was then (for she was seducing me with words as well as actions) or when she reached out her two hands to touch my bare breasts and hot feeling rushed through me. Could I have turned back, grabbed my T-shirt, and run out of there? I don't know. This is my secret, what happened with Sally, and I've never wanted to look at it too closely. It happened—what the hell. Things do. I was so lonely, and there she was. I don't think I could have stopped . . . for now the music pulsed softly and the candles flickered, and Sally looked at me as no one ever had before.

Willy

It's not all bad, Dinah's anomaly. Of course it's not normal. But after all these years as a physician, sometimes I wonder what normal really is. No two human bodies are exactly alike, and there's an unbelievable variety within the normal range. Some people have two ureters. Hearts have little differences that we don't consider pathological. And is anything more marvelous in its infinite variety than that globe of mystery, the human brain? For a period in medical school I seriously considered neurosurgery. But something, possibly humility, made me back off. To take on the brain you have to think you're the Lord himself. And besides that, their malpractice insurance rates are unconscionable.

I got a healthy respect for the brain living with Poor Liz. I watched her change before my eyes. Some sick, sinister force invaded my beautiful wife. Sometimes she just sat and stared at the wall while the kids ran all over the place unattended. And sometimes she talked a blue streak, telling me everything that had happened to her since the age of three, for God's sake, which got less than interesting. I tried to be sympathetic, but she was too much for me. I even went into therapy so I could handle her better. She did

a lot of strange things, like leaving weird messages around
. . . I don't want to go into all that. Jessie began acting
out in a hostile way, and Con started with the compulsive
behavior that threatens to become a character disorder.
Christ, it was a mess. I don't know where we'd be if it
weren't for Dinah.

So, to tell the truth, after I got used to the idea, I saw
that a girl with amnesia might have certain advantages. It
probably sounds—God forbid—male chauvinist piggish.
But at the risk of being run out of town by the bra burners,
I'll bet most men, if they were honest, wouldn't mind a
wife with no parents, no sisters or brothers, and no ex-
husbands or kids from the previous marriage. No belle-
of-the-ball memories to make married life look dull, no
ex-lovers to make comparisons with. Or even—now I'm
really ducking the Bettys and Glorias!—some heavy, intense career to keep her out from eight to eight and wring
her dry. I know damn well they wouldn't! Bill Goldstein
told me once, sotto voce, that if I knew another one, he'd
trade Ellen in, Ellen with her seventy-five relatives and all
their weddings and funerals and bar mitzvahs and Cousin
Mortie who goes to the rich doctor whenever he gets out of
jail to get on his feet again. What man wouldn't be tempted
by a clean slate?

I didn't know any of this when I met her at the party
where, as usual, Mother beeped me to say the place was
falling apart. I'd been talking to this pretty, dark-haired
girl—quiet, a little mysterious, wasn't always interrupting
—and I just grabbed her and took her along.

In the cab I explain. No wife, two small kids (one with
earache), flaky mother, domestic chaos. She doesn't bat an
eyelash. The place looks as though it's been bombed—toys
and kids' clothes and half-chewed carrots all over the place.
Conrad's talking nonstop; the dog's barking; Mother's holding Jessie, who's dribbling jelly doughnut down her back.
Mother's never adapted to life without servants. Stockings

bagging, blouse falling out of her skirt, the hat and hatpins of course.

"Oh, Willy, you shouldn't have brought a guest home with all this mess. The agency girl demanded her money at ten o'clock and just stamped out. Why, I couldn't believe it. I'm so pleased to meet you, Miss . . . Miss . . . Jones, did you say?" The TV's turned up; the cat's yowling. Jessie begins screaming. Mother starts to fall apart. But Dinah's just as cool and sweet as you please, shaking hands with Mother, picking a couple of toys off the floor, persuading Conrad to put down the cat so it'll stop yowling. Mother calms down. I take Jessie's temp. We're going to live. I throw the dirty laundry off a section of the sofa and give Dinah a glass of wine, apologizing for it all.

"Maybe I shouldn't have brought you here. But I didn't know what else to do." Crash from the kitchen. "Mother, just leave everything. Somebody will be here in the morning."

Dinah's taking it all in, wide-eyed. "Did your wife just suddenly . . . leave?"

"Oh, no. There were warnings. First the sounds of liberation. Then heavier problems. She was . . . disturbed. The rest we'll have to save for next time, Dinah, because I have to scrub early in the morning."

She says good-bye to Mother, as nice as you please. I take her home. Then in the morning Mother asks, "Where does she come from, Willy?"

"She said Colorado."

"She seems perfectly nice." The kiss of death from Mother. No breeding! From nothing! "Well, I probably shouldn't say it. But whatever happened to Liz, she came of *fine stock*. The Flanderses were impeccable. Liz could have been DAR any time she wanted, but I never could get her—"

"Call the agency this morning, Mother, okay?" I'm slugging down Mother's weak, pale coffee. That's the way Hattie, the old family retainer, made it! Oh, for Hattie now!

"Of course it's none of my business, Willy. But there are so many nice young women in this city; if you'd just accept some of those invitations that . . ."

Mother could use a touch of amnesia. She's still in Virginia in the twenties. By invitations she means exactly two Old Virginia dinner parties I couldn't go to because I was sewing up somebody's ankles. In Mother's world doctors stop for dinner and ladies go to tea parties . . . and some women are not ladies, and don't ask what *they* go to.

So Mother Charlotte and Dinah don't start out too auspiciously, right? But Dinah's so damn sweet and nice that the devil couldn't resist her. At Sunday tea (I've warned her Mother has fangs) she draws Mother out about olden days and starts on the kids. Jessie's hiding under the bed; Dinah coaxes her out. She listens to Con recite his long poem for school. She slips out and does a load of wash. I'm in love already.

This was before I knew about the amnesia, which Dinah was not exactly up-front about. Not that I blame her. She waited till I was hooked, then told me one unforgettable rainy night. Well, I put on my pants and left.

Then I remembered hearing about her around the hospital a year or two before. I think Mike Portoff mentioned it. The police had found her wandering around the street; they brought her in and did a lot of tests on her. She and Chris Portoff were roommates for a while.

Well, the prognosis wasn't great. But there was something about Dinah, I couldn't shake her so easily. I just felt good when I was with her. She wasn't always asking for something. She was obviously a girl who came from nothing, in some situation she couldn't handle, then blacked out. And crazy about me, and dying to get married. And grateful! The only grateful woman in town! I'd heard enough complaining about the female condition. Well, they're right about some things. But grabbing the chair out of your hands when you try to pull it out for them, like your mother taught you—for Christ's sake. And orating about some poor sap of an ex-husband who "couldn't confront his feelings." When I met Dinah she was living hand to mouth, practically starving. She was ready to kiss my feet.

I suppose none of this would win me the New Sensitivity Prize. Well, if I composed ditties or grew gladiolas for a living, it might be something else. But I've got serious work to do. There's too much misery out there, too much sickness, too many people crying for help. I need a helper, not a revolutionary.

Two months later I was back. I couldn't get along without her. We agreed to let the past lie buried, but we cooked up a story for Mother elaborating on the divorcée-from-Colorado line she'd given me. So now Dinah comes from an old—possibly *Mayflower*—Massachusetts family who went to Colorado during the Gold Rush. The very best people but financial reverses—Mother melts over poor but proud. She went to fine private schools in Colorado Springs and came out at an elegant ball, then married Mr. Wrong, whose memory she was trying to erase. I thought it was pretty ingenious.

"But if she's quality, Willy, why does she act like the maid? She's always picking up."

"They were poor, Mother."

"I thought they went west for gold."

Think fast, Willy. "They did but they lost it. It just ran through their fingers. Dinah hardly remembers when they had servants, she was so young."

So by now Dinah thinks she comes of fine old New England stock and grew up in Dry Gulch, Colorado, on the fringes of the Old West, swinging a lariat.

It's impossible to know if Dinah will ever get her memory back. They don't know much about memory. Every

time they think they have it cornered in a certain area of
the brain, it pops up somewhere else. It seems to be all over
the place. If the brain is like a glob of chocolate mousse, as
my neurology professor described it, then memory's the
chocolate. And everything's brain hormones now; who
knows what they'll find next week? They might find something to clear up the mists.

Then what would we do?

I mentioned this after a few drinks at Cheerful Men (from
Sir William Osler, who advised physicians to "seek the
haunts of cheerful men"), a dinner club I belong to with
Bill Goldstein, Mac Valpey, Portoff, Bertie Mood, and a
couple of others from Episcopal. We meet at a different
restaurant every month for jolly repartee and good clean
male company. We usually don't talk about personal matters. I might have laid a rotten egg—total silence. Then
the usual raillery.

"Hope you're bigger than her last husband!"

"Hit her over the head again!"

"Call Alfred Hitchcock!"

Portoff smirked. Maybe I shouldn't have said it. But isn't
the question in everybody's mind, Dinah's included? I can
only hope that whatever she remembers can't compare to
her life with me. For haven't I given her everything? Well,
nobody took it very seriously. I suppose there is something
comic about it. And something strange and mysterious too.

I'll bet they all envy me like hell.

Dinah

I woke up late in an empty bed and staggered into the living room to see a new Sally, neatly dressed and crackling with efficiency into the telephone.

"Yes, baby. I know, darling. Of course. Don't give an inch. We'll push 'em till they bleed. I tell you, this is beautiful." She saw me and gave no sign, and I felt like a fool, staggering naked into this pristine office scene, for there were no signs of last night's bacchanal. "I know, baby. I know. Well, I know that. Hold on." She covered the mouthpiece. "There's a robe in the bathroom. There's clean towels on the shelf over the tub. There's coffee in the kitchen." Back into the phone. "I stand firm, Bernie. I mean it. I mean they can fuck themselves. I have a gut feeling about this."

After I'd bathed and was drinking coffee in the kitchen, she marched over.

"Ready to work, Dinah?"

"Well, sure."

"Okay, drink up. You can borrow some of my clothes."

I looked at her, at those dark eyes I'd kissed in the night. They had become hard as little jewels. "What are we going to do?"

"You'll talk and I'll tape. I want some primary material. I want to finish the proposal today and messenger it to my agent this afternoon."

"Sally," I said.

She gave a small smile. "Nice night, baby. Now it's time to get to work."

Wearing some pants and a shirt of Sally's, I sat on the couch and talked into the tape recorder. There was a sad, sick little twist in my stomach. Sal, in a black sweater, was jade-hard, her fingernails, lacquered the color of coffee ice cream, moved purposefully on the buttons of the tape recorder, and she took an occasional note on a yellow legal pad. I couldn't keep my mind on what I was talking about. I kept looking at that clipped white hair, that firm jaw, her pale mouth clamped around a menthol cigarette. My eyes traveled down her body to her feet in little tan boots.

"So you slept in the park." Her voice was cool and neutral.

"First near the playground."

"Then what?"

"Then . . . I heard footsteps. I guess. Or I woke up . . . Why won't you smile at me?"

A sigh, a phony smile masking impatience. "Sweetie, we have work to do. I get serious when I'm working. It's called professionalism."

"That's not what you said last night. You said that work and love were all the same thing, the same living, throbbing thing."

She stared at me for a frighteningly long time. "Dinah, I'd really like to get this done and to the agent. So we can get going. So we can have bucks. Understand? I'm sorry if I'm like this. I'll talk about anything you want later."

"Well, yes. But frankly I find it hard to talk when you look so grim. I mean if it wasn't for last night, it wouldn't make any difference. But last night existed and so it does."

We argued, hassled, drank more coffee, and made love again as the midday sun poured in from the garden. What a life—lying naked on Sally's white flokati rug, drinking champagne and eating chicken sandwiches ordered from the deli.

Then she said, "One extension, Dinah. That's all."

"Let's do it now. Get the tape recorder."

"Don't be an ass, baby."

"Why shouldn't we?"

"Because I can't think straight. And there isn't any veritas in vino."

We had to work dressed, sitting in chairs, with Sal's armor on. I'd dry up, my nose and mouth would wiggle with incipient tears. Sal grew fierce and finally possessed.

"Oh, fuck it. Get lost. I'll use what I've got. So we throw fifty thousand dollars out the window, what the hell? Or I'll make it up." Finally, around the middle of the third day, she left for the Xerox place. "Well, it's the best I can do. I'll be back in a couple of hours. Listen, run out and get a chicken for dinner, okay?" Throwing some money at me, she ran out the door.

I badly needed some time to myself. I needed time to think; all this intensity was wearing me out. Things in my new life were happening too fast; I felt like a rudderless boat in a vast, complicated sea.

It was strange to be there alone. I was very aware of how few people I had and how badly I needed them. There was nothing to clean up or put away, for Sal had a way of whizzing things out of sight almost before I noticed. I read for a while in the yard, where a sullen yellow square of afternoon sun was blocked out in the middle of the gray city shadows. Then I went to the phone and called the apartment.

Chrissie answered, her voice shooting up two octaves when she heard who it was. "Di-nah! Where have you been? You won't believe what's been going on around here. When are you coming back? I've got to talk to you, it's real-ly important."

We met at a bar on Madison. Chrissie was sitting in a

booth, wearing a raincoat. Her Shirley Temple curls were a-tumble, and there was a beer in front of her. "Honestly, Dinah, I never do this. But I feel as though I'm at a cross-roads or something."

Mr. Rapp had paid a surprise visit in the middle of the night, surprising Chrissie and Portoff in their skivvies, lit-erally out of breath from their recent exercise. He had threatened to write Chrissie out of his will and was stopping the money immediately unless she and Portoff got married immediately. What an uproar! Tears, rage, disbelief, etc. "And Dinah, then Michael started getting mad because if you'd been there it never would have happened, because then he wouldn't have gotten suspicious enough to come. I honestly don't understand."

"Lord, Chrissie. That's terrible."

"The place is just crazy! Mother phones about every half hour from some pay phone. 'Chrissie, I think your father is starting to relent.' Then Michael screaming that you ran out on him. Meanwhile Daddy didn't send a check this month and I can't pay the rent."

Portoff wanted to do the honorable thing and start plan-ning the wedding right away. But Chrissie had been think-ing. She'd read an article; she'd seen a TV show; she'd been talking to a couple of girlfriends. She was beginning to see that all her life she'd been Daddy's girl and now she was supposed to be delivered into the next stage as Michael's wife—a slave like her mother. She'd begun putting things together: how Michael always left his dirty laundry and dishes for her to do. How whenever they discussed their future, Michael was always out being a brilliant doctor and Chrissie was home wiping oatmeal off the kids' faces. How, whenever they were out with friends, Michael had this way of making her sound a little stupid—cute, but on the dumb side—when she asked a question or made a comment about something serious. And it wasn't just Michael, all the guys did it. It was absolutely amazing how, once you got the

idea about the oppression of women, you found it *everywhere.*
She'd pretty well decided not to marry Michael at all.

At that point, tangling as I was with a new and complicated world, there were certain suppositions I hadn't questioned: that people without money had to be helped by
those who had it, that there were such things as loneliness
and sexual attraction, and for those reasons and more, people often elected to marry or live together. Nor did I want
to question them, and I didn't like what Chrissie was saying
at all, because it was one more complication. So I told her
that being a woman was neither here nor there as far as I
was concerned. What I needed was money in the bank and
a few friends I could trust.

Chrissie's big blue eyes widened and she put her little
white hand on mine. "I'm your friend, Dinah, if you want
me to be. I owe you an apology for the way I've acted,
because I guess I treated you like an object and I'm sorry.
For nineteen years I've been a rotten, spoiled brat. And yet
in a sense you're the one who opened my eyes to everything." She waved at the waiter and ordered two more
beers.

"But why?" I asked.

"Oh, because you're so free. You have nothing, nobody.
And nothing in your head, no parents shaking their heads
and saying don't do this, don't do that. You don't know
what it's like, being brought up brainwashed. It's like
being a cripple . . . Maybe I even resented you a little for
being so free. Even those same old jeans . . . This morning
I looked into my closet at all those clothes, and I thought,
'This is all so I can dress up and attract some man who will
victimize me.' I guess if I were truly liberated I'd throw
them all out." I got a little lost as she talked on and on
about the Sisterhood. And—"Oh, Dinah, please don't call
me Chrissie anymore. It's a baby name Daddy always used.
Call me Christine."

"But Chrissie . . . Christine, I don't understand that. If

you marry Michael, you'll never have to worry about money again, probably. Maybe I think on kind of a basic level, but that doesn't sound bad to me. If you don't marry him, you'll be broke, and that isn't very free—which I know because that's exactly my situation."

She took another swig of beer and tried again. Maybe I couldn't see it yet; maybe I had to experience it in a relationship of my own. There were such things as fulfillment and identity . . . Money was the weapon of the patriarchy, and I had to rise above it.

"Listen, Christine, I have to get back to Sally's, because I'm staying with her while she writes this book that's going to make all the money."

"Dinah, promise to come and see me. And—oh, I only have a dollar or so, could you pay the check?" I paid with the chicken money. Then she pulled a scrap of paper out of her purse. "I almost forgot. This is a message I found on Michael's desk." She pushed it across the table to me. "You're supposed to go over to the nineteenth precinct. There are a whole lot of people there saying you belong to them. I guess Michael forgot to tell you."

It was Gil's number. "I don't want to see them. Things may be tough, but I'm not about to go over there and be claimed like a package." I started to tear up the paper, but she grabbed my hand.

"Don't you dare do that. Your family could be waiting for you over there!"

"No family I want to see. You just told me how lucky I was not to have any parents!"

"Well . . . I don't know if I mean that entirely. But Dinah, it's cruel not to go. Your mother could be there . . . or your loving husband, or your darling children!"

"If they'd been so wonderful, I wouldn't have run away."

"Please," she said, "just keep the paper. You might feel differently another time."

On the way back I stopped at Gristede's for a very small chicken, then rushed back to the apartment. When I got there it looked its best. Lights on, table set. Champagne in a bucket of ice. The painting of the doll-children softly lit by a flock of hurricane candles on the sideboard below. She'd shaken out the flokati rug, and now the flattened places where we'd lain were upright and fluffy, soft and inviting . . . and I knew this was all for me. Glenn Miller was playing softly.

There was a slam inside the bedroom, and Sal strode into the living room in a short white terry-cloth robe. She folded her arms and planted her brown legs apart.

"Well, how nice of you to turn up, Your Highness. I hope you weren't inconvenienced."

I didn't understand sarcasm. "I got the chicken, Sal. And met Chrissie for a beer."

"Chrissie! Who the fuck is Chrissie?"

"She's that girl I stayed with, remember? I told you about her. It seems that she and Portoff—"

"Don't tell me, I'll fall asleep." Her voice was icy. "Our interests are different. Our tastes are different. Oh, you remembered the chicken. How considerate."

I took it into the kitchen and unwrapped it while she watched me. "Looks nice. Shall I cook it?"

"Oh, madam will do the cooking! I'm overwhelmed!" Her voice was thick and strange.

"Sal, cut it out. You're being weird. And if you think you're funny, I'm not laughing."

I heard a strange sound behind me and I turned and looked at her. At first I thought she was having some sort of fit. Her face grew redder and redder and swelled up in a strange way, as though it was about to burst, and the skin got shiny and stretched, like a wet balloon. The cords in her neck stood out, her teeth were clenched, and her brown eyes bugged out of her head, all in violent color-contrast to the white robe, white hair, and white crotch, which flashed occasionally through the bathrobe, surrounded by her flawless head-to-foot suntan.

I was looking at her nervously, wondering what to do

next, when she shrieked, "You lousy, no-good cunt. I have
put my career and my life on the line for you—on the line,
I tell you!—and you have the nerve to go out for a beer
with *Chrissie!*" She whined the name in a terrible voice
while I stood hanging on to the refrigerator, stunned. "I
picked you up off the street. Before me you were nothing.
I fed you, gave you the clothes on your back, took you in.
For days we've worked together so I could complete my
book proposal. I rushed out *myself* to the Xerox place because we were late because dear Dinah just couldn't go any
faster—and rushed to the agent and ran around town and
delivered copies to twenty publishers"—she was screaming
at the top of her lungs—"to be in time for the auction with
the one-hundred-thousand-dollar floor, and you can imagine how *that* looked in the august halls of Knopf, Random
House, and Simon and Schuster, Sally Pendleton and Bernie
Berkowitz screeching in like a pair of fucking maniacs to be
on time because dear Dinah couldn't get her ass together
and talk faster. They thought we were crazy but it isn't the
first time . . . And after all that,"—she took a step toward
me as I quailed—"I thank Bernie from the bottom of my
heart for breaking his ass. I grab a cab, stop for champagne.
Because I'm coming home to celebrate with *my Dinah.* Who
I did all this for. Out of love. Out of karma. Out of the joy
of creativity." Her hands were on my shoulders and there
was a tight, crazed smile on her face. "We're going to drink
champagne together, cook dinner, make love. Join hands
for this beautiful book. I come home, open the door—
nobody. I tidy up, put the wine in the bucket, start the
salad . . . I light the candles." Her eyes hardened as she
moved closer, and I smelled her sweat-and-Paco-Rabanne
smell. "But time passes, a lot of time. Because Dinah is
having a beer with CHRISSIE!" A wild, demented howl.

Then her hands moved up to my throat and grabbed me,
as I thought, This is it. She's stronger, I haven't a chance.
Her eyes and thumbs dug into me, then her face moved

close and her mouth closed on mine, her tongue pressing
and digging into my mouth, and . . . "Can Chrissie do
this, Dinah? Can she make you feel like this?"

I was beginning to come to a few conclusions about sex,
such as that it was crazy as hell. Sally and I ended up on
the flokati rug, and I ended up with a few more bruises,
and we cooked the chicken and drank the champagne.
What I didn't know was, was this an ordinary evening at
home for everybody else too? If so, how did people have
the energy to do their work? For I fell into bed that night
and slept for ten hours, as exhausted as if I'd just fought
a war.

The next morning there was an expression of unaccus-
tomed cheer on Sally's face as she ground the coffee beans.

"I see Chrissie's good for something," she said, as I sat
down sleepily on one of the kitchen stools. She put the little
scrap of paper with the phone number in front of me,
anchoring it with a piece of honeydew melon. "You could
have told me, sweetheart, but never mind. I should have
thought of it myself. We'll go right after breakfast."

"Go where?"

"To the nineteenth precinct, baby. It'll be intense."

"I don't want to go to the nineteenth precinct."

"Please, Dinah. Don't be an asshole." She carefully put
coffee into the glass pot and poured boiling water on top.
That was the thing about Sally. She surrounded herself with
so many things that looked good, smelled good, tasted
wonderful. At the same moment that her voice was making
my flesh crawl with anxiety, she was making fragrant coffee
or lighting her Rigaud candles or tossing me a velvety robe
to put on after my bath.

"There isn't a chance that any relative of mine will be
there. My relatives obviously hated me. I'm lucky to get
rid of them." Sally's eyes hardened. God—how complicated
everything was. All I wanted to do was hang around here
for a while, grow up a little, make some money.

"We have an agreement," said Sally through clenched teeth. "We are writing a book. This is the material."

"The whole idea scares me to death. How do I know what kind of creeps are going to be there, claiming to be my parents or my long-lost husband? And how do I know they aren't? And even if they are, I don't want—"

"You don't have to find anybody you don't want. You can be a lost orphan forever for all I care. I don't give a shit. But we are going to *look*. This is the *material*. Surely you understand. Anyway, darling,"—she poured me some fresh coffee—"your very search is a story in itself. Your conflicts. Your fears, fantasies, maybe just a little flutter of hope that there'll be that wonderful face that will open the curtain! The mystery of the past! Want a croissant? Rough-cut lemon marmalade?"

"I don't want to open the curtain," I said.

"Oh, you'll get over that. You have to, it's the climax of the whole thing. How about an egg—fluffy-scrambled?"

Of course Sal prevailed—Sal and a Valium. After all, I was in a position of control. If I recognized somebody I didn't want to, all I had to do was play dumb. And wear sunglasses. It might even be fun.

Gil—Sergeant Gilhooley—was there.

"It's time you turned up. Not only do you have more relatives than Howard Hughes, but I have a stack of mail for you, in response to the AP story."

The news story had read, "A young woman was found today wandering around Manhattan's east sixties, claiming memory loss for all but recent events. Five feet six inches, 120 pounds, she has long dark hair, hazel eyes, and is approximately twenty-three years old. Her only distinguishing characteristic is a mole on her left calf. She showed cuts and contusions on her face and arms and wore a silver bracelet with a heart-shaped charm saying DINAH. Anyone with information please call the toll-free Dinah hotline, 1-800-IMDINAH, or write DINAH, P.O. Box 287, Manhattan."

Gil said, "Now listen, Dinah. Dinah Jones, is that right?"

"I guess so."

"Okay, Dinah. There have been a lot of nuts here. The really obvious ones we threw out, but I made a list of them all."

"I don't like this," I said, as Sally grabbed the list.

Gil pulled me over behind the desk and said softly, "There are a couple here right now. They've been here every day for a week. Just look in the mirror here." I saw, dimly reflected, a pair of people sitting over in the corner—a wrinkled old lady in black, fingering a rosary, and a morose-looking thin guy with little round glasses who was reading a newspaper. "They claim to be your mother and your brother."

I grabbed Sally's hand. "Oh, my God."

"Easy, baby. I'm right here."

I said to Gil, "Even if they're mine I don't want them."

"Come on, Dinah," Gil said. "Think how they feel. A lot of people ain't got no family at all."

We set it up carefully. I waited in an empty office in the back, Sal stood near the door with her mini tape recorder. Gil brought the two in and the three of us stared at each other. I don't know what was in my head at that moment. Nothing and everything. No three faces ever devoured each other the way we did.

Mama's face broke first. "Oh, Maria. Oh, *mia figlia*. Maria, where have you been? Why you stay away so long? Every Sunday I pray"—coming toward me.

"Mama, you blind," said Brother. "This ain't Maria. She don't even look like Maria." Mama ran her cracked hand over my face and hair. Her face had a thousand wrinkles; her eyes were half buried under folds of flesh; her lips sank in where her teeth were missing. A few white hairs escaped from under her black scarf. She smelled of old clothes and garlic. "Maria would be older than this person here. There would be gray in her hair. And Maria was always heavy.

This person here is a thin person." It sounded as though he'd said it all before many times.

Mama's filmed brown eyes examined me. "Are you Maria? Tell me now." Tears welled into my eyes.

"She can't see too well," Brother explained. "Her hopes go up every time." He put his arm around her shoulder. "Come on, Mama."

Now the tears were rolling down my face. "I'm sorry," I said. "I'm so sorry. I hope you find her."

"Sorry to take up your time," Brother said as they left.

I heard her voice from the hall: *"Luigi, non è Maria?"*

The only one who wasn't crying was Sal, who was crowing over the tape. "Oh, that was beautiful . . . beautiful! Oh, Jesus."

"I can't stand it," I said, when I'd pulled myself together. "This is too hard."

"You'll toughen up," Sally said briskly.

Gil looked from her to me. "You're a nice lady," he told me.

I was so depressed after this that Sally took me to lunch at The Four Seasons. She blew kisses around the Grill Room and ordered champagne.

"To *Uncharted Places*—how's that for a title?"

"Fine. Terrific."

"Stop looking so moldy, Dinah. You're on display."

Several people came over to the table to be introduced. Sally said they were editors and agents. I knew I was supposed to be polite and charming, but I couldn't get that poor old woman out of my head. I tuned out most of what was said until a nice-looking gray-haired man named Ed, hanging over the table, began speaking to me. "The most exciting part of the project will be your hypnosis and your Amytal interview on tape. I'm impressed by your courage in allowing this."

"What?"

Sally kicked me. "She's fabulous, Eddie. Brave and won-

derful . . . I hate to be rude, but this superb mousse de
truite is cooling."

Lord, I was slow—and Sally was fast. "I never told you
I'd do those things on tape."

"Dinah, dear, you may not have in so many words. But
you implied it . . . darling. That's the subject of the book.
What else would I fill four hundred pages with, nursery
rhymes?"

I was furious with myself. I dreaded the thought of my
past spilling into Sally's hands while I sat there semiconscious. The psychiatrist taking notes. Sally taping it all and
grinning.

"You know something? I think I'm in over my head." I
waved my arm at the glorious room with its famous food
and Manhattan's best people. "I don't belong here. Whatever my life was before, I know it wasn't this."

"Nobody belongs here, stupid," she said, soft as a cat.
"We all start at the greasy spoon. We all break our asses to
get here. You just don't happen to remember, and that's
why you're interesting."

"And I'm not so sure I want to." I put my napkin on the
table, all appetite gone. I stood up.

"You can't run from your past, Dinah. It'll catch up
sooner or later, and you might as well get the pain over
with now—and get paid for it. It'll hurt more later. Most
of us don't have the choice."

"I'm leaving."

"Sit down," she said in a voice like a knife.

I turned and ran—ran as well as I could, zigzagging
between tables. Sal threw a bill on the table and gave chase.
Out of the Grill Room. Down the stairs. Out into the
street, up Park. We were about evenly matched: I was
younger but Sal was in better shape, and we both wore
high-heeled shoes. Somewhere around Fifty-ninth I began
to flag. My heart was pounding and I could hardly get my
breath, but she was still behind me, half a block back.

When I thought my chest would explode I sagged into a doorway. I heard her voice before she got there.

"You're a fool, Dinah. I'll sue you for breach of contract. You're mine whether you like it or not. I love you—passionately. Whatever your past. Trust me, baby. We'll face it together whatever it is." She touched my face.

Like some manacled animal, I got into a taxi with her.

By then I was convinced I had something terribly wrong with me. A normal person (if there was one) would never have gotten into such a mess to begin with or would have left when it became clear that Sally was quite crazy. But I wasn't normal and she and I both knew it. In a way I was as bad as she was—though I thought that if I could leave her, I wouldn't be. I learned what I still believe, that craziness is a shared operation. It's possible—but a lot harder —to be nutty alone in the dark.

The bids began to trickle in. They were fewer and lower than she had thought and she finally accepted one from a smaller house for fifty thousand dollars.

"How much is for me?" I asked.

"Ten thou."

"That's not much compared to what you get."

"Without me there isn't any book. Let's get back to the letters"—which she insisted on reading to me. I didn't want to hear them, but she was merciless—even standing outside the bathroom door when I was inside or following me down the street reading them.

"Dere Dinah, I feel sure you must be my beloved long-lost wife who left me so pressipusly ten years ago. Surely yore showing up is a sign . . ."

"Dearest Heart, you don't have to pretend with me. I can accept you the way you are, for now I understand the folly of trying to make another person different from what God intended. Please don't play this amnesia game anymore, but come home to . . ."

"Dear Mommy. I knew you weren't really dead, but just forgot where you lived and went someplace else. I'm sorry I took the cookies. Please come home soon . . ."

"Dinah: You can't get away with this. I have all the papers and letters, and I've retained an attorney. I'm rich and powerful and I'll get you in the end . . ."

"Dear Miss Jones: Are you, by any chance, the charming lady I talked to at the dry cleaner on Columbus Avenue on April twenty-fourth? If you can't remember, I am five foot ten with blue eyes, red hair, and a small mustache . . ."

"Deer Mama pleez come get me they dont give me good food I cant eat it its cold in bed and i have only won blanket. I miss you so bad i cry every nite . . ."

"Darling, the pig is dead. I swear it. We'll draw up a contract and share all the housework equally. Please come home. The kids miss you and I love you . . ."

"They're fabulous," Sally exulted, gathering up another handful.

"You can't use them."

"Jesus, Dinah. You're impossible. They're ours to use."

"Mine!"

"What's yours is mine, partner." She ripped open another one. "Oh, boy. Listen to this. 'Dear Dinah, how do you like it, in your mouth or up your ass? I aim to please. Ten inches long when fully extended—' "

"Give it to me," I shrieked, grabbing it. "Stop making fun of them."

"What do you care? You told me you're not looking for your past anyway."

"Well, I'm not. But you're cruel. You don't have any feelings."

"Honest, baby, you've got to get some detachment about this. A professional attitude." She kept all the letters in a gold-tooled leather box on her desk, where she sat reading one after another, laughing at the human misery that spilled out of them. "How about this? 'Dear so-called Dinah: Pretty clever, Diana. You always thought you were smarter than me. Well, your guilt will follow you to the grave if the police don't get you. We both did Mother in and you know it.' And this: 'Darling Dinnie—Only come home and I'll give you everything you asked for, including the Silver Cloud . . .' "

She dragged me, protesting, back to the police station. I remember one man in particular. Tall, suntanned, and custom-cut, he had wings of silver hair and a mouthful of teeth that almost matched them. He wore a pale beige three-piece suit and a silky shirt, and he carried a Gucci attaché case. He stood there looking me over with slightly out-of-focus eyes and appeared to be trying to swallow a lump in his throat. He held out his arms.

"Dee darling, I knew it was you, you rascal. What an amusing idea, dearest Dee. But please come along now, we've got to be in Montego tomorrow night. They simply won't wait a moment longer."

"Well, to tell you the truth I don't recognize you."

"Oh, fuck. Well, if you change your mind I'll be at the usual villa at Round Hill. Just call Manny at the office and he'll make your reservations." And off he went.

"Maybe I should have gone," I said thoughtfully. "He seemed rich at least. But a little strange."

"Stoned out of his mind," Gil said, while Sally nodded sagely. "He seemed all right when he came in. He must have gone into the bathroom and snorted."

Later, Sally and I argued about him too.

"He's sad, Sally. He's tragic. Can't you see it?"

"Dinah." Sally put down her papers and looked at me over her half-glasses. "We've been fucking around about your therapy for too long. You're overreacting to all these creeps."

"I just have a little sympathy for them."

"I want you to make an appointment with this man in the morning and go." She scratched something in felt pen on one of her bright pink note papers. "He's agreed to do your hypnosis with me and the tape recorder in the room. They aren't all so cooperative; I called ten of them."

I froze—at my own waffling indecisiveness. I was learning that you could get yourself in worse and worse trouble by just going along and doing nothing, avoiding decisions. I knew problems didn't melt. But they also didn't stay the same size. They multiplied, ballooned, proliferated like cancer cells. To stop them you had to face up to the situation and risk the anger of others. It was a hard, complicated world I'd been born into. Sally was absorbed in what she was doing, and I don't know what I would have done if the phone hadn't rung and she hadn't answered it, handing it to me as though it were a dead rat.

It was Chrissie, highly upset. While I listened Sally kept working, but her whole body grew rigid. Chrissie and Michael had had it out; she'd broken the engagement. He was rigid and hidebound and she suspected he was in league with her parents. The whole situation had become desperate —particularly since another rent bill had come. If I was her friend—her sister—would I meet her over at Snapper's? She'd be through in twenty minutes.

"You go and I'll kill you," Sal said in her coldest voice as I put down the phone.

"Oh, don't be silly. The poor kid is in trouble."

"She can go fuck herself."

"I can't believe the things you say. Don't you have any friends—other than the gang at The Four Seasons? Do you ever do anything for anybody?"

Mistake—she began to swell up again. "You sleazy little bitch. How dare you ask me that? If it weren't for me you'd be in jail or starving in the street. Get away from that door."

I'd decided to nerve it out. "You don't own me, Sally. Just cool it. I'll be back in a couple of hours. Stop making such a big deal out of it."

"Chrissie." She spat out the word. "The doctor's wife.

How cute. What's she going to do for you, Dinah? Not what I do. Not to mention the ten grand you're throwing down the toilet. You're so stupid you don't know how good you've got it." It was amazing how hideous she got when she was angry. Her face over her bright blue blouse had turned a sickening red. Her mouth worked in a strange way and her eyes popped. She scared me to death, but at last the choices were clear: either I stayed or I went. I couldn't waffle any longer.

"I'm leaving," I said.

"Oh no you're not, Dinah." Her voice was chillingly calm. "You signed a contract. I'll have you in court in an hour."

"Take your contract and shove it," I said. "Go to the shrink yourself." Then I thought, The letters. I had to rescue them from the tiger's jaws.

Everything happened with insane speed. I moved toward the desk, and at that very moment Sally reached deftly into her drawer and took out a gun—a nice little gun, ladies' size, which she pointed at me. Silver, it sparkled in the light from the bean-jar lamp.

"Put down the letters," she said. I thought she was kidding. I thought it was a toy or a joke.

"No." I was clutching the leather box. "Come on, Sally. Put your cap gun away."

She planted her feet apart, aimed the gun with both hands, and I'd be dead except there were no bullets in it. All that it produced was a tiny click. I dashed for the door as Sally screamed, "I'll get you, you bitch!" clicking away with her useless gun as I ran out of the room. I knew she was fast, she'd caught me before. I heard her feet pounding on the floor of the hall, but I managed to get out the front door, dropping half the letters from the box. I didn't dare pick them up but took the three steps up to the sidewalk in one leap. There, delivered by God, was a ready taxi; I bolted into it and slammed the door. We screeched down the street as Sally jumped up and down in a fury on the sidewalk, screaming, "You'll never get away! I'll get your memories yet! Your memories are mine!"

Chris and I lived together for almost a year. Finding what we could afford on waitresses' salaries was a blow to us both. We were innocent about the ways of the city. She had more practical knowledge; I had more wariness of the human scene. Together we got along.

I didn't mind working at Snapper's. It was one of those trendy singles places with a glass front and the menu on a blackboard. We wore white shirts and black pants, and most of the people were pretty nice. It was steady work and you got a meal a day free. You came home with money in your pocket, which I preferred to empty promises of a hundred thousand. Though there wasn't very much of it.

We had a dark, roach-infested, three-flight walk-up in the west seventies. The block was bad, but it was all we could afford. We didn't dare come home alone at night, and there was a crazy woman who screamed in the next apartment and the landlord couldn't or wouldn't do anything about her. Everything always smelled of stale Chinese food from the restaurant below. With Chris's furniture the place didn't look bad, though we couldn't seem to do much about the roaches, which Chrissie's stupid cat ignored or hid from in terror.

We lived on macaroni and tuna fish, drank cheap wine, and shopped at Woolworth's and the thrift shop. It was hard on Chris, who was used to running to Bloomingdale's whenever she felt like it. I must have been poor in my life before, for it felt very natural; in fact I sometimes hid the pleasure I got out of this new life from Chris. As she sighed and mourned in front of Putamayo, sometimes weeping over her plight, I browsed around Canal Street or lower Broadway with twenty dollars in my pocket, feeling like a millionaire. I found treasures in junk shops and thrift shops, which Chris admired tolerantly: a purple velvet skirt, a string of jet beads, an old Army overcoat with epaulets and insignia, beaded barrettes. I was thrilled with these little finds that were so clearly, purely mine, bought with money I'd earned, chosen purely for my own pleasure. I mended and altered them and found my own funky style.

I liked cooking and shopping for food too and got the same sort of pleasure poking through the markets in Chinatown for fish or vegetables, and afterwards cooking us some dollar-ninety-five wonder from a little piece of nameless sea life and some cellophane noodles. I was prouder of these meals than of the ones I made later for Willy out of much finer ingredients, and perhaps they were more delicious. I was pleased with myself when I successfully unstopped the kitchen sink and when I repaired the exploding upholstery on the sofa. If Chris got bored and frustrated on weekends because she couldn't go to lunch and a matinee—even movies had to be budgeted—I joined the library and read in the park, or wandered around Lincoln Center and listened to whatever free music was in the air. Alone or with Chris, I walked everywhere—over bridges, around SoHo, along the rivers, through the canyons of the financial district. To me it was all new and exciting.

Being in control of my own life coursed through my veins like wine. I was no longer dependent on people who wanted to take advantage of me. Unlike Chris, I had no memory of better times for comparison. My goals, when I began thinking about them, were modest and well within my grasp. I might work up to being headwaitress, take a test to find out if I'd been to high school or, less likely, college; perhaps I'd study more. I liked children and baby-sat from time to time for a woman Chris knew. Perhaps I could take care of the children of some woman who worked, or perhaps even be a nursery-school teacher! Something about helping others . . . for though I'd never wanted to go back less, I was

haunted by the letters and some of the faces I'd seen at the
police station. I knew what it was to be lost and helpless; I
felt I must have things to tell people in the same situation.
I pondered all these things tramping through the snow in
my three-dollar Canal Street rubber boots or later at home
curled up in a fat armchair by the radiator. I felt so free
during that period, sifting through the world's possibilities.
And often, during that year, there were times when I knew
I was happy.

I suspected it wouldn't last. The materialistic longings,
the discontent and anxiety that filled everyone else was
bound to get to me too; I'd start wanting money, success,
a lover, or the freedom and fulfillment that obsessed the
women in Chris's consciousness-raising group, which met
once a week. I couldn't live in such air and not breathe it.

The group—five or six women mostly older than Chris
who sat on the floor drinking wine, eating cheese and crackers, and complaining about their men and their parents—
fell upon me as an authentic Free Woman. I had no mother
who'd cramped my interest in masculine things, no father
who expected me to wait on him, no brother who went to
college while I took cooking classes—though whether such
dark influences lay in my unconscious remained unknown.
No wonder I was so cheerful! So optimistic! But in time,
exposure to the patriarchy would fix that. I found them
both bewildering and funny, and annoying when Chris
piled derision on her mother for her cramped and archaic
way of thinking and her blind adherence to the principles
of patriarchal society.

"But Chris, we wouldn't be here if it weren't for her," I
said. "She paid for the move. She comes over with briskets
and sweaters and fruit and offers of free visits to Cousin
Marvin" (the dentist), "and your father would break her
neck if he knew."

"It's all guilt," Chrissie said. She'd grown out her curls
into a fluffy blond Afro and gotten herself a pair of little

round metal-rimmed glasses. She wore painters' overalls in an attempt to look political, but it was one of the ironies of her life that no matter what she put on or did to herself, she always ended up looking like a cute, cuddly little doll. It made her frantic, while at the same time she argued passionately about the importance of accepting your body as it was.

"She doesn't have to come here," I said.

"She comes by rote," said Myra, a forty-five-year-old lesbian up to her jugular in therapy. "There's no love. No acceptance of Chris as a person. No karma. There's only duty and money, the weapons of the patriarchy. Blind protection of the blood kin. It's all that poor woman knows."

I laughed. "Ridiculous!"

The atmosphere turned malevolent. "The suffering of millions of women is ridiculous?" Myra shouted.

"It's hard for Dinah," Chris said loyally. "She hasn't had any experiences." I had never told her what went on between Sally and me.

"Of course she has; she just chooses not to look at them. But the day will come, Dinah." Myra wagged her finger. "Pandora always opens the box."

The truth was they envied me. They were all so heavily burdened with their "baggage." The tangled knots they'd tied, the memory of a hundred mistakes and wrong turnings, the resentments etched so deep it seemed they'd never be erased. They even hinted at this occasionally; one of them told me I had something everybody else wanted. "I'd give anything to be like you and be able to start again with a clean slate." Only Myra shook her head.

"It isn't clean and she knows it." And in the deepest part of my mind I knew she was right and that sooner or later, whether I liked it or not, that dark cloud would start to dissolve.

Of course the fresh, polished innocence of that first charmed state didn't last. I started wanting things I didn't

have. In the most natural way, I began eyeing some of the
men at Snapper's as I never had before. This one wasn't
much, but the one over there was definitely attractive. The
one at table six was trying to strike up an acquaintance, but
he didn't really turn me on. I went out with a couple of
them. Those were the days of easy sex, and I was no exception—particularly after having been with Sally. I decided I
liked men better. The Sisters told me I should always be on
top. I should insist on my own orgasm. There was no
difficulty about that! The Snapper's men seemed endlessly
willing to please; they'd all read books on the subject or
been to sex therapists, they told me as recommendation.
None wanted to go beyond sex, however, toward love. And
soon I began to want that too.

I grew tired of my velvet and fringe from the thrift shop
and longed for some real clothes. I fixed on a pants suit—
the newest thing then—with near desperation. My favorite
was black and cost a hundred dollars, the silk blouse another
twenty-five. One day after I'd been paid I bought the outfit
and was short for the rent.

"I'm sorry, Chris. I went crazy."

"It's okay, we'll make it. You'll owe me, that's all." She
had become a much nicer person in the past months, probably from a little hardship. "It's beautiful, Dinah. Here,
put the collar like this. Oh, you look gorgeous! And next
time you have a date, pull your hair back like this."

"A date! You'll never make it as a feminist." I laughed,
but she looked shattered.

"It isn't easy to sweep out twenty years of conditioning."
She slowly folded the tissue paper and put it back in the
box. She wore a Matriarchy T-shirt, a pair of bikini under-
pants, and sheep-lined slippers. Her little mouth drooped.
It was still an effort not to call her Chrissie.

How serious they all were, the furious Sisters, sitting on
the floor, glaring over their Almadén. Those anxious dates
so frantic to perform sexual miracles. And Mrs. Rapp's

long, polished nails tapping on the table a little more rapidly every time as Chris made no move to return to the fold
but instead talked pointedly of "sexual experimentation"
with her little jaw tensed, her round specs on her nose.

Mrs. Rapp whispered, "I hardly know how to say this,
Dinah, but I'm so worried I can't sleep at night and Irv is
starting to notice. Does Christine . . . well, do you think
. . . is it possible that she has sexual relations with these
men?"

"Very possible, Mrs. Rapp."

"Oy vey. I was afraid you'd say that."

"She's an adult, you know."

"But Dinah, you've been married. You know the risks
and the consequences. And worse, if they're not clean. I
once read you can't always tell, if they're not clean."

I wasn't really surprised when Chris started seeing Portoff
again, which she did on the condition that he wouldn't tell
her parents. He'd been waiting for this. He looked at me
appraisingly the first time he came to the apartment, and I
annoyed him by greeting him with a big, cheerful smile.
Chris was in the bedroom dressing.

"Mike, how nice to see you!"

Portoff looked sour. "I knew she wouldn't last. Her lib
ideas won't either. This isn't her style"—indicating, with
a scornful gesture, our tenement home. "I'll say confiden-
tially that I'm sorry I ever got the bright idea of moving
you in with her. There's been nothing but disaster ever
since. Have you been going to Frank Liverwood?"

"Of course not. He charges seventy-five dollars an hour."

"So now we're learning a little about financial realities!"

"I'm supporting myself. I'm doing fine."

"You're at risk, Dinah," said the little bastard. "You
could go psycho"—he snapped his fingers—"just like that.
Then who'd take care of you?"

Chris came into the room wearing her little round glasses
and a long ethnic dress, looking rather like an earnest little

blond gypsy. She sensed the hostility in the air, looked upset, and steered him out. Who would take care of me? But then, who took care of anybody? You did your best, that was all. God knows the world was full of evil and despair. I remembered the old wrinkled Italian mama and an elderly pair from New Jersey I'd liked very much. And I imagined those who wrote the letters: a little girl with pigtails ("I'm sorry I took the cookies. Please come home soon"), a poor skinny pale child in some foster home, shivering in his bed ("its cold in bed and i have only won blanket"), a black-haired man in a dark suit and a gold watch ("I'm rich and powerful and I'll get you in the end"), a man in a kitchen, making sandwiches for two kids ("Darling, the pig is dead. I swear it"), two women putting a pillow over the face of an old woman in bed. Even the coke-snorter who wanted me to go to Jamaica. That they all wrote to me in their misery made them part of me in a way I couldn't explain. I stored them in my heart, and they gave me a strange kind of strength, like protective spirits. Perhaps they made up for my missing life.

Dinah

___

'Ve gotten to know my neighbor a little, the one in the black bikini with the young blond lover. One day she took off her earphones and wandered over while I did some long-overdue exercises on the terrace.

"I'm Geraldine Varennes. I should have come over before, but you never know, sometimes people like their privacy. Usually the kind that comes to St. Pet's do, anyway."

"I'm Dinah Wakefield."

"Oh, I know." She seemed to know a lot. She knew the house and the servants almost better than I did, greeting Christophena with a cheery wave and ordering herself a rum punch. "I suppose everybody knows everything here because nothing ever happens. We knew who you were before you came, and Jerry says he's heard of your husband."

Jerry was the beachboy. I'd heard her calling him early in the morning—and seen him lying on the terrace ignoring her. "Jerry . . . Jerrrry . . . Jerrreee. Come in, please, sweetie. Come in, Jerrreee." Whenever I heard those seductive tones I went into the bedroom. I couldn't bear to see his magnificent young bronze body stretched out on a lounge chair, still as a statue, while she called, "Jerry . . . Come in, honey. I'm waiting for you. There's time before breakfast, lover." She was second fiddle to the tea or the Bain de Soleil, which Jerry sometimes reached for and slowly stroked on his chest and loins. Or his face, closing his eyes and moving his face from side to side rather than his hand. I'd listen in spite of myself.

"Well," I said, as Christophena brought the drinks, "I can't think why anybody would have heard of Willy."

"Well, he's famous, isn't he? A famous surgeon?" I looked at her carefully, but she seemed to be hiding nothing. "I truly feel doctors are God's helpers, the most noble of all the professions. A long time ago I studied to be a nurse." She lit a menthol cigarette. "In fact I'd work at your husband's clinic if I thought they'd take me."

"I should think they would."

"I never did finish the course, so I don't have an R.N. degree."

"They probably don't care." Did she want something of me, or was I getting suspicious in the heat? Indirection seemed to be in the air in St. Pet's—roundabout thoughts and hidden approaches. "Do you want me to ask him if they need somebody?"

"Oh, no." Geraldine sat up straighter, running her hand over the row of neat little rubber tires on her stomach, as though to smooth them out. "I wouldn't think of bothering him with something so unimportant. I know how busy he must be. He shouldn't have to think about my stupid little idea."

"But if they're short of help . . ."

"Oh, please. Promise me you won't mention it." She rooted me with her brown gaze, coming out of slightly softened flesh around the eyes. Her hair was pale straw-color, but her plucked eyebrows were dark and she wore dark false eyelashes. "I hope you don't think that's why I dropped by. It was stupid of me to mention it. I just wanted to make a neighborly call. I hoped we could get to know each other a little." She looked distressed.

"How long have you been here?" I asked to get out of the mystifying muddle we'd gotten into.

"Close to ten years." She was only too anxious to tell her story. She'd come down to the islands with her husband, who had a drinking problem, very common in these parts. They'd run a restaurant on St. Thomas for a while, then a beachside bar on Nevis and a boardinghouse on St. Kitts. By the time they were at The Parrot Fish (a dump in English Town), Artie was on a bottle of rum a day. Then everything fell apart. The place went down and they had to sell out. Fights. Nights of booze. Brutal beatings—once he'd even cut her with a knife (showing me a picturesque gash on her inner thigh). Finally Artie left, stealing all their money, but Geraldine was so glad to see him go she didn't care. But then the black moods of depression. Two suicide attempts—she'd even failed at that! Then medication, and then God, which had worked until she met Jerry, who was an atheist—though she retained certain spiritual beliefs. But what a body, in case I hadn't noticed. Nobody had ever made her feel the way he did. In ten years of marriage to Artie she'd never felt it inside her the way she did with Jerry—that big swollen thing searing her insides like a hot poker. She was hooked on it, crazy for it. He said he'd never had a woman like her . . . and on and on with more graphic descriptions of their sex life, while in desperation I ordered two more rum punches and smoked a couple of her cigarettes, which I only do when really unhinged. And thanked God for the invention of sunglasses, which hide one's expression so well.

After a while she wound down. She was a tall, hefty woman with big thighs and big tits and silver toenails, which shone like coins. Her dried hair was tied back with a red scarf, and there was something wrong with one tooth, which she was aware of and tried to keep her mouth over.

"Well, I don't want to take any more of your time. I'm
very glad to have made your acquaintance, Dinah. You
know, we're all shipwrecked here and it's not bad to have
friends. Maybe you and your husband will come for dinner
sometime. Sometimes people here are a little standoffish
and I think it's too bad. I certainly wouldn't want to impose. Jerry says I'm too pushy." I thought she was going to
get up, but she just kept looking at me. "I just want to be
sure you didn't think I came to hint about a job."

"Oh, no," I lied.

"Actually, there's something else. It might sound funny
to you." A slight pause. "They say you're charmed."

As she said it I was aware of Christophena behind me.
The swish-swish of the broom she'd been wielding stopped,
then resumed very slowly, as though the air had thickened,
slowing all movement.

"I don't understand."

"Well, the Petinjans have a lot of beliefs, you know.
They think some people are mounted by the spirits." She
was watching me. "I don't know if you think about those
things. I mean, maybe it sounds silly to you."

Not at all. So what else is new? "Well, Geraldine, I'll
tell you. There is something odd about me, though I
wouldn't call it a charm. I have amnesia; there's a part of
my life I can't remember." It was so still I swear the wind
stopped; the birds and clatter of the palms and the waves
and the voices from the road were, for a moment, hushed.
"And at home I had some funny experiences with . . ." I
stopped. I couldn't remember what I was going to say.
Geraldine was like a statue. "But maybe *that's* what they
think the charm is. Maybe it seems like a charm." I laughed
nervously, and everything snapped back into place.

Geraldine got up. "Well, maybe. But you know, this is
a very spiritual place. There's a lot of that kind of energy
around, and it's part of people's daily lives. What I'm saying is, you're safe with it here." I couldn't think of anything

to say. "And Dinah, I know it's none of my business. But the people who go along with it get along better, and sometimes bad things happen to people who fight it. You know, it's like the food; it's better to let them cook their way than trying to make them cook American. It's the same thing." She put her hand on my arm. "It helps me. Sometimes I think I'd die without them."

She turned and walked slowly back across the stretch of sand between our houses. I turned and looked at Christophena. Her lucent black eyes looked straight into my soul. When our eyes met the darkness lifted, and I knew that this was not all there was.

Dinah

—

I didn't think I could bear it the night Willy got up and left my bed. Chris's and mine—that same squashy double bed, now minus most of the lacy pillows, that barely fit into the tiny bedroom. On the bureau was an empty bottle of Mersault in a bucket of cold water and a couple of sticky glasses. Never had there been such an empty room.

"Nothing, Dinah?" he had asked. "Not some dim image of a mother's face or a pet dog . . . Dad coming home from work? Nothing?"

"A big blank."

"And the Colorado marriage?"

"I made it up." God, the way he'd looked at me!

"I'd better go home," he'd said. "To tell you the truth, I don't know how to handle it."

Crying didn't stop him, though he waited till I'd stopped choking and weeping before he left. I sat there listening to his footsteps going down the three flights. Then I started again.

I'd had to tell him, as Chris had reminded me a dozen times. This wasn't one of the Snapper's lovers, looking for an evening of play. There was a whole life here I was dallying with, several in fact. The kids had gotten attached to me, and I loved them dearly—almost as much as I loved Willy, who would never again look at me with adoring need, never again reach out his fine surgeon's hand to move my hair gently off my face. They'd filled my life. When the phone rang, it was Willy, or had been; when I looked out the window, it was his car I saw parking across the street, or had once. How unendurably I'd slid back! The black pants suit hung in the closet like a shroud . . . and now Chris was going out with Michael again, which made it even worse.

During that wet, dreary spring I relived my new, unbearable memories; Sunday mornings when we'd lie close in bed until footsteps came down the hall and one of the kids ran in and jumped into bed with us, giggling and pulling the covers, till Willy got dressed and went to the deli for bagels and Nova. Sometimes we'd go on an excursion—the zoo or Staten Island ferry or Chinatown, Jessie riding on Willy's shoulders and Con dragging me by the hand. We'd have lunch at a Chinese restaurant or a hot dog stand. Later, at home, when the kids were in bed, Willy and I would eat dinner together, early if he had to scrub in the morning, quickly because we wanted each other so badly. We'd make love as though we'd invented it, and indeed, in a sense, we had. In the morning, when the latest agency nanny arrived, Jessie wailed miserably and hung on to my leg to keep me from leaving. I'd extricate myself, feeling horrible, closing the door on her red, tearful face and Conrad's baleful glare.

I'd organized the whole household—scheduled the laundry, the dry cleaner, the diaper service, Gristede's, even started looking for a maid. Sometimes I took a bag of groceries over and cooked dinner, leaving in time to be at the restaurant. Willy and I didn't have much chance to be alone, but I didn't mind. I just wanted to be with him. When he asked me to move in, I knew I had to tell him the rotten truth.

I was doomed either way. Either I kept up the lie or I lost him, and now he thought I was a liar anyway for telling him I was a divorcée from Colorado. I'd closed my eyes and pretended he accepted me with all my peculiarities. Now I paid the price. Everything reminded me of Willy—the store where we'd shopped for vegetables, the white monumental blaze of Episcopal Hospital by the river, a restaurant he'd taken me to. A couple of times I even walked by the house, but the windows were dark. I almost rang the bell . . . and then I didn't.

I spent a month brooding, while Chris clucked and consoled and scolded and said Willy was so desperate for a wife he was bound to come back, unless of course he met somebody else, which she was almost sure he hadn't yet.

Then one night I got drunk and called Sally.

She was cool and friendly. "Dinah, how nice to hear from you. What luck, I just got back from Rio—one of those impulsive trips. It was fantastic . . . and I rethought our project and decided it just needed a little more time. You were so wise and right to see it when I didn't."

"I didn't see anything. And I still don't remember a thing."

"Oh, well, you will, sweetie. Hey, I have a friend's car for a few days. How about driving out to the country for dinner? The azaleas are just coming out."

At that point I would have accepted an invitation to a dog fight. A cock fight. Why not? It would be no worse than being in town, where each budding tree made me want to weep.

Of course I'd kidded myself; there was no such thing as an innocent evening with Sally. By the time we were on the Merritt Parkway I knew what we were going for. The car seemed to be full of that dirty red light Sally generated, and my head was full of, well, gay pornography. I told myself that it was just misplaced longing for Willy, fastening on whatever was at hand. But even so, this feeling for her was different, riskier, more of a high dive off the cliff, knowing you had to hit the water when the wave was up or smash yourself to pieces. In comparison, making love to Willy was like swimming off a safe beach at high tide.

We had dinner on the terrace of the Rivertown Inn. She was so smoothly kind, so attuned to my feelings, that I wondered if that crazed woman clicking her silver gun had been a dream. Now she listened to my sad story with a wise, sympathetic smile. When I told her how Willy had left, she reached over one finger, with Wine-on-Ice nail, to my eyes and removed the tears hovering there, carrying the drop of salty moisture to her lips—carefully, as though it were a tiny jewel—and licking it off delicately. Over the Vandermint I cried a little more, over what I wasn't sure.

In our room, which had dotted swiss curtains and a curly maple bed, Sally made love to me gently and tenderly, which I couldn't recall her doing before; I only remembered us attacking each other. This time it was like floating in a cloud. Sally's white hair seemed cloudy, as did the white curtains and a fluffy blue and white quilt. I watched her face against it when she came, her skin brown with tiny wrinkles around the eyes, like some ancient Egyptian goddess crying out to eternity.

In the morning I lay naked in bed, staring at the ceiling, while Sally took a bath. Sadness, if that's what it had been, turned to anger at Willy for running away from me, for not being courageous about unfamiliar things—and he a physician! Now that my body was quiet, I was irritated at myself for coming on this stupid trip. When she popped out of the bathroom without a towel and came toward me, I told her I'd had enough.

"What's the matter?"

"Frankly, this whole trip makes me feel like I was sent back to GO."

She laughed. "You've got your rules mixed up, Dinah. You don't need this stuffy doctor with his houseful of brats.

He'll be driving a Porsche and giving you fifty dollars a week to run the house on."

I sat up. "I can't believe the things you say. Willy's a kind, brilliant, honest person. I respect him more for backing away if he can't handle the amnesia"—Sally hooted with laughter—"instead of lying and pretending to be cool about everything like *some* people."

"Bullshit." She was enjoying this exchange, and in a sneaky, secret way so was I. She was the only person who called for neither politeness nor consideration, who had no feelings whatever to worry about. While the rest of the world cried, sulked, or bruised easily, Sally only laughed, a response not without appeal when I thought about Willy brooding over my lack of past. "Darling, I love the way the world is brainwashing you. You're much more fun than you used to be."

"You thrive on misery, don't you? You've lived so long in the jungle you've forgotten there are ordinary, good people in the world—if you ever knew it. You pull everybody down to your own rotten level."

Her voice hardened. "Look who's calling who rotten. Just look. I was straight with you. I trusted you. I took you in. I busted my ass for you, and you walked out—and by the way, you're still under contract."

"I walked out because you made my life hell."

"Some hell, baby. If that's hell give me more. I'll burn forever."

"I walked out because you tried to kill me."

She looked at me in honest amazement and amusement. "Jesus, you've got some imagination. With what, sweetie —a dildo?"

The phone rang; she always brought her work with her. I paid no attention but took a leisurely shower and was pulling on my jeans when the bathroom door opened and Sally stood there, still as a statue. It took a moment; I'd forgotten her signals. Not a muscle moved; her eyes were

fixed as stones. Her white bathrobe was open in the front.
The only thing that moved was her belly, which moved
rapidly in and out.

"What's the . . ." But I couldn't get the words out.

"I'll tell you what's the matter. We've been scooped,
that's what. How darling of Bernie to call and let me know.
You cunt."

How she confused me! On one hand I wanted to kill her;
on the other all the old feelings of terror came back. I hung
on to the door frame and shook, and she stepped forward
and grabbed me by the shoulders.

"Get your hands off me," I said.

"Oh no, sweetheart. We're in it together. You're going
to listen and share the grief. They've terminated our contract—thanks to you. No memory, no book contract. See,
darling? It's amazing I could drag it out as long as I did.
Well, I can't push her, I can't force her, I kept saying. But
now, Bernie tells me, we're *dumped,* because Doubleday has
bought another book about an amnesiac woman who got
her memory back and it's six figures and paperback and
feature film and big publicity tour, big fancy party with all
the right people, and *the whole Goddamn fucking thing could
have been ours!*" She was screaming and shaking me at the
same time.

"For God's sake get your hands off me, you bitch."

"I won't. The whole thing is your fault because you're
such an asshole you flushed it all down the toilet. You never
tried. You took the money under false pretenses because
you never meant to remember, you only meant to rob me."

A last try at reason. "That's not true. You got the money.
I never saw a penny of it. I don't know why you even care;
you have plenty of other projects."

She pushed me so hard my head slammed against the
door frame. "Shall I do it again? Maybe it'll make your head
work better. Because now I have to give them back fifty
thousand dollars—understand? Fifty thousand, every penny
of which is *spent.*"

She was strong, but I managed to get away from her, or free enough to duck over to the window. Sally and I edged around the room like prizefighters.

"Not so fast, Dinah. You're not going to get out of this so easily. Your name's on the contract too. You're liable. I'll have the police after you in an hour."

"I'm leaving here. You don't scare me anymore"—a total lie. "What makes you so sure I'd even tell you? I could have remembered everything all this time and never said a word about it. Did you think of that?"

She hadn't. Nor had I until that moment. I've made plenty of mistakes, but that was one of the worst. She began to turn red and swell up. A little tantrum had become murderous rage. I edged near the door; on the bureau were the car keys. I'd make a run for it. I had no top on, but the car was pretty close. I'd just have to exit like Lady Godiva.

"I'm going to kill you, Dinah," Sally said, her eyes frozen, her voice cold and calm. "You won't get away this time. Maybe I'll cut off one of your tits and stick it in your dead mouth, like they did in Nam."

Then everything happened very fast. I got the keys and wrenched the door open. For a moment she wasn't there, and I thought, She's getting her gun, this is it. I froze with terror, then heard a sound and ran down the hall toward the exit. Then down the stairs—the wrong stairs—slamming in and out, maids a-goggle, and Sally giving murderous chase not with her gun but with a silver knife, screaming, "I'm going to cut you up, Dinah."

Somebody might have grabbed us if there'd been a main lobby, but it was a motel kind of place and our entourage —me, Sally, and a couple of wild-eyed maids—swept out the back door and into the parking lot. There was a heart-stopping moment while I looked frantically for the car, then saw it and ran for it, managing to get in and slam the door just as Sally arrived and began pulling at the handle.

I closed both doors and locked them. It was a hot day and the temperature in there must have been 110 degrees.

As people came out of the motel to watch this curious drama, Sally flung herself on the fender, bathrobe flapping. I started the ignition and we rolled slowly out of the parking lot. I would have gone to the police station if I'd known where it was. I didn't go fast because I didn't really want to kill her; I just wanted this red face with its white hair and bulging eyes away from my front window, this half-naked body off the car. Or maybe I did want to kill her, I don't know.

We rolled down the hill to a major route where we passed McDonald's, Midas Muffler, Toyota City, Friendly's, and so on, past Rivertown Mall—Macy's, Bloomingdale's, Neiman-Marcus—and Sally was still hanging on. The air-conditioning didn't work, and when, desperate for air, I opened the far window slightly, Sally threw herself across the hood and stuck the tip of her knife in, screaming threats and obscenities.

I veered around, because I couldn't see past that brown body, which blotted out the entire landscape. I couldn't see very well and never saw the car that was coming from the other direction (very fast, they said later) because somehow I'd gotten into the wrong lane.

I woke up in a hospital. I was disoriented but comfortable enough—if you didn't count the aching muscles. A nice sunny room. I lay flat on my back on a white-sheeted bed, staring at the ceiling, arms by my sides. At first I wondered if I was dead . . . but if I was dead everything wouldn't hurt so much. I raised one hand and found a bandage on my head.

Chrissie was sitting on the end of the bed, watching me with a puzzled, frightened look. She put her hand on my arm, pulled it back. Arranged the cover, moved away. She was white as a sheet. For a moment there was that terrible blank I remembered so well, that glassine lens. I knew her and yet I didn't; she was real yet in a dream . . . Then she snapped into place.

"Dinah—oh, Dinah."

"What happened? Am I dead?"

"No, but it was close. It's a miracle you're alive . . . Do you know who I am?"

"Chris, my roommate." She had some reaction I didn't understand. "I'm pretty confused. I haven't the faintest idea how I got here."

"Well, you were . . ." She took a deep breath. "You were in a car crash with Sally."

"Sally?"

"So you don't . . ." She looked upset. "Dinah, you have to rest. But everything's going to be okay, and nobody knows but me. The police called me, because of your Snapper's ID. But don't worry, I didn't even tell Mother and *certainly* not Michael."

I hadn't the slightest idea what she was talking about.

I wasn't hurt badly, and soon I checked out of the hospital, making up a social security number and a Blue Cross number. I didn't really like doing it, but what else was I to do? We drove off in a taxi, leaving them scanning and muttering and phoning and trying to summon me up out of the computer—efforts all doomed to failure, of course, because I didn't really exist.

Back in the city, Chris helped me up the three flights and put me to bed.

"Dinah, Sally was killed."

"Oh, I'm sorry." Was I? My memory was a little off— again. I only remembered Sally as a woman I'd had some kind of business dealings with.

"Dinah, you still don't remember it?"

"No."

"Well, the police wondered why she was riding on the hood of the car. Instead of inside."

"The hood?"

"Yes, right in front of the windshield. In a bathrobe."

She pressed my memory lightly, and then one day it began to come back. Oh . . . Sally. The drive in the country, the dinner, the Vandermint. The curly maple bed, the dotty curtains. There had been something silver, something she had. I'd run away . . . Oh, she'd gotten angry again, swollen up and turned red . . . turned red . . ."I remember part but not the crash."

She was still avoiding my eye in a funny way. "Well, there have been a few newspaper stories, and even something on TV—I think it was Channel Five. It wasn't in the *Times,* though there was something on page three of the *Post.*"

"Newspapers?"

"Well, they might have exaggerated, Dinah. I guess. 'Lesbian Love Nest' and stuff like that. 'Naked women flee motel wielding knives.' "

Then she explained that the bizarre accident had taken place almost under the nose of a reporter from the local paper, who had been in a roadside Wendy's. She'd looked up to see a passing car with a half-naked woman draped over the hood, waving what looked like a knife. Inside, at the wheel, was another naked woman. So she dropped her cheeseburger and ran out just in time to see this curious vehicle veer into the other lane and, a moment later, smash into an oncoming car. She'd seen the whole gory thing and was shortly on the phone to her editor.

"But the stories were mainly about Sally, Dinah. After all, you're nobody," and Sally was famous, mainly for her recent best-seller in which she proved beyond all reasonable doubt that Marilyn Monroe had been murdered by the Kennedy women. "They focused on the corrupt literary establishment and stuff like that. One of the reporters asked me about you, and I said you were just this orphan waitress. I even gave him the wrong name, though they have your name from your wallet; that's how they got to me. But I think it's okay; it's been a week now, and I'm sure Willy doesn't read anything but the *Times*. He'll never hear about it in a million years."

I must have looked blank. "But even if he did . . ."

Her expression stopped me. "You're *gay*, Dinah. And you never told me." She looked at me with bereaved eyes. "You're better now and we have to talk about this."

"I'm not gay."

"But you were . . . gay with her."

"Well, yes. It was part of the whole thing and now it's over."

Poor Chris. How sorely she was tested. Though she'd defended Sister Myra's sexual orientation to the death—her right, her body, her self-expression!—when it came closer to home it was different. I'd never told her about Sally and me. She'd been sleeping on the living-room couch, to let me have the whole bed, she said.

She moved away from me till she was backed up against the refrigerator. "You had sex with a woman," she whispered.

"Well, so what? It was just something that happened."

"You didn't tell me, and we've slept in the same bed the whole time, until the accident!"

"Where else would we sleep? We have only one bed." It was perfectly ample. Neither of us was that big, and we didn't thrash around much.

"It must have been hard for you," Chris said in a thin voice.

"I never missed her, if that's what you mean. She's crazy as hell . . . Was crazy." Then I got it. Looking at her little blond bush of hair, her curvy-doll body, I got it. "Chris, you can't believe what I think you believe."

"I know you get turned on by women."

"It means I was, by one woman. But honestly, the idea of making love to you never entered my head."

"Well, Dinah, *that*'s hard to believe."

I said frantically, "Well, maybe it did, but just kind of theoretically. The idea doesn't interest me. Not that you aren't cute and all that. Oh, shit. Everything I say comes out wrong, and you're the one with the problem, not me."

She sat down slowly on the kitchen chair and reached for a cinnamon doughnut, which she brought to her face and stared at intently, probably to avoid my eye. "I guess that's true, Dinah. I can't make the leap. I'm going to end up like my mother sure as the sun's coming up tomorrow."

"So, is that really so bad? I like your mother."

"I forget sometimes, Dinah. You don't have the context. You don't have the voices in your head. In a way you're sort of amoral."

"I'm trying to function in a very confusing world, where people don't usually say what they mean."

She looked at me for a long time. "Of course. To you it must seem that way. You don't even have much sense of right and wrong."

"You're making me feel horrible! Of course I do; I'm not a criminal. I do my share of the housework and I try not to hurt people's feelings."

"Is that why you went to bed with Sally—not to hurt her feelings?"

Back and forth we bickered, until I was pretty well recovered.

"I'm your friend, Dinah, and I'm glad to take care of you. But I can't stay here any longer."

"I'll sleep on the couch, I don't care."

"Our whole relationship has changed, and now that you're well, I don't feel comfortable here any longer. A person can't keep stretching and stretching out of shape forever. You always go back to the same old shape you were in the beginning. Now I think I was made for a very conventional life."

I felt dreadful, watching her pack. She was my only real friend, the only person in the world I could trust. I didn't

know how I'd survive without this solemn, sweet little
person, her funny advice and her mysterious conflicts—not
to mention her share of the rent.

"Chris, aren't you making too big a deal out of this?"

"Yes, probably. I'm just tired of fighting my true self.
I'm really sorry, Dinah. I'll never forget this year. I like
you. I even love you, sort of. You're the one I thought . . ."
A choke. "It just wouldn't be fair to you for me to stay here
because I couldn't be natural anymore." She pulled an arm-
ful of dresses out of the closet—dresses she hadn't worn
since the old apartment. "And whatever you do, Dinah,
don't tell Willy."

"He's not around to tell," I said.

It was after she left that the first memory came back, just
as I was getting out of the shower. I was a child playing by
a stream in some country place. A small village . . . I knew
where the post office was, and the school . . . Then it
stopped. I didn't even know where I had lived.

I got back into the shower, thinking more details might
fall onto my head, but that was the end of it. But I must
have had a fine childhood, playing by a babbling stream
with a field of wildflowers nearby! Not what I'd dreaded at
all. I thought—though I wasn't sure—that it might be
Vermont, though I didn't know the name of the town. It
made me very excited. I could even go there on a bus, if I
could just remember a little more! It was something to look
forward to and save money for—which was now virtually
impossible since Chris had moved in with Michael. I began
looking around for another roommate.

Then one night I came out of Snapper's and there was
Willy, standing there with the kids.

I'd recovered somewhat from Willy. Not forgotten about
him, of course, but faced what I'd thought was the inevit-
ability of getting along without him, for I never dreamed

he'd return. I'd been out with a couple of other men. One
of the other waitresses needed a place to live, and I could
start saving for going to Vermont . . .

Willy said, "Dinah, we need you." There he was, tall,
pale, with his wavy hair sticking up. He was wearing a
raincoat and holding a child by each hand. Jessie's nose was
running and her hair was in snarls. Con was wearing a
sweater I was sure was Charlotte's. It was well past bedtime.
It was poignant, and necessary—Charlotte was visiting her
cousin in Maryland.

"Well, Willy. What a surprise. It's been . . . let's see,
a couple of months." (It had been sixty-one days, twenty-
three hours and seven minutes.) I greeted the kids affec-
tionately while he watched with rueful hope. Whatever
happened, I wasn't going to make it easy for him. I could
stand on my own feet.

"Con, I'm so glad to see you. You've grown an inch at
least. I've really missed you both."

"We can't do the laundry. The washer's broken," Conrad
said. "And we can't find anything."

Jessie said, "Dinah, we miss you. Grandma cooks yucky
food and everything's horrible. The agency nurse made me
eat liver."

We went to Maxwell's Plum, where Willy ordered champagne. I looked at him and in his eyes I saw apology and
appeal. Well, I never could resist him. I looked at his
beautiful hands, one of which was wiping Jessie's nose. His
hands choked me up. I couldn't resist him at all.

They hadn't exaggerated. The house hadn't looked so bad
since the night I'd met Willy. But I would have been glad
to be there if the ceiling had fallen in. I quit Snapper's and
moved right in—a double act of commitment which might
have given me pause if I'd found another roommate, which
I hadn't, and if the manager of the restaurant hadn't made
a serious pass, which warranted my leaving on the spot.

The first thing I did was to resume the search for a maid, rewarded one morning by the appearance of Emerelda at the door. She came from Haiti and was a little vague about how she'd gotten to us. Nor had she a green card. But two cross, whiny children turned sweet and docile when this little dark lady walked in, and her first dinner—lime chicken and peas-and-rice—was delicious. And she kept the children (and me) spellbound with voodoo tales.

While Emerelda got the household under control, I spent most of my time with the children, who were in desperate need of consistency and love. We went to the playground, the zoo, or the market, with the dog on its leash. On rainy days we'd stay in the big playroom in the basement, which Liz had furnished with a mini gym and some old, comfortable furniture. We'd curl up with books or toys and play tinkly tunes on the little record player. We sang songs, read, and played games. At night after their baths I'd tell them stories or sing to them in bed, sometimes for so long that Willy would come up looking just a touch annoyed and say it was time they were asleep.

"Don't they wear you out?" Willy asked. "Don't you get tired or resentful at taking care of kids that aren't even yours?"

"Never. Why should I care whose they are?"

He marveled, "You're pure. You're innocent. You have no jealousy. I didn't think a woman like you existed."

"Am I so different from other women?"

"Yes, you're different from everybody. Somehow you walk alone."

"But I feel shallow and limited," I said. "I'm envious when people talk about their lives before."

"Darling, what you don't have I'll give you."

He thought I was remarkably free of the expectations that haunted most people, about what life should be for a woman, or an American, or a wife, or a taxpayer, or whatever. Well, I could only go on what I'd learned, which was if you couldn't do for yourself, you pretty well had to find somebody else to do for you. In return for his supporting me, it seemed the least I could do for Willy was take care of his house and his children. For a long time it was a fair exchange. We loved each other with a special gratitude for having saved each other's lives. We'd come along just when we needed each other most, and it took us very far along the road.

Of course he checked me out thoroughly. "Dinah, I hope you don't mind that as a physician I took the liberty of talking to Mike Portoff and Frank Liverwood about you. Nothing confidential, of course, just your prognosis. They both felt there was a good chance you'll always have the amnesia."

"Suppose it changes, Willy? Suppose I remember more than that little country town business?"

"I've never believed, Dinah, that things just *happen*. Your getting your memory back or not is largely a matter of *will*. I hope and expect that your life will be committed to me and not devoted to chasing will-o'-the-wisps in Vermont or around the police station or collecting letters from strangers. I need a wholehearted life partner. In return for this I'll give you everything—my devotion, my home, my children, your own if you want. Every material comfort and life in Manhattan's fast track. And I'll always be true to you. I don't have the time or energy for fooling around or for another divorce either."

Well, it can never be said Willy didn't lay it on the line. And how neatly he circled, and evaded, the possibility of my remembering, so when that dark cloud started dissolving like a clarifying solution, he could tell me to just *not look*. But that was all later. Neither of us believed the amnesia would clear up—the idea was too incredible—and what Willy offered was far more compelling.

We had a small wedding at home, then went to Jamaica for our honeymoon. We'd never been alone together for more than a few hours at a time till that trip. Said Willy, as we made love in our hotel room in Ocho Rios, "I want to fill you up with me." He meant more than his engorged penis and my waiting insides. Now I heard all about whatever parts of his life he hadn't told me before. His conflict with his father. His father's conflict with Charlotte because she was a Southern gardenia and he was a self-made guy who'd pulled himself up from nothing. His brother Phil and how Dad loved him better, how Charlotte had protected Willy from Dad because he was sensitive and different. Charlotte's palpitations, hypochondria, hysteria, and castrating behavior. Dad's death ten years before.

"There's something I want to tell you, Dinah." We sat on a candlelit terrace overlooking the sea, a bottle of wine on our table, while the steel band played "Yellow Bird." He took my hand in his. "I was in therapy for a while, just to get straightened out during the divorce. Some of my own conflicts surfaced—nothing serious, but I'd like to share them with you."

"Of course, Willy."

"Maybe I should have told you before, but it's hard for me to talk about. Doctors have the illusion they're indestructible, you know. It was hard on my self-image, but a revelation in many ways. My childhood was the typical suburban American dream. Sure, Dad drank too much at the club sometimes, but so did the other guys. And if Charlotte was helpless, I thought that was how women were supposed to be. So amazingly enough, it wasn't till I was over thirty years old and married to Liz that I found out in therapy that there was serious pathology in my family. Really bad stuff."

He looked so upset I held his hand tightly. "What do you mean?"

"It was very, very subtle. The way Charlotte would flick her eyes over Dad's suit: let's see if you pass or if you look like the *inferior redneck* you really are. Then he'd pay her back by getting drunk at the Peabody family reunion. In their quiet, veiled way they were trying to destroy each other. For instance, when she read him something from the morning paper, she'd slow her speech to make sure he understood—as though he were slightly illiterate. He'd get it all right. So he'd fail to compliment her cooking—she used to be a great Southern cook—or he'd ostentatiously *add salt.*" I guess I still looked blank. "Try to understand, Dinah. Once she knitted him a beautiful sweater in maroon, his favorite color. He said, 'Charlotte, this is the nicest sweater I've had since the one my mother made me when I was twelve.' Can you believe he'd say something so hurtful?"

"Why was that so bad?"

"Because he compared her to *his mother!*" Willy's voice got louder. "That's got to hurt her! And then, inevitably, her revenge. One night I heard them talking in the bedroom, and he said, 'Charlotte, do you feel like being intimate?' He was a pretty old-fashioned guy. And she said—I heard her with my own ears—'Not tonight, Frank. I've got a headache.' "

It certainly gave us something to talk about, though after a while I would have given anything for another subject. Snorkling on the reef as the hot sun beat down: "Since Charlotte was obviously frigid, she developed an unhealthy attachment to me, and Dr. Chalmers said it was a miracle she did so little damage. Apparently I have a lot of ego strength." Sprawled on the sugary sand under the banyan tree: "At my graduation from Yale, when Dad, Charlotte, my brother, Phil, and I were having dinner at a restaurant, Dad and I both ordered lobster. But they only had one left. And Charlotte said, 'Let Willy have it, because it's his big day.' Taking the penis away from Dad and giving it to me, you see."

"It wasn't a penis. It was a lobster." My eyes were closed.

"Dinah, you're refusing to understand what I'm telling you—unless you have some defect in metaphorical thinking. Hey, I never thought of that." He kissed me. "I'm sorry, darling. I'll be more patient. But it's very important that you grasp this."

Later on I found it simpler to just agree with Willy, but at the time I found all this very confusing. "You're saying that your parents were crazy but you're not—is that right?"

"Not *crazy*, Dinah. Acting out a pathological marriage. In our family poor Phil got the brunt of it. He has a deeply buried homosexual problem because he felt he had to be macho with Dad. Whereas I accepted my femininity because I partly identified with Charlotte. Which of course was the source of Dad's hostility, and the reason Phil lives in Borneo."

"People don't go to Borneo because of their femininity." Or maybe they did. What did I know?

"You're just going to have to accept what I say. I know more about it than you do."

As we walked through a coffee plantation, Willy said he was sorry he hadn't told me all this before we were married.

"It doesn't matter, Willy. Really it doesn't."

"Well, it does. People should tell each other these serious things beforehand. Just accept my apology, okay?"

Foolishly I said, "I just don't see what's so serious. I mean if you told me about another woman or *man* or a couple of kids you hadn't mentioned, that would be one thing. Or a crime or some dread disease; *then* it would be serious. But as far as I can see, you're pretty much as advertised. You've had a pretty normal life."

Willy's eyes darkened and for a moment he said nothing. Then, "Dinah, on this subject you have no basis whatever for offering an opinion. Any opinion *at all*. You've had no experience with marriage."

"That we know of."

We arrived back at the hot, tarry road. "We've decided to assume and live *as though you haven't*. Because even if you have, it's *erased*, which is why you're unable to take this in.

Marriage is like one of those gigantic structures made of toothpicks or matches. A million tiny strokes that make a whole. And we're already laying the foundation."

Somehow his words scared me. "Willy, let's go back to the hotel and make love."

And we did, in our white-painted room with the blue curtains that fluttered in the breeze and the smooth tile floor where our clothes lay. As I lay next to him, my arms locked around him and our bodies tightly together, the foundation was strong. But I knew I'd disappointed him in some way I didn't understand. I was glad to get back to New York and so was he. We'd been too exposed there in Jamaica, away from all the daily things that made us work well together.

Though Willy's assumptions, presented as truths, were no less ludicrous than Sally's or Chrissie's, I knew it was in my best interest to make them my own. Diligently I studied them, like an anthropologist studying another culture. His terrible childhood, from which he'd emerged unscathed because of remarkable ego strength. The sanctity and peculiar morality of the medical profession, his work as vital top priority. His high expectations for his children and our obligations to them—the best schools, fine character training, a warm home environment with firm scheduling, which would make them into secure but competitive and ambitious adults of fine moral fiber. My relationship with Charlotte, which he assumed to be very difficult and taxing —"I hate to inflict her on you, Dinah, but what can I do? Phil went to Borneo and copped out on the whole thing"— when in fact I liked her very much. Even certain sexual practices that he thought would give me pause—to which I found it simpler to feign objection than to see his look of slightly shocked disapproval. This was delicate territory. It wasn't that he really wanted me to object when his head moved down my body and between my legs. But if I registered a gentle protest, easily overcome, his passion doubled.

I learned to say (like Chrissie), "Oh, Willy, do you think we should?" and, "Darling, you mustn't," a few times whenever our lovemaking ventured into new territory.

The matter of Liz was, to say the least, more complicated. She haunted the house. She had left her imprint everywhere: we sat on furniture she'd chosen and ate off her plates, and I cooked in her pots and pans. And it had been she who created the strange disorder I found when I first came—the fondue forks under the sofa, the typewriter in the refrigerator, and a huge pile of pennies in the basement toilet. It makes me sad to record these things now. The typewriter was not in the regular refrigerator, but in an old one in the playroom where Liz had kept snacks for the kids. I suppose Willy hadn't looked into it since she left. I opened it one day and there among the rotten fruit and moldy cookies was a portable Olivetti. There was a piece of paper in it and the words, "I'm cold."

I called Willy down; it was in the evening and the kids were in bed. He looked at it without saying anything, but his face changed and I thought there were tears in his eyes.

"I never get used to it," he said. "Close the fridge."

"Don't you want to take it out?"

"I'll do it this weekend. What I really hate is that you saw it."

"But why? It isn't your fault."

"Somehow it is. I should have seen the signs sooner; there might have been a better treatment. I shouldn't have put the kids or myself through it. I'm sorry, Dinah. It was very negligent of me not to go over the house, but I've just been so damn busy."

The strange thing, which I didn't tell him, was that I immediately understood why she had done these things. I could see into her crazy mind with an eerie clarity, and in her context, it all made sense. The old fridge was full of unexpressed words, she thought, and if she put the typewriter inside, they could put themselves on paper. The fondue forks were under the sofa because that's where Switzerland was—for anybody with sense enough to see it.

I had a feeling I was getting a look at things I had no business seeing. Not that I tried. When I found the dead parakeet in the medicine chest, I knew it was because budgies have the power to cure headaches. Most of these unbidden interpretations showed her motives to be benign or peculiar at most, but one day in the backyard I found a little circle of white stones and immediately knew she'd tried to kill Willy. The stones were a necklace. Every day she'd remove one so it would tighten slowly around his neck until . . . I can't say the rest.

I scooped them up and dropped them into the next yard, where they've lain ever since. But it shook me up. I didn't know why I could understand her, and I didn't like it at all. I knew I was different from other people. But a blank is one thing, and a blank with strange, deep holes in it is something else. I tried to explain the parakeet to Willy, and he gave me a funny look and said, "I read somewhere that certain native tribes believe that."

He had removed all pictures of Liz. He wanted to erase her from our lives.

"But what about the children?"

"It's better if they forget her completely. She can never be a mother to them again. That's what you are now."

"But Con talks about her." Though only indirectly. Around Halloween, Conrad had told me a story about a little boy who was bad and his mother turned into a witch and left him and never came back. And the little boy, very sad, looked out the window for her every night to see if she was crossing the moon on a broomstick.

Willy said, "Well, fantasies are normal. Let him imagine her as a sort of fairy godmother. Though this must upset you."

"Why should it?"

Said Willy slowly and deliberately, "Many women in

your position would resent the ex-wife, Dinah—the mother
of the kids you're stuck taking care of. The maker of the
home you live in. And you only have to give me the word
and we'll move. I'm not married to this place; I'm here out
of inertia."

"No, I don't want to move. I love this house." Later I
asked, "Why doesn't she want to see the children?"

He tightened. "I don't want her to see them. She's not
responsible. She'd put them in the refrigerator along with
the typewriter."

Then, late one morning after we'd been married only a
few months, the doorbell rang and there stood Liz—tall,
handsome, rather fierce, with a mane of wild reddish gold
hair and burning green eyes. Very white skin, wearing a
black turtleneck and a big raccoon coat. A rather
frightened-looking man was with her.

"I'm Liz Wakefield. I suppose you're Dinah. I've come
to see my children. I have a court order."

"Oh, Liz! Come on in." I opened the door and she looked
surprised.

"You want me to come in?"

"Please do. I'll make some coffee. They'll be back in a
few minutes."

Looking a little stunned, she introduced Harry Gideon,
her lawyer. "Don't you want to look at the court order?"

"The judge has found Dr. Wakefield's refusal to let the
mother see her children totally unreasonable," said Gideon.

"What refusal? You're free to come any time you want."
Liz and Gideon exchanged glances. "I mean, as far as I'm
concerned. They're terrific kids. I really love them."

I went into the kitchen to start the coffee, Liz trailing
slowly after me. I had the strangest feeling of familiarity
about her, as though I already knew her—though it might
have been because we shared Willy. And a curious fondness
and affection. I smiled at her, and she looked at me suspi-
ciously.

"You've changed the kitchen." Her voice was accusing.

"I've changed a lot of things. It was all sort of a mess."

"By which you mean, no doubt, that I was a mess too. Which I'm distinctly not anymore!"

"Oh, I believe you!"

While we were drinking coffee, the door opened and Emerelda came in with the kids. Con flew into her arms and burst into tears, which caused Liz to do the same.

"You went away, Mommy. Are you going to stay now?"

"Not today, darling. But I'll be back soon."

Jessie wouldn't talk to her.

"Come on, Jessie. Give your mom a big hug," I said.

"Not my mommy," she said, clinging to my legs. "Dinah is my mommy and you're a bad witch."

"Just a half-bad witch, Jessie. I love you, you know."

When Emerelda had taken the children into the kitchen for their lunch, Gideon explained that Liz was suing for custody of the children. She'd taken a sublet and had several job possibilities lined up. It was just a question of orchestrating everything. They should be with their mother, it was extremely damaging for me to tell the child her mother was a witch, etc.

"Oh, I'd never say that. Willy thinks Jessie says it because you left her."

Liz and Gideon chorused, "He would say that; that's typical; that's just what he'd say."

"Come on, Dinah," Liz said. "How could she even know the word?"

"From a Halloween book."

Gideon's function was to bait me. First he implied that I neglected the children, and when I protested, he said I was trying to take over Liz's maternal function. I'd never encountered the legal mind before and didn't like it at all—particularly when he threatened to prove in court that Willy and I were unfit parents.

"But I'm sure Willy will be fair," I said to Liz.

She looked at me for a long time. "You really don't know, do you?"

"What?"

"Willy has refused to let me even see the kids in the last year, the whole time since the divorce. I mean, I was crazy once, but . . ."

"Strike that," Gideon said. "You were never crazy. You were going through an identity crisis. You've got to get this straight, Liz. You and a million other intelligent, well-educated women trapped at home with small children and no stimulation, not to mention an unavailable, unsympathetic, workaholic husband. It's a cut-and-dried feminist case; we just have to give the judge some ammunition."

"I'll talk to Willy," I told Liz. "Now I know why you never came till now. And let's not fight. I *hate* fighting."

Willy heard about Liz's visit almost before he was through the door. I heard his footsteps coming down the hall to the kitchen, where I was broiling the lamb chops.

"You let Liz in here, Dinah?"

"Of course. You never told me not to. In fact you haven't told me much about this at all."

"All right, I am now. Liz is very charming; everybody likes her. And she's completely delusional. Think of the things you've found around here. The pennies. The typewriter. The fondue forks. The toenail clippings"—complete with polish, in a pepper mill, fortunately unused. "The whole chaotic mess was all Liz. Once she dyed Jessie's hair black, for God's sake. Do I have to go on?"

"No, but honestly, she seemed as sane as you or me."

He sighed with his I-must-be-patient-with-her look. "Dinah. The lawyer is probably some boyfriend. The court order is probably from one of those places where they make up things like that for gags. Maybe she thinks it's funny, I don't know. It's cruel to Con and Jessie to let her in here."

"Sometimes crazy people get better."

"Sometimes. Her prognosis was extremely grave. I'm a doctor and I know." We looked at each other and Willy stretched out his arms. "Oh, God. Listen to us. We're letting the past get in the way, and all that counts is you, me, and the kids." Leaning my head on his shoulder, I smelled the faint ether scent he always picked up around the hospital. "Promise me you won't let her in here again."

"But Willy, if she wants to see her own children—"

"She's the wolf in sheep's clothing. You've got to trust me. Isn't that what marriage is all about?"

To Willy's embarrassment, his lawyer called and confirmed the custody suit.

"I'm simply stunned. But it won't go very far after the judge has a look at her hospital records." We were in bed reading.

"Willy, if Liz were sane, would you give her the kids?"

"That's an impossible question. I can't separate her from her illness."

"Well, try."

"I can't. If she were sane she wouldn't have left me."

"But Willy—"

He put down the *New England Journal.* "If you don't mind, Dinah, I've had enough of this conversation." In his pale gray pajamas he loped across the room to the bathroom, where I heard him clinking around in the medicine chest. A tap of the plastic glass, a slosh of water, a gulp. A Valium or a Quaalude—Dalmane was for later, more serious sleeplessness. Then I heard him brushing his teeth. I lay down in bed, running my hand over the hollow his shoulder had made in the pillow beside me.

On Christmas Eve I made roast prime ribs and a pumpkin pie, feeling very proud of myself. We ate it near the tree we'd decorated that morning. After dinner Willy took the kids up to put them to bed and Charlotte helped me clean up—putting clean dishes in the dishwasher and dirty ones on the shelf.

"Well, Dinah. This has been very nice. You're a very talented young woman; the potatoes were delicious—almost like Hattie's. Thank the Lord the children have a normal home life again, and Willy too. Though I wouldn't feel right talking about what went on before. But Liz came from excellent stock; I couldn't believe it when . . . Now who could that be?" as the doorbell rang.

I recognized the silhouette of her raccoon coat and her mass of hair through the glass curtain on the door. I let myself out onto the stoop.

"Let me in, for Christ's sake," said Liz. She smelled strongly of alcohol. "I want to see my children."

"Liz, please don't come in now. You've been drinking. You'll screw up everything."

She stared at me in the light from the door. "Do you have any children, other than mine?"

"No."

"Then don't be so superior. I want to come in. It's Christmas Eve, for God's sake. Is Willy cruel enough not to let me in on Christmas Eve?"

"It's not cruel. Listen, I could close the door in your face. But I want to help you."

"Don't patronize me, *Dinah*." She gave my name a scornful emphasis. "I don't need your fucking help. I want to see my kids. I brought some presents for them." She was holding a large shopping bag from F.A.O. Schwarz. The city was hushed by snow, and a man and child walked by, carrying a pine tree. A taxi was double-parked a few doors down the street, and I heard the motor hum and whine and the spin of a wheel locked in slush. Then the door opened and a man leaned out.

"Liz, for fuck's sake let's go." Not Gideon, another one. "The meter's ticking and we'll never get another cab tonight."

"I'll be there in a minute." While I watched nervously, she scooped up a handful of snow in her mittens, made a snowball, and threw it up at the kids' window, while I shrank back against the door.

The window opened and Con called, "It's Mommy! Hi, Mommy!"

Her face broke into a big, happy smile. "Hello, darling. I love you so much. Have a merry Christmas. Where's Jessie?" The man hanging out of the taxi began to sing "Good King Wenceslas." We all waited a moment.

Then the upstairs window crashed down.

"That's Willy. Will you *go?* Keep the presents till next time."

She caught my eye and went over to the cab where her friend waited.

Willy came down the stairs as I closed the front door. "Con said Liz was out there."

"Not Liz. Some drunk woman who looked sort of like her, as a matter of fact."

"What are you doing here covered with snow?" He brushed it from my shoulders.

"She rang the bell all full of Christmas spirit and I had a little trouble getting rid of her. She had the wrong house is all."

It was the first lie I told Willy, but not the last. The first of the toothpicks of deception, the ones destined to collapse the whole structure. Though I don't believe I was wrong. Willy says the word *wrong* is not in my vocabulary. Not true—it's just that we never agreed on what it means.

Liz convinced the judge that she was sane enough to see the children once a week. Willy fumed, "She managed to get some Goddamn female judge. Jessie'll never go." But she did. Not that she'd changed her mind about Liz being a witch, but she'd heard on TV that there were good witches as well as bad and she was willing to give it a try—as long as she didn't have to eat liver.

Liz started out with enthusiastic plans. But it was a bitterly cold winter, and soon her weekly expeditions flagged. One afternoon they came back early, faces and fingers red. We all sat by the fire and had hot chocolate.

"Liz, you don't have to freeze," I said. "It's fine with me if you want to hang around here."

"In other words, don't take them back to my shitty apartment." It was strange how little such remarks bothered me. I knew it was just a matter of time until we'd be friends. She was blowing on her hands.

"Why are you so hostile? After all, this was your house."

"I'm aware of that." Her eye flickered over me. By then I was visibly pregnant with Jason, and she seemed to soften a little. "Usually I like to try to make it different and a little crazy for them. Unusual things they don't do every day." She'd taken them to Mexican restaurants and Chinese teahouses, led them through obscure galleries and odd bookstores.

"They're lucky kids," I said.

She gave me another long, appraising look. "There's something about you, Dinah. I don't know what it is."

I said hesitantly, "Maybe we have some kind of funny connection, ESP or something."

She burst out laughing. "My butt!"

After she left, Emerelda said, "I believe the first Mistress Wakefield to be mounted by a loa—probably Ogoun." Loas were Emerelda's voodoo spirits.

"Well, maybe she was before, but she isn't crazy now."

"There are some in which the spirit lies low. Perhaps it is Erzilie; she bides her time for years. Then breaks out." Emerelda not only believed all this but worried that I didn't.

"But you're a devout Catholic, Emerelda."

Her round eyes grew bigger. "Of course, Mistress. It is all one. Someday you will see." She put her little brown hand on my stomach. "I think it is a boy."

I couldn't help listening to Emerelda's ideas about the loas, though Willy not only disapproved, he thought they were a dangerous influence on the children. So I didn't mention Emerelda's stories, or that she thought I too had been invaded by some sort of spirit. If it couldn't be proved, Willy was deeply suspicious. He was a scientist through and through.

I got so used to Liz coming that I was amazed when, after Jason was born, she missed a couple of Wednesdays.

"She's dropping the ball; it's her pattern," Willy said. "The custody suit is as good as over." We were having breakfast in the kitchen. I was drinking coffee with my free hand as Jason lay draped over the other forearm like a muff, face down, arms and legs dangling, a position he seemed to find soothing. "It isn't just a struggle for the kids. It's a struggle to be normal and she can't win."

There were times when Willy gave me the chills, though I didn't know then exactly why, and I wasn't sure I cared. Now Jason and I were at the center of the world. What a pair we were, my little muff and I, so busy admiring each other. His beauty, his clear-eyed stare, his tiny, miraculous digits. His silky sweet skin and pink satin gums that bit my breast, his small, plaintive cry. I'd sit by his crib, staring at him, writing his life. I'd been unprepared for such feelings, thinking I'd just sweep him into the pot with the others and mix him into our household brew. I hadn't known how eagerly I'd run into his room in the middle of the night, breasts aching; that I'd spend so much time admiring his feet, his hands, arranging his few hairs, or fussing over his food; or what absurd capers I'd go through to get him to smile. I hadn't known what this love would be like, and like anybody in love, I thought I knew everything.

Liz appeared next when she was not supposed to.

"Can I see the kids?"

"Of course, why not?"

"You don't care, you have everything. Suppose it was him?" indicating Jason. "Suppose somebody else had him. How would you feel then?"

I looked from Liz to Jason, then back at Liz again. "Actually I hadn't thought of it that way."

"Obviously not."

"I can't even conceive of being separated from him in the first place."

"Neither could I," she said, "but it happened. You aren't as safe as you think. It's amazing how the rug can be pulled out from under you, and it's so hard to get it back again." Her voice shook. "I'm dropping the custody suit. I already owe the lawyers more than I have."

"I'm sorry . . . I'm sorry," I said.

"Sorry? What for? You and Willy have won." She took a Kleenex from a box on the table and blew her nose. "I thought I could hold on and prove neglect after you had your baby, but Gideon won't go any further till he's paid."

Like a blurry picture coming into focus, her situation really became clear to me. "Are you telling me your children were being kept from you because of money?"

"Well, what the hell else?" She stared at me.

"I just thought . . . just thought there was some kind of justice about things like that."

"Well, maybe sometimes. If you can afford to get where they dispense it. If you're perfect. But I started dropping the ball, as you know. I drink a little too much sometimes. I have a new lover, which is always distracting. Speaking of drinking, I wonder if I may have a little gin and an ice cube or two."

"Of course. It's over in that cabinet."

She made us each a drink, which I took rather guiltily, thinking of Jason, whose dinner would be flooded with Tanqueray and Noilly Prat.

"Look, Liz. Come whenever you want to see the kids,

any time. I'm just keeping them for you for as long as you want. As far as I'm concerned, they could live with you."

"Now that you have one of your own, you'd kiss them good-bye."

"No, I said that before Jason was born. And it isn't just Willy. You make everything hard because you're so hostile."

"Of course I'm a little hostile. You have everything I want; you've taken over my life. It's not that I want it back. I don't mean that. But oh, the comfort, the security, the status. The freedom. You can't be free if you're broke."

"I could have told you that."

"And there's an aimlessness about my life, a pointlessness. All the jobs and projects . . . I can't seem to find what I want to do. I think of something, or I meet somebody with a great idea, but nothing works out. I'm always scratching to pay the bills and I get tired. You wouldn't understand any of it."

"Don't tell me what I wouldn't understand. We all have our problems."

When I told her about the amnesia, she said, "You're joking."

"You must think I have a pretty strange sense of humor."

"Amnesia," she murmured. "I wish I could work that."

The front door burst open and Emerelda and the kids came in from the playground, followed by Charlotte and the dog. The kitchen was all fuss and babble, and Jason's crying got more serious. When he'd worked up to fever pitch, I extracted one breast and nursed him sitting in the rocker. Liz undressed the other two kids, and Emerelda began peeling potatoes for dinner. Charlotte sat rubbing her feet—"Good Lord, I'll never get used to these pavements." I felt peaceful, as I always did when I was feeding the baby, a little drunk, a little hypnotized. Jessie's cheeks were still pink and her hair damp from playing outdoors. I felt as though I were at the center of the earth. The kids buzzed back and forth as though having two—or three or four—mothers was quite natural. After a while Emerelda said, "I think Mister Doc will be home soon."

Liz stood up. "I'd better go."

"Yes, you probably should."

Nobody mentioned Liz's coming by that day. A few days later she called.

"Listen, I lied to you, Dinah. In a way I had to drop the custody suit because of money. But in another, I had to admit to myself I don't really want them. I know it sounds terrible. I don't want the confinement, and the poverty to go with it, always trying to fight money out of Willy. And the fear of going crazy again is always there. I don't think I could handle all that. I'm grateful they have you, and even with your own baby you were loving to them, I saw that. Don't think I wasn't watching you."

Willy

I've done what all physicians dream of. I've evolved a technique that makes history of everything that went before. Polyester epoxy adhesive for severed nerves opens up new vistas in digital surgery! An application tube the size of a thread fits over the nerve and leaves a minute droplet of the nerve conductor in exactly the right place. It dries in four seconds.

I fell on it almost by accident. I was called to the emergency room one night to see a girl whose hand had been lopped off by a subway train; some crazy had pushed her off the platform. She told me with a look I'll never forget that she played the violin. Boy, I froze in my tracks. Too often we forget there's a person attached to that wound! By God, I was going to save that hand. There was this stuff around I'd seen Mac use on bones. I thought, What the hell? We have nothing to lose. We were in the O.R. for seven hours. It didn't work the first way, so I added a little adhesive stuff we found in the dental clinic. The scrub nurse had some nail hardener in her handbag. We were running all over the place, trying this mixture and that. Finally we got one that adhered, so I put it on. I did all the nerves, bones, and vessels and sewed it up.

I never expected it to work. I thought I was giving her a presentable but useless hand. I'll never forget the day she moved her fingers! The kid was in tears. "Dr. Wakefield, you've saved me." That was six months ago, and today she's playing the violin again!

There was a little noise from Mac Valpey, who said he'd cooked up his bone glue years before and it was probably as good a nerve conductor as mine. But I'm the one who made it work, right? Mac is always blowing off and trying to steal other people's credit.

Well, that was the beginning. Cooper, who invented the operation for Parkinson's, and Cooley and De Bakey tell me it's the same thing. They won't let you sleep. There's the demonstrations. The films and lectures which I've now given at seventeen major hospitals in the U.S., Europe, and the Far East. The teaching, of course, and the usual hospital committees, and more lectures and journals than ever before, because I have to keep up. Suppose somebody comes along with a better nerve glue? You're only as good as your last operation.

This is the time a man needs a wife he can lean on. I've always known that there are some peculiar things about Dinah. I've tried like hell to understand her limited perceptions and odd point of view. But why in God's name is she such good friends with my ex-wife?

I know Poor Liz is better. She was sane enough to drop the custody suit. She's stayed out of the hospital, and she manages to get along. She's trying to start a little business of some sort. I hope she gets on her feet; it's better for the kids.

I just mentioned it once. I asked her why she didn't see more of Ellen Goldstein, Vicky Valpey, and the other Episcopal wives. Then I said, "Dinah, why don't you hate my ex-wife?" I should have put it better. She got that strange look and said she likes Liz and loves the children and that's that. It's a perfect example of her off-the-wall responses. I didn't say this, of course, but if Liz was the way she used to be, she'd be light-years ahead of Dinah—looks, brains, personality, gumption. What do they find to talk about? As if I don't know!

Then Dinah says, "We don't talk about you, Willy, if that's what you're worried about. Or hardly ever. I promise, we wouldn't do that." In that soft, sweet voice. "It started because of the children."

"I feel it's disloyal."

She looked right through me. "I'm sorry, Willy." I knew she'd go right ahead and do whatever she wanted. There's nothing I can do. She's deceptive. I'm not even sure it's her fault. I think it's because she's forgotten certain moral and ethical precepts. She's all twigs and no stalk. She just rides the wind, and when she's up against it, she lies. It's sad, it really is. The amnesia has given her a real wall-to-wall character disorder. I could send her to Frank Liverwood, but I know this kind of pathology isn't very responsive to therapy.

And her reality testing is lousy. She has trouble drawing the line between real life and never-never land, and to make it worse she pulls the kids right along into her fantasies. Mother's tea parties, for instance, that Jessie was telling me about. Well, fine. Dinah's been wonderful with Mother. They dig out the big tea service every Thursday and have high tea, and Mother's tickled to death.

But instead of leading Mother gently but firmly back from Birdland, Dinah flies right off with her and encourages the kids to go along too, as though it's a game. If it weren't for Jessie they'd all float off into a time warp. I'd come home to find Scarlett and Aunt Pittypat and Leslie Howard.

Now Dinah's starting to have some kind of witchy spells, I think when I disagree with her. The other night we were in a cab on the way to the knuckle dance, where I had to make a speech. We were dressed to the nines. Dinah was wearing a new dress she got at Saks, but something was wrong, I don't know what. She never looks the way Vicky

Valpey does. I don't know whether it's the way she does her hair or what. I think she's just one fashion behind. I was grousing because the tux was too tight.

"Here, darling. Pull it down a little. There." She clucked in that nice way she has. "You look so handsome. I'm so proud of you." She's considerate enough not to plant a lipstick kiss on my cheek, just gives a little rub that leaves no track. "You're so brilliant and I'm not. There are so many things I'm trying to understand . . . I was wondering, Willy, do you believe in the ability of people to see into each other's minds?"

"No way, José."

"But I've heard that in Texas there's a whole college that studies ESP."

"There are probably colleges for left-handed leprechauns. Somebody's making a buck."

"But there are so many people that say—"

"In here, driver." The asshole's just about to pass the Hilton back into another twenty minutes of traffic, and Dinah's shoes consist of two straps of gold spaghetti. His fare box is broken; we have to argue about the amount. I wasn't paying any attention to her. Then I noticed she was still as a stone—not reaching for her handbag or the door. She's leaning against me stiff as a mummy. She was absolutely out. Her pupils were fixed and she was comatose. For a minute I thought she was dead. My heart and stomach lurched into my mouth. I grabbed her and shook her, grabbed her pulse, and opened one of her eyes. Then she came to.

"What are you doing, Willy?"

Whoa. "Are you okay?"

"Of course." She began combing her hair. "Why not?"

"Because . . ." The cab had stopped. "Because you were just out cold as a mackerel."

She laughed. "What are you talking about?"

Out on the sidewalk hundreds of medics and their glossy

wives are making for the bar inside. "You were just—not for long—unconscious."

She looks at me in a funny way. "Well, I did have a . . . an unusual sensation."

I threw a few bills at the driver. Christ, she's got epilepsy. "Darling, we have to get through tonight, but we'll get you to Bertie Mood first thing in the morning."

She laughed and said no dice. No neurologist. And that was the end of it, except there's nothing like giving a key professional speech while keeping half an eye on your wife to see if she's going to convulse. But she was perfectly pleasant and chatty. She even carried off the you're-dowdy glances from Vicky and Ellen. I grabbed Chrissie. "Hey, give Dinah a little fashion advice, okay?" Anything, Willy, anything! She's so proud of her matchmaking she almost carries a sign. I told her what happened in the cab.

Chrissie said slowly, "You know, Willy, I love Dinah, but she is very . . . strange. She seems to attract . . . um . . . peculiar episodes."

Terrific, a big help.

Dinah refuses to go to Bertie Mood, Frank Liverwood, or anybody. She swears she hasn't passed out again. I have to trust her, what can I do? Meetings, conferences, papers— I'm always running back and forth to the airport. I'm crazy half the time. So she fainted for a minute in a hot taxi, so what?

I look at her around the house. She's aiming Conrad toward his homework, listening to Jessie's criticisms of the whole society. She hugs Jason, checks out whatever smells so good in the kitchen. I'm going to a meeting so she's fixing me a plate, answering the phone, giving Mother a pat, sewing a button on somebody's sweater, talking about ordering tulip bulbs for the garden.

I need this doll. She's my life.

Dinah

———

or the next several years the children took a great deal
of my time. They went to three different private
schools, all of which expected me to chaperone the
Winter Frolic or fund-raise or supervise Thanksgiving Do-
nation Day or go on the class trip to the Museum of Natural
History. They had doctors and dentists and tennis lessons
and guitar lessons and Jessie had ballet and Con had the
therapist. I policed their social life and made sure the families of their friends had no rampant psychopathology (as
defined by Willy) that would harm our young, and that the
neighborhoods where they lived were acceptable. They
needed more and more attention from me over the years
because the more successful Willy got, the less time he
spent at home, and when he got there he just wanted to
flop and drink a martini and read the paper and not think
about anything much, so we all got into the habit of protecting him from our more difficult passages. So it fell to
me to have the talks about drugs and sex and friendship and
homosexuality, though I certainly wasn't any expert. I just
happened to be available.

As the children grew up, so did I. I developed a social

self necessary for our increasing social-professional obligations. I became easier with people, smoother, more tactful.
At Willy's direction, I volunteered for work at the hospital
gift shop ("You have to do it, Dinah; it's just one of those
things") and joined a fund-raising committee and another
committee to plant geraniums and petunias around the
main entrance.

Now, with money and time, I learned how to dress, cook
gourmet meals, and redecorate our home. I got all the
people at Episcopal straight and learned to make chitchat at
all those dinners and receptions. I was much more confident; after all, I was Mrs. Willard Wakefield, wife of the
brilliant surgeon who had invented the landmark operation
for reattaching digits. Now Willy was always demonstrat-
ing his operation and traveling around to lecture on it and
show films and lead conferences, so I was left more than
ever in charge of things at home.

After the debacle of the custody suit, Liz went off to
Europe for a year, one of several impulsive disappearances.
Then one afternoon she walked in unannounced. Jessie
looked at her mother and a couple of tears crawled out of
her eyes and down her cheeks.

"Why did you come back? Why didn't you just stay
away?"

"Because I love you," Liz said, looking as though she
might cry herself. "I'm going to try New York again."

This time it had been the rich Italian photographer who
wouldn't get a *divorzio* from his wife (he'd warned her, but
she didn't believe him) and left her with the apartment in
Trastevere and the bill for two months' rent . . . and another broken heart. And there was the job with the New
Age publisher in Monterey, and the partnership with the
musician, after which Liz ended up—as usual—the loser.
If I, as a parent, supplied the steadiness and dependability,
Liz supplied the excitement, the daring, and the willingness
to take risks. Willy never knew how often and how freely

she came to the house (or that she had her own key). She and I became good friends, as I'd known we would, and the kids got used to having at least two mothers—Jason included, for when he was older, she often took him along on their excursions. We all tacitly edited our reports to Willy.

Liz desperately needed an outlet for all her talent and energy, and I happened to be the one who gave her the idea for Finders Keepers. I'd told her about Gil, and the interviews at the police station, and the letters—which I still had around somewhere. I told her I still had an on-and-off correspondence with a couple of them, just because they were lonely, even though I'd turned out not to be their long-lost sister/mother/wife. One woman thought she was better off writing to me than having her real sister turn up, because the truth was they'd always hated each other anyway and she'd only tried to find her out of guilt. She liked having me as a sort of "quasi-sister." We could write and tell each other things but didn't have to get involved, or even meet.

It was this story that gave Liz the idea of starting a lost and found for people. There were thousands of lonely people, she reasoned, millions really. Almost everybody in New York was lonely and a lot of people in other places too. The problem was that they were often lonely on purpose, in a way. They'd gotten divorced or chosen not to go back to their old mother in Brattleboro, or they'd moved from Alabama and left family behind, or they'd kicked out the last roommate because he didn't bathe or waffled on the rent. So while they chose to get rid of the people in their lives, at the same time they chased around to singles bars and had joyless sex and spent Christmas day stoned.

"So what's the problem?" she asked.

"God, I don't know."

"Come on, Dinah. They don't want just *any* people; they want the ones they pick themselves. They don't want to go home to Brooklyn for Easter because they can't stand that maundering bunch of Irish Catholics getting drunk and fighting and doing Eugene O'Neill. What they want is a nice older couple they don't know too well, or some kids to take to the zoo once in a while or even to have stay for the weekend, without having to be a full-time mother. I understand that perfectly! Or maybe they want a nice half-relationship with a guy without getting into the whole bag of worms which is marriage. Maybe they just want a friend or sister like that woman you write to." She looked at me expectantly. "Even Charlotte. Tea parties on her terms, don't you see?"

At that moment I really realized how smart she was. I never would have thought of this. I thought I didn't understand a lot of what Willy told me because he was so incredibly brilliant and a scientist and all that. But now I suspected it was more because I wasn't all that bright. It wasn't the first time I suspected I was in over my head.

"Dinah, one more little step. Your people. Your letters. Don't you see, we could start a business matching people up with other people. The childless single career woman with the poor orphan kid. The lonely old couple with the nice young man who doesn't want to go home to Brooklyn. Even dates—but carefully screened by us to make sure people were getting what they wanted. Special services for runaways, parolees, and amnesiacs."

It was thrilling to see inspiration take hold, like it must have been for Willy that day in the O.R. "Liz, you're a genius."

"No, no, just common sense. It's been partly done already. They get grandmothers together with strange kids and little boys with Big Brothers and computer dates . . ." She was pacing excitedly around the kitchen. "And at church socials and singles parties you take the same risks. But in this case we do the screening so everybody saves time and grief. We charge a flat fee, and if it doesn't work out, we find another kid or boyfriend or grandpa or whatever."

So that was the beginning of Finders Keepers—A Lost
and Found for People, which Liz built up from the ground,
and which today is a thriving multimillion-dollar business.
My function from the start was silent, because we both had
a hunch Willy would hate the idea. So I worked on my part
of it in the mornings when nobody was there, and Willy
never knew about my letter, for instance, which was the
leadoff for the "lost" part of our two-pronged approach:

"HAVE YOU LOST SOMEBODY?

"I am an amnesiac. Five years ago I 'came to' in front of
a Manhattan subway station—nameless, homeless, and
broke. Today I have a husband, children, happiness, and
fulfillment. Will you be as lucky as me?

"Whether you are an amnesiac, a refugee, a returning
Viet vet, or just plain lost and lonely, you may need our
help in finding your family or loved ones. We are an agency
dedicated to finding those crickets that have strayed from
the hearth. To reach into the past, just fill out the enclosed
form . . . ."

The letter didn't last long; Liz thought it sounded like
an ad from a funeral home. But it did for a start, and we
sent it out to everybody we could think of, including my
people, and later to churches, schools, and hospitals.

The other prong, the "found" part, said

"WOULD YOU LIKE TO FIND SOMEBODY? We all need
somebody to love, especially if we can't stand our relatives.
How about one of our custom-picked Faux Familles? The
mother, sister, husband, child you wish you'd had!"

We had a cute picture of a child, captioned, "Susie needs
a Mommy," and one of a sweet-faced old lady knitting a
sock, which said, "Eleanor is a Grandmother in search of a
Grandchild. Are you it?"

The response was so enormous, especially after the ads in
the *Voice* and *New York Magazine,* that Liz could hardly
handle it in her apartment, a dump near Columbus Circle.
She didn't really know anything about running a business,

and the whole thing almost collapsed because of her inex-
perience. But she managed to save it with the aid of a
psychologist friend, who helped her read letters, and of
course me, though I didn't have much time and didn't
know what the hell I was doing anyway. And she was lucky
that nothing disastrous happened, because a lot of nuts
applied—dirty old men looking for nice little boys, that
sort of thing. But she went very slowly and cautiously with
the first pairings, and they worked out pretty well, partly
because she always warned her clients not to build their
hopes up too much: she wasn't selling miracles, just com-
panionship.

Besides the Faux Familles (at that time Liz still thought
anything European was classy), she managed to find a couple of real ones: a runaway wife who changed her mind and
wanted to go home but couldn't track down her husband,
and the parents of a runaway teenager referred by Covenant
House. She was there when they came to claim him. He'd
been on the street for three months, but he must have been
very strong because he kicked it all and was ready to go
home, and the parents took him back with open arms. It
made it all worth it. What had seemed like a wild idea to
make money has proved to be a service to humanity.

All this took several years, of course; building up a business from the ground is a slow and tedious process. But it
turned out to be exactly the sort of thing she's good at. She
was smart and she wasn't afraid of hard work. She always
stayed on the good side of the police and made it clear that
she wasn't running an adoption service or anything like
that. She only put people together, and what they did after
that was their business.

I couldn't keep it a secret from Willy, particularly after
I started to put money in the business, which I had to do
or the whole thing would have collapsed. But I didn't want
to hide it; I wanted him to be as enchanted with the idea as
I was. So I told him about it one evening while we were
reading in bed.

Willy had a way of lowering his book very slowly, turning his head toward me, and rolling his eyes up over his reading glasses with an expression of great pain, then staring silently. Finally I said impatiently, "Well, what do you think?"

"Dinah, what exactly do you expect me to say?"

"I don't tell you things because I *expect* you to say a certain thing. I tell you because I'd like your opinion."

"Knowing my feelings about my ex-wife, you must have some idea how I feel."

"Willy, sometimes it's really hard to talk to you. I don't know why we're discussing what *I* think you're going to say, which is neither here nor there. I simply want to know what you *think*."

"There's nothing simple about it. I think the whole idea sucks, as Conrad would say." Willy was pressing his fingers together in a new way he had. Press-release. Press-release.

"Okay. Why?"

"Because frankly the notion of Liz starting a business is terrifying. I'd trust Jason more. She's incompetent and psychotic besides. Second, the notion that I'm putting money into it makes me want to throw up."

"No, I'm putting money into it."

"Academic, Dinah. I earned it. I sweated for it."

"True, but you gave it to me, for my account, telling me it was mine to throw away as I chose."

"I meant on yourself. Clothes. Hairdresser. Christmas presents. Taxis. Lunches with the girls. It never occurred to me that you'd spend it on flyaway business ventures with my ex-wife. I suppose the worst of this, Dinah, is your friendship with Liz, which I find *extremely upsetting*"— shouting the last words and flinging his book on the floor. "But go ahead. Enjoy yourselves! Compare bed stories. Have a good time."

"Willy, we don't talk about things like that. It's more about Liz's search for her identity. Or the kids. And she never says anything against you" (only half-true). "Finders

Keepers is the sort of thing she's wanted to do all her life, and it's too bad you can't be happy for her."

"Happy? Aside from a general Christian feeling of well-wishing to her as a human being, I don't give a damn what happens to Liz Wakefield."

"Liz Flanders. She's gone back to her maiden name."

"Oh, of course. Naturally. It follows."

"Honestly, Willy. After all, she was your wife. Jess and Con's mother. She was terribly sick and now she's well."

"The prognosis is lousy. She could go psychotic again, and down the drain will go this ridiculous business, which by the way sounds delusional in itself. Liz playing God. Terrific. The halt leading the blind." He got up and started toward the bathroom.

"Willy, don't. Don't take anything. Come here, I'll rub your back. Come on."

But once he was zeroed in on the medicine cabinet, it was hard to stop him. It was a habit that had surfaced as life's stresses intensified. His navy blue pajamas with white piping moved across the floor.

"I'm just going to take a couple of aspirin," he said, but I heard the clink of two or three containers, and I felt sad and frustrated. He appeared in the doorway holding a glass of water, still gulping. "Dinah, I can't lie about my feelings, can I? But I'm not going to try to stop you or cut back your allowance. Just don't tell me about the Goddamn project, okay? By the way, how much have you put into it?"

"Three thousand dollars."

"*Three thousand dollars?*" He stared at me as though beyond ordinary rage.

"One hand repair."

"Two," Willy said. "I only keep fifty cents on the dollar."

"Willy, I'll pay you back sometime. Please don't take anything else," as he turned back to the bathroom again. I

felt tears well up. "Oh, shit. How did we get like this?
Why do you always make me feel so guilty?"

"That's your nature, Dinah. As I've said before, my medication has nothing to do with your character. It has to do
with the stress I live under—my wife financing Poor Liz's
crazy business venture, and the Looney Tunes tea parties I
hear about. For God's sake, a man's room is supposed to be
a haven of calm and peace, and mine is like Disneyland."

"You're changing the subject. You take too many pills."

"I'm a doctor. I know what I'm doing."

He decided to cut my allowance down after all. "I'm
perfectly willing to pay for clothes and all that. But Dinah,
three thousand dollars for the Lost Grandma Agency when
my own mother is sitting here losing her marbles . . ." A
connection I failed to grasp. "From now on I make the
decisions about money matters." I argued, pleaded, tried to
reason, but nothing would change him. It was Willy's
money, his house, his life.

Very slowly Willy and I were moving apart. We func-
tioned well as a team, but sometimes the teammates hardly
communicated. As Willy sat in his study working on *Digital Detachments: No Longer a Tragedy* for Basic Books, I was
searching for Jessie's gym tunic and arranging Conrad's
swimming lessons. I told myself I didn't mind Willy's
grumpiness, but I did. I was past the point where I accepted
being talked to as though I were a moron or a crazy person,
especially when I knew he couldn't do without me.

I knew there was no perfect husband, and expecting un-
ending sympathy and devotion from Willy was unrealistic.
I was, in fact, lucky to have him. But I was lonely a good
deal of the time. Chris and Portoff had moved to Scarsdale,
and I'd never really gotten along with the other Episcopal
wives. The amnesia was no longer a secret, and I think it
made them nervous. They didn't quite know what to say to
me. They looked wary, as though I might explode. We'd
have luncheon somewhere, and somehow, in the middle of

the quiche, conversation would flag. Either they'd ask me about my memory or they wouldn't, though they were dying to.

The only person I could really be myself with was Liz, but she was more and more involved with FK. Even when she had an office and a couple of full-time assistants and a part-time psychologist for in-depth interviews, she knew it wouldn't work unless she was there to supervise it all. She wasn't around to spell me with the kids, and I resented it a little, besides missing her company. I hinted about it and she said, "Dinah, I feel bad about it and I'm sorry, but there isn't a thing I can do about it. Unless you want to run the business for me."

Which I didn't want to do at all. I didn't want a career, or to change anything really. It was just that I got tired of orthodontists' waiting rooms, and conversations with short people, and picking synthetics out of the dryer while they were still damp, and little pieces of plastic all over the floor, and the smell of watermelon gum. Charlotte, instead of being the company she had been, was increasingly out of touch, nodding and smiling and having conversations with herself, so I sometimes felt as though I had four children instead of three—five, if you counted Willy.

I didn't belong anywhere. And sometimes as I looked at the kids, I'd feel a little stab of envy for the rich childhood tapestry of birthdays, of Christmas mornings, of dinners by candlelight, of ball games and weekends in the country and dogs and cats and reading by the fire, all the little pictures they'd have forever. I knew they'd be better, wiser, and richer for these memories. It was not in my nature to feel sorry for myself, and I was contented most of the time. But sometimes, just for a moment, I'd feel adrift in the universe.

When Jason started kindergarten I had time alone every day for the first time. It was very strange to have the children gone and only Emerelda and me around the house.

There was plenty to do, so I never got bored. But every once in a while, when Emerelda was ironing, for instance, and I was having a cup of tea in the kitchen, looking at a book or newspaper, I'd get the curious feeling that we weren't alone at all—that the room was full of people. There would be the kind of silence that is just barely a silence. Imagine that scene in *The Sound of Music* when the whole Trapp family is hiding from the Nazis. They're quiet, all right, but they're *there*. I'd get the same feeling. I'd look at Emerelda, and she'd either be looking at some point in space with her bright brown eyes or half mumbling to herself as she ironed Willy's shirt. If I asked her what she was talking about, she'd just smile and drop her eyes.

"I don't know, Mistress. My mommy talked to herself too."

Then a couple of times when I was alone I had more of those peculiar visitations, or whatever they were, that I'd had in the taxi with Willy and never explained. I knew if I did, he either wouldn't believe me or he'd drag me off to Bertie Mood. I couldn't have passed out, or I would have found myself in the hospital. But one day on my way back from picking up some theater tickets, on one of those grim, grubby blocks between Sixth and Seventh, I felt, all of a sudden, as though I were being painlessly, rather delightfully *electrocuted,* a champagne fizzle from head to toe. Then a . . . a difference came over me, like a weight. I felt peculiarly heavier, then as though somebody had gotten into my head and was making me think in a certain way. And what a way . . . I was actually eyeing some sleazy guy outside a bar, and wondering whether to pick him up or wait for a better one! Then a whole headful of fantasies of the wildest sort! And my God, I was swaying along, swinging my hips, undoing a button or two of my blouse . . . till the drunk's rheumy eye had cleared up and he was staring at me and leering. Luckily I'd picked one who could barely stand up. Then in a few seconds it was over, and I was striding up the street as though nothing had happened at all.

Had anything happened?

But then there was the other time when I was in the backyard cutting back some shrubs, and that strange sensation came over me again . . . and this time I was looking at the pruning shears and thinking they wouldn't do at all for the murder I was planning! But then I seemed to be flying around a graveyard or cemetery, and a lot of dark people—a whole bunch of Emereldas—were looking up at me. And there were three guys beating drums . . . and then it passed. I never told Willy about either of them.

I did tell Liz about these peculiar experiences, but she didn't seem to take them very seriously. "Of course you aren't going crazy, Dinah. Maybe they're memories."

"Maybe I was a hooker or a murderer or a graveyard ghost! Oh, great!"

"Well, dear, I just don't know." She looked at her watch. "Listen, everybody thinks crazy things from time to time."

"What would you think if I told you I could see in your head during the time you were crazy?"

That got her attention. She listened while I told her that Switzerland was under the couch and the ring of stones and all that. I know it got to her. But she wouldn't admit it.

"I don't know what I thought. When I try to think back I just see mix-up, like a kaleidoscope. So I don't look back. I don't want to, Dinah. It was too painful. I was rotten to my kids and Willy and myself. Please don't ask me to think about that period. I was like a tornado, destroying everything." She stood up. "And don't you give in to this shit, Dinah. Everybody needs you. There's too much on the line. If any monkeys come into your head, throw them out. Out!"

Liz believed you could will anything. It was one of the reasons I liked her. It was so different from the way I thought. She hated things that couldn't be clearly explained, she was so frightened of that part of herself. She was, in fact, very like Willy.

Well, *I* wasn't afraid, not after all this time. Though I'd scarcely been aware of it, my feeling about the amnesia had shifted around. It was no longer a defect I avoided, but now more like a tantalizing present under the Christmas tree— there to open when I felt like it. Instead of looking away from it as I had at first, now I looked toward it more and more, touched the ribbon, slid my finger under the paper and out again. Even if I never opened it, there was something about having it around that gave me courage.

As often happened when I was alone . . . Well, that's wrong. I never was alone, or never felt alone. Even if nobody else was in the room, I often sensed ghosts—murmuring, elbowing, nudging ghosts. Never mind that ghosts don't exist. The room would get that shimmering, faintly electric, inhabited feeling, the air thick with vibrations . . . Sometimes I'd look to see if they gave a sign, or moved something or made a noise, but they never did. Often they parted suddenly, letting in that one little memory that I carried around, with the sunlight and the smell of grass and the sparkling stream, and in time they let me know that it was a place called Bell's Corners, Vermont.

Willy didn't mind that I went, given his increasing tendency to love me for leaving him alone. And I think the children were glad I had a project. Jessie had hinted more than once that I needed to find my own "identity."

Bell's Corners is a tiny hamlet hidden in the folds of a mountain. Scarlet and gold leaves skittered off the hood of the car as I drove along. There was a square, a peeling white church, a boarded-up store—a ghost town. I wasn't sure if it felt familiar or not: I'd had some confusing experiences about things that felt familiar but weren't. But it was a lovely place, and I hoped it had once been my home. I thought I found the bright crystal stream I remembered, winding through a field. The whole trip had a dreamlike quality. Especially what happened afterwards.

There was only one sign of life in Bell's Corners, a battered pickup truck in the driveway of one A. Hood. A knock at the door produced a wizened little woman who agreed to rent me a room for a couple of nights. It was a nice spot, whether she had anything to tell me or not. The shadow of the mountain fell over a small family graveyard, where, I saw, a space awaited A. Hood next to her husband.

Mrs. Hood didn't give away a thing at first. In a housedress and homemade sweater, she sat in the kitchen with a bottle of Jack Daniel's and a pack of Marlboros. She listened to my story with no expression, then let it be known that she'd sure appreciate a dinner at the steak place in the next town. When you were old and alone it was hard to get a square meal together. So Mrs. Hood—now Ada Grace—added a padded jacket and knitted ski hat to her ensemble, and off we went.

I was Robert Morrow's girl, she thought. He used to be postmaster. My mother, Mildred, had been a little too fond of the bottle. They'd moved New York way, to Troy, when I was about sixteen, and been killed in a car accident about two years later. (I measured myself for emotion and found none.) Over dinner I heard about how Dad was a wicked shot, how Mildred's apple pie had won two contests, about square dances and church suppers.

But when I prodded her for something darker, she snapped, "Listen, girl. Don't turn over too many rocks. You might not like what crawls out. If the good Lord took away your memory, maybe he did it for a good reason." That was all she'd say—though I wondered if her silence was from discretion or gastric discomfort, for she'd tucked away a lot of food, this tiny little woman whose stomach must have been the size of a teacup.

The next day Ada Grace and I worked in the garden together, which I enjoyed enormously. From time to time she threw me a tidbit about the church choir or my bad case of scarlet fever or how Mildred had always wanted a son. It was like hearing about somebody else.

"You were a funny little critter. Robert used to say he thought you were haunted. And Mildred was right skeered of you sometimes."

"Did they love me?"

"They was good and dutiful parents. Folks in these parts don't show their feelin's much. They took good care of you, girl."

Unless it was some other girl entirely.

That evening we went to a French restaurant a few miles away, Ada Grace in her usual attire plus a pair of flopping rubber galoshes. Over another substantial meal and a bottle of wine, she delivered only the rosiest information about my Norman Rockwell childhood, at the same time hinting that certain skeletons inhabited my closets.

"Mrs. Hood—Ada Grace—if you know any secrets I beg you to tell them to me. Whatever happened is very important."

"No, 'tisn't. And it's not your business anyway."

"Whose, if not mine?"

"Good Lord, girl—nobody's but those that was there. Ain't got nothin' to do with you 'tall." She wiped her mouth, then summoned the waiter and ordered chocolate mousse. "My granddaughter comes up here, wants me to talk into some tape recorder about bygone days. It's none of her Goddamn business, that's what."

I'd stopped eating and drinking in the name of getting us home safely, but Mrs. Hood put away an astounding amount of food and had to be half carried out. In the car she belched and sagged sideways, her head resting on my shoulder. When we got back to the house, which I had trouble finding in the darkness, I took her in and laid her on the bed, first removing the hat, the jacket, and the galoshes. She mumbled and hiccuped.

"Do you feel all right, Ada Grace? I'm afraid you've eaten

too much." She murmured and mumbled and appeared to sleep, and I left her and went to bed.

The next day Ada Grace took me on a tour of the area, showing me where I'd done this or that, then at night we went to a very fancy Italian-Continental place. I didn't understand the curious game we were playing but didn't dare stop it. Ada Grace put away inordinate amounts of mussels, pasta, veal scallopini, and Lachrima Christi. I remonstrated with her; she didn't look at all well, and there was something strange about the whole business anyway. I sat and stared at her as she ate some impossible pink and green dessert. Her face, so white and wrinkled when I'd first seen it, was pink and puffy, as though she were storing the food inside against the long winter.

"Ada Grace, I'm leaving in the morning and I'd like to thank you for everything." Her fork moved more slowly. "I'll never forget this visit, and maybe I'll come back and see you sometime."

She said, "Robert was untrue to Mildred with another woman, and that woman was Ada Grace Hood." She belched slightly as she said it, and I stared, thinking I'd misunderstood. "I never told Joe or any living soul, and Robert and Mildred died with the secret. But I don't guess it makes any difference now." Her sharp old eyes met mine. "You resemble Robert, girl. He was a fine-looking man."

I was moved and troubled, and I touched her hand. "Is that why Mildred was unhappy?"

"It is. She never could forgive him. So they left Bell's Corners for Troy."

I paid the seventy-five dollars and half dragged Ada Grace out to the car, for indeed she seemed semiconscious. Slowly we drove home.

"He was a fool to tell," she mumbled. "I told him never to breathe a word, but he was dog-honest, Robert was. Too damn much tellin' nowadays."

Was this my father's lover, his mistress, this crumpling

doll next to me? At home I put her into bed again, removing jacket, hat, galoshes, and that huge-stitched, uneven
sweater. She lay on her back, eyes closed, breathing heavily
through half-open mouth. She could have been my relative,
an aunt or a sort of mother once removed, as though the
connection of sex was forever.

I slept deeply and tranquilly and woke to one of those
clear, cool country mornings that quiet the soul. The twit-
ter of birds was the only tiny, surface interruption of a
silence as deep as the pine forest. From the narrow little bed
I could look out the window and see the mountain with its
fall patches of red and gold. Through the open window the
air felt sharp and fresh.

There was no coffee in the kitchen, nor any sign of Ada
Grace. I packed up my few things, then gently opened the
door of her room, tapping as I did so. She was lying in
more or less the same position as the night before when I'd
tucked her in, but something was different. She was very
deeply asleep—so deep as to be motionless. I began shaking
her gently and saying, "Ada Grace, I have to go. I've come
to say good-bye." I shook harder and then drew my hands
back as though I'd been stung.

"How did you know?" Willy asked me later.

"I held a little mirror in front of her mouth and there
was no breath."

"Dinah, you've seen too many movies." But you can get
an education from movies.

I sat down and held her hand, lifeless as a piece of rubber.
Her face was no longer that puffy, shiny pink, but gray and
ashy. She'd eaten herself to death. Confessed herself to
death.

I stayed there for three more days, till they buried her.
I'd wanted to stand by the Hoods' graves, and so I did. The
minister came from the next town, and a little handful of
people who'd known her. We stood on the thick grass near
a fence covered with wild roses. It was a clear, chilly day.

Somewhere a dog yelped, and I heard the buzz of a chain saw from across the road. The daughter, who was quite upset, told me how devoted her parents had been to each other, how perfect their union. In a sense we were sisters— I and this thin-faced, middle-aged social worker from Urbana, Illinois.

Willy

—

Dinah's in Vermont chasing her memories. Well, here it comes, I suppose. When I was younger and a lot less secure, I thought any returning memories would threaten our marriage. In fact we agreed she'd never go looking for them. But a lot of things have come out I couldn't have predicted. The amnesia has led to some bizarre pathology. She refuses to make an appointment with Bertie Mood. I'll have to do it and drag her there bodily. But when do I have time? The chairmanship of the American Society of Surgery of the Hand and Limbs is a full-time job in itself. I'll talk to her again when she gets back, assuming nothing out of the ordinary happens in the meantime. With Dinah you never know.

The other night the kids and I are eating dinner at the kitchen table and Emerelda is serving. I'm trying to make up for being an absentee father, which I'm guilty as sin about. The kids hardly know me; I'm a workaholic blur running in and out. They're not saying a word, but it's something else too. They're all chewing away with eyes as big as saucers, watching the maid. Even sensible Con is looking worried and hardly eating a bite.

Then something's going on behind me, and the kids are staring white as sheets with their mouths open. "What's the matter with you?" I ask. Nobody answers. I turn around and there's Emerelda looking like Mammy Yokum having one of her spells. She's making strange gestures with her hands and she starts talking mumbledy-jumbo. Her eyeballs are gone. It's some kind of voodoo trance. She begins singing peculiar songs, while Jason drops his chicken leg and Jessie almost falls off her chair, saying, "Erzilie, Erzilie!" Conrad's face registers total confusion.

I'm a physician and I know it is better to let her come out of it herself. Jessie and Jason are looking a little peculiar too, kind of rotating in their seats. Conrad grabs his fork and slams it on the table in anger. Then bang, it's over, and Emerelda's back to fixing the salad and Jason's gnawing on the chicken leg again. I ask what the hell happened, and the kids look like I'm talking Chinese.

"Jessie, I asked you a question."

"What, Dad?" All innocence.

"Emerelda, come over here."

"Certainly, Mister Doc." She brings the fruit salad.

"That was an interesting little number you just did for us. Are we to have floor shows with dinner now?"

First she looks bewildered. Am I going crazy, am I hallucinating from the two martinis? But then she bites her lip and looks down.

"Oh, I am so shamed. It is the loas."

"The what?"

Then she explains a lot of stuff about voodoo spirits and how she usually knows when one is coming along the path, but every once in a while, in a highly charged spiritual situation, one will sneak up and surprise her. Most of the time she doesn't even know afterwards that it's happened. She's sorry, Mister Doc.

Nobody could be more loyal and devoted than Emerelda. But I'm fed up with the voodoo bullshit. I have already put a stop to the storytelling and told her her beliefs were her

own business, but to please keep them to herself. She said
she'd try. I have said that I disapproved of superstitious
stuff except for the organized church, and since she worked
in my house she had to respect this. She'd do her best, she
said, looking worried.

Now I run all this by her again and she looks worried
again, and so do the kids.

"Mister Doc, I greatly respect you and the Mistress and
I love these children dearly. But I feel there is a strong,
mysterious charm upon this family. The Mistress's lost
memories are being held by powerful loas who struggle to
keep them hidden and—"

"Emerelda." I stand up. She comes about to my chest.
All three kids are looking terrified. "Mrs. Wakefield has
amnesia. It's a documented mental condition. I want you
to tell the children right now that there is no such thing as
a loa."

Her eyes widen. "Oh, Mister Doc. I dare not do that."

Jesus Christ. "All right. I will. Children. These are
Emerelda's beliefs. They come out of her primitive culture
and background. That's fine for her but not for us. *We* do
not believe in loas."

Their knees are practically rattling. Jessie says, "Daddy,
please don't say that."

"I'll say anything I want!"

"But Daddy . . . ," Jason wails. He looks scared to
death.

Emerelda has been watching me. Then she suddenly says,
"Children, you must listen to your daddy, even if you cannot understand. He is a man of great power. He was put
here to do great and sacred works. He must be protected
and surrounded and trusted by his family." She starts serving the salad. "Jessie, eat your beans."

"Well, Emerelda." That's better! "I certainly appreciate
that. But—"

"Your family is loyal to you first, Mister Doc, as I am
myself."

Everybody's finishing up their dinner as though nothing's happened at all. Jessie's picking at her string beans. Jason is noisily scraping his plate. Next they're all smiling innocently, talking about school like model TV kids. Nobody's even bitching. We have a nice evening together. I help with the homework. Emerelda acts as though nothing happened. But later I hear Jessie talking to herself in bed, and she's saying, "Erzilie, Erzilie, take me with you, Erzilie, please, please!"

I'm living in a bughouse.

I told Mac about this and he just laughed. Well, his wife screws around.

"Terrible, Willy. You're breaking my heart."

Why can't people be objective? Why do they have to refer everything to their own problems? I said, "Try and detach your mind as we were taught in medical school."

"Were we?"

"If we hadn't learned that we'd cry over every patient," I said.

"The patients are one thing," Mac said. "It's real life I cry about."

I told him I just wanted a rational, objective opinion.

"There isn't any, Willy. Haven't you learned that yet?" He grinned. Good old Mac. "Listen, you're married to a kook, that's all. It could be a lot worse. A lot. I'm telling you. I know."

There's been a wake in psychiatry because Liverwood lost his NIMH grant—a blessing for medical research. Now there's some strange shuffling around by Portoff, who's been angling to get on the medical board for years but always gets voted down for reasons obvious to everyone but himself and Frank Liverwood. I can't explain this mutual back-scratching, but I can guess the script:

Patient: Oh, Dr. Portoff, my legs hurt and my left ear is bleeding and my heart has stopped beating.

Portoff: You need a complete physical workup, plus years of intensive therapy with my colleague Dr. Liverwood, just to rule out any psychosomatic component.

And:

Patient: Oh, Dr. Liverwood, I cry all the time and I hear voices telling me what to do and I'm convinced people are following me and sometimes I run around the house shooting my revolver.

Liverwood: You need at least five years of analysis, plus monthly workups by my colleague Dr. Portoff, just to rule out any physical component.

How's that for holistic medicine?

The day he arrived, Portoff told me he'd run the hospital someday. He said it jokingly, but I'm beginning to think he means it. He's always involved in some little power struggle, besides being full of secrets and weird little plots.

The other day I walked into the physicians' cloakroom and there were Portoff, Liverwood, and Bertie Mood, all in a huddle, and when I came in they all immediately shut up and Frank and Bertie took off like roadrunners. Portoff was in his throat-clearing, ahem-ahem mood. I tried to ignore him, but it's like trying to ignore oncoming traffic.

He struts over and starts nudging and ahem-ing and hinting and staring into space. Then he starts some ridiculous speech about the physician's image and clean hands and we should keep our problems tucked out of sight—better still not have them at all as he, in his perfection, does not —and patient confidence and . . . *clippings*. I tell him I am on my way to the office, where eighty-five surgical patients are beating down the door for the privilege of being carved up by me, but Portoff only puckers up tighter than ever and says, "Everything's a joke to you, Willy. But I think you'll find you can't stay on your high horse forever, laughing at everything. Sometime soon, when you aren't in a hurry and you're prepared to be serious, there's a matter I'd like to discuss with you."

I'm halfway out the door. "Sure, Mike. Listen, I can be as grim as the next doctor."

"The whole future of the hospital is at stake," he's caroling as I run down the hall, "not to mention certain reputations."

My butt! It's Portoff's power trip he thinks is threatened, or I'll eat my hat. I wonder what he wants to talk about?

Dinah

———

here was a funny atmosphere when I got back from Bell's Corners. I hadn't expected Willy or the kids to be more than politely interested in my trip, but this was different from yes-dear-I-have-to-go. Willy wouldn't even look me in the eye, and he wouldn't make love to me but cringed over on the far side of the bed as though I had an infectious disease. The rest of the time he was a blur—dashing frantically from one thing to another and avoiding me in the most depressing way.

A couple of times I grabbed him, made him sit down, and forced him to listen to a rundown of the demise of Ada Grace. He sat and stared at me as though I were Medusa of the snaky locks, then bolted and ran as soon as he possibly could.

Then one night around midnight, while Willy lay in his drug-induced sleep, I went down to the kitchen for a glass of milk. It was one of the nights Emerelda slept over, and I found her there sewing and drinking tea. The air in the kitchen crackled, almost moved with the energy. She was watching me closely.

"Mistress, I must say something of the utmost importance. I have never told you this, but I am a mambo."

"What's that?"

"A high priestess. Certain things are revealed only to me. I preside at the hounfort." The loas again, bless their hearts! "I have such a feeling about you, Mistress Doc. I can't sleep for thinking of it. I feel there is something sacred in your head."

"What's a hounfort, Emerelda?"

"Oh, a special temple for our ceremonies. I most respectfully invite you to come there with me. It is in Brooklyn."

"The hounfort . . . is . . . in . . . Brooklyn."

"Please listen, Mistress. I believe the loas to be holding your first twenty-three years. This is a very strange thing. It might be Damballa or the Gran Mait himself. So far you have not been mounted—or only briefly. Though the first Mistress Wakefield was, indeed she was." She nodded, her small face grave and wide-eyed. "It is even possible that you drove her spirit away and that your emergence cured her."

I'd come out of the subway at about the same time Liz recovered. "Coincidence, Emerelda."

"Your wanga is the most inscrutable I have ever seen. But I believe that your memories have a malevolent power which has already caused harm. The Country Mistress died from the force of them. The Mistress Sally died in search of them" (she even knew about that!), "and I have the greatest fear that others will suffer or even die until you accept them back wholly and with love."

Wholly and with love. It was dark in the kitchen except for the pool of light we sat in. Her words were strangely compelling—even more after she got out a bottle of rum and poured a slosh in my milk and one in her tea. I could almost see my memories like a dark, malevolent cloud floating over us, eluding all attempts to penetrate.

"But I'm not sure I want to."

"Oh, but you have no choice, Mistress. You must be true to your memories—the material of your heart that was given magically to the first Mistress Wakefield to hold."

I gave myself a shake. "Emerelda, this is giving me the creeps. I just don't believe in the loas. I don't think." I said it nervously, because I was beginning to wonder. And as I did I suddenly choked, for no reason at all, and had to get a drink of water at the sink, as Emerelda watched with interest.

"I beg you not to close your mind without coming to the hounfort one time."

"No. No hounfort. And besides, it may sound funny, but I have had a sort of agreement with the doc not to go chasing memories. I wanted my life to start over again with him, and I really don't want to remember what might have been unhappy. Though of course if things start coming into my head, I can't stop them." She looked at me in silence. I felt pretty confused. I'd already gone chasing memories all the way up to Vermont. "Anyway, you can't make people believe."

"Yes, Mistress, but I must ask you, do you find something new in your head? A familiar white house?"

You know what? I did. Just as she said it. My house, and my bedroom at the top of the stairs, and everything in it. And out the window, the mountain at Bell's Corners. I avoided Emerelda's eyes for days afterwards.

I hardly know how Willy told me. Perhaps I knew without knowing, and then, one day over breakfast, our eyes met. I was devastated at the hurt and betrayal I saw there. He was close to tears—far worse than anger. I shook my head as though to deny . . . what?

Willy croaked, or gagged, "Clippings."

Then he got up, went upstairs, and came down with an envelope, which he thrust into my hands before stamping out of the house, perhaps forever.

Clippings . . . clippings!

My hand was shaking on the receiver as the phone rang, rang, rang in Scarsdale.

"I thought we were friends!" I shouted when Chrissie
answered. "I would have died with my secret if it hadn't
been for the fucking accident! I would have died with any
secret *you* gave *me!*"

"Oh, Dinah. I deserve every word you say. I'd deserve it
if you came here and killed me. I'm so sorry . . . It was
just that Michael—"

"Was going through your drawers as usual."

"You can't keep secrets from your husband," she wailed.
"And Michael didn't *mean* to. I had them in an old cereal
box up on a shelf. Oh, Dinah, we should have burned them
years ago."

"I suppose it's all over the hospital too!"

Shocked silence. "Oh, no! He wouldn't do that. It's just
that Michael feels that information like this should be, uh,
handled, I think that's what he said, for the good of Episcopal's image, because physicians are supposed to present
an example for the rest of society, so he feels he *has* to
suggest to just a few people that there are some doctors
who . . ."

I was dead.

". . . and Dinah, Michael said one thing I wondered
about, that people are *always* gay . . . and just as your
friend I think you should go back into therapy. You have a
husband and kids and there's going to come a time when
you have to choose between the life you have now and
coming out of the closet and living on Christopher Street"
—Chrissie's concept of the gay life.

"Michael's wrong. I'm not gay, and you'd better go back
to the Sisters' group because your brain is softening out
there."

Hysterical denials and defense of her perfect life. Then,
"Dinah, do you really like having sex with men?"

"Of course. I love it."

Chrissie said, "Well, I'm damn sick of it myself."

Leveling with Willy was the hardest thing I ever did.

But I knew I had to, if our marriage was going to survive. That night I put Jason to bed early and came down to the living room, where he was sitting, staring into space. His two white hands rested on the arms of the chair.

"Willy, we have to talk."

"Excuse me," he said, and went out of the room. I heard him running water in the bathroom. Then he came back.

"All right, Dinah. Let's talk."

So I told him all about Sally and me, and how she'd seduced me, and though he might hate me for it, in all honesty I didn't see anything wrong with it, but our marriage came first to me. I loved him and I was truly sorry all this had happened.

As I watched with horror he began to cry, covering his face with his hands, leaning his elbows on his knees as he sobbed. I knelt next to him on the floor.

"Oh, Willy, don't. I can't bear it."

"Neither can I. That makes two of us."

"Have I hurt your career so badly?"

"Oh Christ, that's not it. Nothing can hurt it. People forget. It's that I keep picturing you making love with her."

"Oh, darling. I've made love with you a thousand times better and more often."

His eyes opened suddenly. "How could you do it?" he whispered. "I swear I've tried to understand it. I can't. It's just . . . not . . . normal."

"It was just sex, Willy, plain old sex. And it happened at a time when I had nobody. It's not really so strange."

He said, "The worst part is, I want to know about it." His voice dropped to a low whisper, even though there wasn't anybody around to hear us. "It's probably sick, in fact I know it is. But I feel as though I can't forget it until you tell me what it was like."

In telling this I've condensed several evenings. It wasn't easy for him to say this, or for me to tell. But tell I did, and as I told him about the things Sally and I did together, Willy's hands crept around me and under my sweater and into my pants, and the whole thing made me so hot and wet I could hardly wait, and we ended up fucking in the middle of the living-room floor. And Willy pinned me down with his hands and his cock and growled, "She couldn't do this to you, Dinah, could she? She couldn't make you feel like this." And it was true, she couldn't, and when he asked me which I liked better, I said him, because I needed him inside me. I wasn't sure if it was really true, because I'd more or less decided it didn't really make any difference and wondered why people broke their lives because they thought one kind of sex was better than another. They were just different—and not even that much different —and it seemed funny that everybody thought it was so important.

Later I looked at those old newspaper clippings again. They didn't seem all that bad, compared to a lot of the stuff you see in the paper. One of the stories called Sally "the penultimate professional, who had died in pursuit of her story." It was hard to think of her interest in me as primarily professional, but now that I look back on it, I suppose it was; she just picked up what fun she could along the way. Now I understood her peculiar attraction. Even if she'd tried to kill me a couple of times, I'd known there was one person I could be as rotten with as I liked. I could be bitchy and mean and unjust and perverted, and she only laughed. More and more my life with Willy involved an effort to hide or cover up parts of myself in order to get his approval. And even though we'd come together in a way that was almost a miracle, and though Willy had not only accepted my "gay" affair but turned it to advantage in a way I'd never thought possible, he didn't forget. Not my Willy. I suppose he had to make up for me by having a memory that was twice as good as other people's.

We'd go along for a while, then something would happen

to bring it up—along with the rest of the steadily increasing list of my crimes that collected in Willy's mind like
dust balls.

There was, for instance, the business about Philip, when
he finally came back from Borneo after twenty years. He
was Willy's older brother, a shaggy, bearded innocent from
deep in the jungle. He wore burlap sacks and strange-
looking sandals and a lot of beads and bells and pieces of
leather and metal. Willy picked him up at the airport and
brought him home, looking agonized, and the next morning dispatched me to Brooks Brothers with him to buy him
a suit. So I fitted Phil out in gray flannel and cordovan
shoes, which didn't help much because he refused to shave
or have a haircut.

Willy wanted to show him a good time, so we took him
to the theater and to Lutèce, and during the day I took him
around the city with Jessie and Jason. He was a sweet,
gentle soul, as unlike Willy as anybody could possibly
be. He was into New Age thinking, the afterlife, playing
the flute, something called the music of the flowers, and
of course all kinds of drugs. The kids loved him because
of his endless patience and good nature, though Jessie pronounced him "weird." He and Charlotte spent a lot of time
together, Charlotte serving tea to dead DAR members
and Phil strumming Hindu songs on a little square
guitar.

After he'd been here for a few days, he announced he had
to meet a friend at Kennedy Airport and returned with a
small Bornean lover—male. His name was Ping and he
smiled constantly and understood nothing, which, it turned
out, was fortunate. Over dinner Phil announced that he had
long been homosexual and had decided to let the world see
his true feelings. Having seen what open, tolerant, and
understanding people we were, and how open and tolerant
a place Manhattan was, never again would he bury his heart.
So he'd phoned Ping—it seemed there were phones in Bor-

neo—and told him to hop on the next plane so they could share this moment of going public, and so forth . . . Phil was rather long-winded.

None of this surprised me particularly, or the kids either. I'd always given them pretty frank answers. So I only smiled and was giving Ping more shrimp when I caught the look on Willy's face. He was deeply shocked. This, after all, was his brother, no matter how much he resembled Obi-Wan Kenobi. That his brother was gay affected him more than all the other much stranger things about Phil. Even if you were gay, you didn't say so, and God knows you didn't announce it at the dinner table.

So he said tightly that "we've discussed it enough for the present," giving Phil and me warning looks. Poor Phil looked crushed, and Ping, who fortunately didn't understand a word, just kept beaming. When he patted Jason (then about six) on the head, Willy's face got red and tight and he said to Phil, "Please tell your friend to keep his hands to himself."

"Daddy, you're not being very nice to Uncle Phil," said Jessie, arbiter of good taste and appropriate behavior.

"Really, Willy," I said.

He turned to me. "Have you something to contribute, Dinah? This is a specialty of yours, isn't it?" Zap! Jessie turned and gave me her deep Scorpio stare. I returned it to Willy.

"I think people's sexual orientations are their own business and—"

"Couldn't agree more," Willy said.

"—and shouldn't be criticized, especially when they're guests in our house," I finished, patting Phil on his burlap arm. He saved his suit for going out. I told him I admired his honesty and he shouldn't be hurt, because Willy just needed time to get used to it.

Willy said, "Please don't put words in my mouth. Don't tell me what I'll get used to. I don't care how many people are jumping out of closets in the name of honesty, I don't approve of exhibitionism about sex. And it's my house and I won't have it."

So Phil and Ping were packed off to a hotel and then Willy and I had a big fight. I said, "How could you do it? What's the matter with you?"

"It's my house and I pay the bills and I have the last word."

"Is that all you have to say—that you're the big boss? Is that what we're reduced to?"

"I'm the only one, it seems, who can keep any order in our lives, which can only be done by firmness and control."

I said, "Willy, we have always had *order*. Because I've created it. When I met you, you had no order, and I brought it to you. Have you forgotten?"

"You're the one who forgets, Dinah. Conveniently. Don't deny that. The computer grandma agency. The mad tea parties. The Lesbian Love Nest. My name and reputation smeared all over the front pages. And now"—he waved his arm—"this. Phil imports his little slanty-eyed boyfriend with your approval."

This took place in the kitchen one night over a bottle of vodka in which Willy had put far too big a dent, so some of this can be attributed to the grape, or the potato. But not all. Willy was confusing a great many things. I was willing, I said, to accept a certain amount of blame for some things, but not a speck for the ones I had nothing to do with.

"Willy, you told me yourself about Phil's problem with his femininity. Now it's solved and you should be glad for him. And I'd say Phil's being gay is the *least* strange thing about him. I mean here he is dancing barefoot around the house, tootling on his flute—"

"You will not insult my brother!" Willy screamed so loud that we both glanced toward the stairs and the kids' bedrooms. "No matter how peculiar he is, he's *mine*. You will

not say anything about him. Because everything you touch *shatters!*"

I put my hand on his. "Willy, please don't do this. Don't do this to our marriage. I care about you, you care about me. Treat us more gently."

I was always the one who raised the white flag, which I guess was all right. But I was doing it more and more— apologizing for things I hadn't done, smoothing out the wrinkles of Willy's rage. It was I who moved my hand across the sheet to his rigid, sleepless body, I who covered things over for the sake of the kids. Afterwards he apologized for losing his temper.

"Forgive me, Dinah. I don't know what came over me. I'm going crazy with the responsibilities of the knuckle committee. And the speech for the conference. Suddenly it seems that everybody's jumping out of the closet all at once. The best scrub nurse at Episcopal has declared herself a lesbian and now it's impossible to work with her."

"But why?"

"She has a way of swiping that scalpel at me when she hands it that makes me nervous as hell. I wouldn't put anything past her."

"Willy, please forgive poor Phil. He feels terrible."

"I will, Dinah. But I need a little time. I don't know, I suppose I'm old-fashioned. Or I'm getting to be an old man. It takes me time to get used to these things."

Then a few months after all this had settled down, there was another catastrophe. Willy was in London, and I had dinner with Liz one evening. Emerelda couldn't come, but I'd decided the children—now fourteen, twelve, and seven —were old enough to stay by themselves with Charlotte, who spent most of her time smiling and nodding to invisible people but still managed to take care of herself and help in the kitchen a little. So I made a meat loaf and some baked potatoes and got everything ready for them, then left amid their assurances that everything would be just fine.

I got back later than I'd expected. Actually, Liz and I

had gotten rather drunk on white wine. When I staggered in around midnight I found the lights blazing and the three kids jumping around frantically, all talking at once.

"Dinah, we didn't know where to call you. We couldn't call Daddy because he's away and we called Dr. Flumetti" (the pediatrician) "but only got the answering machine . . ." Jessie was half crying.

At around ten, they told me, the three of them were upstairs, just kind of fooling around, while Grandma was supposedly reading in the living room, having her cup of tea. They thought they heard a voice and assumed she'd turned on the television. Then Jessie said, "That sounds funny. I'm going down and see." And down she went and found Grandma having a tea party—teapot, cups, saucers, slices of lemon, cookies, the whole thing. Except there weren't any guests.

"Here, Mindy Sue, lighten it with a little milk, the way you like it. And try one of these molasses cookies. I tried a new recipe; it's the one Cousin Dorothy used to use on holidays. They're very nice, not too sweet. I can't eat much sugar anymore." But Mindy Sue stubbornly wouldn't take her cup, which Charlotte was patiently holding out to her. "Mindy, please take hold of this, honey, my arm's getting tired." Crash went the cup on the floor. "Oh, my, you're a clumsy. Never mind, I'll get Hattie to clean it up." Another cup. "And yours now, Miss Daisy. Now let me guess; strong with one lump, isn't that so? I seem to remember from those nice teas you had in Charleston. Well, my heavens, take it." Crash—another one. "Good Lord, where's Hattie? We seem to be having a terrible time here today. Hattie!" No answer. "Well, she'll be along. Now, Roberta, how do you take yours? I can't quite recall."

There were several guests, and by this time each had dropped her cup and saucer, demolishing half of our good china. Con and Jason had come down too and were watching horror-struck. Jessie got it first.

"Grandma's flipped completely," she said, and Con's face

stretched and paled as it does when things go wrong. Jason was the one who tried to reason with her.

"Grandma, the tea party's over. Your guests are too messy; they can't even hold their cups. Tell them to go home." Like me, he's willing to enter the fantasy.

"But Willy," said Charlotte, "that wouldn't be polite. Why, Miss Daisy came all the way from Atlanta for our little gathering." It was some grand all-South tea party. "As soon as Hattie comes she'll tidy up. Here's your cup," which he tactfully took. "Miss Daisy, you remember my son Willy. I brought him up to Bobby Lee's wedding in Memphis. He looks like me, I think. Philip resembles his father." Jason wasn't even bothered when she moved back yet another generation. "Mother, do I have to sit here? I want to go out and play. Daisy has a new jump rope."

"Now, Charlotte, finish your tea," said Jason. "Then you can go. What a pretty pink dress."

At which point Jessie screamed, "Jason, stop! You're going crazy too!" which Charlotte didn't seem to hear. Somehow they got her to bed, taking off her shoes, and when they covered her up she went peacefully to sleep.

After that Charlotte never came up North again; she remained forever in Virginia. For years she'd checked back into the present and been part of the household, and there had been plenty of times when she and I had sat down together and had a perfectly ordinary conversation. But now she didn't even know who we were, or she'd turned us forever into Bobbie Lee and Mindy Sue. And having started with the china, she started dropping and breaking other things too, and lost things and got confused and started to cry at mysterious times. She had to be cared for full-time.

We dreaded having her "lock-up," as Emerelda said. But luckily the upstairs tenant was leaving for a big screenwriting job in Hollywood, so we did the apartment over and put Charlotte in it, and Emerelda's friend Prudie came to take care of her. I'd gotten very fond of Charlotte and was used to the sight of her rocking gently in the corner by the fire. But now when I looked into those cornflower blue eyes, I saw only corridors leading back forty or fifty years.

All this upset Willy, and he tended to take it out on me. Though he was grateful to me for being so good to her, he still couldn't resist a few digs about how she'd come unwrapped while I was out getting drunk with Poor Liz, leaving the family neglected, exposing the children to the onset of Charlotte's senile psychosis, and so forth.

Then one morning Emerelda came in rather late, looking wild-eyed and rumpled—unusual for this neat little person. I'd gotten everybody off to school and was rinsing the breakfast dishes, and Willy was finishing his coffee and flipping through the paper and scratching notes for an article he was writing on fingernail diseases, getting up occasionally to wash his hands, which he did more and more often. After he washed them he'd squirt on hand lotion and rub it in carefully. Then the hand lotion felt sticky, so he'd have to wash them again . . . All of which, with the pills, kept him in the bathroom quite a lot.

When he was in there, Emerelda grabbed my arm. "Mistress, I have to talk to you very urgently."

"Is anything wrong?" I asked, alarmed.

"I will explain when Mister Doc leaves."

Willy appeared, gathering up his possessions. "Got to run, Dinah; I have a wrist to do in twenty minutes. Check on Mother, will you? She seemed particularly gaga last night. And Emerelda, would you give a little more attention to the bathrooms? They don't seem as clean as they might."

As soon as the front door slammed, Emerelda said, "Mistress, I have been visited by the loas in the most extreme way. All night I lay awake listening to their voices telling me about you. They refuse to hold your memories any longer. You must understand, our people put no value on memories. But some of the loas have been playing with yours like a new toy, and now Legba says they must be returned as soon as possible." She was quite agitated. "I beg you, Mistress. I know how dangerous it is to displease them. It is far better to make them your friends." Her little round face was frightened.

"Emerelda, are you telling me you want me to go to Brooklyn to a voodoo ceremony?"

"Yes, Mistress, and the first Mistress Wakefield too. It would be terrible if she were mounted again and returned to madness. You could both be punished. And what would happen to the children?"

"Emerelda, listen to me. Do you know what a psychiatrist is?"

"A doctor of the mind."

"Right. How would you feel about visiting one?"

"No, Mistress. I have no need. Mistress Charlotte has been mounted and is kept a prisoner in her memories. I feel it is another malevolent sign and that as your memories float free they put others in great danger. You must fasten them to your heart."

"But Emerelda, I couldn't even if I wanted to. I can't make them come back."

"They will come back at the hounfort, Mistress Doc. If you will not come with me, I can stay with you no longer. For I fear what would happen, for you and myself both."

I sat down and poured myself another cup of coffee. "Emerelda, are you threatening to quit?"

"It is so, Mistress."

"But we couldn't live without you, and the children would be heartbroken!"

"What would happen to them if you will not come will be far worse. They could have no mothers at all, or only mad ones. You are not safe, Mistress. You must believe me. I could not bear to see what could happen, and perhaps to me too. When the Gran Mait is not obeyed, he is merciless."

I watched her as she stuffed a load of wash into the machine and poured detergent on top. I didn't think I could live without Emerelda. She'd been with us for eight years, since I'd first moved into the house. Jason knew no other maid and Jessie, if not Conrad, had long forgotten the string of nannies who had once paraded through their lives. Not only was she quick and efficient, and loving to the children, but there was a calm at her center that was good for all of us. Now as she dropped the plastic cup and stuffed the dark clothes in with the white, along with a purple blouse of mine that was sure to run, while mumbling worriedly to herself, it was obvious that there was something really wrong with her. And if Emerelda wasn't happy, neither was I, nor would any of us be.

"You understand, Mistress, that I have suffered with this for many weeks. It is not a passing thing. Even if I no longer work for you, I cannot escape the consequences. It is too late to go back. I even wish"—the bleach was sloshing out of the cup—"that the Doc would come too."

"Not a chance of that, Emerelda."

"Perhaps the Gran Mait would be appeased by the women alone." Half the soap went on the floor. "Perhaps Mister Doc and Mistress Liz picked up a spell when they were in the Caribbean, early in their marriage."

I phoned Liz and explained the situation to her.

"I see. A voodoo ceremony. Emerelda would quit. I'd relapse, and you could blank out or worse . . . I'll go. In fact I wouldn't miss it for anything. For God's sake don't tell Willy."

"I won't. I'll think of something."

"And Dinah, ask Emerelda what we should wear. Would jeans be appropriate, or should I wear my new Halston?"

We chose the week when Willy was in St. Louis and left Prudie in charge. The hounfort was in some unreachable part of Brooklyn, though I admit that all of Brooklyn seemed unreachable to me. The taxi wound around blocks, advised and misadvised by Liz, who thought she understood where we were going. It was a fine, clear evening in May, and we were to dress upon arrival in traditional costumes supplied by Emerelda. As the driver got more and more lost and we were on the verge of giving up, we drew up in front of an old warehouse in an abandoned neighborhood. Light came through a small door on the side and we heard the faint thump-thump of drums.

"Dinah, I don't like this. We'll never get out of here alive. Oh my God, the meter says sixteen dollars. All I can say is the show better be worth it."

Emerelda appeared in the little doorway, barefoot, wearing a white ruffled dress and a red scarf wrapped around her head like a turban. She led us inside, quickly locking the door after us. We were in a huge, gloomy room lit by flickering torches. As our eyes got accustomed to the darkness, we could make out people flitting about, all looking very busy, the women in the same costume as Emerelda—the same as she now handed us and told us to put on in a dark corner. Her manner was different—detached yet authoritative, and very serious. It was strange to be given orders by Emerelda, instead of the other way around. We wouldn't have dreamed of disobeying.

In the center of the big room was a rather moth-eaten, weary ficus tree in a pot, minus most of its leaves and hung with what looked like old rags. Nearby three very black men beat on high, narrow African drums—the drums of Dahomey—and placed around were all sorts of pots, jars, bowls, and other mysterious odds and ends. The sound of the drums was very loud and insistent, and echoed in the cavernous place.

"Emerelda, is this legal?" I whispered as she led us to where she wanted to put us.

She looked at me gravely. "Are the gods legal?"

"What do we do now?" Liz asked.

"Just follow me," Emerelda said. She shook each of us by

the hand—a very firm, specific handshake, three times downward.

Looking back now, I find it very hard to describe that evening. It started out being slightly ridiculous; here were Liz and I hanging around in our white dresses and red turbans ("like the sixth-grade Christmas pageant," Liz said later), while all around, the others—similarly dressed women and sexy black men in tight pants and knotted-up shirts that revealed brown satin midriffs—were filling pots, pouring water, and tending to a small bonfire, which was being kindled near the tree. Now there was the sound of rattles and the tinkle of bells. Two women were kneeling on the floor, drawing pictures with fingers dipped in flour; Emerelda said these were the vévés, symbolic pictures of the loas. Tonight they were making a particular bid for Damballa, one of the rougher ones, and Erzilie, who was inclined to be shy. When I'd agreed to come, I'd reminded Emerelda, again, that I couldn't believe, nor could Liz. That was all right, she'd said, as long as we respected what was going on. And, "Please do not fight it, Mistress. Let whatever happens, happen." Now when I asked her what we should do, she said whatever we felt like.

Now the drumbeats filled the air and most of the people were swaying and dancing around to the rhythm, stamping their feet in a dance that was impossible to resist. Liz looked strange, with her white face and wisps of curly red hair sticking out of her turban, and so, no doubt, did I, among these small, slender, dark people. We towered over most of them. It wasn't long (though I lost all track of time) until I was captured by it—a butterfly by a net, a marionette whose strings were suddenly taken by the gods. A lazy stroller swept into a parade, a car pulled by a massive magnet . . . I try to think of comparisons and none are exactly right, though all are partly true. The dance flooded the mind with strange thoughts, perfumes, sounds, yearnings. First I felt heavy, then extraordinarily light. It played games with time, and even with consciousness, which time depends on—or is it the other way around? To this day I don't know how long we were there. It was a little like being stoned, and later on, people couldn't believe that Liz and I had taken nothing but a couple of swigs from the rum bottle, which was passed around like a kind of loving cup. Sometimes it was glorious, sometimes painful. It was like nothing I'd ever experienced. I felt again as though someone had gotten into my head, but this time it was some gay, lighthearted, mischievous being, or several beings, who only wanted to sing and dance.

Images flickered in and out of my head, including Liz doing a wild, whirling dance, feet bare, eyes closed, holding a torch from the bonfire, which scattered sparks over all of us, sparks that didn't burn. She sang a strange, guttural song, and the Haitians seemed to draw back from her as though pushed by some immense force. I saw my own arms, mysteriously covered with cuts which neither hurt nor bled, and my bare feet actually standing in the burning cinders of the bonfire. After that I must have passed out, and I came to after I was doused by Emerelda in a trough of water and leaves.

Then there was a terrible banging and yelling, which seemed to come from another world, so different was it from the sounds and music of the hounfort. Emerelda embraced me—she only came up to my nose—and said, "Oh, Mistress, I am so happy. I know the loas have favored you. There has never been such a visitation . . . I believe it was the Gran Mait himself." She had Liz in the tub now and seemed to be half drowning her. Liz's red curls were wet and stringy, and her dress, like mine, was soaked. We both felt very giggly and light-headed, jumping around and laughing like kids. Then there was more thumping and yelling and sirens this time, and the door burst open and in came the police.

It's incredible to me that with all the crime in New York —the murders, robberies, burglaries, muggings, and rapes that take place every single day—the police waste their time raiding a hounfort. For a while they leave the Haitians alone, and then they start saying it's sinful or pagan or whatever, or the old ladies in the neighborhood call it devil worship, or the local priest won't have it in his parish. We'd hit a bad night. Later I was tactless enough to ask Emerelda why she and her friends didn't grease a few palms, and she said they were all so poor they wouldn't be able to buy a single policeman.

Anyway, they took us to the local precinct to be booked. Liz and I sat in the patrol car like naughty children, alternating between uncontrollable giggles and panic.

"Oh, God. I hope Willy doesn't find out. He'll divorce me."

"No, he won't, Dinah. Willy puts up with incredible amounts because he doesn't want to be bothered, you know that."

"But this is bothering. Oh, my God, they'll kick him off the hospital staff."

"Well, maybe he won't find out," Liz said.

Sergeant Estevez seemed bemused. "What's this, the latest thrill for society wives? Just out of curiosity, what the hell were you two doing there?"

"The maid threatened to quit unless we went, and our poor old mother would die without her," Liz said. "We had no choice."

"Yeah, I'll bet."

Willy might never have found out if . . . Oh, of course he would have. He reads the paper, and even if he didn't, somebody would have told him. Somebody who remembered every detail of the car crash and the Lesbian Love Nest —Portoff! He called St. Louis and told Willy under the guise of being helpful. He knew I was of fragile mental health, and he felt it his duty to tell the other members of the medical board. He didn't want Willy to hear it from any lips but his.

Chrissie and I inevitably had a falling-out over this, because she felt guilty about it and was lying all over the place to protect the little prick.

"You've got to look at it the way Michael does, Dinah. It's not just the trustees he has to answer to. He feels strongly that doctors should maintain an image of stability because of their important place in society. He thinks it's a shame that a fine physician like Willy has these blots on his name, and that his domestic difficulties—not just you, Dinah, but the first wife too—all serve to wear him down by attrition and to debilitate his skills, when in fact his home should be a source of strength."

I was so furious I could hardly speak. "Chrissie, that's a lot of shit. His home is a source of strength, because I *made it that way*. Michael's being a bastard and you know it."

"Dinah, I'll always be your friend. But you are a *strange person*. You can't pretend your life is normal and stable, I don't care what you say." I ended up slamming down the phone.

The whole business at the police station turned out to be a joke, because there wasn't anything they could book us for. There's no law on the books forbidding voodoo, and there weren't any drugs around. They'd looked. How could we all have been having such a great time with nothing but a few bottles of Mount Gay rum? They considered locking us all up for disturbing the peace, but there were about forty of us, counting the hounsis and the houngans, and they didn't have the space. They decided to skip it and let everybody go with a warning, and that would have been the end of it except Liz got mad and socked one of the cops she said was feeling her up, and there was a big business about that, and Liz and I ended up in jail for the night.

I love Liz but sometimes she goes too far. She's very excitable, and she always thinks somebody is feeling her up. She's terribly high-strung and I think that's one reason why she can't cope with the kids all the time—things that don't bother me make her frantic. We flopped in the cell like a couple of rag dolls or pale-faced Aunt Jemimas in our soaking wet houn clothes. It upset Liz, but I didn't really mind. I thought maybe Willy would never find out, and I wanted to talk to Liz about what we'd experienced. But after Liz calmed down and resigned herself, she grew sulky.

"Well, I didn't think it was so wonderful. I thought it was boring. I'm just glad it didn't last long."

"But we were there for hours."

"We weren't. As soon as those people started jerking around to the tom-tom, in came New York's finest. In fact the whole thing was a fiasco." She yawned. "I'm exhausted, God knows why."

"But Liz, you were dancing around and whirling and singing and waving that torch. Don't you remember?"

She laughed. "I was dancing and singing? Hey, kid, the houn's got you. You were seeing things."

"No, I swear it's true. I remember standing in the fire, and look, my feet aren't even burned."

"Darling, they're black."

"Liz, it was incredible. It was like being carried by the gods. I wish you remembered too."

"What are you talking about?" She stared at me.

"Do you remember my telling you about my house that I remembered?"

"No—yes—I guess so." She was rubbing her head in a puzzled way.

"Now I remember everything in the whole house—living room, basement, bathroom, kitchen, everything. And my father's voice. My mother cooking. And a pink dress I had, and playing by that stream. And now I remember the village." I was so excited I was pacing up and down the jail cell. "My father was the postman. There was a field with cows and just beyond the church . . . a white church. On Sundays the bell rang and we went, and my mom sang in the choir."

I began to cry, and Liz grabbed my hands. "Oh my God, do you mean your memory came back from tonight?"

"Well, not all, but it's starting. I went to school up a

dirt road past some very tall elms, and the teacher's name
was Mrs. Wilson, and there was a boy in the next row I
thought was cute but . . . Oh, it's so wonderful. I feel
differently about it now. I don't care what bad things I
remember; the main thing is they're mine."

She had a funny expression on her face. "Well, are they?
I mean, I remember the dirt road and Mrs. Wilson too.
And the pink dress." I didn't immediately understand what
she was saying. "Your mother made apple pies, right? With
crisscross crust. There was a blue tablecloth on the dining-
room table. Your room was upstairs, a dormer room. You
took piano lessons from Mr. Walling. The pink dress had
four pearl buttons on the front. Once you tore it and your
mother spanked you."

I was frightened. "What else?" We were both staring at
each other.

"Mrs. Wilson played favorites and you weren't one of
them, because you were lousy at math. And the house . . .
There was a Magnavox record player and a stack of little
forty-five records, and you'd play them and dance around
the room. And sometimes Carol came over and you'd dance
together. Carol . . . Carol Whiteside."

"You can't know these things," I whispered.

"Well, I do. I always thought I was making up stories
when I was crazy, my head was so full of bullshit. What
about all the boyfriends and the . . ." She stopped. "I don't
want to talk about this anymore."

Later I wondered if I'd made up the whole thing. God
knows strange things were happening to my mind that
evening. Liz threw herself facedown on her cot and turned
to the wall, but I sat there for a long time. It was a long
night in that dirty and uncomfortable cell. I was cold but
excited as I'd never been before. There were no burns on my
feet, only a black crust of dirt. Liz didn't sleep either; she
kept thrashing around and saying, "Shit."

"How long have you known these things?" I asked finally. There was a long silence.

"Since I was crazy. And Dinah, I *never* want to talk about this again."

I remembered what Emerelda had said about being true to my memories. I knew it was important not to confuse the real ones with what I would *like* to have happened or was afraid *might* have happened . . . or what Liz had said, which she refused to discuss. I'd written down what Ada Grace had told me in order to keep it all straight, and now things began flooding into my head, things she'd never mentioned and probably didn't know about: how I'd broken my leg when I was nine climbing a tree, and they'd set it, and I found the place where they made the incision—a scar I'd never understood. How my best friend Carol and I walked two miles to town, how my mother and I had picked strawberries for jam, and how good it had smelled when it was cooking. And more about school, the nice teacher and the mean teacher, and Uncle Seth down the road, who let me help him milk the cows.

For a long time I didn't tell Willy, but it was hard. Memories were pouring into my head every day, and it was all I could do to calm him down after the hounfort business and keeping him from firing Emerelda. In the wrong mood he might not believe me. He'd say I made it all up or was having some hallucination about the perfect childhood I'd never had, inspired by Ada Grace.

But then my life had changed. Another house, this one in Troy, New York, larger and gloomier and sadder somehow. Now we seemed to be richer, for my mother and I had more clothes. But I would come home from school and find my mother sitting in a chair crying or sometimes drinking whiskey by herself. Sometimes at night I'd hear my parents arguing in their room. My name was—had been—Dinah Morrow.

I went to a big, ugly urban high school where I seemed to have been a rather indifferent student. I spent a lot of time at the movies or watching television, and I often went to roadhouses with pimply boys, where we drank beer and stuck nickels in the jukebox. I seemed to have lived on cheeseburgers, french fries, and black-and-white milk shakes. I remembered what must have been a favorite outfit: a short shift with large squares of green, vermilion, and grape, which I wore with yellow panty hose and green high heels. I had an anklet with a heart on it, a charm bracelet, and somebody's class ring hanging on a chain around my neck. My hair was teased into a mound, my lipstick was white, and my eyes were encrusted with black mascara. I smoked Chesterfields. When I tried to remember what I thought about, I got mostly movie plots and popular songs. Then I remembered fucking one of the pimply boys in the back seat of a car. He was panting and sweating, and I was lying there waiting for it to be over and worrying about messing up my clothes.

I had no time to edit any of this, which I was tempted to do. It shot out at me like a moviola gone haywire, with all the film flying wildly out and piling up in a tangled heap on the floor. Nor could I stop it anymore; every day brought forth a new and sordid incident. I'd see myself at the movies with Ron or Don or Chuck, and he's holding the popcorn with one hand and has the other up my skirt. I'm coming in the front door much too late, adjusting my clothes, and there's my mother passed out in the chair with an empty bottle and glass nearby. I'm at the roadhouse, jiggling around to Bobby Darin, thinking I look cute. I'm in the classroom; the history teacher has just handed back another failing test. Worst of all, I'm shoving one of the pimply lovers off just before he comes, because he doesn't have a condom, and he has his orgasm all over my new, beaded sweater—my last memory.

Willy

Cheerful Men met this week at the "21" Club. They put us upstairs and the food was lousy. I had mushy shrimps, a wet, gray steak, and soggy potatoes. Even the martinis were no good. I could have used some good horny-guy jokes, but Christ, everybody's getting serious. Conversation was all about tax shelters and money managers and legal fees. And of course malpractice suits. Two people are suing Bill Goldstein. He mangled some woman's breast and fucked up an eyelid. So all he could talk about was his Goddamn lawyer, but I suppose that's better than the usual complaints about how much money his wife spends—which of course makes the rest of us weep with pity.

At least we used to have a few laughs. We'd have a couple of drinks and tell some stupid jokes and fall off our chairs laughing. We'd torture Portoff a little, share a few secrets. We'd really enjoy the food, knowing we didn't have to be Mimi Sheraton over every bite. Liverwood says the reason he's crazy about take-out food is that he doesn't have to look at his wife's lip quivering when the dinner's no good.

He's not the only one whose home life is less than perfection. Liverwood should have my problems, he'd be back at analytic school.

I must say my colleagues have been very tactful about not mentioning the unmentionable, i.e., the predilection my wife has for getting her insanity into the newspapers. She doesn't even have to try; she's a walking PR firm. If only her talent could be turned into good, solid bucks instead of a trail of destruction! It's amazing how things happen to my sweet, innocent Dinah, who is missing half her brain—or a quarter now that her predictably dull and unexamined background is surfacing.

She just happens to be in the Lesbian Love Nest with her old dyke lover, who chases her out with a knife and climbs on the car in the nude, and the car just happens to smash up in front of the reporter from the local paper. Gosh, Willy, is that the craziest? I don't even know how much of it's true, and neither does she. Is she here? Is she there? Is she queer or straight? Is she real?

Well, we lived through it, because life goes on and there's too much else to do and I haven't got the leisure to sit around and cry over bullshit. We put a Band-Aid on the gaping wound and limped onward. Thank you, Michael Portoff, for anonymously sending me the clippings! And thank you, fate, for killing the story before it got to New York, so the only people who know Dinah's a dyke are the ones Portoff told, i.e., everybody at Episcopal Hospital and a few dozen others for good measure.

We didn't even need Portoff's help for "Voodoo Queens Jailed" (*Daily News,* p. 2) or "Society Women Dance in Trance" (*Post,* p. 1) or "Wives of Prominent Surgeon Arrested in Brooklyn: Pagan Ceremony Creates Furor among Residents" (*New York Times* Metropolitan Section). Now does that headline have punch? Note the *wives:* plural. And the word *pagan* is always good for some knee-jerk indignation.

I admit this didn't get me in the groin like the Lesbian Love Nest, but it didn't improve my appetite. I'm arriving home early from the hand convention in St. Louis, and a taxi pulls up and Dinah and Liz crawl out looking like a pair of bedraggled Raggedy Anns. "Oh, Willy," Dinah trills, "we've been in jail!" Liz, the old sharpie, tells her to shut up. I drag them inside and get the story out of them. I put them on the carpet and give them both hell while they stand there like a couple of naughty kids, giggling and nudging and glancing at each other to compare editing.

"I'm not going to listen to this, Willy," Liz says. "Your wife's got her memory back and you should be happy for her." I throw Liz out and say I never want to see her again. "Fuck you, Willy," says my ladylike ex. "My visits are court-ordered and there isn't a thing you can do about them."

When I tell Dinah I'm going to fire Emerelda, she bursts into tears and says she's sorry about everything—typical Dinah, throwing out blanket apologies to cover herself— but she can't live without her and neither can the kids and especially since this miracle which has taken place in Brooklyn. Honest, Willy! And Liz advised her not to tell me, but since she feels we are "drifting apart," she thinks it will bring us closer if she "shares" her new memories with me, which I'm about as interested in as last year's phone book. Having, as she well knows, been through it with Liz ad nauseam, and having spent most of my patience (what little is left) on little tales of rejected childhood love and cruel parents—some almost identical! "But Willy, this is different."

My butt it is. I have another loony wife. Portoff's shifty little eyes caught mine over the cigars at "21," and there was more truth in his dirty look than in anything else. And a question was there too. Can you cope with it all, Willy? Can you keep flying? For a minute I envied him his nice little Chrissie in Scarsdale.

The other matter inevitably came up at Cheerful Men. And that's Miss—oh, excuse me, *Ms.*—Bingham, who died of an embolism after surgery last week. After, not

during, for God's sake. She came in on an emergency basis
after her arm was caught in the crusher of a Department of
Sanitation truck. Of course this caused the boys to rock in
their chairs with their customary black humor.

"That's one way to get rid of your wife, throw her into
the garbage!" chortles Goldstein.

"Was she in a Hefty bag?" asks Liverwood gleefully.

"Too bad it didn't work," says Mac, who's been hostile
as hell since his divorce.

It took fully ten minutes till my chowder-headed colleagues had calmed down enough for me to explain that
Ms. Bingham was not part of the garbage but rather a
garbageperson, new on the job, who had fallen off the
top at the wrong moment. Which doesn't make any difference anyway. I got to repair the arm, five hours in
the O.R. knowing I'd have to accept assignment from the
city's shit insurance—and knowing this would be the
beginning of God knows how many other procedures
to get the arm decent-looking. As for functional, forget
it. Even Willy's glue has its limits. So the operation is
finished at four in the morning (Why the hell are they
picking up garbage at midnight?), and by eight o'clock
she's dead. It wasn't anybody's fault; she got proper care.
I did my best, which of course I always do. But I'm
having trouble shaking it, and I remember how Mac felt
about Mr. Morales.

"It wasn't anything you did, Willy," Goldstein says.
"For God's sake. There's no grounds for a suit. The insurance company will pay 'em off and that's that."

"They'd sue Mother Teresa if she had good coverage,"
Mac says. "They make up grounds, you know that." He
waves for another round of cognacs. "You've been lucky,
Willy. You low-risk guys can't stand the gaff. Let me tell
you about . . ." and off he goes on his latest murder, a
nine-year-old girl he's disemboweling and she dies, but he's
blaming the anesthetist. I don't even want to know the

details. I have enough fucking problems; who needs this crap?

The dirty truth is I'm not really sure I did my best work on the garbageperson's arm. I have a feeling if it had been the first lady, I would have done a whole lot better. Well, I'm only human. How can you do decent work without decent pay?

I've got to keep on an even keel. There's been too much going on. You study hard, work hard, do what you think is right. Somehow the ground goes out from under your feet; everything gets crazy. How does it happen? Physicians have enough professional stress, so when personal problems get rough it's twice as hard to take. Dinah's all right most of the time. I can't go through another divorce; I think it would finish me. I just have to keep an eye on her and be braced for the next beau geste . . . and pray it doesn't make the six o'clock news. If things have calmed down in a month or so I'll cut back on the Valium. Or only take them at night.

Bill Goldstein says, "There's something about getting older that makes you appreciate what you've got a lot more."

It could be a whole lot worse. If Portoff won the election for head of the medical board.

I never thought he'd get on it, but he ran around and kissed enough asses and there he is. Now he wants to unseat me. The whole thing would be a joke except that I know for a fact Bertie Mood's behind him, and probably Liverwood, though of course he hides behind his face and denies everything. And Mac told me the other day that he might get the votes.

We were eating lunch in the cafeteria. I asked, "Is it Dinah?" Mac looked blank. "Don't make me spell it out. Do you think there's something to this physician's-family-image stuff?"

"No, Willy." Mac was studying his BLT. "It's you. I'm

behind you all the way, Willy. I know you've got the stuff, even if other people don't."

It wasn't the kind of thing you can talk about. Mac and I looked at each other. I thought I was going to be sick, and I got up and ran out of the lunchroom. I just made it.

Dinah

---

told Willy all of it, including the Troy part, or everything but the sex.

"I was awful. Sometimes I wish the memories had stopped when I was young."

"Not awful, Dinah. A typical teenager from a certain background."

"I never had a serious thought or even a generous one. I was shallow and conceited and selfish. I was stupid and worst of all, I didn't know or care that I was stupid."

Willy didn't deny this. "Well, darling, the early part was sort of nice. Concentrate on that."

"Sort of nice! It's not a movie, it's me!"

Willy said, "You're getting awfully upset by this and you seem to be increasingly depressed. How about a few visits to Liverwood?"

"*Liverwood!* You're the one I need to help me cope with this."

Willy's face was tired and strained. "It's not that I wouldn't like to, Dinah. It's that I can't. I have a demanding career which leaves me very little time for anything else, you know that. I know I'm not a very good hus-

band or father, because I'm away so much. I love you and I
don't have the interest or energy to chase other women.
But my work comes first. Take it or leave it. I have only
so much emotional capital. I never promised you anything
else."

I was touched when he said that, if a little disappointed.
And amazed—his reaction was the last thing I'd expected.
I thought he'd be angry or threatened by my returning
memories. But he seemed just . . . spent. I've never forgotten that he was so honest, and in a sense it released me
from feeling that I had to share what was going on with
him.

I was on my own, really. I suppose people always are in
the end, though they don't know it.

The children weren't impressed with my new childhood
either. When I told them how contented and secure I'd
been, Jessie said, "Unlike us."

"I didn't say that, Jessie."

"Well, it sounds as though you think you were this
terrific, lucky kid from this perfect *simple* background, and
we're just a bunch of spoiled city brats." This one night at
dinner. "Just because you were *poor* and lived in the *country*
doesn't make you any better."

"I never said that, and I didn't mean it either."

Said Willy, looking at his watch, "Don't be rude, Jessie."

Con said, "She never said that, what's your problem?"

"Mom, is there any more roast lamb?" Jason asked.

"Sure. You know, my mother always made shepherd's
pie out of leftover lamb, all cut in little pieces in the gravy
with mashed potatoes on top. Boy, was that good. I'll make
it some time."

Silence. Jessie said, "I'll send out for Chinese."

"Jessie, watch your tongue." Willy looked at his watch.
"I have to go. I have a meeting tonight. You should all
have some respect and sympathy for Dinah; she's very ex-

cited about getting her past back. Now, how would you
feel?" I must say Willy was good about sticking by me in
front of the kids, no matter how he really felt.

"You're right, Dad," said Conrad the Righteous.

"How can we know how we'd feel?" Jason asked. "The
whole thing is pretty weird."

That hurt. "I'm not weird."

"Not you, Mom. But the forgetting and remembering
stuff is."

"Dinah, it's not personal or anything," Jessie said in a
Liz-like voice, "but sometimes these old things that happened to you are sort of boring."

And so forth. Willy was bored too, even when new memories came back at odd times and I couldn't resist telling
him.

"Willy, I had an Uncle Jim who always brought chocolate almonds at Christmas," I told him while we were making love. He was having an orgasm, and he only replied,
"Uh-uh-uh-oh God." Then he fell asleep, while I lay awake
remembering the paper chains we made for the tree, the
candy apples, and the carol singers outside our front door
in the snow.

Soon Willy was tired of hearing any of it. "Dinah, I'm
trying to read ten journals in forty-five minutes. Instead of
just saying whatever comes into your head, why don't you
try to understand why you forgot and then remembered
again? Try to think constructively about it, instead of com-
pulsively chattering about ice-cream cones and the church
supper. There's an explanation for everything. Everything
can be dissected and understood. Try to find out how,
Dinah."

I'd foolishly hoped Willy would become interested in my
returning memories and even pull them out of me the way
he had the things about Sally. But he cared as little about
them now as he had when we were first married. Now it
irritated me that he denied half my life, and we argued a

lot and were less careful about keeping up a good front for the children.

"I hate it when Daddy treats you like shit," Jessie said.

"He doesn't, Jessie. We disagree. He gets mad. He and I are different."

"In spades!"

"He's pretty straight," I said lamely.

"Well, that's all right. What I really mind is that you always give in to him."

"He's tense. Frankly he can't take a lot of things. I give in because I don't really care."

Jessie's brows knitted at me, just like Willy's. "That's the trouble, can't you see that?" All this in a taxi coming home from some kid's party in the Village. She smelled of pot. "What do you care about anyway, Dinah?"

"How can you ask that? I care about all of us. Our family. Our welfare."

She leaned back, one arm tragically over her eyes. "Everything but your identity! God, I can't wait to get to Miss Porter's."

"I resent what you're saying. You have everything. Parents who would do anything for you—"

"I know, two mothers and a father. There's something wrong, Dinah. Look at poor Conrad."

"What do you mean, poor? He has a B average at Andover—"

"He's depressed," said Jessie, "and no wonder."

"You aren't going to provoke me, Jessie. You kids are lucky."

"Does that include Jason?"

"Of course," I said.

"Jason's lucky; his mother is at home. My mother is too busy matching kids up with fake parents because their real ones don't care about them."

She'd cornered me again. She wore me out the way Willy did. It was their intensity, their coiled-spring energy, their constant need to argue. And Liz had something like it too, a drive that kept her working sixteen hours a day. Ever since I had a family of my own to refer to, accusations such as Jessie's got to me more. Now I had pictures in my mind: Mildred weeping in bed as Robert went out to meet Ada Grace. Robert and Ada Grace making love in that silky-grassed field. Cries of love, tears of despair . . . The great human experiences were now part of me. Now pictures were projected on the blank wall of my mind.

I was careful to keep memories sorted from speculation. I remembered being sixteen, that jiggling bubble-headed layabout in the minidress, but not the car accident that killed my parents. "Your ma was at the wheel," Ada Grace had told me, "and she'd had a drop too much, they said later. Went right into a furniture van. Don't reckon they felt much pain." I could see my sad, sloppy-faced mother at the wheel, my father next to her, no longer in his post-master's uniform, but in a Troy businessman's suit. The car careening around. Their voices arguing . . . "Mildred, go slower. Pull over, I'll take the wheel. It's not safe." And she: "Don't talk to me about safe. I don't give a damn, I have nothing to live for. You've destroyed our marriage." Then the van barreling toward them. A rainy night, the truck driver oblivious. Closer and closer, him trying to get the wheel away from her. Then—too late. The truck like a monster face in the front window, then the horrible, heavy crash. The crunch of metal, the shatter of glass back when it really shattered, before they put Saran Wrap in it. A cascade of glittering fragments. Screams, the spurt of blood, the last sight. Maybe they cried out each other's names for the last time, looked at each other, that last minute, with great love—like Bonnie and Clyde in the movie.

But I began to understand that as I gained memories, I was losing something else. My mystery, my crystal ball was yielding . . . I was just another ordinary human being. I wasn't so sure I wanted to be like other people now. Behind the dark curtain had been possibilities, hints, haunting suggestions of the extraordinary. It was an afterlife that had taken place before, a realm of mystery, spirits, the soul. Now the door to God's house was opening and inside were a lot of ordinary, unhappy people. I began to think I was losing a treasure.

I knew the amnesia had given me certain peculiarities, endlessly pointed out by Willy. I was ingenuous, naive, childish, besides being curiously amoral and as fatalistic as the most primitive peasant. Since I had no past myself, the pasts of others seemed unimportant; I'd never resented Liz because I'd never pictured her and Willy together as a family. Now I began to wonder about them. What had it been like when they were happy together? Had Willy loved her more; had she been a better lover, mother, companion for him? I'd never felt I had any control over my life. Things were going to happen in a certain way and there was nothing I could do about it, I assumed, because this had been my experience. Having had difficulties, I'd be a fool not to appreciate what I had. Now as memories poured in, fears came with them—fears I couldn't identify. I felt a new wariness, even suspicion. The more I had to lose, the more I had to be protected.

Unlike Willy, I'd never been afraid of death. Hadn't I returned from the dead once? If there was a realm of the spirits, which I sensed every day, I would return to it again some time. But as my past life revealed itself, I began to worry about death for the first time, fretting about my health, ecological dangers, epidemics, and nuclear war, just like everybody else. I could make a fair guess that the years still in shadow would not reveal me to be a lost princess, heiress, goddess, or anything but dull Dinah Morrow plodding on through an unexceptional life. And how many things I'd missed, how many things I hadn't done, what emotions I'd never experienced! Now in my mid-thirties, I'd always thought I was pretty lucky. But now I began to look at my life from another angle, even remembering some of the feminism of Chris's Sisters. I was married to a cross, preoccupied man obsessed with his work who popped pills and washed his hands all the time. Our sex life left a lot to be desired, and sometimes he hardly seemed to notice me, and he certainly took me for granted. It was frightening to consider any other life but the one I had. But as the memories flooded back, my eyelids were forced back, so I had to look farther than I ever had before.

It frightened me, and I couldn't even talk to Liz about it. She didn't want to talk about the conversation we'd had in the jail cell and denied remembering any pink dress with four pearl buttons. And something in her green eyes warned me to drop it.

She'd told me once that when she was crazy, she'd had too many memories. Her whole life kept flashing before her eyes, hers and about six other people's too. She said all the strange things she'd done around the house—such as putting the pennies in the toilet—had been efforts to stop the frantic spill of film in her mind, to try to appease whatever gods were causing it. I'd tried to tell her I knew why she'd done these things, and now I tried again. I told her I understood why Switzerland was under the couch. But she wouldn't talk about that either.

"You have to understand, it scares me to go back to that stuff."

I knew that she and I had some kind of mental connection, which Emerelda said was because of a wanga the loas had put on us, and that she could help me negotiate this difficult passage. But she was busy, she was sorry, she was frantic, she loved me and all that, but the new L.A. branch of FK was making her crazy. It was hard being an ordinary person; you had to have something *not* to be crazy, and FK was hers. I needed something, a job or a shrink or . . .

She was right. I was becoming an ordinary person and I hated it. I didn't want to remember any more, even if the last memory was shoving the pimply lover off my lap. It wasn't exactly that the rest might be worse. It was that the rest would be all there was.

"Willy, I don't want to remember any more."

"It's up to you, Dinah. You're probably right, it doesn't make you any better."

"What do you mean, better?"

He closed his eyes wearily. "Better—best—worst. Go look at the doctionary. The dictionary."

He was at his desk; I was standing in the doorway of the study, bored with everything, irritated, full of mysterious churning miseries. "I don't just get memories, I get a whole lot of shit."

"Dinah. The conference is in the morning and the paper is due at the conference and—"

"I'm sorry."

I looked at his bent, anguished back. I was going to be like Willy—unhappy, fretful, desperately chasing shadows and fleeing fears, but without ennobling work to blame everything on. If I'd felt forlorn before, different, now I was headed toward a darker fate. I wondered seriously how I was going to live the rest of my life.

One fine fall afternoon—it was just after Con started at Yale—as I was working outside in our little patch of garden, Liz arrived.

"Dinah, I've got to talk to you. Is Willy here?"

"He's away. What's the matter?"

She seemed rather upset, and I put down the trowel. Inside, in the kitchen, Emerelda was folding laundry and humming, occasionally talking to herself or to a recalcitrant undershirt.

"Where are the kids?"

"Jason's playing baseball and Jessie's at the shrink. Remember?"

"Lord, that's right. Look, Dinah. A man was in today who says he's your husband."

I looked at Liz, standing on the dirty bricks in a pale linen suit and perfectly round spectacles, her curly, flame-colored hair glinting in the late light. It was dusk, when everything seemed to happen to me. It had been dusk the first time I went to Sally's, dusk the day Willy and I had taken the kids sledding and I'd fallen in love with him. And dusk when I'd come to Bell's Corners. Now it was dusk again.

"But I have a husband," I said.

"It appears you have two."

"But Liz, there have been little errors like this before. I've had mothers and children and aunties, and three other husbands, all lemons."

"Well, I know that, it's all in your file. But I have a feeling this guy might be for real. His name is George." The air seemed to turn chilly.

"George," I whispered.

"George Dickenson, do you remember him?"

"No, I don't remember anything after screwing around in those cars. George Dickenson . . . George Dickenson," I mouthed silently. From the kitchen window, Emerelda was watching me intently.

We came into the kitchen and I washed my hands.

"Why did he come to FK?" I asked. "Is he looking for a mommy or a little child to take to the zoo?"

"Don't kid yourself, Dinah. He's looking for you. He saw one of our ads in the *Boston Globe*. He lives around there. He said he'd written you a few times starting right after they had that first AP story—"

"Liz, that was twelve years ago."

"An example of unusual constancy."

"He's got to be a nut," I said.

"Well, I'm not so sure, Dinah. Don't forget I've been in this business for a while."

I sat down slowly at the kitchen table. "What makes you think George is for real?"

"I don't know—a gut feeling. He's a country lawyer. Sort of rumpled and confused and wondering what the hell he's doing here."

"He sounds like an idiot."

"Not an idiot, but not the kind of person who usually comes to Finders Keepers. He's got a full life. That's why I can't help wondering about him. And you know, there's something familiar about him. I could swear I've met him before."

"Is he married?"

"Only to you," she said. "He seems very nervous about the whole situation, but he wants to see you and talk to you."

"But what for?" A desperate feeling was working its way up to my chest. I had a lot of them now. Some worked up, others down. Some just stayed leaden in one spot.

"I don't know. I told him you were married to somebody else and had children. I don't think he expects you to drop your whole life and go running back to him. Probably he just wants to lift a few for old times' sake, and I'll bet he drinks bourbon with a beer chaser."

She was smiling broadly. Sometimes Liz had a very strange sense of humor. And she'd always enjoyed shaking me up. She held out her arms to Jessie as she came in, but Jessie, having just been to the psychiatrist, only sat and brooded, just as I was doing.

"Everything's so complicated," she complained.

"Indeed so, darling." Liz moved the tea over and poured us each a glass of wine. Emerelda was making voodoo pie for dinner. "Dinah, he can't do anything to you or even make you remember. But give the guy a break."

Jessie said to Liz, "You care more about Dinah than you do about me."

"That's not true."

"But you talk to her more. You have more things in common with her."

"Only because she's a grown-up. People have a different kind of love for their children," Liz told her.

"Some love you have. I'll bet you don't even want me. I'll bet you wouldn't want me to come and live with you."

The question pierced the troubled kitchen air. If Jessie had been looking for attention, she got it. I felt a clutch at my heart: fear of change, I guess, and of losing her. How quickly whole lives could turn inside out. Liz, Emerelda, and I froze, staring at her—so young, so old, presently so troubled. Green eyes, tumbled sandy hair with glints of red. A defiant expression like Liz's that first day she'd come, dragging her lawyer. Now her chest was sticking out under her white sweater. I felt like crying.

Then Liz said, "Jessie, I would love it. I would be honored."

I gasped involuntarily. Jessie looked at me, then at Liz. "Is that true, Mom?"

"Of course it's true."

"Where would I sleep?"

"We'd figure out something. We'd build you a room. Or I'd get a bigger apartment."

"What would I do after I came home from school, when you were still at work?"

"You'd be a latchkey child. Or maybe we'd get a baby-sitter."

Jessie turned to me. "If I moved in with Mom, would you be hurt? I mean, you had all the dirty work, and now that I'm starting to be better, you wouldn't enjoy me."

I gulped. "I'd miss you but I wouldn't be hurt."

Long, long pause, while we all stared at her and I started to perspire.

Jessie said finally, "I think I'll stay here."

She got up and went to her room, leaving the three of us

trembling. Liz and I both grabbed for the wine bottle at the same time, and I let her win.

"All right, I'll meet George," I said. "What the hell. Everything's on shifting sand anyway."

Liz said, "I could swear I met that guy somewhere before."

George and I met under the clock at the Biltmore, because he was coming in on the train and didn't want to get lost. It was a curious situation; he'd know me but I wouldn't know him. I'd dressed carefully in ex-husband clothes—a businesslike navy blue suit, the sort of thing Joan Crawford would have worn. He was pacing up and down nervously, and at first he didn't recognize me. Then all at once he did.

"Dinah. Oh, Dinah. It is you. Thank you for coming."

"I guess you're George."

He looked nice. Rumpled, as Liz had said, and a little breathless, as though he'd been running to keep up with the world. Around my age, stocky, a little bald, actually a little wild-eyed. He grabbed my hand.

"This is a very emotional moment."

"I'm sure it must be," I said.

"Very emotional. Very strange."

"I'm sure." I smiled politely. It was all so one-sided.

"Do you remember me at all?" he asked. I looked at him carefully, taking my time about it. I put him in a stronger light. I squinted.

"I'm afraid not. I'm sorry."

We sat down at one of the tables and ordered drinks. A vodka and tonic for me, a beer for him.

"Dinah, just what do you remember?"

I was ready for that. "First let's see if you can tell me my name and where I came from."

He smiled. "Dinah Morrow from Bell's Crossing, Vermont . . . but I met you after you moved to Troy." My hands began to shake. "When you were sixteen. Actually we weren't married. I just said it because I thought it would sound better."

I began to giggle. I giggled and snickered and choked. "I'm sorry, I'm very nervous."

"Well, so am I. I've never been so nervous in my life."

"George, did we live together, or what?"

He looked at me sadly. "It just breaks my heart . . . I mean that you don't remember. I remember it so well. We had a whole life, you and I. We might as well have been married. We did the things married people do. We fought, we made love, we went shopping together. I used to wash your back . . . I'm not embarrassing you, am I?"

"I don't know." I was looking at him, but not quite in the eyes.

"We had a lot of laughs. We didn't have much money, but we didn't really care."

"How old were we?" I asked in a low voice.

"Seventeen, around there. We were pretty young for all that."

"How long were we together?"

"Well, seven years on and off." Oh my God. "It was a bumpy ride, Dinah—as Margo Channing said. There was a lot of Sturm und Drang. A lot of fighting and making up. We couldn't live with each other, and we couldn't live without." He took out his handkerchief, which had green and white stripes, and mopped his face. His eyes mostly. I was holding on to my handbag, white-knuckled.

"Where did we live?"

"In a crazy little shack near the woods. I painted it white. It had two rooms. Just enough room for . . ."

"The two of us," I said.

"Three." He looked at me with his sharp blue eyes. "We had a baby."

I felt a wave of nausea; then I began to shake. "You know something, George Whoever? I didn't have to come here today. You aren't the only so-called husband who's turned up. The others had good stories too. I came as a favor to Liz. I could have ignored the whole thing." I was holding back what promised to be a storm of tears. "I don't believe you. I have three kids. I have a whole life. How dare you threaten it?"

"That's not why I came. I know you're upset and I'm sorry." He wiped his face again. "Jesus, it's just like it was before."

I grabbed my handbag, slamming it against the table. "Just one question before I leave. Why are you doing this to me?"

He said, "Because it's time you took some responsibility for her. I'm not trying to attack you. I can't believe you aren't curious about the time you don't remember."

"I remember enough to dampen my curiosity. I wasn't a very nice teenager." My lip trembled. George had doubtless been one of the back-seat lovers.

"You weren't as bad as you thought," he said.

I turned and ran out of the Biltmore. I suppose I expected him to follow, but he didn't. Half dazed, I flagged a taxi and got in. In the taxi I wept with rage. Through my tears and the dirty window the city was shrill and ominous. It was still early and hot as hell. We were supposed to go to our house in Connecticut, as though nothing had happened.

The next morning I took a long walk across the fields alone. The purity of the sky and the earth and the whipping wind failed to calm the things that were churning around in my head. I wished I'd never gone to meet him, this damn George, the lumpen reality of the lost seven years . . . though I tried to tell myself he was a fake. Somehow he'd found out about me. But why would he lie?

As I came back to the house Jason said, "Mom, you shouldn't wear tight jeans anymore."

I put my arms around his shoulders, which were higher every year. "Only you could get away with saying that."

For a lightning moment he leaned his head against my breast, then jerked away as though body contact might give him some terrible disease or suck him back to helplessness. Men were all alike, even this one who was all mine. I still got a lump in my throat when I looked at him.

Later we went to the station to meet Willy. I noticed, as he got off the train, how pale he looked, drawn up almost, as though he'd been immersed in water for too long. His smile for me was faint, more heartfelt for Jason. I put my arms around him and held him tight. I hadn't done it in just that way for a long time. He was surprised and stiff. First he pulled back a little, then he said, "Christ, I'm tired."

We had dinner on the deck—the first time in weeks that all five of us had eaten together. In the yellow bug-light that bathed the table where we sat, Jason and I turned pale green and the other three became a silvery apricot, as though we were fruits from different vines. I got a little drunk on the Beaujolais we had with our steak.

"We're a good family," I said. "A loving family. No matter what happens we have each other." Conrad, now seventeen, was giving me glances of acute embarrassment. He was still greatly bothered by behavior that seemed out of control, which included a little friendly inebriation. I wondered when, if ever, the waves washed away the fears of the past. Though he'd seen his mother pull herself together, adhere, and grow strong, the lesson was lost on him at the deepest level. No matter how much therapy he'd had, he'd go through life seeing her fall apart. And Jessie would try to manipulate everybody so she'd always be in control.

I began to cry. "I've given my best years to you guys," I sniffled. "Sorted the laundry, called the baby-sitters, helped with the homework. Loved you and gave up things for you. And Willy too—we've given you a stable home. And you're still frightened, both of you. I don't know what to do anymore." I wasn't talking to Jason and they knew it. Jessie gave her brother a dirty look, then came over and gave me a brief hug and kiss.

"Dinah, we love you. We appreciate you. You're our favorite stepmother. We discuss our fears with our therapists. We can't help it if we're not perfect."

"You've been great, Dinah," said Con.

Willy said, "What the hell is all this, Dinah? Self-pity isn't your style. Is there any more steak?" As usual I leapt up and got him some, staggering a little. I was a weepy drunk.

"I just don't want anything to happen to us. I think we're just wonderful the way we are."

Later, in bed, Willy's penis remained as soft and limp as a baby animal, an increasingly common occurrence. I worked and worked but nothing happened. I was doing it out of duty rather than excitement and probably it showed.

Finally he sighed, "Forget it, Dinah. I'm tired out from the trip. And I think I caught something; I don't feel well." Off to the john—in the Connecticut house it was down the hall. Through the thin wall I could hear the rush of water, the snap of small plastic containers.

"What did you just take?"

"Just some Bufferin and a Chlor-Trimeton. Why?"

"Willy, stop lying to yourself. It's one thing to lie to me, but it's immoral to lie to yourself." I didn't immediately notice the irony of my words. Willy flopped into bed, his long, palely fuzzy legs outlined in the moonlight from the window.

"Get off my case. I know what I'm doing."

"If you do, that makes it worse."

"What the hell does that mean?" Willy asked falsely.

"It means you take too many pills and it scares me."

"Keep your voice down. The kids can hear every word in this place."

I said, "Good, let them hear. You want to force us all to be accomplices in your drug taking."

"Dinah, *I do not take drugs.* I don't take cocaine or angel dust or LSD or heroin or marijuana. I medicate myself for allergies and take an occasional Valium or a Lomotil. Now and then a Dalmane or a Quaalude to sleep. And once or twice I've taken a little Benzadrine to get through an operation."

"Christ, I didn't know that."

"If I had a problem, which you seem determined to believe, I would *hide* it from you. As you can see, I'm perfectly open about it. I'm a doctor and I know what I'm doing. I lead a high-stress life. If we lived in the sticks, like in your Bell's Corners for instance, and you grew vegetables and I delivered mail like your recently remembered and therefore perfect daddy, I probably wouldn't need these little aids to get along. But I happen to be in the fast track —of which you are the prime beneficiary."

My eyelids were drooping. "Willy, let's go to sleep."

"That's right, go to sleep. The sandman will fix it all."

At breakfast in the quaint, thirty-year-old kitchen, grim looks from the kids.

"Dinah, does Daddy take too many pills?"

"Ask him."

"I did. He says no."

"Then that must be the answer. Why do you ask me?"

I was relieved when we got home. I didn't like weekends either. I was happiest on Monday mornings—Emerelda and I buzzing around, the phone ringing, the reassuring stir of activity, the satisfying concerns of food and shelter. The latest from loa land—the Country Mistress had become a zombie and was walking around Bell's Corners at night. (I could see her in the padded jacket, the ski hat, and the unbuckled galoshes over her homemade socks, walking on the moonlit village green.) The Mistress Sally had become a guedé, which she wouldn't define, and had miraculously grown a zozo, which was voodoo for cock! Guedés flew around cemeteries on Halloween and did all sorts of obscene

things, and the loupgarous came down chimneys and
sucked the children's blood if you didn't watch out.

What fun the loas were—a lot more fun than my life,
when you got right down to it. As I sat over my grocery
list, idly staring into space, Emerelda said, "The other
husband lives in the Mistress Liz's memory too, you must
not forget. So for this reason, I believe he is real, and only
waits for you to speak."

"We were both very young," George said. "You were about
sixteen, and we hung out at a roadhouse called Elmer's."
We were in a coffee shop at Grand Central, and I was
wearing another Joan Crawford suit. He had been eighteen
and working his way through college. He'd grown up in
Hoosick Falls; his father was a policeman. He was working
in a record shop when we met. "The beginning's a little
difficult," he said. "I'll move ahead."

"Why is it difficult?"

"Oh, God, the whole thing's painful. I've never talked
about it much—a little to Jackie, the woman I live with.
It brings it all back, is all. It wasn't easy, Dinah, any of it.
And we were so young."

"All right, then tell what happened later."

He'd lapsed into a reverie. "What?"

"How did I end up covered with cuts and bruises in front
of Bloomingdale's?"

"Well, I suppose you . . . Bloomingdale's?"

We'd had a fight, George and I, and not the first. I'd
stormed out and taken the car, which I was inclined to do
when frustrated. I was gone for hours, much longer than
usual. There was a crash. The people in the other car were
badly injured and one was killed . . . Our car had been
totaled, but I wasn't in it. I'd vanished. There was a little
blood on the seat, but not much. Somehow I'd escaped.

"I wrote you when that AP story came out, Dinah. I

wondered if it was you. Did you ever get my letters?" I
hadn't. Sally could have had them. They could be molder-
ing away at the nineteenth precinct. Even if I'd gotten them
I wouldn't have believed them then.

As he talked I could picture—though not actually remember—the scene. George standing in our tiny kitchen,
a sinkful of dirty dishes behind him. I'm in my jeans, my
yellow T-shirt, and my Keds. I could smell the burned
frying pan from the hamburgers and the ashes from a
hundred cigarettes. The beer cans bent in half falling out of
an overflowing garbage can. On the kitchen table a bottle
of Old Crow, a loaf of Wonder Bread, for George and I
hadn't any style.

Elvis is on the radio.

At the table sits Rosie, our daughter, finishing her Jell-
O. She's five, and she watches us with big hazel eyes like
mine. She's heard us a thousand times. George feels
trapped, I feel trapped. He's trying to get started as a lawyer
and doesn't have any clients. I work at the dime store.
Someday we'll have money and status, but it's taking forever. We cramp each other's style, interfere with each other's dreams. We hurl insults at each other, and finally I run
out and get into the car. I'm mad and a little drunk. I'll go
drive around for a while, let him stew. I feel the anger
rising like a tide, feel the car wheels grind in the dirt and
gravel, see the lighted dashboard of the old Ford Pinto. I
screech onto the highway, but even when I push my foot to
the floor, the car won't go very fast on the hills. On the
level I can make it move. The wind whips through my hair
and I feel a lot better. I step it up: fifty-five, sixty-five,
seventy-five. I don't see the car coming from the other
direction . . .

Somehow I'd gotten out of that wrecked car and left,
already out of it. In dreamland. Xanadu. I'd gotten myself
to New York and onto the subway. I'd read about amnesia
and fugue states. I'd fugued myself right out of my life and

into another one. Bruised and bleeding, I'd managed to make a fresh start with a completeness few can manage. Left an unsatisfying life . . . if it was unsatisfying. It was just as possible that I'd loved him—adored him. Or, like my mother, been unable to forgive him for something. And, like her, found forgetfulness in the rain of shattered glass, the screech of brakes, the crash of metal bodies.

We watched each other warily in the bright light of the coffee shop.

"So I just got up and walked out on my daughter."

"That's right," George said.

"Leaving you to take care of her."

"That's right."

"How do I know you aren't making it all up? How do I know there even is a daughter?"

"How do I know you have amnesia?" He waved for the waiter and got the bill.

"Where is she now?" I asked.

"To tell you the truth, I don't know. A few weeks ago she just dropped out of sight. I'm a little upset about it."

I said, "I have to go home now. I just can't handle any more today."

The next day he wanted to go to a museum, as long as he was in New York. So we went to the Metropolitan. We looked at the Monets and Picassos, strolled through the Egyptian section, and ended up in a small, darkish room of tiny medieval paintings: madonnas clad in hot blue, linen white Christs on crucifixes, ruby bishops' robes. I stole glances at him as he bent to look at minute details.

"Did you always wear glasses?"

"Not all the time."

"Did you have more hair before?"

"A little more, not much. I started going bald when I was twenty. You know, Dinah, you look great, finished. You were always good-looking, but every which way. Now it's all smoothed and pulled together."

I asked, "Were we very much in love?"

Staring at a Memling he said, "We were crazy about each other."

A chill went down me and a guard walked in. We scrutinized a triptych. I kept trying to stand slightly behind him so I could stare all I wanted at him, searching for familiarity. He had dark brown hair on the long side, a heavy neck over his wrong-colored shirt. A good broad back. I stood closer to him and our hands brushed. "It took me a long time to get over it."

"But Jackie helped," I said. I felt a surge of completely unexpected anger. "Didn't she?"

"Oh Lord, I waited for you for so long."

"But you knew Jackie before the accident—didn't you?" I was surprised at my ugly tones. We went into a big, airy gallery and he turned to me and smiled.

"You might say so." The room echoed and the anger abated.

"George, did we have a fight about Jackie?"

"Yes," he said. Now I was sad; a tear stood in each eye.

"So she came between us." I gulped.

"Listen, Dinah. You should know that . . . Well, no reason you should. I'm not one for fooling around. I'm a very domesticated male. I like peace and quiet. I like my work but I don't kill myself at it. You and I were wearing each other out."

I laughed. "Always excuses." Then, "I'm sorry, I seem to sound vindictive. This is very funny, this whole thing. I mean, to you it's probably a nuisance, being here. The whole thing is probably a nuisance."

"Oh, no," he said. "You mustn't think that."

"Well, that's good. If you mean it."

"Sure I mean it. After all, I came here. I sought you out."

In the bright, waning afternoon we walked down Fifth by the park, George with his hands in his pockets in a way I liked.

"Who does Rosie look like?" I asked finally.

"Like you."

"I suppose she hates me."

After some thought he said, "I think that's probably true." I half choked.

"Does she like Jackie?"

"Not particularly. She's an angry kid. She likes me all right, or else she tolerates me in an affectionate way. I guess she loves me." I took his arm and felt a little better.

"George, tell me more about our house."

"Is that all you want to hear about Rosie?"

"At the moment, yes."

The little house was near Troy. We'd rented it from a woman who kept bees. George was crazy about roses, and he was always trying to grow them. Not that he had much time between law school and working in the car rental place. He'd study at night, but it was hard to do with me around. On Sundays we'd sit out on the grass and drink beer and maybe have a barbecued chicken, and George would garden and I'd put the baby down on a blanket on the grass to play with her toys. We had a little dog named Rags, part Yorkie.

As he talked I felt as though I were waking up after a long sleep. And perhaps I was, though never before would I have so described my marriage to Willy. But for neither of us was it the tender core of the world it had once been. We were both smothering in familiarity and incapable of generating anything new. But the saddest part was that I remembered those early days with Willy, and they were very much like this one—clear, sparkling, fresh with promise. I remembered holding on to his arm too and believing I would never want to let go of it, as though I'd been dead or asleep or in another world before I'd found him. Each awakening seemed to trivialize everything that came before it, one of nature's cruelties. How dangerous these days of self-renewal.

We went into the Oak Bar of the Plaza and ordered martinis.

"When did my parents die?" I asked.

"In nineteen sixty-two," he said.

"Was I sad?"

"Sure you were. You loved them. It was a terrible shock. But it brought you to me, because after they died you really had no place to go."

"I wonder why I came to New York."

"Oh, you were dying to," George said. "You were always talking about it and reading about it and bitching about being stuck in the boondocks. So I guess you just managed things so you got there. I would have brought you here, you know. I would have done anything for you."

In the silence I felt the slow pound of my heart. He reached over and ran one finger up the back of my hand. "You must have hitchhiked. Later on a guy turned up and said he'd picked you up somewhere around Kinderhook and taken you farther south. If it was you. He thought of taking you to a hospital, but when he stopped for gas you disappeared." I was staring at our two hands, hypnotized.

"I don't know whether it's you or not," he went on. "It's half you and half somebody else. I guess it's what everybody wants—the familiar and the mysterious. The old and the new. You're different than you used to be, more accommodating. You used to fight about everything."

I worked up all my nerve, and the gin helped. "George, did we used to screw in the back of a car?"

"Yes."

"And I got pregnant."

"Yes."

"But George . . ." I stopped. I'd been about to point out that Rosie might not be his child, but there were times to be quiet and this was one of them. It didn't make any difference anyway.

"What?" he asked.

"I was going to say, well, neither of us must have been very happy about that."

"We weren't at first, but there wasn't much to do about

it at that time, in that place. On the money we had. I
began to come around first. I was only nineteen, but I'd
always wanted a baby. Kind of strange for a boy, but I
wasn't your average kid. Anyway, Dinah, it was another
way to be part of you. Which I wanted desperately."

"What was I like?" I asked.

He smiled. "You were irresponsible. You had a chip on
your shoulder. You were a baby. You were lucky you found
me."

"What did you see in me, then?"

"You were fun. You were interesting. I never could pre-
dict you. Or resist you either."

We were sitting on a banquette and he turned and kissed
me—a long, serious kiss that shook me to the core. But as
he drew away and my half-drunk eyes skittered around the
room, there in the doorway stood Portoff and Chrissie, just
arriving with friends. Portoff with his little plastic Ken-
doll smile and Chris with her oh-God-real-life expression.
They stared at me. They put their heads together. I could
imagine their conversation: "See, Chris? I told you she was
no good. A tramp. A trollop. She'll ruin Willy yet." And
Chris: "Oh, Mi-chael. I don't believe it, it must be her
long-lost brother or something. Anyway, Dinah wouldn't
fool around with men because she likes girls." "Whatever
she likes, she's a slut and she owes me ten thousand dollars."

I could have killed them for spoiling my moment, my
life, my old/new passion, whose clean flames were burning
off old grievances and old skins.

"What's the matter?" George asked.

"Nothing. I thought I saw somebody I know. Guess I'm
jumpy." I decided to brave it out. The last thing I wanted
was to have this magic beclouded. Not tonight, anyway;
tonight was ours.

He asked, "Do you want to think and worry now, or save
it till later?"

"Save it. Maybe we won't have to."

"Dinah. If there's one thing I'm sure of, it's that we will."

As we left I felt their eyes boring into our backs and saw them whispering as we went out the door. We had dinner at a nearby restaurant and then walked to George's hotel, a couple of blocks west, a sharp wind whipping us as we walked along.

In the elevator he put his arms around me and we kissed ferociously, tongues tangling, drinking each other up. I ran my arms around his shoulders, his back, his broad strong back, so different from Willy's. We moved down the hall, holding on to each other. By the time we got to the room he had half my blouse undone, and when we were closed inside the dark room, I looked down to see one breast, lit white by the streetlight outside, in his hand. We both looked at it in surprise, as though it were a treasure he'd picked up somewhere, a seashell on the beach, a coin by the side of the road. His hand, large and dark, held its delicate burden tenderly. In the dark room he murmured my name and began kissing me all over. I felt his tongue burn me with each kiss, and I imagined that it would leave marks all over, little sears of love that I would find tomorrow.

Then, frantically, we began to undress each other. Buttons, zippers, a hopelessly knotted necktie stubbornly anchored by a tie clasp. A belt with an unfamiliar buckle, a new kind of hook and eye thing at his waist . . . Ah, it was all so new; this was what I'd craved! He yanked at my panty hose. Off with our shoes, socks, buttons at the wrists and neck. At last I found my treasure, and as we flopped on the bed I ran my tongue along his penis (different from Willy's, shorter and broader) until a crystal drop appeared at the tip, which I put in my eye: it would guide me through a dark world. I reached for George's hairy testicles and held them to my breasts.

We sat together on the bed, naked at last, clothes spilled

on the floor, looking at each other in the single shaft of
light. He was broad and dark, my new lover, my old husband—heavy chest, shortish legs, black hair. I might have
chosen Willy in contrast, so long and light was he, and at
the moment, so uninteresting. George's hands were blunt
and strong, with none of Willy's delicacy; now I liked these
better. And such blue eyes and such low, heavy eyebrows.
We stared at each other, feasting, as his hands reached out
to my two nipples, now aimed at him in two hard little
points. With thumb and finger he rolled them back and
forth, the tiniest bit, in the gentlest way. I felt a sort of
low hum starting deeply inside me. George's cock started
up from between his legs like a magnificent weapon. I got
up on my knees and moved over onto his lap, aiming it at
that hot, wet place; now I could smell our rank animal
smell. The hum inside me started to pulsate, and with my
arms around his neck I moved up and down, up and down,
in a grand dance of love.

Willy came back a day early. I found him sitting in the
kitchen when I came back in the morning. Nobody else was
home. Both Jessie and Jason were at friends' houses for the
weekend, a piece of luck that had enabled me to be so free
and romantic. I was in that loose, unvigilant condition that
often follows a night of love. I almost skipped through the
door. Then, a briefcase. A raincoat. I tucked in my blouse
and ran my hands through my hair. I couldn't kiss him—I
reeked of sex. Hair, clothes, everything. I'd been cooked in
it.

   "Hi, darling, I see you're back. I'm just going to run up
and change."

   He looked up. "Where have you been?"

   "At Liz's." No, that was no good. "I don't mean Liz, I
meant Alexandra, this girl I used to know at Snapper's. I
ran into her on the street."

"Where's Jason?"

"At John Kilty's. I'll just run up and . . ."

Willy got up and walked toward me. "What's the matter? Why are you so jumpy?"

"Not jumpy—dirty. Same old clothes as yesterday."

"Why didn't you take a nightgown?"

"Because I ran into her on the street, I told you. It was just a sudden idea; we had dinner and it got late." We stood staring at each other, I cringing backwards toward the stairs. Don't let him inhale. I prayed he wouldn't cross-examine me, but he looked more puzzled than accusing.

"Is anything wrong, Dinah?"

"No, nothing."

"Give me a kiss."

"Yuck. No. I'm filthy. I'll kiss you when I come down." I raced up the stairs, leaving him looking a little sad, shoulders sagging. Oh God, don't let him be sad. I'd counted on anger and accusations to justify what had happened. Instead he closed his eyes for a moment and went back into the kitchen.

He'd gotten back around midnight, he told me when I came back down. He'd missed me, that was all. I was free to go where I wanted. Not a big deal. It was just that he'd grown accustomed to my face, as the song went.

They'd finished up in Houston a day early and he'd driven around a little and gotten depressed. It was one of those rootless places; everybody there came from somewhere else. The grandmothers were all in condos in Florida. The kids were all at boarding school sniffing cocaine. The dads were hustling and the moms were shopping. What the fuck was happening to everybody?

"And I thought about Charlotte up there thinking it's nineteen fifteen and poor crazy Phil and even Poor Liz"— Willy continued to regard Liz as hopelessly psychotic, in spite of the fact that she now ran a multimillion-dollar business—"and even your people, moving from one place to another and lying unmourned in some upstate graveyard. Jesus, Dinah, the whole world is falling apart."

And the divorce! Bill Goldstein was splitting after twenty years of marriage and three kids, and so-and-so after twenty-five years and two kids, and so forth. The point being that he and I had done well with an unusual situation and we had to hang on to each other. We two were a multitude. We five. The kids were terrific on the whole, in spite of a few problems here and there. They'd be okay. Especially Jason—the apple of his eye. "I don't mean this to sound as bad as it will, Dinah, and I'd never say it to anybody but you. But sometimes I worry about the other two inheriting their mother's crazy gene. More and more mental illness is being found to come from brain hormones." He'd die rather than have Con and Jessie know he ever thought such a thing. He loved them; he'd pay for the shrinks forever.

"And Dinah, I love you for taking care of them the way you have. Of course I've said this before, but somehow driving round and round those Houston freeways made me think how easy most people find it to run away from responsibilities and think only of their own pleasure rather than taking on a tough job, as you did. Bill Goldstein was just saying the other day how much he admired you for doing something that ninety-nine percent of women wouldn't have done for anything, and not out of some masochistic sense of duty but because you were really able to love them out of your own generous spirit. 'Willy, you're a lucky man,' Bill said. His wife has fallen for a rock singer half her age. The poor guy is really having trouble functioning. He said, 'Willy, divorce doesn't solve anything.' Think about that, Dinah. It's true. Mac Valpey has been married three times and . . ."

Willy didn't usually talk that much, and I wished to God he'd shut up. As it was, I was having trouble loading the coffee maker; my head was full of vivid, full-color pictures of George and me going at it, and I would have given anything if Willy were not there. All I wanted to do was sit around with some coffee and my own dirty mind.

". . . not only haven't I been a very good husband or father, but at times I've been unappreciative, hostile, unsympathetic, suspicious, and downright paranoid," Willy was saying. "I've even thought I was having some sort of mid-life crisis, and I've decided to go back into therapy for a while. Not that I think therapy is the big answer to everything. The main transaction is between us, Dinah—you and me. But at the same time I don't want to burden you with a lot of crap that comes from my childhood stuff with Charlotte and Phil and all that, which is essentially my problem, which you've had the grace to listen to enough already. So I'm starting with this Zigler tomorrow. He had an hour open today but I wanted to spend today with you." He took my clammy hand. "And Dinah, stop with the memories, okay? Somehow things got worse when they started to come back, I don't know why."

The phone rang and my heart slammed in my chest. I would never manage this double life. Already I was miserable and it hadn't even been going on for twenty-four hours. Already Willy was frowning at the voice in the receiver and handing it to me; already I was manufacturing lies. "Hello . . . Oh, I didn't know you were in town. Lunch is difficult today. How about tea—or a drink?" Willy gestured that I should go ahead. Not for an instant would he interfere with my life. But later he'd like to take me out for a really nice dinner—Le Perigord or La Côte Basque. In my head were black clouds with SHIT written on them in dripping yellow paint. I told George I'd meet him in the bar of his hotel. I poured the coffee, hand shaking. I could think only of George's cock sliding in and out of me at 5:15 P.M.—and why hadn't I made it for lunch? Slippery. Shiny. Leaving a trail of bright stars in its wake. Nudging me ever so gently till I exploded . . . I dropped the cream, which Willy stared at for a moment, then began mopping up.

"Who was that?"

"A client of Liz's from out of town." It wasn't even a lie. "He thinks he might have known my parents."

"I'll reserve a table for eight o'clock at La Côte Basque," Willy said. "No kids—imagine our luck. Will that give you enough time? We can meet at the restaurant."

Willy seemed to have wound down for the time being, to my relief; I'd even wondered if it was the pills talking. But pills alone do not a mid-life crisis make. Nor do they cause such contrition and consideration.

"Dinah, let me make us some sandwiches for lunch. You go ahead and do whatever you have to do." I'd been frantically weeding the garden, which seemed as good a way as any to let off steam and make the time pass. "Now let's see. Do we have any tuna fish? And where are the onions?"

"No onions, Willy."

"Don't worry, I'll have them too." Slicing away. "We'll reek at each other."

I could have cried. I don't know how I got through the day—or the next and the next and the one when George went back, a combined tragedy and relief. The single, solitary lucky thing was that Willy continued more or less impotent, another reason for going back to the shrink. We had to try once or twice to celebrate the new era, but the shrink suggested knocking it off for a while to "de-cathect the sexual situation," to my boundless relief. And one night Willy had a meeting that he mercifully couldn't get out of, and George and I ordered dinner from room service at his hotel and spent the whole evening in an orgy that made me understand why sex has been said to turn the brain to custard. I wanted to stay with him badly, but I didn't dare.

As I dressed at midnight he said, "Now what?"

"What do you mean?"

"Now you go home to Willy."

"And you go home to Jackie." Her name turned bitter in my mouth.

"Of course. I live with her. I even love her."

I'm not sure what I did then. In my mind I tried to kill him. He grabbed my two hands.

"Oh, God, I hate you for saying that," I wept.

"Listen, Dinah. We both have to live with this. We should have talked but we've been too busy fucking."

I was crying. "I don't know what's the matter with me. I've never been like this. Nothing used to bother me before. Now everything makes me crazy."

He held me to him. "I was afraid this would happen. I didn't want to come because I was afraid we'd end up just the way we were before."

I saw him off at the train station. He strode cheerfully down the platform, waving good-bye. Good as sex had once seemed with Willy, it had been nothing like this. With George all controls were off. It was age, he said: neither of us had been this loose at eighteen or at twenty-five. I walked back through the station feeling as though my entire insides had been pulled out, washed, aired, and reinserted. It was exhilarating; it was remarkable. But I didn't know how I was going to live my life.

It was incredible that Willy didn't find out about George, since in some perverse way I tried to arrange it. When George was in New York I'd manage to make some blunder or slip which to anybody but Willy—the new Willy, that is—would have been clear proof that I was lying. When I went to Boston to stay at a motel near George, telling Willy I was going on another roots trip, and Willy even suggested changing his schedule so he could go along and participate in this crucial journey into my past —the past he'd hoped to ignore—I forbade him with such force that anybody but a moron would have gotten the picture. Or anybody who hadn't seen the light driving around those endless Houston freeways. I grew pale and lost weight. The house went to pot while I sat around day-dreaming. I started smoking. I went for long walks by the river. I dreamed about George and woke in terror, hoping I hadn't talked in my sleep.

But as much as Willy talked about us, our marriage, our family, and our unity, whatever was going on with him was so essentially his own that he hardly noticed me at all. He thought he did. He sincerely believed that he was restructuring himself so he'd be better for me as well as himself. But he was so busy talking about his psychic breakthroughs that he was oblivious to the fact that I was pretty strange myself, either exhausted from the state of semi-orgasm I was in most of the time or else charging around with manic energy, cleaning out closets, buying clothes, or rushing Jason around town. He believed everything was for him. If I sparkled it was because he loved me, if I was hangdog it was because he'd been unconsciously rejecting. I could do nothing wrong. In a way I missed his old suspicious self; I knew where I stood, at least, when I couldn't do anything right. It would have been helpful to have my guilt excused in advance by his anger, which would have justified my passionate affair with George. If anything could. Every night I swore I would break it off; every morning I awoke with my body electrified, counting the days or hours until I would be with him again.

During the Christmas holidays Willy had an erection, presumably the first one in months. I watched it, that Saturday morning, with a despair that bordered on panic. I could not, would not make love to Willy. I belonged to another. Willy walked out of the bathroom and locked the bedroom door while I feigned sleep—usually a sign to lay off, but not this time.

"Willy, I've got so much to do I don't know where to start. Christmas shopping and phone calls and arrangements for the party, and if I don't do it today—"

He sat down on the bed while I tried not to look at his cock, long and pale like an Indian pipe. Brownish tan fuzz. "You'll do it today."

He reached out and touched my breasts and I could have

cried. George, I prayed, George, save me. But, God forgive
me, I was as excited as Willy. I was excited all the time
anyway and anybody would do. We made love in hasty
silence—hasty because he was concentrating on keeping the
erection, and silence because I was so filled with self-loath-
ing I couldn't speak.

Afterwards he said, "God, Dinah, I thought you'd never
stop. Are you finished?" He moved his mouth down between my legs. No, I wasn't. I never would be, never; I'd
go into a state of permanent orgasm. I'd sit around going
uh-uh-uh all the time. Anybody would do, or nobody at
all. They'd have to sedate me. Wrap me in wet sheets.

"Dinah," Willy said one night as we were reading in
bed, "there's something on my mind."

When was there not? But this time as I listened my hands
began to perspire on the pages of my book. Willy believed
—truly believed—that people owned their own bodies.
He'd thought a lot about what would happen if either of us
slept with anybody else, and he'd discussed it with the
shrink. He'd decided if I were ever untrue to him he could
probably handle it, as long as he was satisfied about my
motives. That is, if I wasn't doing it out of boredom,
irresponsibility, or revenge, but out of an honest desire to
grow. Even passion might be understandable. What he
wouldn't be able to stand was duplicity and lying and
sneaking around. I should tell him or he should tell me,
whichever applied. Maybe if married people came to each
other in the beginning, when they just started being turned
on by somebody else, so they could talk about it . . .

"Willy, it's very hard for me to imagine you running to
the hospital phone and calling me and saying, 'Dinah, I
just got an erection looking at the scrub nurse's tits and I
think we should talk about it.' " The longer I could keep
this ridiculous conversation going, the longer it would take
him to ask me the dread question, which I was sure he was
going to do.

"I didn't mean *run to the phone*, Dinah." The old familiar

irritation was back in his voice, and it made me feel better. How tired I was of vast understanding. "You make everything into a cartoon. I meant later, at leisure. I might say, 'Dinah, we have a problem about so-and-so and I'm worried about it and I'm starting to look at other women. In fact today I got an erection, et cetera.' "

"But we might not have a problem. And anyway, don't men just get erections looking at girls anyway, and so what?"

"Sometimes they do. But I have a feeling that a man who's satisfied at home really wants his wife more than anybody." I couldn't stand the suspense.

"Do we have a problem, Willy?" A long pause.

"I don't know, Dinah. Do we?" He retired behind the AMA journal. Then, "Zigler thinks every extramarital affair is a metaphor—a blueprint of the psyche. He said, 'In the heart's complex reasoning, sometimes the cuckold is complimented.' "

"This Zigler has a way with a phrase, doesn't he?"

"A very insightful guy." Willy nodded thoughtfully. "He told me about a woman who cheated on her husband with a guy who reminded her of him as he used to be but no longer was. It was a kind of inverted compliment and message at the same time. Of course it would have saved everybody a lot of grief if she'd only said so instead of acting it out."

I guess I fell asleep; Willy clearly wasn't going to give me the satisfaction of an out-and-out accusation but only plant little seeds of guilt in my heart's complex reasoning. But he knew, Willy did. He knew, somehow, when George was in town, that my so-called roots trips were phony. He'd look at me as I left for some made-up tea or dinner with so-and-so, one of the endless FK clients who seemed to demand so much of my time, or yet another cousin from Albany. Our eyes would meet, catch . . . and mine would drop or flicker away. He didn't get angry, only sadder and more depressed. It was around then that he started to talk about retrenching, getting out of the rat race. Leaving the city and starting again somewhere else, maybe in some tropic place where the evil would bake out of us. Where we could cast aside civilization's dreck and rediscover simpler values. Where Dinah would be thousands of miles from George.

Meanwhile, George began to press. "Dinah, we'd better talk."

"About what?"

"The whole thing, for God's sake. I'm exhausted; I can't keep running back and forth like this. And I'm sick of lying to Jackie."

"Fuck Jackie."

George was all forbearance. "I think we should decide what we want out of this and where we're going. You must have some thoughts on the matter."

"Well, you have been doing most of the traveling. I'll go up there more."

"Dinah, let me ask you something. How do you see your life, say, five years from now? Or ten?"

"More or less the same. Why?"

"That's what I was afraid of." Then one of us would touch the other and that would be the end of serious, sensible talk.

Willy said the key to understanding me was that unlike others, I moved in *trajectories*. I'd go along in one direction until somebody came along and pushed me into another, and unless somebody else came along and deflected me again, I'd keep going forever into infinity. I lacked, he said, my own *motor,* which probably lay forgotten in my past. If he'd understood this earlier he would have done things differently—exactly how, he wasn't sure. Luckily he'd been the one to come along, because I'd have trotted off just as happily with the Godfather. Now he worried about who was going to come along next, and if that person would have force enough to send me off into a different trajectory

—in spite of all Willy's love and strength. He prayed that I wouldn't be hurt.

Then one night six months or so after we'd been on this slippery path, Willy walked into the house looking particularly ghastly. It was earlier than usual and Liz was just leaving after a visit and a fast cup of tea. He still disapproved of Liz's and my friendship. Now he looked at her as though she were a ghost, then from her to me and back to her again. His face tightened.

"Well. Isn't this chummy."

I flashed the placating lie: "Oh, Liz was just dropping off some stuff of Jessie's."

Liz said, "Willy, we've been divorced for over twelve years. Can't we be friends?"

Willy seemed to be having trouble breathing. "You destroyed my house once before and now you're doing it again."

Liz huffed, "I'm not destroying a fucking thing. And I'm sick of protecting you and lying to you, which I only do for Dinah's sake."

Willy closed his eyes as though the world were too painful to look at. "Yes, I understand."

"You don't and I'm going to explain it to you," Liz said angrily. "Dinah's and my friendship has been the greatest good fortune for Conrad and Jessica and Jason too. They have two mothers, and Dinah and I have three children. I think it's lovely and I'm convinced that more people should—"

"I know what you think. You founded an entire business on the ridiculous notion that nobody can get along with their relatives, which is in itself an indictment of the family as an institution. As for the children, I don't know how you can dare mention them to me when I know that Jessie at least has suffered from your and Dinah's so-called friendship."

"What are you talking about, Willy?" I asked.

He said, "You know damn well what I'm talking about, both of you." And he stormed off upstairs.

"What was all that about?" Liz asked.

"I don't know. I don't get it."

"Find out, okay? Maybe Jessie's been playing games."

Liz left and I went upstairs to the bedroom. Willy was in the bathroom clicking his pill bottles. I sat down on the bed.

"Willy, Zigler said no."

His angry face appeared in the doorway. "I know what Zigler said. It so happens that I've had a rotten day and a pretty horrible piece of news. Which on top of this other business is making it hard for me to cope right now, to tell the truth. I'm anxious as hell."

I got up and went over to him. "Willy, what happened?"

"A digital detachment."

"What?"

"One of the early operations has gone sour. The finger fell off."

I had a strong desire to laugh. "Where?"

"What do you mean, where?"

"I mean in the street or in bed or out the car window . . . Is it lost?"

Willy screamed, "Are you crazy? Who cares where?"

"Well, I just meant if the person still had it you could put it back on again."

"Dinah, it was gangrenous. It went bad. It didn't work."

"It worked for what—eight years?"

Willy snarled, "Oh, Christ, there's no talking to you, it's hopeless." He flung himself on the bed, face up, staring at the ceiling. His Italian cotton shirt strained over his chest and he yanked his tie loose. "Dinah, I can't play these games anymore. I can't take it. I'm going to break in pieces. I've told myself it can't be true, then something like today happens and I know I'd be a fool to deny it any longer. The ridiculous thing is I still love you." Tears were in his eyes.

"Willy, what is it?"

"You know, you know. Do I have to say it?"

"I don't know," I lied.

He said with effort, "It's been with great struggle and difficulty that I've come to accept your bisexuality. But why, with all the women out there, must you pick my ex-wife?"

I stared at him as he lay there, across miles of vast misunderstanding. "You can't believe that. You can't have said that."

"For Christ's sake don't lie." He covered his face with his hands. "Have you heard anything I've said to you in the last weeks? I've struggled to accept this. If you have any respect for me at all, have the decency to tell me the truth. Don't degrade me."

"Willy,"—I tried to pull his hands down—"I don't sleep with Liz. I have never. Or any other women."

"I can't believe you won't be honest about it," he moaned. "Zigler said you wouldn't. You can't deny it. Sneaking in and out, and you both look guilty as sin when I catch you. And Jessie knows without knowing."

"Knows what, for God's sake?"

"She's told me things, put as a child would put them. Mom and Dinah are such chums. Mom is here all the time. They phone each other. They have secrets . . ."

"But there's nothing to tell!"

"Have the decency to listen when I tell you the truth. Don't you know it when you hear it?" He looked at me, drawn and puffy-eyed. "I want to believe you. I need you, Dinah, now more than ever. I need to trust you. And yet I sense something. Tell me I'm imagining things. I'd rather be paranoid than right."

"You are," I lied. "Our marriage is no worse now than it's ever been. Which might sound kind of lukewarm but it's true. *I am not sleeping with Liz.* Thank God you didn't say it in front of her; she'd faint." I looked deep into Willy's

dark brown eyes. The urge to tell was strong, but if I gave
in to it I would have to choose between him and George,
and this I could not do. At last he sighed and flung an arm
over his face.

"I don't know, I just don't know. I feel old—old and
cold and alone."

It was that evening that we picked out St. Petin.

"Let's dream a little, Dinah. Let's pretend we're going to
find ourselves a tropical island to live on. Someplace where
the hot sun beats down and the bright green bushes burst
with ripe fruit. You're in a mawmaw or a pawpaw . . ."

"A pawpaw is a fruit."

"Or a muumuu. You're making poipoi."

"Willy, quite frankly I don't want to go to an island." I
was stunned at the look of deep pain that crossed his face.
"Dinah," he whispered, "please play with me, just a little.
I need to play."

So we had a bottle of wine and got out the atlas and
found St. Petin.

"We'll live on the beach in one of those thatched straw
huts. I'll cure the sick and take fees in coconuts. We won't
have a telephone and the mail boat comes once a month. In
the evening people come around and strum things as we lie
under our mosquito netting."

"What do we do all day?"

"We fish. We catch crabs and cook them over a charcoal
fire. We eat fruits from the trees. We dance to native
drums. We make love."

How hard this was; what a price I was paying. "Is this
what you'd really like?"

"I don't know," Willy said. "Probably not, but sometimes I feel there's too much here and I wish we could go
away somewhere and start again."

Which sounded all too much like what I'd done, and I
wondered if it really made any difference. Look at the grief
I'd caused and was still causing.

Dinah

Geraldine and I have become friends of sorts, mostly out of loneliness. She does most of the talking, often about astrology. She's a Cancer and Jerry's Scorpio, a bad combination. Poor Artie was a Pisces. Years ago I made up a birthday, which she tells me is Aquarius, and then George told me what my real birthday is and I'm still Aquarius. She said she thought I might be psychic and wondered if I'd ever read other people's minds. I couldn't tell her about Liz, I don't know why. Geraldine said, "Well I thought you might because in my chart there's a strong ray of female communication around now, and I thought it might have something to do with you."

Willy puts astrology in the same category as the loas. He gets harder and harder, more buried in himself, even angrier. Now he's reading about Nazi concentration camps, which he says he got started on because of our Waffen SS neighbor. Maybe, says he, he can make a case and catch the man. So he's always writing to Barnes & Noble and the Strand and everywhere else for Holocaust books, then going down to the post office (such as it is) to pick up the packages. The living room is strewn with *Mein Kampf,* Toland,

and so forth. Once I asked him why this was worth more
time than voodoo, for instance, and he said, "Only you
could ask that question."

"All right, so what's the answer?"

"Because I'm looking for the truth, and bonga-bonga has
nothing to do with the truth. And this, Dinah, is our
problem in a nutshell."

"No, it isn't."

"Then what is?" All this over rum punches at The Parrot
Fish. Willy looked sad and tired.

"I wish you'd tell me, Dinah. After all the therapy and
all the trouble and all the talk, I swear to God I still don't
understand why we can't get along well enough to have a
decent marriage."

"Neither do I. We're both pretty unhappy."

"I'm unhappy because our marriage is a failure."

Round in circles we go. We have the same conversations
here in our white shorts and gaudy shirts that we did back
in New York in our pinstripes and gray flannel. Maybe it's
because we're so stuck with each other here. Willy's only
friend is Mister Bagnold and he's as strange as Willy. I have
only Geraldine. Old Charlotte smiles, but she thinks I'm
her Aunt Daisy from Atlanta.

Geraldine went down and presented her nursing credentials at the clinic and was immediately hired—proof of their
desperation, because she only had a year of training when
she was twenty and flunked half the courses. She said I'd
inspired her to stop depending so much on Jerry and to try
to find her own fulfillment—which I didn't remember saying at all. Now that she has something to do, she drinks
less and smokes less pot. And instead of that pining cry in
the mornings, she's up and bustling around in her white
uniform, having a quick breakfast before going down to the
clinic on her motorbike. Willy's offered her a ride a couple
of times, but she says she doesn't want to impose. With
Willy she's almost servile. She thinks he's Cooley and De

Bakey. I guess she's only heard about the first part of his career.

So when she asks me why, being married to this perfect creature, I'm obviously unhappy, I can't tell her about George. Though George is just part of it. I'm right back to where I was before I met him. He just gave me a little respite.

Geraldine had her dinner party the other day. Just the four of us. Not a successful evening. Geraldine talked too much and Jerry tried to shut her up and got nasty and we were all embarrassed. Then she got drunk and cried, and Willy tried to get me out, but I hated to leave her like that. I sat on the beach with her for an hour listening to her woes, during which time Jerry made a pass at Willy— but a subtle one he could deny later. This had never happened to Willy before and he went wild and took a poke at him, ending up with a black eye because, of course, Jerry is younger and stronger. The next day we all pretended nothing had happened.

This is life on our tropical island. I drag myself through all of it.

Geraldine's new job means I don't see much of her anymore. And now Jason seems blue. He misses Jessie and Con. I've told him I'll take him anywhere or do anything to help him make friends with the other kids at school, but they're a motley crew too, like the adults. St. Pet's is a melting pot of unmelted elements. We've become waifs. We've lost our roots and our community by coming here, and I'm too sad and sick to do anything about it.

Dinah

—

The affair with George made everything extremely difficult, but I don't know how I would have coped with Willy without it. He seemed to be almost splitting in pieces. Now there were several Willys: the strong-minded, truth-seeking man of science, restoring order to a chaotic world, or the weepy and depressed child, begging me to save him. The Freeway Philosopher or Robinson Crusoe. Or he'd go back to that old stuff about Mom, Dad, and his masculinity. And if I didn't manage to keep track of which Willy was currently presiding, he'd be furious and say I didn't love him and didn't understand him. The whole thing confused me and wore me out, especially since Zigler's so-called therapy didn't seem to be doing much good. And nobody kept track of how many pills he was taking or what kind. Plus another digital detachment.

Then the thing happened that in some corner of my mind I'd been waiting for, though I didn't know it until the doorbell rang that snowy night. Willy and I were by our fire, knitting and reading, if not content, not actively miserable. I went into the hall. Through the glass curtains was a female silhouette, a woman holding something.

I opened the door and saw a girl standing there, dark-haired and guarded in manner. She wore a cape and was holding something under it in front. We stared at each other, she and I. I felt a faint stirring. One of those half-memories again. What was left of my soul. I pulled her inside. She wore a blue knitted hat dusted with snow, and under the cape, in a canvas sling, was a tiny baby. Neither of us said anything. Down at the end of the block a car started up.

Willy called, "Who is it?"

"I think you might be my mother," the girl said quietly. Though I didn't remember her, I knew she was right. A wave of love rose in me like a tide.

"I think you're right," I said, my voice breaking. I wanted to take her in my arms, her and the baby. "Did George explain why I left?"

"Yes," she said, "but I don't believe him." I reached out and started to touch the baby's head, and ever so delicately she moved the child out of my reach. It cut me like a sword, that gentle gesture.

"Why are you here?" I asked.

Rosie said, "Because I don't have anywhere else to go."

As I stood there digesting this piece of information, Willy walked into the hall. He looked a little unkempt in an old bathrobe and his bedroom slippers—once-impeccable Willy. Also grouchy and apprehensive. Now what? He stared at Rosie and I closed the front door behind her. In the hall light I got a better look at her. A nice-looking but not really pretty girl. She had George's deep blue eyes, but otherwise I knew she looked like me, though harder and more sullen. A haunted look. Now that she was inside, she clutched the baby instinctively and stared at Willy and me like a captured animal. I saw her dart a fearful glance at the door and I felt tears start to press behind my eyes. I had done this. A strand of her long brown hair hung out of her hat, and I wanted to reach over and tuck it back.

"Well, who's this?" Willy asked rather grouchily.

I took a deep breath. "Willy, this is Rosie . . . What did you say your last name was?"

Rosie said, "Dickenson."

No husband. "Rosie Dickenson. A long-lost relative of mine, Willy, what a surprise!" Rosie stared at me incredulously. "Where did you say you come from, Rosie?"

"L.A.," Rosie said. "On the bus, Mom."

"Oh, I forgot!" I laughed falsely. "Rosie stayed with us a lot and sometimes she'd call me Mom, just for fun. Her own mother disappeared when she was just a kid." I was helping her off with the cape.

"When you were fifteen and going to the roadhouse?"

"Well, just sometimes at home." I was rapidly painting myself into a corner. If Willy hadn't been so preoccupied with his own troubles, he would have done a little counting. I could feel Rosie's scorn.

Then Willy said briskly, "Well, Rosie, is that your baby?"

She said, "Who else's would it be?"

"I don't know, but it ought to be in bed." To me he said, "Is she staying?"

"Of course. I'll put her in Jessie's room," Jessie now away at boarding school.

Then a rather ridiculous argument began between Willy and me, supposedly out of earshot, about how Jessie would feel about somebody sleeping in her room. So maybe Con's . . . No. The old sewing room would do very well after I cleaned it up.

"Dinah, for Christ's sake. We don't run a foundling home."

"Now, Willy, Rosie has no other place to go."

"Exactly what relation to you is she?"

"Well, a sort of half-cousin. It's hard to explain."

"She could have phoned or something," said Willy grouchily.

"We have to take her in, Willy. The poor girl's obviously in trouble."

"I'd say she was in trouble over nine months ago."

Back in the hall. Rosie had sunk into one of the chairs that flanked the hall table. She looked exhausted, and the baby was starting to whimper. Her face was flushed and she felt hot. It was Robert Frost who said, "Home is where they have to take you in."

Rosie's fever had a good effect on Willy. He stopped grumbling and turned back into a doctor. To bed with aspirin. And how about the baby? Once in Jessie's room, Rosie started fumbling with the buttons of her sweater, but Willy said she shouldn't nurse if she was sick. But by now the child was yelling lustily and her instincts were stronger than Willy's medical advice. Glassy-eyed, she lay back on the bed and put the child to her breast.

"Okay, Nepenthe," she said. Nepenthe? Later when I got to the dictionary I learned its significance: "anything inducing a pleasurable sensation of forgetfulness."

Meanwhile I had to get to a phone, one well out of earshot. "Willy, I'm going to run out and get some Similac."

"That's ridiculous, Dinah, until the baby's been seen by a pediatrician. I'm not about to go flipping through pediatrics textbooks at this hour."

"It isn't ridiculous, because four hours from now she could pass out and the baby would still be hungry."

"Well, I'll see if I can get Reg Flumetti on the phone. There's always the all-night drugstore down on Fiftieth Street."

"Willy, it's snowing. Sometimes I think you aren't very practical. I'll be back in a few minutes."

Jesus, he made me feel trapped. I flung on my fur coat and went out the door, came back for boots, ran out again. I got the Similac and then closed myself into a pay phone.

"This is Dinah. Is George there?"

Pregnant pause. "Dinah?"

"Yes, Dinah. Dinah Wakefield, and it's important."

Then George, in a half-hiss, "You shouldn't have done that."

"Don't tell me what I shouldn't do. Rosie's just arrived with her baby."

"Oh my God."

"Did she go to you first?"

"She called from the bus terminal, but Jackie said no."

"Jackie said no. She's all heart, isn't she?"

"Don't give me that shit. She's had Rosie on her back for years."

"Do you always do what Jackie says, like a good boy?"

After a pause, "You know, Dinah, you try my patience. What would you do if Willy said no?"

There was a long silence while I thought about that one. Then I said, "I'd tell him to go fuck himself."

"I wonder if that's true."

"Just try me."

"Did you tell him who Rosie is?"

"Of course," I lied. "Listen, I have to go . . . Grandpa."

Back in the room Rosie and the baby lay quietly in the half-light, Willy hovering in the door.

"I took off her boots, Dinah, but I wasn't about to start pulling off jeans and all that. You'd better take over. Do you suppose she'd eat some soup?"

I put my hands on his cheeks and kissed him. "Thank you, darling. I love you." He looked a little surprised. I thought, I'll just pretend he knows who she is and accepts her, just for tonight. I'll pretend she doesn't hate me. That we're all a big extended family.

Before I went down to heat up the soup, I looked at these two new/old members of my family as they lay curled up on the bed together. The girl's lovely jawline, her slender neck stretched out in the hall light. The long curly unkempt hair, the ratty sweater and blue jeans. The baby's

alabaster skin and tiny perfect hand like a little white
flower. Rosie's knapsack, on the floor, hung open. A few
disposable diapers and a couple of T-shirts. A pair of jeans.
They were all mine, the two of them.

I went down to the kitchen. *Do you suppose she'd eat some
soup?* I doubt if any words Willy ever said gave me such
pleasure. Nor had we been as happy in ages as we were
during those first days when Rosie was so deathly ill. We
were a team again, doing what we knew how to do. It was
a period precious even in its deceptions. I was joyfully
delivered from the question of whether memories, or the
lack of them, justified my affair with George, and if so,
why I was so guilty about it, and if not, what *did* justify it
. . . and whether I'd ever remember George, and if I even
wanted to . . . and what the hell I was going to do about
everything anyway.

Our household fell under the baby's spell. Emerelda (who
looked at Rosie and guessed the truth immediately) moved
in to help. Reg Flumetti came, and Dan Holland, the
internist, possibly the last medical house calls on record.
Rosie had pneumonia, anemia, and possibly pleurisy. There
was a chilling moment when Dan looked at her arms and
legs.

I asked, "What are you looking for?"

Dan said, "Needle tracks."

I felt my blood turn and change direction. "Are there
any?"

"No. But I suspect she's been doing something to get
herself in this condition."

"That's a value judgment," I said angrily.

"So what?"

We fed the baby Similac and Rosie homemade chicken
soup. We fed them both antibiotics and vitamins.

"I have made a special Haitian guava paste for the new
daughter to build up her strength," said Emerelda, "and a
poultice of pawpaw for the baby."

Penny had a bad diaper rash, which occupied a lot of our attention, including Jason's until I realized that he was less interested in dermatology than in having a good look at a little girl's privates. Later I heard him on the phone with his friend. "It's like a slit with a couple of little pink buds sticking out."

Willy looked at the squished pawpaw. "It's working, Dinah. There has to be some scientific basis for it." He was as silly as the rest of us. "Penny, Penny Penny Poo, I see you, kitchy kitchy koo!" When the child's tiny face peered at him with adult profundity, he laughed delightedly. "I think she looks a little like you, Dinah, she has the same looks Jason had. The big eyes and the nose and the jawline. The dark lashes and straight hair. Here, Penny, Uncle Willy's here. Grandpa Willy or sixth cousin or whatever it is. Penny, Penny, pudding and pie. Kissed the boys and made them cry. Ooooh, what a heartbreaker this one is going to be!"

I'd cry too when this was over. I hadn't seen Willy so happy in ages, maybe even years. Now he ran into the house, briefly greeting the rest of us and running for the baby's room, which was also Rosie's. At the door he'd shyly knock until Rosie invited him in. We'd hauled up Jason's old crib and scrubbed it up for Penny. I'd gone to Saks and bought sheets and sleepers and stuffed animals and a baby mobile that played "Lullaby and Good Night." When I went up I'd find Willy mooning over her, chattering nursery rhymes and trying to get a smile.

"Hello, sweetheart. How's my little dewdrop today? Look at those feet—bigger than ever. Dinah, look. Rosie, look at her. She's got her toe in her mouth. Will you look at that? She's trying to suck on it. Penny Penny Poo, Henny Penny Wenny." Then, "Bill Goldstein was saying today they shouldn't have those tie-bottom gowns, Dinah; his grandson's pediatrician says they inhibit growth. Why don't you get her more of the ones with feet? And Zigler says they need lots of stimulation early. How about more toys and some of those floppy picture books?"

"Willy, she's only a month old."

"I'll read them to her every night. And Dinah, the best quality Mother Goose you can find, one she'll have all her life. One with the good old-fashioned color plates. Maybe I can get down to Scribner's myself tomorrow. And what about a little record player?"

What strange forms punishment takes; mine was severe. I'd look at Emerelda in the kitchen rocking chair, Penny asleep on her lap. The evening fire laid, the snow piled in the yard. Jason on the floor doing algebra, and nearby Charlotte, who talked to the baby in some mysterious sign language. Rosie resting in her room, sometimes Liz, who dropped by occasionally for an admiring visit. Shaking her head at me, she'd say, "Dinah, you get into the worst messes. And without doing anything."

I knew it but I couldn't bear to change it. There was too much joy in this present, more than when Jason had been a baby, really, for then my obligation to him seemed overwhelming. I'd fussed and worried over him, sure that every fold of his diaper would influence his future. This was a purer happiness.

Rosie was the first to pierce this state of enchantment. I'd sit with her as she ate her dinner from a tray; a lamb chop, a baked potato, green beans. Salad. Whole wheat toast. Apple pie and a glass of milk. Said Rosie, mouth full, "When are you going to tell him?" She was so direct. I suspected life had taught her it was the simplest and most effective way to operate.

"I don't know."

"Are you ashamed of me?"

"Oh, no. It isn't that."

"Maybe you think I didn't have any right to come." Looking carefully at me she said, "You really don't remember me at all?"

"No, Rosie, I don't. I'm sorry. It's nobody's fault; something's wrong with my memory."

"Would Willy throw us out if you told him?"

"He might want to, but I wouldn't let him."

Rosie said thoughtfully, "It's funny, but I don't believe anything you say." How different I must have been in my other life. Nobody in my Willy-family enraged me the way either George or Rosie could with no effort at all. The little bitch—we'd saved her life, hers and Penny's. Here she was eating my food and living in my house, but gratitude never entered her head. I choked down the words. She still wasn't well. Then she said, "If you don't tell Willy the truth, I'm going to. He's a nice guy and he deserves it."

I stared at her sallow face with those dark blue eyes. "That would be a very foolish and destructive thing to do."

"The truth is never destructive."

"That's what you think. And I must say you have a nerve."

"I just can't stand the way you keep protecting him, as though there's something wrong with him."

"It's not that. Willy's very straight. He doesn't know about George." I could have bitten my tongue. "I mean of course I'm going to tell him everything, but I want you to get better and Penny to get a little older. You're both so vulnerable now, and we need the happiness you've brought to this house. You have a whole life ahead to be honest and miserable in, Rosie. Enjoy this little period of kind lies."

Then one morning George called as Willy was saying good-bye to Penny, a fifteen-minute ritual.

"Hi, darling, I'm here. Couldn't get away till now. I'll be over as soon as I change my shirt."

Oh God. "George, you can't come here."

"Now look, Dinah. I'm sure that under the circumstances Willy would . . . Haven't you told him?"

"Of course not. What with the baby and Rosie being sick—"

George's voice rose. "Sick? Why didn't you tell me?"

The truth was I'd forgotten about George. "She was very run-down and had pneumonia. She's all right now. It was hardly the moment to confront Willy about our marriage when the house has been full of doctors and Penny had a diaper rash and—"

"You don't understand," said George. "You don't have to tell Willy about us *now*. But you *do* have to tell him that we *used* to be married and had Rosie."

True. "You're right. Somehow I keep thinking it's all in one package."

"Well, it's really two different things. Now tell him, okay? I'll see you in a little while." Slam.

"George!" I screamed into the silent phone. Frantically I dialed the Warwick, where he usually stayed, but he wasn't registered there. For the first time he'd gone to another hotel.

Willy ran down the stairs. "I'm running, Dinah. I'm doing a knuckle this afternoon, but I'll be finished at five or so and home for dinner." He gave me a big hug. "My Dinah." A kiss. Jason, who didn't see this sort of thing very often anymore, glanced at us in surprise. Willy actually looked happy. "You know, I'll be sorry when they go. I told Rosie she was welcome to stay as long as she wants." My heart sank as he loped out the door with a merry farewell to Emerelda.

"Mistress," Emerelda whispered as the door closed, "I am very worried."

"*You're* worried. You don't know the half of it!"

"No, Mistress, it is more than the matter of the first husband."

I said, "Emerelda, is there anything you don't know?"

She dropped her eyes. "Hardly, Mistress. That is why I am a mambo. But this is a matter of great seriousness. The loas are locked in combat, which is very dangerous. I have had three visions which carry the gravest messages. Damballa holds the rest of your memories, but Ogoun threatens the life of Mister Doc if they are ever released. As it is, the unremembered memories are riding your life, Mistress. I am fearful that the new daughter or the old husband will tap the closed door of your mind and allow them to flood out." She looked tired. These nights of the loa visitations left her worn out. "Oh, Mistress, you must be very careful."

"Now, Emerelda, you've been worried before and nothing has happened. We have a mother and a baby to take care of. How about making some lime chicken for dinner?"

I poured myself some coffee with a shaking hand. Jesus, the unremembered memories. Let them stay there, I had enough problems. And I wasn't crazy about being a normal person. I was exhausted from all this passion and secrecy and fear and guilt. I'd lost my peace of mind. Though on the other hand I might be better off with memories than with George, Rosie, and Penny in the flesh. Memories you could stuff around somewhere; people you couldn't.

Emerelda sighed. "It tries my powers as a mambo in the most extreme way. In Haiti people care little about memories. Sometimes we forget our age and even whose children are whose. The sharing of memories that you have with the Mistress Liz is quite common. Here the memories have a powerful religious force and are worshiped by the doctors of the mind. I feel they even have a value like money."

I stared at her as she went back into the kitchen. But before I could even absorb her latest enigma, the doorbell rang and in came George, having introduced himself to Jason, who was on his way out. It was so interesting around here these days he had trouble tearing himself away. George was red-cheeked from the cold and in grand spirits. And horny. He didn't notice Emerelda, who was stooping over sorting laundry, and he grabbed me in his arms. Tongue. Strokey hands. Full-fledged erection.

"Congratulations to us," he whispered. "I've been wanting to come for two weeks. Is there an empty bedroom?"

"George, for God's sake cool it." Emerelda purposely kicked the trash can, which restored him to sanity.

"It's been a month, Dinah," he whispered. "Oh God, I want you." He looked at me. "I see the feeling isn't mutual."

"It's not that, George. I've been so busy. I've had so much on my mind and Penny's had a diaper rash . . . Don't you want to see her?"

"The baby . . . Oh, sure." He closed his eyes and concentrated. "Okay, Grandma. Where's the kid?"

The reunion between George and Rosie was touching. A big hug. Her eyes were wet.

"Why didn't you tell me?" George asked her.

"First I wasn't sure. Then after I was sure I decided to handle it myself."

He was sitting by her, holding her hand. "That's a lot to handle. No job. No money. Pregnant. Is it Bruce's child?"

Rosie said huffily, "Well, of course. I was with Bruce for three years." All this was news to me. We'd behaved as though Penny was a virgin birth.

"So where is he?"

"He split when I told him I was pregnant. He said he was going up to Big Sur."

"I'll kill him," George said.

"Look, Dad, he just doesn't want to be involved, see? He never said he wanted a child. He always told me he wanted to stay loose. I don't blame him. He couldn't confront the idea of being a father."

"I'll hire somebody to shoot him in the knees," George said.

"Dad, cut it out. Bruce and I were all right when we were living in Venice. It's over, that's all. He has trouble with intimacy."

"Suppose you had trouble with intimacy?" George asked. That stopped her.

"Well, I'd say I got fucked." She looked at me standing in the doorway. "What do you think, Mom?"

"I agree that Bruce should be shot."

For the first time she smiled at me. Then she said to George, "She's scared to tell her husband, Dad."

George said, "Don't you ever speak disrespectfully of your mother. And don't try to play us against each other."

We had lunch, and I spent most of the afternoon nervously smoking cigarettes.

"George, you don't know Willy. He's a little unstable, or maybe the word is high-strung. You see, he married me for the amnesia and he got very threatened when my memory started coming back. Or something."

"You never told me that."

"Well, as a matter of fact I never realized it until now. But I know it's true. He had two babies and an old mother and he needed me. He was completely helpless."

"If he was helpless, then he still is. And this is a damn strange discussion, Dinah, because frankly I don't give a damn about Willy's feelings, considering the way things have evolved."

"Only about Jackie's."

He said, "The truth is you've created this whole mess by just doing nothing. I agree with Rosie, though I won't say so in front of her. And I'll be damned if I'm going home until something gets straightened out around here. She's my kid too and my grandchild and this is ridiculous."

In other words he was going to sit it out. And Rosie wouldn't promise silence. While George sat in the rocking chair with Penny, singing her nursery rhymes, I agreed to meet Willy at the hospital, sit him down somewhere and tell him the truth, before he arrived home to find George, who refused to leave. Probably I could have gotten him out by threatening withdrawal of sexual favors, but he convinced me that it was the only reasonable thing to do and that Willy probably would be able to handle the whole thing perfectly well. If Willy couldn't stand the notion of a first husband, he and I didn't have much of a marriage anyway.

"Maybe not, but it's a bird in the hand, so to speak. And I don't think I could function without a husband. I'm not used to it."

George asked, "If there were no Jackie, would you give up Willy for me?"

"If there were no Willy, would you give up Jackie?" Neither of us could answer.

Sitting in the taxi, I knew my worry about Willy went beyond the possibility of his anger into deeper dreads that only Emerelda would have understood. Her suggestion of danger to Willy had been preceded in me by an almost indefinable fear for his safety, which George had attributed to my guilt. "Good God, Dinah, the man's one of the most successful surgeons in the country. You can't accomplish what he has unless you're pretty strong. You talk about him as though he's a frail flower, which you'd understand if you ever had any therapy."

"He is frail. I don't know why, but he is."

Which all blew away when I arrived at the hospital. I hadn't been there in months, and the atmosphere was encouraging. All was hustle and bustle, here in Willy's world, clean and efficient and direct. If there was death, there were lives saved too, and Willy was on the side of the saviors. As I swept in trailing my Blackglama mink, a couple of nurses fluttered over to me. "Oh, Mrs. Wakefield. The doctor is in the O.R." Willy was doing the knuckle. "Would you like to wait here? Can I get you some coffee?" It was odd that after all these years as Mrs. Willard Wakefield I still sometimes felt like that tattered waif crawling out of the subway. The mink was like a Halloween costume. As I took it off and hung it over a chair, I saw one of the young nurses stroke it softly with her fingers. Probably I had everything she wanted, except the sense of security she thought went with it. But never mind. It was nice to be here in this timeless place where day faded into night, where doctors' names crackled over the PA system, where I was on the side of the healers.

Shortly Willy and Mac Valpey appeared in their green scrub suits.

"Dinah, what a nice surprise," Willy said, peeling off his shower cap. "Is everything all right at home?"

"Fine, Willy."

"Is Penny all right?" To Mac he said, "She had a little colic this morning, and I suggested to Reg she might need a change of formula. He said it was time to start her on cereal. Can you believe it—cereal! At a month!"

Mac winked at me. "Ever hear of an overpossessive great-uncle once removed?"

"Actually it's a . . . What is it, Dinah?" Willy gave me an affectionate smile. "I still haven't got the relationship straight. Not that it matters a damn."

My nerve was failing fast. "Willy, will you be finished soon?" Now his followers were beginning to flock around: nurses, assistants, the anesthesiologist, the knuckle's parents. Plus he had to change and write orders on a couple of charts. If there had ever been a confident and secure man it was Willy, exuding power and strength and ability. Solving six problems at once with grace and authority. I thought, I should make a point of coming to the hospital more to remind myself of this persona. Plus handsome and sexy in his green scrub suit and Corfam shoes. I watched him as he wrote out orders and smiled at a pair of admiring nurses. How funny I never got jealous of Willy, though there must have been women after him all the time. I never thought about them, yet the thought of Jackie brought a black coil of fury to my heart.

Finally he appeared dressed. "All right, darling, let's go. You're sweet to come and meet me; you haven't done it for years."

I gulped. "Willy, let's go to a bar or something."

"A bar?" He stared at me. How middle-aged we'd gotten. "Can't we have a drink at home?"

I said, in craven tones, "Well, I think we're out of gin and I forgot to get wine and . . . it's so chaotic around

there with the baby screaming and Jason and Rosie and
. . . I'd just like to be alone with you for an hour. Without
all those other people."

Said poor, gullible Willy, "Dinah, I never thought.
We'll have some champagne at the Regency, just the two
of us." I could have wept. I wished he'd hit me instead of
kissing me. Or that I'd bang my head and get amnesia all
over again.

At the Regency I ordered a martini extra dry straight up.
With a twist. The last time I'd had one, Willy had to carry
me home. I took one sip and put it down; the furze that
started to coat my mind scared me. I sent it back and
ordered a glass of wine.

"Dinah, what the hell's the matter with you? You're
nervous as a cat. Say it. Is something wrong?" His eyes flew
open in alarm. "It's Penny! She's sick! Something's happened to her! Say it quick. Don't stall!"

"Penny's fine. Nobody's sick. Nobody's dead. Everything's the way it was this morning except now we have a
. . . er . . . houseguest."

"Oh, who's that?"

"Rosie's father."

"No kidding."

I said, "His name is George Dickenson. From Quincy,
Massachusetts."

"Well, that's fine, I guess. If you can find a place to put
him. We'll just have to use Con's room. Now what relation
is he to you? I'd better get it straight before we go home."

"He's my ex-husband."

Willy's face stiffened for a moment, then broke into a
grin. "You're cute, Dinah. You don't have such a thing."

"But I do, Willy."

"Jesus, some sense of humor. That would make Rosie
your . . ."

"My daughter. That's right."

The Regency bar was very dark but not too dark for us
to see each other's faces. He began to believe me. I watched

belief fight with disbelief for what seemed an incredibly long time. I was perspiring. I wriggled out of the mink coat and still he didn't move. Finally he said, "You never told me you were married before."

"Willy, I didn't know. Which you know very well."

"And Rosie is your daughter." He was speaking very slowly. "And Penny is your granddaughter."

"That's right."

Then he yelled, "How do you know? How do they know? How do I know you're not all lying?"

Heads turned at other tables. There was a wild look on Willy's face. I said, "Telling the truth is as difficult for me as it is for you to hear it."

"How long have you known this?"

"Since the night Rosie came."

Willy smiled a sickening smile. "So a strange girl comes to the door on a snowy night, carrying a baby. She says she's your daughter and you believe her."

"No, Willy. I knew she existed because George told me about her."

"George. Our houseguest."

"That's right."

"May I ask why you didn't tell me?"

"George came through FK and he's the fourth husband, you know that. I thought he was another faux mari. But he convinced me he's real."

"How did he do that?" Willy asked. "Did he produce any credentials? A marriage license? Any proof at all?"

"Well, no."

Said Willy, with the air of having solved a perfectly simple problem, "So it probably isn't true at all."

The discussion seemed to be sprouting heads like a hydra. "George and I weren't actually married, Willy. But we lived together for many years and had Rosie."

"Do you remember any of this? Anything at all?" Willy asked.

"No, the curtain drops when I was around sixteen."

"So a strange man turns up and says he used to live with you and sends a strange woman with a baby, who moves into our house. Dinah,"—laughing thinly—"don't you understand? We're being flimflammed."

"What do you mean?"

Willy explained, "A guy knocks a girl up. He wants out. He hears about the lost grandma agency and figures it all out. He lucks into somebody as gullible as you and as incompetent as Poor Liz." Willy shook his head and gave a laugh that was more like a cough. "Jesus, Dinah. You scared me to death. I don't like this situation and I've gotten fond of the baby. But it's perfectly clear what happened." He waved for the check. "All we have to do is go home and clear them out."

"But Willy, if this were true, then why would George have come to the house?"

"Well, I don't know, Dinah. They must have some plan to take advantage of us, and this is probably a phase in some sting operation. If it weren't so late I'd call Milt Crossway" (his lawyer) "on the phone. Maybe I can still get him."

I said, "Willy, this is completely wrong. The story is true. For God's sake, you said the baby looks like me. And look at Rosie."

"That's why the plan worked so well," Willy said. "But resemblance is largely in the eye of the beholder. Objectively she's just another dark-haired, big-eyed girl. But her body build is completely different—shorter and stockier than yours."

"Exactly. Like George. It's undeniable, you'll see. You'll have to see." Of all Willy's possible responses, I'd never dreamed of this one, the wildest of all. "Willy, you have to believe me. Look, I have certain . . . memories of when I was fifteen and sixteen that I never mentioned, I guess because I was ashamed. But I used to make out with boys in the backs of cars."

Willy slowly got a twenty out of his wallet. "Oh, you did. Isn't that a little young for that sort of thing?"

"I suppose so, but I did. And one of them was George, I think." A slow, fearful doubt was flooding me. I kept losing track of what I was supposed to tell and what I wasn't.

"You never told me this."

"Well, I guess I didn't. You never wanted to know."

"Want to tell me about it?"

"Not really. I said it to prove a point, because I'm almost sure one of them was George."

"Is this supposed to please me?"

"Willy, the subject is not whether you're pleased but whether I'm telling the truth."

Then he hardened. "You don't know what the truth is. I think the whole thing is a lie. I think you were a poor, sad, unpopular orphan kid and you never fucked anybody till you married me. I think you married me for my ready-made family and you loved appropriating Poor Liz's kids to make up for your own terrible sense of inadequacy, and this whole story is a feeble effort to compete with me in some way by pretending you were married too and had a child. It's pathetic, Dinah. It's sad. Plus the voodoo. Zigler has been telling me you have serious emotional problems, and now I believe him. This whole fantasy of yours has opened my eyes. Now I see that I've been protecting you and blaming myself for things that are really functions of your *mental illness*. Which has largely to do with your *desperate pretense at heterosexuality*."

The wine in my mouth turned to ashes. Willy had cast around and found an approach to all this that put him in the driver's seat, and with that smug expression that Sally had once called the mask of male WASP professionals in the fifty-percent bracket, he shoved his wallet back in one pocket and his charge cards in the other.

Then he said, "Dinah, I don't mean to be cruel to you. Zigler's given me the names of a couple of people and I have

them here somewhere. But I'm not going to close my eyes
to pathology the way I did with Liz. If help is needed *it
will be given*. Or else *there will be a divorce*. Con and Jessie
have suffered enough, and I'll fight to the death to protect
Jason from a destructive situation."

The room was swimming around, and the three glasses
of wine I'd had out of sheer nervousness didn't help, particularly since Willy had been drinking Perrier. I kept rum-
maging around for some thread to grab on to, but the ball
of wool was shaggy and full of knots. Something had gone
wrong, but I really didn't understand what.

I said feebly, "Honestly, Willy, whenever we have a
problem, all you can think to do is summon lawyers and
shrinks."

"Thank God we have them to help us with our difficulties."

We left the Regency: Willy tall, straight, custom-cut,
me hollow-eyed and bewildered, scuttling after him dragging my fur coat. Affluent Manhattan couple out on the
town, taking an hour away from the kids to talk over a few
matters. Round one—Willy. We got into a taxi, and as
the driver started through the park, Willy leaned back with
a little smile on his face. I was too frightened to talk. He'd
never used the word *divorce* before. Willy had always said
he'd die with this marriage no matter what happened. We'd
survived the truth about Sally. But therapy had given him
backbone. He'd fight me and get Jason. He'd done it with
Liz. I began to sniffle, groping in my handbag for a Kleenex. It couldn't happen. He was talking about what a relief
it was to get the truth out at last, or at least to start.

"Zigler has pointed out to me that the amnesia was really
a brilliant device to block out a sad, empty life, screwing
around in cars. You had nothing till you knew me, and the
amnesia was a convenient way not to tell me what a basically
ordinary young woman you really were. It made you mysterious and interesting, especially to a doctor."

I was stunned. "You don't believe the amnesia is real?"

He said, "Well, let's put it this way. I think it's *gotten* real."

As the cab drove up to our house I felt as though I were going to puke, and so I did, into the gutter. Willy stood there and watched me as I threw up. It was my lowest point. His face was a study.

"Are you all right?"

"I guess so," I said. He waited for me to pull myself together before we went in. He even loaned me his Binaca. Now what would happen? And what would happen to me?

We walked into a peaceful domestic scene. Emerelda cutting up fruit into a bowl. Delicious smells of lime chicken. Rosie by the fire reading the paper, Penny nearby in Jason's old cradle. George was arranging cheese and crackers on a plate with Jason's help. He'd put some champagne flutes on a tray, so we could all celebrate this happy occasion. At times George had a baffling optimism. As we came in he walked over to Willy for a big handshake. By God, he was going to do it.

"Willy, I'm George Dickenson. I hope you'll forgive my barging in on you like this, particularly under the circumstances. But I thought the sooner we talked, the better. And I want to thank you for taking in my family." He glanced at me, puzzled. I must have looked like the wrath of God. I looked at Willy, holding my breath. He looked stunned. George plowed on. "I know the whole thing is a little unusual, but I've seen crazier arrangements than this. The stepfamily has gotten pretty common, but what makes this one a little offbeat is Dinah's amnesia." Laugh. He glanced at me for help. "I'm touched and grateful to all of you for taking Rosie and the baby in. I've been talking about future plans with Rosie and—"

"Mr. Dickenson. George." Willy's voice was thin and stiff and his smile was skull-like. "Let's get down to business. Do you have any credentials?" He was going the scam route. "Do you have any proof at all that this story of yours is true?"

George looked puzzled. "Story?"

"As far as I'm concerned you're a stranger who walked in off the street. Dinah told me some fabrication about a distant relative that I never believed for a minute. Your plan —whatever it is—isn't going to work. Tell me, are you one of those psychopaths who can't resist returning to the scene of the crime, or did you suddenly begin to feel guilty about your infant child?"

George paled and there was a frightening silence in the room. Even Rosie's customary cool was shattered. She stared at Willy and slowly reached over to Penny as though to protect her.

George said to me, "Dinah, did you explain everything to Willy?"

"Well, of course, but it's kind of a shock. I mean Willy and I had never thought I'd been married before and the whole thing—"

"Dinah," Willy said, "the only reason I have any patience at all with this situation is that I understand why you're caught up in it. But what's exploitative to them is very dangerous to you. You were not married before. This young woman is not your child. Jason and Jessie and Conrad are your children. You're a person of simple interests, and the idea of having a baby around appealed to you. You're gullible and you believed what they told you."

George bristled. "Now, look here. Dinah and I lived together many years ago and Rosie is our daughter." He sounded nervous, no doubt unhinged by Willy. "Dinah, tell him, for God's sake."

"He doesn't believe me."

Willy turned to me. "Do you remember him, Dinah?"

"Well, no. But I'm absolutely sure that—"

"You're an attorney," Willy said. "Would that stand up in court?"

George barked, "This isn't court. And you have a problem, to say the least. You can't face the fact that your wife had a life before you came along."

Willy laughed his dreadful cough-laugh. "What you can't face, Mr. Dickenson, is that my wife never saw you before in her life. That you've been caught at your sleazy little game and you're going to have to take responsibility for your child and this young woman you've gotten into trouble. And not in my house."

Several things happened then. George began muttering that he had a picture of him and me somewhere. He'd meant to put it in his suitcase; if he hadn't he'd bring it to Willy and show him. But I looked at Willy and saw madness written in his face, and Rosie must have at the same time, for a strange, thin cry came out of her, a wail like a wounded animal. I ran over to her and put my arm around her, but she shook me off.

"I can't stand this," she said, sobbing. "You're all crazy. Maybe you're not even my mother. How do I know what to believe?" Then Penny started crying and Emerelda bolted out of the kitchen like a shot and picked her up. I was shaken by a full, clear anger as Willy stood in the middle of all this laughing.

"You're crazy, Willy," I said. "You're a bastard and you're crazy."

Rage leapt into his eyes. "Get all these people out of my house."

"I will not. Rosie isn't well and they need me."

Willy screamed, *"They aren't our people!"*

I was furious. "So what? Who cares who they belong to? This morning you loved Penny, and now you want to throw her out in the street."

Willy screamed again, *"She's not ours!"*

I'm not even sure what we were arguing about. I was skating on the thin ice of Willy's mind. How badly I wanted to remember George and Rosie and convince Willy they were real. But that last door remained locked and might never be opened. I could have said I remembered George, but I couldn't lie about my memories. Really they were all I had. If I started compromising them I'd end up insane, floating around in a miasma of lies and dreams. I'd known that when Willy suggested I'd made up my amnesia. The tape of my mind stayed stubbornly locked in the middle of some back-seat screw, and that was all there was to it. And George knew what I was thinking.

"Dinah, are you absolutely positive you don't remember me from before?"

"Positive. I've told you."

"I think it might be a good idea if I took Rosie and the baby and left," George said.

"Oh, no, George. I've said they can stay, and that's that."

"Either they go or I do," Willy said in a strangled voice. "And if I do I'm calling Milt Crossway first thing in the morning and we start divorce proceedings."

"Then you'd better leave." My voice trembled, but I meant it.

Willy left, though not immediately. After all, he'd lived in that house for almost twenty years. He left in an hour or so, after he'd packed a suitcase and yelled at me some more upstairs, where we continued our argument in privacy. Round and round we went.

"You've completely lost your mind, Dinah. You're breaking up your marriage over a band of gypsies. And that George is obviously a con artist." His crosspatch tone was as familiar to me as the plane trees outside the windows or the oak wardrobe I'd bought so long ago on Amsterdam Avenue. "And I'm not abandoning you. I'm just going to a hotel for a few days till things calm down. Until you come to your senses. In fact I think I'll write a note to that effect and have it notarized at the drugstore." He was sitting on the bed, scribbling something at the bedside table as he'd

done a thousand times before. "Here are the names Zigler
gave me. I wouldn't go to Liverwood; he's being sued by
several female patients for exhibiting himself." In the
meantime he chanted a litany of my crimes. "The Lesbian
Love Nest. The dating agency for orphans and runaways.
Voodoo spells on my poor old mother and the old woman
in Vermont. And now this—the baby flimflam. I've been
patient, Dinah. I've waited and tried to reason with you. I
don't know what it is exactly. You aren't a *bad person*. It's
just that . . . you have no center. No organizational principles. Everything flies off every which way."

The trouble was, I still loved him, and it wasn't easy to
watch him walk out the door. Or for him to go. I wondered
if all marriages were as baffling as this, as undefinable.
Willy wasn't able to say specifically what the matter with
us was any more than I could. I was beginning to see why
people were so often unable to explain their divorces, even
Liz, who was so smart. She said somehow love turned into
fear and distrust, like countries that spend their money on
arms while the people starve. "We starved love and spent
our energy and resources trying to protect ourselves," she
said. "I don't know how to put it any better."

I sat on the bed as Willy grabbed shirts from his drawer
and piled them in his suitcase, along with the contents of
his medicine chest: Valium, Dalmane, Quaaludes, plus a
few uppers, downers, shakers, and calmers. He caught my
eye.

"I can prove in court that every one of them has a medical
justification."

"Oh, Willy. We're not going to court."

"I hope not, Dinah, for your sake, since I have the
money, the power, the reputation, and the medical proof of
your psychiatric problems. And everything in my name. If
your lawyer has any sense we won't even make it to the
courtroom steps."

Jesus. Down the stairs we went, and just when I was

working up the anger necessary to see him out the door, I heard a step behind us and there was Jason with his knapsack on over his down jacket. In the front hall the three of us stood staring at each other. I reached for Jason, and he gracefully moved aside and stood next to Willy.

"I'm sorry, Mom. It's nothing against you, but Dad doesn't have anybody on his side. You have that whole gang in there." He might as well have stuck a knife in me.

"But Jason, this is your home. It's where you belong."

"Well, I'll be back to see you." He was almost eleven—long, lanky, desolate, just beginning the lonely physical leap into adulthood. I grabbed him and hugged him, though he held back. I couldn't help the terrible things I said.

"Jason, you're mine, don't you understand? Con and Jessie are Willy's. You're mine. You can't leave me." But he wouldn't budge.

"Okay, Jason," Willy said. "Let's go."

Jason said, "Good-bye, Mom."

And they left, leaving me with the family I didn't even remember.

Willy

—

'm not going to waste time on regrets. I'm a busy physician and father of three children, and the main thing is
to handle this deplorable situation with the least possible
pain. It's clear to all the children that Dinah is deeply
disturbed. I've spoken to Con and Jessie and told them it's
just a matter of time until Dinah is hospitalized. I've had
several talks with Jason, who of course is distressed that his
mother is mentally ill. I allow him to visit the house every
few days, but the rest of the time I keep him with me at
the Stanhope, or whenever I'm at the Stanhope. We have
dinner together and play chess, or he does his homework
with my help, or we look at something on Channel Thirteen. He's already benefited from being away from that
playpen of crazies at home.

On Milt Crossway's advice I've taken everything out of
the joint accounts and stopped all her charge accounts. I
send her fifty dollars a week, which should be plenty for her
if she's careful. When Jason remarked that she didn't seem
to have much food around, I reminded him that it was
inevitable as long as she insists on feeding the woman and
her child and even that demented maid. If she comes to her

senses she'll throw them all out. The girl can go on welfare, along with the thousands of other young women who get themselves in trouble.

Dinah has gotten herself an attorney, which probably won't last long when the man finds she can't pay him. His name is—ha ha—Billings! Milt said he knows him pretty well and called him a sensible, reasonable guy. So far, Billings's less-than-brilliant advice has been to tell Dinah to Xerox my income tax forms going back ten years, thinking I'd be stupid enough to keep them at home instead of in the office safe. Billings also told Dinah that Milt is "the biggest gun in town—a merciless bastard." That ought to keep her on her toes.

Dinah has a few pill containers which she intends to show to the judge to prove I'm a drug addict, but no judge would deny a few Valiums to somebody in my situation. And he's going to hear everything. The lesbian affair with my ex, voodoo spells, the boys from Borneo, driving my mother into senility, killing the old woman in Vermont, and turning my home into a haven for welfare mothers and flimflam artists. It's too bad Dinah insists on going through the charade when we all know it will end with her incarceration. In the meantime let her hit up her ex-husband or whoever he is for some dough. He certainly never gave her a nickel before.

The whole situation is so bizarre that nobody I've told can really grasp it. Zigler is useless. Whenever the shrinks run into something they can't comprehend, they start the old "Do you want to talk about it? Why are you so threatened?" shit. That asshole Zigler can't think his way out of a paper bag. The only half-useful thing he did was to order me to take some Dalmane. I need it to get through everything that's going on.

I started the Valium after that first digital detachment. Now there's been seven of them. Not a single one has responded to reattachment. Well, what the hell? It doesn't undo the benefits they've had. They're lucky they got a few years' more use. With all the medical progress these days and the lasers and CAT scans and all the new diagnostic tools, people have come to expect miracles, and when we can't deliver they sue. The age of expectation. A hundred years ago they wouldn't have lived long enough to complain. Anything the doc did was terrific—leeches, bleeding, anything. Now we're society's whipping boys. Freeze our fees. Sue us. Raise our malpractice premiums. Drown us in regulations. Fine, we'll stop practicing medicine except on each other. That'll fix 'em!

I told Mac Valpey the other day that I was pretty sure there was collusion between the state and the insurance companies—payoffs, that sort of thing. The governor's involved and it's all going to come out. Apparently he had a bad medical experience once, and he's going to get his revenge on the medical profession. Mac doesn't believe it. But it's obvious they're after physicians and have been for a long time. We're too successful. We make too much money. They want to bring us to our knees. They've actually infiltrated the AMA and our lobby in Washington, disguised as doctors. It's undeniable. Their purpose is to erode the power of the medical establishment.

And that's not all. A long time ago the President himself knocked a girl up and she got a quiet little D & C at Episcopal, back before the law changed. Later the woman threatened to expose everybody until the abortionist—a prominent gynecologist still practicing—and the Prez paid her off! And the President blames the doctor, *not* the woman. The first lady still doesn't know!

Mac almost fell off his chair and asked me again if I could prove what I'd said. We were having coffee in the cafeteria. I said it could easily be proved by things I'd heard and what people had said, though Ellis, the gynecologist, denies everything. Mac screams, "Duncan Ellis?" I told him to for God's sake shut up, if the story gets out Ellis is as good as dead. Then Mac gets very slit-eyed and soft-voiced, the way he does when he's being smart. I don't look well. I look tired. I need a vacation. And all about his latest divorce for the fiftieth time. How sometimes he thought strange things and imagined things that weren't true . . . The bastard. Well, I told him to go fuck himself and left.

There are plots everywhere. As soon as you grasp that simple fact, things fall into place. There's no such thing as an innocent person. (There's a line in a song of a Broadway musical that makes me think of Dinah: "That child ties knots no sailor ever knew.") People manipulate. They remember. They hold grudges. You live with it. You learn vigilance.

Dinah

—

osie's attitude about her situation was relaxed, to say
the least.

"Mom, I'm really sorry we caused you all this
trouble."

"It's all right."

"Willy's such a patriarch, you're better off without him."
She was putting carrots into the food processor. Now that
she was better, her countercultural traits were starting to
come out. "His values are basically materialistic."

"These materialistic people are often good at paying the
bills."

"Don't worry, you'll find something."

"*I'll* find something, for God's sake. How about you?"

"But I have Penny."

George, who found the lawyer for me, was of course
pleased about the separation. If Willy saw the world as cold,
unfair, and dangerous, George bounced forward to meet it
with a big smile of hope. He was less help about money.

"I don't make very much as a small-town attorney,
Dinah. I suppose I could lend you a little."

"Couldn't you give Rosie some every week to contribute
to the household?"

"Jackie wouldn't like it."

"You're a wimp, do you know that?"

"You're probably right, but I don't feel like getting into a big mess with her right at the moment, when things with you and me are so unsettled."

"George, either send some money or I'm going to call Jackie up and tell her the whole situation. If Jackie can't take the notion of a first wife, you don't have much of a relationship anyway. She's one of the most successful third-grade teachers in the country—you can't accomplish what she has unless you're pretty strong. You talk about her as though she's a frail flower."

"Pretty funny," he said.

"I mean it. The washer is broken and the baby needs clothes. And I've got Rosie talked into taking classes in computer training, but I can't pay the tuition. Come on, George."

I was desperate enough to mean it. Emerelda came one day a week out of loyalty, but she'd taken another job, so Rosie and I were doing most of the work. She wasn't a bad girl, just a little stunned by everything that was going on.

"I guess I was unrealistic about a lot of things in California. I'd been into a lot of drugs and having Penny was like a drug too. That's why I named her Nepenthe; she was supposed to make me forget all the bad stuff. And to remind me never to forget her the way you forgot me."

I said wearily, "Rosie, how much do I have to do to make up for being in a car accident?"

"It's so hard to believe a person could forget their own child."

"I've taken you in now, haven't I? I even kicked Willy out for you. What do you expect?"

And I wondered then why I'd turned in a perfectly good life and husband for her. And a son, though Jason came by fairly often because he got tired of hanging around Willy's room at the Stanhope. I even wearied of Penny with her fussing and her endless dirty diapers. It was depressing to realize how many things depended, finally, on a steady income. Somebody had to pay life's electrical bills. I felt deserted too. Jessie was in Fort Lauderdale for her spring vacation, and Con visiting a friend on the Cape. I talked to them both; avoidance was in their voices.

One evening when we were gathered in the gloom (to save electricity) the doorbell rang and there stood Liz in a Chanel suit. She'd just come back from a triumphant international tour of the FK offices in London, Paris, Rome, Tokyo, and Riyadh. She'd talked briefly to Conrad.

"Dinah, this is horrible. I didn't know any of this." She looked around. "Good Lord, the place is falling apart." She looked at Rosie, who was chopping up vegetables for a salad, our spare supper. "Dinah, come upstairs with me. I want to talk to you."

In the bedroom she said, "Listen, all you have to do is call the office."

"I don't want to borrow money from you."

"Not borrow. Your investment in FK—that original three thousand—has gotten a lot bigger. It's been reinvested because you said you didn't need it."

I'd half forgotten it. "But why should you do all the work and I get the money?"

"I have plenty of my own, dodo-head. FK wouldn't exist if it weren't for you. When you made me that loan I had no other resources."

So I had a few thousand, anyway, which made me optimistically believe that Willy could not starve me out and force me back into the marriage—which Billings said was his game. On the few occasions I talked to Willy on the phone, he sounded strange somehow, and I didn't like the way Jason's face closed down when he talked about his father.

"He's fine, Mom. I told you."

"What do you two do in the evenings?" I asked.

"We go out to Côte Basque or somewhere. Jackson Hole. We play backgammon in the room or watch the tube."

"Are you doing your homework? Your last marks weren't very good."

"Sometimes."

"Jason, you and I have always been pretty honest with each other. Is something on your mind?"

Jason struggled not to cry. "My parents are getting divorced."

I called Billings. "I can't take it," I said. "I'll do whatever he wants. It's too hard on Jason."

Billings asked, "Are the girl and the baby still there?"

"Well, of course."

"You have to make concessions, Dinah. I told you that. He gives a little, you give a little. Willy is very unhappy about this other family of yours. If you want to reconcile, you have to get rid of them."

Then I'd look out in the garden, where Rosie was putting Penny in her carriage in the spring sunlight, where she was optimistically planting seeds in our sour soil. She looked better and happier than when she first arrived. And Penny, now five months old, waved her arms and legs and greeted me with a big, beautiful smile, as though I were some life-giving angel rather than just Grandma. How fragile she was; how perishable they both were. The alternatives were not pleasant—Rosie on welfare or in some minimal, dreary, low-skills job. She was only nineteen. Nor could I endure the thought of Penny in a day-care center. Every trouble-free day I could provide for them was insurance for the future. And Rosie needed the mother she'd never had. I could never live with myself if I threw them out.

I decided to try talking with Willy, and since Billings/Crossway didn't want us to meet, I went to his office. Cathy, the nurse, hadn't been warned and believed me when I said I was surprising Willy. After an hour's wait I walked into his dark and leathery office. Willy was reading something, and in the moment before he saw me, I noticed that the paper was rattling in his hands. When he saw me he slammed it down on the desk.

"Dinah, I must say this is a surprise. You look well."

"Thank you." I couldn't say the same for him. He looked terrible.

"Can I do something for you?"

"I'd like to stop this whole rotten divorce business. It's too hard on Jason."

"Jason's perfectly fine," Willy said. "In fact he's much better off out of that nursery atmosphere at home, all women and babies. With me he can be freer about his masculine identity, and Zigler agrees."

"He's not fine, he's terrible. And as for Con and Jessie, Liz says—"

There was a demented smile on his face. "Ah, Poor Liz again. Milt Crossway said you wouldn't be able to resist mentioning her. Tell me, Dinah, is your relationship with her satisfying enough to make up for a normal marriage?"

"Willy, I can't believe you think what you think. It's so wrong it's ridiculous."

Willy's voice was hard. "Get that crew out of the house and we'll talk. I'd consider trying the marriage again if we had a contract to control your spendthrift habits. A strict budget and certain irrevocable rules about how we live. Order instead of the chaos of the last thirteen years." There was a glass paperweight on his desk, and he was slowly turning it round and round while I stared at it, mesmerized. "If Jason sounds more serious, it's because I've been strict with him for the first time in his life."

"Too bad he's flunking out of Dalton."

"Those two bad marks are entirely the fault of a certain disturbed pair of teachers, who have since been dismissed," Willy replied.

"Are you happy at the Stanhope?"

"Nobody's *happy,* Dinah. We wrest what contentment

we can out of whatever life deals us. I don't want a divorce either. But I simply refuse to live anymore the way we've been living, in a garbage heap of loose ethics and no standards and no control and waste and steadily mounting charge accounts." Then the usual litany of my crimes, finishing up with "turning my home into a haven for unwed mothers and flimflam artists."

How boring he could be. Did I really want him back? "Look, Willy, I can't turn Rosie and the baby out. I'd be absolutely miserable if I did that."

"Rosie and the baby go. And the so-called friendship with Poor Liz ceases, or we go straight to court. You'll end up with nothing."

"I don't need your money because I own a piece of FK."

This was putting it rather grandly, but I've never had a head for figures. The effect on Willy was stunning. He was holding the glass paperweight, and when the phone beeper on his desk suddenly lit up, he dropped it and cracked the glass top of the desk. He reached out one finger to test the damage and misaimed and cut himself.

"Willy, what's the matter with you?"

He screamed, "Get out of here! How dare you come here during office hours. It's typical of your inappropriate behavior that you come here during my working hours and start a hysterical emotional scene when you know very well I'm extremely busy and can't—" Cathy ran in with a baleful look. "Little accident, Cathy. We'd better remove it before the next patient comes in." When her back was turned he hissed, *"Get out of here!"*

When I told Billings about this interview he said, "You've been extremely foolish, Dinah. You've just cut your support down seventy-five percent."

"It's always been hard for me to lie."

"In that case you'll get a lousy settlement."

"I don't care about money."

"If that's true, you're irrational and I'm dropping your case."

Liz said, "Now Willy thinks you don't need him."

"But I do. I miss him."

"Not where it counts."

"What do you mean, where it counts? Is money the basis for everything?"

She said thoughtfully, "I'm just about convinced that it is. It's made the big difference in my life anyway."

This was depressing. I'd thought Willy would be pleased about the FK money because then he wouldn't have to give me so much. But to him, it meant he'd lost control of me. I suppose this was what made him start to "go sour," as they said afterwards, though in fact he'd been souring for a long time. I knew something was wrong with him, especially when Jason told me he'd blacked out one evening in the hotel room, then tried to swear Jason to silence. I told Jason he'd better move back home.

"I can't, Mom. He doesn't have anybody to take care of him."

The day after I heard this, Emerelda came in with that dazed, frazzled look she had when the loas had been giving her a hard time.

"Emerelda, not the loas. God, I have enough problems."

"Mistress, the battle between Ogoun and Damballa must be stopped, or I fear the consequences for Mister Doc. In a dream I saw him being smitten down and I fear for his safety." She'd known even before I told her. "I have consulted Prudie, and she and I agree that the only salvation for this family is a hounfest right here in your backyard. A week from Saturday will be the full moon, and I strongly urge you to do it then."

"Drums and bonfires and spooks *in our yard?*"

"Yes, Mistress. I will arrange the whole thing. I am devoted to this family, and I will do anything in my power to drive away the spell which has been on it for so long."

I said halfheartedly, "It isn't a spell; it's just life problems."

"No, I fear you are wrong. It is a charm of the very worst

kind. I only pray that we can break it." Her dark eyes
looked hard into mine. "You must accept your spiritual
powers, Mistress. I feel they will ride your life forever, long
after your memories are returned. You will not be truly
happy until you open your heart to these things."

Okay. I told her to summon her houngans. I had nothing
to lose. If it meant another night in jail, so what? It would
be warmer than my house. And the house was in Willy's
name. So the neighbors yelled a little. Maybe they'd join
us. I needed a little pleasure in my drab life, and I'd enjoyed
being possessed the last time. And it might be good for
Rosie, who didn't have much fun either. To my surprise
Liz was unenthusiastic.

"Well, it was fun once, Dinah. But I was never as
thrilled about it as you were. I got where I am by hard
work, not voodoo."

She had a point. After a tour of FK's brand-new computer, we were sitting in her elegant glass-walled office
overlooking Central Park. Her good-looking male secretary
was serving us espresso and miniature croissants. On the
wall were framed certificates of her membership in the
Young Presidents' Club and the Fortune 500. She was a
Top Girl and *Cosmo*'s Woman of the Year. She wore a
beautiful silk suit in midnight blue, and her hair, blonder
than before, was expensively casual.

"It took a lot of hard work, plus some plain old common
sense. For instance, a computer survey showed that lonely
people don't trust redheads, so I changed my hair. And that
old couch where you're sitting?" It was the only tatty-
looking piece of furniture in the room. "That's where I sit
with new clients. That's where the truth comes out. I had
a woman last week who thought she was looking for a
husband, but it turned out what she really wanted was a
mother. I don't think we could have discovered that sitting
on the Breuer chairs."

"I suppose you think I'm crazy."

"Well, of course, dear. And that's why we all love you."

The preparations began early on the day of the full moon. Six Haitians arrived in the afternoon and began setting things up in the backyard. It was all quite elaborate. Besides the bonfire there were a couple of charcoal burners and a lot of decking out of our crabapple tree. By evening it was hung with scarves and ribbons and bells, and underneath were a lot of little bowls containing eggs and flour and coal and soap and glass beads and God knows what else. To my horror there were two live chickens in wooden cages that we were going to sacrifice.

"Emerelda, we'll catch poultry fever or something. I'm worried about Penny."

"Oh, Mistress, this will purify the little girl and put rainbows in her heart."

There was something about hounfests that appealed to children, and Rosie was an eager participant, as was Jason, who came over after telling Willy he was going to the movies. And late in the day George turned up with his broad, beamish smile.

"I wouldn't miss it for the world. I came down on the shuttle."

"George, Billings says you can't stay here."

"I know, darling. I came for the anthropology."

As darkness fell Prudie brought Charlotte down in her wheelchair—Charlotte who had physically aged but remained more or less at her previous state of addlement. George, Jason, Rosie, and I put on our costumes, and then the drums started: high African drums, pounded by three tall, black, good-looking houngans.

Our little Manhattan yard, with its dirty bricks and dusty bushes, became an enchanted tropical glade. As the drums beat and the candles flickered, we all danced around the bonfire—Rosie and I and the mambos in our white dresses and red turbans, our bare feet pounding on the hard ground, and George and Jason in brightly colored shirts tied up at the waist. Over our heads, dozens of strands of beads, hanging on the tree, glittered in the firelight, swinging gently back and forth. Tiny bells trilled and the drumbeats got faster and faster, taking our hearts with them. I felt myself start to drift in and out of consciousness in that unforgettable way, and then I felt a sudden weight on my back, and I knew I'd been mounted.

It was only during possession that I understood some of the strange experiences of my mind. Now I possessed *them;* I was finally in God's house, in touch with my deepest self. This deep, mysterious place was not frightening but teeming with life, alive with light and song and populated by innumerable strange creatures. I experienced the pull of Ogoun and Damballa, struggling over the dark cloud still in my head, the unremembered memories. In my possessed state I didn't really care which of them won; the memories seemed unimportant for the moment. What did I care, if I could come back here? But afterwards these visions faded, and I couldn't remember quite what had seemed so clear at the time.

It was only later that I felt surprise that Liz and Jessie had been dancing too in houn dresses, that Liz and I talked together in a language nobody else understood; together we could see straight down the long tunnel that leads to everything. And there was Jessie with a white scarf on her head, eyes downcast, walking slowly along like a bride. Later I learned she had been mounted by Erzilie, most feminine of the loas. And there was George crawling along the ground like a snake and eating the egg from the dish; he was ridden by Damballa. And Jason, staggering around with a bottle of Mount Gay in his hand, Baron Samedi himself! On the fringes of our firelight, other small Haitian ladies tended to Penny and Charlotte, the young and the old. I saw Charlotte's wrinkled old white face smiling and nodding to the beat in the flickering light. I only half remember holding the flapping, screeching chicken and biting off its head.

It goes without saying that a hounfest is a very sexual
experience, what with those drums of Dahomey and the
rum everybody keeps swigging. At some point, apparently,
George and I just ran at each other and fucked over in a
corner of the yard. Emerelda told me later, but I don't
remember. George said he'd had me up against the wall of
the house. It made me realize that a lot of the fun of
anything is remembering it afterwards. Though George
told me it was incredibly exciting, it's as though it never
happened. It was just one more sensation in the kaleidoscope of the evening when I and the people I loved best in
the world danced in possession around the fire, along with
a couple of neighbors who came down and joined us.

And Willy.

I'll never know why he decided to come over that evening, and he has since refused to discuss it. But I think that
he came over to make up, to drop the lawyers and the
divorce and embrace Penny again and let Rosie stay. Or
maybe he only came looking for Jason, who was supposed
to be at the movies with some kid and then didn't come
home. Anyway, he came. Emerelda looked up when George
and I were going at it against the wall of the house and
everybody was dancing around the bonfire to the drums,
and there was Willy looking out the kitchen window. Staring. Mouth open. Wild-eyed. Taking it all in. She says he
screamed, but I should think somebody would have noticed, and Emerelda isn't one for accuracy. Nobody noticed
or heard him except her, but later the whole story came
back through Billings, so I know it was true—Billings who
by that time I had no more need for.

But I knew nothing, only that the spirits had smiled on
all of us and the night was sweet. Emerelda and Prudie
dumped us one at a time in the inflatable kiddie pool we'd
filled with water and magic leaves. A bunch of wet dolls we
were, Liz, Jason, Jessie, George, Rosie, and me. My family.
Charlotte singing a waltz in her old cracked voice; Penny

gurgling and chanting in the arms of one of the houngans
—tiny and pale against his shining mahogany skin. The
last faint beats, the last flicker of the bonfire Jason had stood
in without pain. And an audience watching from surround-
ing fire escapes, too fascinated to call the police.

Liz said in the tub, "If this gets out I'm ruined."

"This is better than Fort Lauderdale," Jessie exulted.

I was sloshy with sentiment. "I love all of you."

I've sometimes thought that if by some trick of the mind
or change of the heart Willy had been able to kick off his
shoes, pull off his tie, and knot his shirt above his waist to
dance with us, things might have ended differently. But he
couldn't. What was easy for some of us was hard for others
and impossible for him. You had to be able to unhitch your
mind in a certain way and just let it happen. But Willy
turned and ran.

We all slept that night more or less where we fell, and
when I woke up I felt peaceful and purged. I was flat on the
living-room rug, and Jason lay nearby on the couch. But I
began to have an ominous feeling as Liz staggered in.

"Dinah, this is the last time we ever do this. The whole
thing is for fruitcakes."

The backyard was a wreck, littered with burned charcoal,
chicken feathers, and blood. It took half the day to clean it
up. Said Jason, "Mom, that was some trip last night, but
what happened?"

"I just had a few friends over for drinks."

It's hard for me to recount the events of the next two
days, partly because I had to put them together from the
reports of others and partly because they were so terrible.
For even if I wasn't there, they had everything to do with
me and Willy and our life together, and some contest which
only Willy had known about and which he, God help him,
had lost.

He must have "gone sour" before he went into the operating room that Monday morning to reattach the two fin-

gers of the famous sculptor Renatti, whose girlfriend, possibly jealous of the nude he was working on, had chopped them off with a cleaver and then, horrified at the magnitude of her act, had sealed the fingers neatly into a Ziploc sandwich bag and delivered them, along with Renatti, to the emergency room of Episcopal Hospital. It was a case tailor-made for the famous Willy's epoxy technique, in spite of the dwindling popularity of the technique because of the digital detachments. In went Willy, scrubbed and gloved and restored for a brief hour to his former glory; then, while everyone stood around and watched, he proceeded to sew the fingers on backwards.

People can hardly believe that such a thing happened at Episcopal, the most prestigious teaching hospital in the country, where the rich and famous from all over the world go with their maladies and which boasts the very latest equipment and the best-funded research programs and the most brilliant doctors. Well, let me tell you, these things happen more often than you think. Willy's misfortune wouldn't have gone past the walls of the O.R. except that Renatti happens to be well known, and his work was currently on exhibition at the Museum of Modern Art, and the girlfriend's impulsive gesture had gotten into one of the afternoon papers.

Now that the whole thing is out, I understand that it was inconceivable to the people in the O.R.—the nurses, the anesthetist, and Mac Valpey, who was assisting—that Willy was actually sewing on those fingers so that they bent and pointed toward the back of the hand, rather than the other way around. It would be like Cooley and De Bakey planting a liver into somebody's chest—so inconceivable that for several precious minutes an observer wouldn't believe his own eyes. But look at the bad books by famous authors praised by critics or the meaningless economic statistics we believe just because they were computed by celebrities. To me it proved how successful Willy was, which I

tended to forget sleeping next to him, sorting his dirty
clothes, buttering his toast, hearing him belch and brush
his teeth. To the medical world he was a genius, and because they were so impressed by him, they bent their minds
around and said to themselves, "I must have seen it wrong,"
or, "I need new glasses," or, "Oh, he's doing it differently
this time."

So they watched while the first finger was done, and then
when he started putting the second one on backwards, Mac
Valpey grasped the incredible thing that not only was happening but that he was assisting with, and he put his arm
gently but firmly around Willy and said, "Willy, I'm taking over the operation." Slightly late, because they had to
undo the stitches and the glue had set and it got all mushy
and it was a mess and he lost the fingers anyway. And Willy
stood over on the side—more or less manacled by a burly
scrub nurse because they didn't want to open the door and
contaminate the "sterile field"—twitching and grinning
with his eyes bright and poppy, saying, "You bastards don't
know what you're doing. I'll have you in front of the medical board and I'll sue you for every penny you have. I'll
advise this man to sue for the loss of his digits."

This in itself might not have finished Willy as a doctor,
because a lot of things get swept under rugs. There's an
ophthalmologist who regularly operates on blind eyes, and
a renal surgeon who leaves in a kidney stone so he'll have to
go back in and get it. Oh, I could tell you stories! But the
trouble is, when the hospital or the good doctors try to go
after them, these creeps turn around and sue for threatened
loss of income—and usually win! So when Willy stood
there babbling about lawyers, everybody in the O.R. swore
silence and agreed to blame the failure of the operation on
the Ziploc bag. It might have worked except for what happened next.

Sometime that day or the next they found all the pills he
had stashed away in his locker. I'd never known, nor had

anybody else, that he'd been stoned out of his mind for
months and that his habit had escalated when our troubles
started. He'd been first spotted a few weeks before by a
nurse who saw him pouring Valium from the hospital store
into the pocket of his lab coat and who, because it was
Willy, couldn't believe her eyes. But she told another doctor and the two kept an eye on him. Then when she saw
him doing it again she reported him, and after the fingers
business the hospital officials opened his locker and out fell
a cascade of many-colored pills, pellets, and capsules. They
paged him ("Dr. Wakefield Dr. Willard Wakefield Dr.
Wakefield pick up please pick up") and when he went to
the hospital administrator's office, there was the chairman
of the board (a post recently vacated by Willy) and the dean
of the medical school and the president of the hospital staff,
two lawyers, and a psychiatrist—not Zigler who was
quoted as saying only three days before "If there's anything
wrong with Willy Wakefield's mental health I'll eat my
hat. The problems are all with the wife." They told Willy
he was fired and finished in the medical community and an
addict and crazy as hell besides, just like that, and put him
in the Dallas B. Schuylkill psychiatric wing and shot him
full of Thorazine.

I heard about it all backwards. First from the hospital,
asking me to come over because Willy was "discomposed."
Then a phone call from Chrissie saying she wanted to explain Portoff's role in what had happened, which I still
didn't know. So poor Chrissie had to tell me about the pill
business and a distorted version of the finger business and
explain that though Portoff had been the doctor who helped
incriminate him, it wasn't anything personal, but just that
Michael felt so strongly about character excellence and how
the medical profession should be above suspicion, etc., and
that he had to turn Willy in.

Worse yet, Chrissie managed to spill, Portoff had let
Willy know months before that he'd seen me kissing a

strange man in the Oak Bar. Which Willy dismissed as
fabrication (due, no doubt, to his belief that I disliked
kissing men), but it stayed in his unconscious mind and
festered there—one more thing to erode what was left of
our love.

Walking into that hospital room was terrible. They'd
warned me, and a nice nurse named Lola held firmly on to
my arm as I walked over to the bed, saying, "Okay, Mrs.
Wakefield, you gotta be strong now." Mac Valpey was
there, in tears. But nothing could prepare me for seeing
him lying there in one of those cribs, glassy-eyed and hol-
low-cheeked, staring at the ceiling and occasionally saying
something that sounded like "glub-glub." Whatever our
troubles, we were still legally married, and I *felt* married,
and I knew I'd stick with him and see him through this.
He looked at me but didn't recognize me at all.

Then Mac and I went to the cafeteria, where we tried to
have lunch, though neither of us could eat anything. He
told me all about what happened in the O.R. and how he
didn't know whether to be guiltier because he was the one
to recognize Willy's madness or because he'd let the whole
ghastly thing happen at all. I told him I was grateful for
his friendship. And poor Mac broke down and sobbed and
said Willy was a great human being, and I cried too, and
so did a few other people who stopped by our table. I was
touched to know all these people had cared so much about
him.

They replaced the drugs in his system with other drugs
and told us to wait. So I went home and took care of the
house as I'd always done. Emerelda blamed herself because,
she said, the hounfest had caused the whole thing and I
hadn't gotten the rest of my memories back anyway, even
though Willy had been smitten down, and she'd done
something wrong and wasn't worthy of being a mambo. She
was going home to Haiti to walk barefoot into the jungle

and consult the high hounpriest, Ti Cousin, who knew everything.

Then Billings called. He said that since Willy had gone mad I had easy grounds for divorce and I'd get everything, hands down, real neat and easy. I said I didn't want a divorce, because I didn't believe in hitting somebody when he was down. I was in legal limbo because Willy had closed all the charges and put the bank accounts and money markets in his name only, so I couldn't pay the bills. I had the FK money, though that wouldn't last long, but Billings said Willy was legally responsible for me. He and Crossway had weighed all the possibilities. Willy could walk out of the hospital the next day, perfectly sane and clear-headed, and direct them to proceed with the divorce action. Or he could rave from his bed that he wanted to stay married, but since he was legally insane, they didn't have to listen, in fact they were professionally obligated *not* to listen. On the other hand, if he raved that he hated me and didn't want to stay married to me, they had to listen because that's what he'd said in the first place. (But really because that way they'd get paid, which they wouldn't at all unless they put it all back in my name, which fact, when I pointed it out, cleaned up the matter immediately.)

We were all deeply affected by what had happened. Liz was very serious and silent whenever it came up. Con and Jessie were more afraid than ever that they were doomed to go crazy like their parents. We were all devastated. It was as though Willy and I had never separated and talked divorce. It didn't matter anymore. And Jessie said we were all behaving as though Willy were dead, when in fact he was just sick for a while. But a staff psychiatrist at the hospital told us the prognosis was lousy and we should be prepared for the possibility that Willy was permanently psychotic and would have to live out his life in hospitals.

Even George and Rosie felt terrible—Rosie because she loved the way Willy had loved Penny, and George because with his undaunted optimism he thought Willy was a hell of a nice guy in spite of everything. George came down whenever he could, and Rosie was a tremendous help after Emerelda left for Haiti, doing her share around the house, taking a course in word processing, and talking about getting a job or going to college at night. But the worst part was that Con and Jessie resented them and blamed them for what had happened. As for George, in loving Willy again I'd never loved him more, as though love regenerated itself when it was being used, like mother's milk. We'd never made love more tenderly, which George seemed to feel too.

After a couple of months they moved Willy from the Dallas B. Schuylkill Pavilion to the Bloomingdale psychiatric hospital in White Plains, where they had antique oriental rugs and grandfather clocks and served martinis on the terrace. Willy improved a lot there. Though he said he hated me and wouldn't talk to me, he recognized me when I came to visit him. At first they only let us be together with an orderly, but after a while, when Willy was calmer and more used to the place, they let us take walks around the grounds together.

It was September by then and the days were still and warm, with a golden bronze light, and the vines and shrubs were beginning to produce autumn berries. Maybe the beauty of nature affected poor, ash-pale Willy, with his strange haircut and his frightened brown eyes. Something in him began to soften. As time went by, I began to get the impression of sickness struggling with health, which is the way Grimes, the staff shrink, defined it.

I'd say, "Willy, Con is doing fabulously well at Yale and has two A's and two B's."

He'd beam. "I always knew he was bright." (Health.)

"And Jessie's doing pretty well too, though her interests are different. She told Liz she wants to be an actress."

"I don't know who Liz is." (Sickness.)

I was supposed to accentuate the positive.

"Our kids are successes."

"They aren't our kids, Dinah. They're mine, strictly speaking." Which Grimes would have called health because it was "reality," but I didn't think it was very healthy because it rang of old troubles. Not so easy to sort it out, and between this and the no-no's (Willy's work, our divorce, madness, illness, and evil in general) I had to do a lot of pussyfooting. Wipe out the disaster and we had no conversation left.

And there were setbacks. Phil and Ping were back in town for what was now their annual visit from Borneo, because New York was where their true happiness had begun. After they arrived, Phil went first to see Charlotte, and Prudie told him where Willy was, and in his distress he went straight off to see his brother without talking to me first. Phil went flapping in with his bells and burlap and a little crown of daisies he wore for the occasion, and Willy took one look at him and began screaming in terror and spent three days curled up in a ball—while Phil narrowly missed being committed himself. (Said Grimes, "I'm hesitant about making these snap judgments, Dinah, but knowing the brother's sexual orientation and Willy's classic response, I'd say we could make a ballpark guess about the basic conflict.")

Being at Bloomingdale, Willy missed the publicity. It was started by some eager little reporter. She saw the story about the girlfriend chopping off Renatti's fingers and knew about Willy's technique, and somewhere in her fertile little brain were memories of the voodoo housewives in jail. She put it all together in a story that caught her editor's eye, though none of us had told her anything, of course, and the hospital was keeping mum. But because of all the current talk about incompetent doctors, malpractice suits, and badly run hospitals, the story picked up steam. *The New York Times* ran a three-part feature on the subject, and *New York Magazine* had a story about us with a lifelike cover

drawing of Willy in his scrub suit, holding up two dismem-
bered fingers and smiling crazily.

Somebody had even told the writer about Liz's having
been crazy and the hounfest in the backyard and our separation and Rosie, and even the Lesbian Love Nest; so much
in fact that I realized there was a family leak—though from
whom I don't even want to know. I can't blame Portoff,
because there were things in that article known only to our
family, which the writer described as "extended beyond Dr.
Wakefield's endurance."

All this publicity destroyed any possibility of Willy's
being able to practice in New York again, or not for a long
time anyway. The quotes from Mac Valpey and Bill Goldstein and the head of Episcopal and Mike Portoff trying to
minimize the whole thing just made it worse, because they
seemed to prove that the medical community would do
anything to avoid disciplining one of its own. So Willy had
to be sacrificed to prove how tough and principled they
were and how they wouldn't tolerate any deviation from the
strictest possible ethic; their comments were laced with only
a few sighs about "the loss of a brilliant mind."

And then there was Renatti's inevitable malpractice suit,
which won the highest award on record—five million—
which sent the malpractice rates up higher, and the physicians' fees jumped twenty percent to cover the new insurance rates and the new tax shelters they had to get for their
increased income, and more people were sick because they
couldn't afford medical care, and everything went back to
the hopelessly escalating spiral where the poor got sicker
and the doctors got richer. The only difference being that
the sculptor Renatti now had five million dollars, and all
the other people with digital detachments were rushing to
court to see if they could come out as well as he had.

Willy only learned about all this very gradually over the
next months as he improved and we thought he could take
it. I knew I had to get him out of Bloomingdale; it was

costing a fortune. He'd become quite docile and agreeable, if a little sad.

"Willy, what do you think of the idea of leaving New York and going to live somewhere else?"

Willy, slowly: "Where do you mean?"

"Well, maybe that island in the Caribbean we found that night, do you remember? I thought we might go there and live for a year or two and see how we like it."

Willy, slowly: "How could we do that?"

"We'll rent the house, pack up and go. All of us. I'll do the whole thing. I'll find a place to live and maybe you could work at a clinic or something, if you want."

Willy, slowly: "How could I do that?"

"I'll take care of everything."

Grimes didn't approve. "Jesus, Dinah, he'll blow up down there, and then what'll you do? He should stay here for another six months at least."

"The insurance is running out, and it's either this or a state hospital. Even if he blows up he won't do anything harmful; he's never been violent in his life."

But after more meetings and examinations they decided that Willy had come together pretty well. There were a lot of people who had one psychotic episode under stress and recovered and never had another. They agreed that life on a quiet tropical island might suit him very well—"Until he's ready to get back on the fast track again," said Grimes, "in the Big Juicy Apple."

The response from the family to this plan was discouraging.

Jessie wailed, "You're destroying our home!"

And Conrad—"God, Dinah. Do we have to go so far? How about something closer, Westport or Oyster Bay?"

I explained again. "Con, the idea is to get him away from everything and let him start again. In Westport every pool and tennis court would be awash with practicing physicians, don't you see?"

Jessie said tearfully, "You're ruining my life. I knew you would. You hate me. You always have."

"Jessie, stop the crap," Liz told her.

Jessie fumed, "Nobody thinks of me and how I have to explain my weird family to my friends. Now I'll be a latch-key child." Liz and I exchanged exasperated looks.

Later Liz said to me, "Don't worry about all this stuff, Dinah. I can make my own schedule now, and I have plenty of room in the new co-op. I'm available for them. You have done a wonderful job with my children—never mind what they say."

We were sitting in the kitchen. The house was half bare of the furniture, which was being auctioned off. The rest Liz would take and distribute to the kids as they needed it. I was exhausted from everything I had to do and teary about leaving. Liz and I sniffled a bit over our tea as the new tenants tramped around upstairs examining bathrooms and closets. "I hate them," Liz whispered. In her jeans and sweatshirt, she looked as young as she had the day she'd walked in with the lawyer, fourteen years before.

"I'm going to miss you," I told her. "I hate change. I can't even invite you to come and stay with us."

It was painful to leave Liz, even worse than leaving George and Rosie and Penny. I loved them and I was concerned about them, but they were newer in my life, and my love for Liz had the resonance of years. But I was pleased with Rosie's plans for living in an ashram for single mothers a few miles from George.

George said, "Don't worry, Dinah. I'll keep an eye on her. And Jackie's softening a little because the baby's so cute."

"Well, she better not soften much. Penny's mine, not hers."

On the last night in the house, George and I made love for the last time. It might have been the imminent separation that made us both so excited, almost insatiable. But even though deep in the night George wept and said he loved me and always had, and he'd tell Jackie to take a hike if I just gave him the word, that I should give up this ridiculous plan and lock Willy up somewhere, I still knew my real love and loyalty were for Willy and whatever future we had in St. Petin. I said, "I'm deeply touched, but I'll bet you wouldn't say it if you didn't know Willy and I were getting on that plane tomorrow." And George couldn't reply.

According to plan, the three children, Charlotte, and I went by limousine to White Plains, where we picked up Willy before going directly to Kennedy Airport. The kids, in spite of their initial grousing, were wonderful; now they couldn't do enough for Dad's rehabilitation, fussing over him with pillows, glasses of water, and whatever else they thought he needed. Meanwhile I fretted over this strange thing we were doing.

So we made it to San Juan, and then to St. Pet's, to our new house on Yankee Beach. It was so beautiful and open to the sea and the breeze was so fresh and sweet-smelling that we all fell in love. The five servants were bobbing and smiling and beaming at us, and most of our luggage had arrived, and the kids were enchanted by the beach and the lizards crawling up the walls and the big white knots of netting over the beds.

And Willy, whose face had been knotted into a frightened, polite grimace all day long, gave me a real smile at last and held out his arms to me for the first time in what seemed like—oh, *years*.

Dinah

———

'd say the fever chart of our life on St. Pet's went rapidly
up and then rapidly down. At first the openness and
freedom of the place was exciting to our Manhattan-bred
kids, who tore all over the island on their mopeds, explor-
ing this lovely place with its cane fields and white surf
beaches and patches of jungle, whose small, dark people
with lilting voices walked barefoot along the road, baskets
of fruit or laundry on their heads. Willy and I went for
walks early in the morning or late in the afternoon when it
was cooler, up the beach or along the road to English Town,
or back up into the hills past the shanties and lean-tos where
most of the people lived. The air smelled of earth and
burning charcoal and jasmine and fishy saltiness.

Willy was, on the surface, contented—so considerate, so
constantly smiling, in fact, that it made me nervous.

"Have you walked too far, darling? Tell me if you're
getting tired; we'll start back. Those shoes don't look very
comfortable."

"They're fine. I'm fine."

"What an interesting island this is, with its cross-
cultural currents. Look at the faces of the servants: you can

see African and Carib and Spanish characteristics. And one
of them—Eureka, I think—looks Mayan Indian. Now
Dinah, you must tell me if you don't like any of them.
We'll just go up the mountain and get another."

"They're fine. I like them all."

"Are you happy here, darling? I don't mean happy,
really. Contented. I suppose I'm asking if you have any
regrets about leaving New York."

"Maybe sometimes. But I do like it, Willy."

"We'll go back for a visit. Aren't you getting a little
burned, Dinah? Your nose and cheeks look red. Have you
been using sunscreen?"

"Yes, I have. I'm all right. I don't burn."

"That may be true at home, but this sun is different. Be
very careful, now—promise?"

"Yes, Willy." And so on.

Sometimes he talked about nothing, only smiled and
hummed as we walked along. The smile seemed to broaden
at some times and recede at others, and I'd wonder if it had
anything to do with me. Sometimes when I looked at him
I felt as though I'd stumbled into a conversation he was
having with someone else.

It was on one of these walks that we first saw the strange
scarred man shuffling along with his walking stick. Sparse
iron gray hair, stuck on his egg-shaped head like dusties
from the vacuum bag, cold pewter eyes in little round
metal-rimmed glasses, a sharp, hard nose, a mouth like a
slot. And dressed in a dark suit, stiff-collared white shirt
and tie, and shiny black boots. Some kind of button on his
lapel that might have been a swastika. The embodiment of
evil, scudding along in the dust of the hillside—and then
he turned out to be our neighbor. He grunted a minimal
greeting, gave us a dirty look, and slammed himself into
his house.

I cringed and Willy smiled.

Sometimes, up in the hills, I heard drums—those un-

mistakable drums of Dahomey. Sometimes I'd hear them at
night when we sat on the verandah after dinner, with the
lights out so the bugs wouldn't bother us too much. I hoped
Willy didn't recognize them. In the dark I couldn't see him
well and might have imagined it when the outline of his
body seemed to tighten as though pulled by invisible
threads. The sound had just the opposite effect on me. It
made me feel loose and sexual, which wasn't always welcome these days when Willy either couldn't or wouldn't do
much about it. Sometimes, sitting in the dark, Willy said,
"Dinah, we have to talk."

"I know, Willy."

Then silence. He'd say, "You start."

Jesus. "Okay. I guess we should talk about everything
that happened—our whole marriage. You know, I think
we were basically okay until the business about the—"

"I didn't mean that so much. I mean, all that was just
acting out the real stuff underneath. You know, there's so
much time to think down here. Things come into my mind
that I'd forgotten for years." Long pause, sighs and false
starts while I waited patiently.

"Yes, Willy?"

"It's so hard to talk about. But I know I have to face
these things." More pain and preliminary. At first I braced
myself for terrible revelations. Then he'd say, "Phil and I
jerked each other off when we were eight."

"So what?"

"Dinah, try to understand. Try to grasp the guilt."

Next time—"Phil and I jerked each other off not once,
but three times"—I had the brains to act shocked. Which
pleased him, so he went on for an hour about his Oedipal,
Charlotte's this, and Dad's that.

Objectively health was in the lead; sickness was held at
bay, though with difficulty, I sensed. The trouble was that
health was so boring. Willy's road back might have been
through his own uncharted places, but I was sick of hearing

about them. So I was glad when he started working at the clinic, which gave him a dayful of interesting things to talk about and think about, plus his new friendship with Mister Bagnold, a one-eyed weirdo who had suddenly left his London practice for reasons, I suspected, similar to Willy's, or worse. Baggie dropped names, titles, and peerages with an offhandedness that might have dazzled, but Baggie smelled of phoniness the way Jason smelled of ganja. Still, we were all losers here on St. Pet's, or we wouldn't be here. That's what Yankee Beach was all about.

It was fine while the kids were still here. Willy would go to work or wander off alone, and the rest of us would go swimming or snorkling or sit under the little straw beach hut, playing chess or poker or reading. Sometimes Lionel drove us to the open market at English Town, where we'd spend hours examining pots, pans, ballpoint pens, bolts of flowered fabric, sandals, straw hats, many-colored beads, and many much stranger objects, and then, in the square, the piles of glorious fruits and vegetables we couldn't resist. Here we'd meet our neighbors, because everybody, after all, had to eat. Jerry from next door, flexing his golden muscles. The Grim Reaper with his walking stick, which we'd decided concealed a tommy gun. The two British gays, the three Dutch whatevers, la famille française. The gays, Danny and Rickie, were the most approachable. If we came without Winnie, they'd advise us what to buy and how to bargain.

"Darling, don't touch the pawpaws, they're no good. But grab those baby bananas! And you know about ackee, of course: eat it only in season when it's soft and bright red. It's a treat with scrambled eggs, but if it isn't ripe it's a deadly poison. Rickie, sweet, pay attention; you're a nibbler and I would like to keep you around for a while."

We'd have hamburgers and beer at The Parrot Fish, in the cool shadow under the awning. Then drive home for the sacred siesta.

Then Con and Jessie went back and Jason started school, and Willy started with the Holocaust, which I looked upon at first as a nice hobby. It was better to see him reading than sitting and staring into space with that smile on his face and his lips moving. It released me from a certain responsibility, but it left me empty-handed. Liz had warned me about being a displaced housewife. And Geraldine would come roaring home on her motorbike. She'd come in, wearing her nurse's uniform, and find me dozing on the verandah.

"It's none of my business, Dinah, and I don't want to seem pushy. But I am so much happier since I found some fulfilling work to do and the opportunity to work side by side with two brilliant physicians such as your husband and Mister Bagnold. And my new career has made a big difference in my relationship with Jerry. He doesn't take me for granted the way he used to. I think he respects me more for being my own person. Shouldn't you think about a career or some occupation . . ."

So far I'd managed to avoid ever going to an office or any other place of gainful employment, and it was my dearest wish to continue. But I was at loose ends since Willy had rapidly begun to retreat into his old suspicious, crabby self. And now he often strolled down to English Town in the evening to have a beer with Baggie. I dreaded the solitude. Shadows and strange sounds gave me the jitters. I'd sit alone on the verandah, and from the kitchen porch on the side of the house I'd hear the girls' soft grave voices and occasional laughter and the sound of their portable radio. If I went for a walk, I'd pass them sitting there barefoot with their legs splayed apart to keep cool, the bright overhead light shining on the little porch like a stage light. They'd greet me politely, "Good evening, Mistress." Silence while I walked by. Then soft chatter and giggles.

Con and Jessie spent Christmas in New York with Liz, so the rest of us did our best together. We dug up a small

tropical tree and put it in a pot and decorated it, or Jason
and I did, and Charlotte helped in her fashion.

"Mom," he said, "do you think this is working?"

"You mean the Christmas tree?"

"No, I mean St. Petin."

I said, "It has to work."

He said nothing. Once a clownlike, expressive child, now
he strove for impassivity. The slight tremor of his lower lip
went straight to my heart. "It isn't much of a Christmas,"
he said finally. I'd thought of having a party, but the oddity
of the guest list was discouraging. Geraldine and Jerry.
Baggie. Danny and Rickie. The Beast of Buchenwald.

On New Year's Eve, when the maids wanted to leave
early to go to their party, I must have looked particularly
pathetic because Christophena said, "Perhaps you and Mister Wakefield and Master Jason would care to come to our
party yonder up the mountain."

I was thrilled. "Oh, we'd love to! Will there be dancing?"

She gave her big, cheerful laugh. "What kind of party is
it that has no dancing?"

Willy wouldn't go and we came close to a fight, which
I'd been carefully avoiding for so long that the bottled-up
anger was overwhelming.

"And why not?" I asked.

"Because we don't belong there. She just said it to be
polite. If we went we'd put a damper on things."

"I don't believe that, Willy. I think you're talking color,
and it's disgusting."

"There *is* color, Dinah. No matter what vision you have
of St. Pet's being some happy Garden of Eden. Baggie says
there are very specific ground rules and we don't know what
they are. If we'd had some notice I could have checked it
out with him. But I'm damned if I want to start a fucking
revolution. Look what happened in Cuba."

I said, "Well, I'm going and you can't stop me." I looked

at Jason, playing solitaire on the floor of the bedroom where we were bickering. "Want to go with me, Jason?"

"Jason goes nowhere. This is the night they all get drunk and throw bombs at each other. If you want to go out and get blown up, that's up to you."

"Oh, God, Willy, they don't throw anything. A glass of rum and a little merengue around the floor. We'll be the only people on the whole island sitting home tonight."

And so on. I ended up going, leaving Willy with his masseters rotating, and Jason came along to chaperone as well as protect me from the murderous Rasties that Willy knew to be running loose in the cane fields. The party was lovely and got me through the rest of the winter. A whole bunch of people, all ages, sizes, and shapes, dancing on a high terrace overlooking the sea. Colored lanterns and a steel band, lots of Mount Gay, lots of flashing white teeth in shiny black faces. I had a multitude of partners, who taught me wonderful new steps, and I would have stayed all night if it weren't for Jason's conscience. So after a couple of hours we left and ran down the mountain singing.

At home Willy was asleep under the netting, still dressed, with *Mein Kampf* open on his chest. When I walked in his eyes popped open and he looked at me in the lamplight.

"Watch out, Dinah. I know."

Maybe he was half-asleep. I said, "You should have come with us; it was marvelous."

He laughed. "That's really funny. You don't know how funny that is."

By spring I was longing for a trip home. But Willy didn't want to *leave the island*—a new metaphor for exposing oneself to great danger.

"Of course I'm not going to try to stop you, Dinah. But I wish you'd think carefully about whether you want to."

"I have and I'm dying to."

"Well, I don't think it would be very good for Jason. It would cause him a lot of guilt, and he doesn't really want to go." Poor Jason didn't know what to do, so we compromised; he'd come and join me for a week or so. "I can't stop you from seeing that man, Dinah. Particularly since everybody would cover up for you, which you know very well. But if Jason lays eyes on him I'm wiring Crossway without any discussion. And Jason won't lie to me to cover your tracks."

"I'm not going to see George. I'm going to see Rosie and my granddaughter."

"Your fantasy granddaughter. The girl is a stranger and you know it. You and she planned the whole thing for reasons it's taken me all this time to understand. I guess I'm pretty trusting. And the fact that you'll *leave the island* just to see her proves it to me."

Oh, how tired I was of these conversations. I counted the days, and not because I was longing for George. Since we'd been here, George and Rosie had receded into the distance like a couple of people I'd once known but might never see again. But not Penny. By now she was probably walking and must have gotten two or three teeth, and I had missed these milestones. I imagined her staggering across the floor, laughing, saying a couple of fractured words. I could see a white pearl pushing its way through her pink satin gum. It would be unthinkable for her to go through much more of life without knowing her grandma.

Probably I shouldn't have left Willy. I wanted to go so badly that I talked myself into believing it was all right. And I'd been so careful, so conscientious for so long. I knew he was clean; there wasn't a pill around the place except for aspirin and antihistamines. He sounded a little peculiar, dropping hints I didn't understand. But how tired I was getting from carrying him. What good was health if it depended on me? I told myself that I was exaggerating my

own importance, that a separation would be good for us. As
the day got closer I quailed a little. There was a look in his
eyes I couldn't decipher.

As it turned out, he made it easier for me. Now he was
writing something, a big research project that would re-
quire all his attention. He had a phone installed, even
though we'd rejoiced in not having one. He talked of hiring
a secretary or research assistant. The dining room became
an office, and he was up at six to write for two hours before
going to the clinic. When research materials began spilling
into the living room, he turned one of the bedrooms into a
study. He should have done this ages ago, said he. Life on
St. Pet's had given him many new ideas that cried out for
expression. He'd reached the stage in life where it was his
duty to write, to make his contribution to the intellectual
mainstream, etc.

When I asked what he was writing about, he only said,
"Darling, I'd rather not talk about it yet. I'm not playing
the temperamental writer, but I'm afraid it'll go up in
smoke. Nonfiction of course. And related to my life. That's
all I'll say right now."

He looked so cheerful and confident that I could see why
so many people write books. It gives the illusion that
they're doing something important, a nice feeling to have
though not always true, considering that most of them go
unread. But as far as Willy was concerned, the result was
less important than his new optimism and his change of
heart about my trip.

"I can't believe I said all those stupid things, Dinah. I'll
have to ask you to forgive me as you have so often before.
You've always been my strength and the center of my life.
I want you to go and have a marvelous time; you deserve a
change. Give my love to Rosie and hug little Penny for me,
and don't forget to take lots of pictures."

It was the dark and the light, the sickness and the health.
Fear turning to trust and back to fear again. We'd probably

go on like this forever, Willy and I. We were people on a
stage where some crazed light director up in the rafters kept
changing the filters—from purple hate to rosy love, from
bitter green jealousy to bright confident yellow. Nice red-
and-blue mornings of industry as Willy made notes on legal
pads. Mauve evenings as we held hands and looked at the
sea. Even a couple of silvery nights. Not golden, silvery—
frissons and fondness rather than madness, but nicer than
we'd had in a long time.

By departure day I was almost sorry to leave. Willy and
Jason saw me off at the airport. Willy hadn't looked so well
in years—tall and straight, suntanned in his open blue
shirt. My Willy. We all stood sweating in the concrete
shack near a hand-lettered sign saying AIR PETIN, where the
personnel was either stoned or asleep and a portable radio
played steel drums. On one side was a little bar that sold
bottled beer and soft drinks, and nearby the rack of greasy
porn magazines, toward which Jason was sidling. Outside
on the tarmac was the tiny plane that would take me to San
Juan, where I'd catch the connecting flight to New York.
Two mechanics in shorts were tinkering with the propellers
between swigs of soda. My nerve failed.

"Willy, I don't want to go."

"Don't be silly, Dinah. Jason and I will be fine, and Con
and Jessie will be here in three days"—part of the plan. "I
can't get a thing done with you hanging around being
supportive, and the kids leave me alone. Between the clinic
and the book there aren't enough hours in the day."

We kissed good-bye—a long kiss, fifteen years long, and
full of our history. All the things that had happened to us
had thickened the texture of our marriage and made it
richer; the plain muslin had become brocade. I knew all of
his dark corners and he mine. Blindfolded, with only my
hands, I could have picked him out of a crowd. Whether
we liked it or not, we belonged to each other.

When they announced the plane, I deflected Jason's interest from a page of naked behinds long enough to kiss him good-bye. "Oh, good-bye, Mom. I'll see you."

I grabbed my suitcase and got into the plane. I was sweating in the white linen suit and high heels I'd put on to get the jump on civilized life. I looked out of the tiny cabin window at my two men. They kept waving as we took off and soared up into the cloudless blue sky. I watched, damp-eyed, till they were only flecks down there on our tropical island, till the island was only a white streak like a brush stroke on the sapphire sea.

Willy

——

et her go. Getting smart at last, Willy!

    For a long time I thought it was better to keep her here where I could keep an eye on her. Before I got the big picture—before I got *it*. When I still didn't understand and still thought it was a matter of having to get rid of crazy wife number two before she drove me out of my head. When I thought it was a matter for the courts. When I thought we were just another sad joke of a domestic tragedy to add to the now endless list of marital laughs at Cheerful Men. When I still thought she was . . . oh, crazy, all right, but on a manageable scale. When I thought my responsibility to my family was to get a divorce and save the kids. When at bottom I felt truly sorry for the poor woman, who'd been screwed since the day she was born. When I was still angry at myself and sick at heart for choosing her in the first place, when I was stupid enough to think memories could be willed away. When I was selfish enough to see the amnesia as some kind of benefit to me because then I could be her whole life. When I still thought half of what she said was true, even if I didn't know which half. When in some pathetic way I still loved her. When I

believed she loved me. When I'd catch myself thinking
every day or two that somehow, someday we could patch it
up. When I still thought that she wasn't as crazy as Poor
Liz and that perhaps Jason could be saved from the mental
illness I watch for with such fear in the other two—Conrad
when he gets all uptight and obsessive and Jessie when she's
a screaming bitch. When I was younger and stronger and
more optimistic. When I still believed . . . oh, in the ran-
domness of things, that if a guy had his fingers hacked off
it was because of Dame Fortune and nothing else. When I
thought that, for the most part, people did their best and
tried hard and if things didn't work out it wasn't anybody's
fault. When . . . when . . .

Where was I?

Oh, yes. That was before I got the big picture.

It was something that happened not all at once but gradually, after we moved down here. New York just didn't
work out. I was working hard; I got tired. We aren't the
first ones to get off the fast track in favor of a simpler life
and nature's wonders. Well, God knows I felt better getting
out of the city. But Dinah brought her troubles in the old
kit bag. I'd forgotten about the damned voodoo. If I'd
thought of it we would have gone to northern Canada. Or
to Montana, which I've heard is nice. Or even Florida, or
why not California? I've always wanted to go to Maine and
see that rocky coast. Mac and his new wife have a house in
New Hampshire. Mexico. Europe. The south of France.
Germany, right around Munich. I liked Brussels when I
was there. Or Switzerland; the kids could have learned to
ski. The Tuscan hills, or farther north in the Dolomites.
Sicily, if you duck the bullets. The Greek islands, one of
those tiny ones with whitewashed houses . . . Is it Patmos
or Mykonos?

Oh, yes . . . The Revelation came slowly, quietly, a little every day. It was like a previously invisible structure
that now fitted over us and our lives. An organizer—like

one of those things that hangs on the wall with plastic slots
for everything. Well, the Revelation, as I'm calling it hum-
bly, modestly—though there are times I could shout and
sing with triumph, just like when the first epoxy worked—
the Revelation has organized everything in the same way.
God, it's incredible. It's like a tiny golden key that opened
that big door of mystery—the one you think never gets
opened. Somebody put that little key in my hand and
showed me the keyhole, and inside was that big, complex
organizer—a sort of huge blueprint, or—no, more like the
control room in a nuclear reactor, yards and yards of shiny
switchboards and knobs and buttons and video screens, all
this tremendous control in one room, everything where it
should be, everybody doing his job at his own desk, and
Willy's got the key and he's in charge!

But Willy's not going to blow up the world—no.

What this is about is understanding, knowledge, making
sense out of all the chaos and craziness and wildness that
swirls through the human brain and threatens our sanity.
How often have I thought, Why does this have to be? Why
are things so unfair? Why are there rich and poor and some
have everything and some nothing? Why is there no justice;
why does evil so often win over good? Well, now I know,
or my James Bond computer does. It answers every question. If I want to understand something abstract, like the
nature of good and evil, the answer comes as a sort of
teleplay on the video. And the answer is always true.

For a while I just fooled around asking this and that,
trying to get a purchase on things. Not so easy. Willy's
magic computer creaked and groaned. I had to learn the
basic program, which took time. It was like learning a new
language, or rethinking physics in the light of new discov-
eries. And the basic premises were strange and almost re-
pulsive at first. But so was the splitting of the atom. The
roundness of the earth. Freud's theory of infant sexuality.
The crucifixion of Christ. The writing of James Joyce. Jog-

ging. Flying. Surgery . . . And all have turned out to be important, true, and useful. So here are the Premises of the Revelation, in all their raw, wild beauty:

1. Nothing is random. Everything is planned.
2. The human mind is naturally devious. This is not bad, but rather our salvation and the crown of humanity.
3. Innocence and trust are quaint, invalid concepts that evolved to idealize human relationships.
4. Everything must be in writing, signed, and notarized.
5. Revelation is *seeing the grand design.* Vigilance is a state of grace.

This is a basic, skeletal summation of an extremely complex theory which will take me the rest of my life to master. I've found the key to mastering thought.

I've always been a pragmatic guy. I had to see it to believe it, or feel it or smell it or hear it. It was hard at first to accept the reality of a vast, invisible infrastructure that organizes everything. And the minute I did, I wondered how I'd gone on so long assuming things were as they appeared and being unhappy a lot of the time, though I didn't admit it or even know it. I was locked into my knowledge and training, the only language I knew. Even therapy didn't help. Or love. Sex. Or marriage—which was pretty good for a long time. Fatherhood, though I love my kids. My work, which was the center of my life. Friendships, like with Bill and Mac. My happy childhood. Mother. Father. Phil. Money and its pleasures. Liz. Dinah. Zigler. Crossway. Billings. Episcopal Hospital. The house. The dog. The cat. Little Penny. Books. Art. Music. The culture of the city. The house in the country.

Soon I began to see the bones beneath the flesh, so to speak. Life through my X-ray machine was almost a vision. I had to struggle not to laugh with happiness, to suppress the smiles that crept over my face. But Dinah is a simple soul who thinks only of whether I appear quiet, contented,

and "good" according to her standards. No, Mommy, I'm
not taking any pills. (A lot you know!) Yes, I like the nice
sunset. Yes, I love my clinic and my poor patients and the
backwater shithole we live in and our asshole neighbors. It's
terrific, honey! It's everything we ever dreamed of! And
f'gosh sakes, we don't even have a mortgage! And meanwhile, in the shadow of my straw hat, behind my sunglasses, I'm smiling to myself.

The first tip was her reaction to Wertzheimer, our not-
so-friendly neighbor. Baggie has his number. Who cares?
says Dinah. The place is full of criminals under assumed
names; that's our Yankee Beach! Let him shake his past. All
he did was murder a few million Jews—that's his business!
So he shoved them into gas ovens. Kept their hair and wove
it into pillow slips. Live and let live! But by then I'm
starting to look below the surface. What's she so protective
about? I mean the woman isn't a murderess, as far as I
know. She's flaky but not evil. Then one day we pass
Wertzheimer on the road and she glances at him and drops
her eyes. He pretends he doesn't see. He's a mean-looking
bugger. This is a little different from her usual horseplay
with voodoo spirits and naked lesbians. That's only mildly
criminal. She mentions several times what a creepy guy he
is, which is self-evident.

Then messages start to arrive. She's folding up a piece of
paper when I walk into the room. Phone calls where there's
nobody on the line. Letters she thinks I don't see from
Boston, where the flimflam guy lives. Not much but
enough.

I push my buttons, pull my knobs! And there it is before
me: the plot of the year, of my life! Dinah, Wertzheimer,
nursie next door with the tits and her fag boyfriend, the
flimflam guy and the girl with the baby, and the unsinkable
Liz are all in on it! And Dinah's picked St. Pet's on purpose
to get into the hookup in a seemingly innocent way and to
join forces with Wertzheimer, who has a basement full of

shortwave radio equipment and computers and God knows what else to mastermind their plot for world domination, along with, no less, the KGB (which of course is just the old Waffen SS in new tutus), gay rights, and the Arab terrorists! The whole bag—torture, kidnapping, stolen nuclear weapons, economic blackmail, you name it. And it's been going on for years! The lost grandma agency is a front . . . Emerelda is an agent . . . And the dead lesbian on the car, that was like one of those gangland murders. And the amnesia was a front, a brilliant lie, to cover up a past that would make Lucrezia Borgia look like a girl scout. My Dinah!

For a while it was pretty bad. I thought about suicide every day but couldn't do it. I tried to swim straight out but always came back at the last minute and dragged myself up on the coral sand of Yankee Beach. I took a handful of pills one night and then puked them up . . . I know where the ackee grows, the poison plant. I got as far as putting some in my mouth, but I was too cowardly to do it. I examined the Revelation again and again to make sure I hadn't made a mistake. The evidence was all over the place. I would have to have been blind not to accept it. There had to be a reason it came into my head. I'd look at her while she slept. Kill her? It wouldn't be difficult.

But something in me began to shift. Whatever love there'd been dried up, and she didn't seem any more worth killing than the lizard on the wall. My first duty was to stop the plot. I'd bide my time, collect evidence, and put it together in a book. No hurry. Always caution, wariness, vigilance. Keep an eye on them; never arouse their suspicions; act crazy if necessary. Dinah's easy to fool . . . though I must say I underestimated her ability to keep a secret. It's sort of sad and ridiculous, Dinah and I spying on each other. She thinks she's fooling me, but I'm fooling her. Slowly, slowly, chapter by chapter. Let the tape unroll in my head; get it all down. Every night I bury it in a different place on the beach. Early in the morning I dig it up and shake it out and get to work. Every couple of days I have it notarized. It'll hit the stands just as I'm on the plane to Washington. I'll get an apartment there, which will be more convenient for the conferences with the President, State, and the CIA. They'll give me police protection.

Who says you can't start again at fifty-one? And D.C. isn't a bad place to live at all. Hey! Georgetown. Foggy Bottom. Arlington or Bethesda, might do a little consultation work at Johns Hopkins if I'm there. The Rock Creek area. The Watergate. Connecticut Avenue going out toward Chevy Chase is nice.

Oh God. The blackness, the pain. The clouds of doubt. What's the matter with me? I pay for the gorgeous clarity, the joy of walking into my control room, where the walls are white and the knobs are chrome and the directions are in red and blue. Sometimes I claw at those white walls; my fingers leave streaks. Sometimes they fall off and I can't put them back on. I'm clawing with bloody stumps. My mind is a shriek, my body a wound.

I try to hide these feelings from Jason, but he's worried about me. He's always asking me if I'm okay. I go to work like a zombie, half there. Old Baggie says, "Hey, Willy, you look a mite peaky. Wot say we get sloshed tonight?"

Always the same solution. It doesn't help much. It does for a while, then afterwards maggots chew at my feet, rats eat my face. Moths and mosquitoes go down my throat. I don't want to talk about the things in my head.

Baggie and I go to The Parrot Fish and drink rum. What a fucking land's-end dump, just like my life. A thatched roof on stilts, a few broken-down tables with oilcloth covers, a couple of naked light bulbs. A cruddy bar tended by that sinister lump of humanity, Bilge. Bilge has a putrifying skin disease and wisely stays in the dark. Baggie swears it's not contagious. And the clientele . . . One night there was a knife fight in there and the guy who lost was dead by the time we got him to the clinic. Thank God we didn't have to patch him up.

We watch Bilge slop rum into a couple of glasses and pray the stuff kills his germs. Baggie talks about his Harley Street practice and how evil people brought about his downfall. But he's got a pedigree down to there, and someday he'll go back to London and be lord or duke or whatever he thinks he is. He just has to get things together for a while. He has about as much chance of getting off this island as I do.

I tried out a little of the Revelation on him and he didn't understand, not that I expected him to.

"Nobody's fuckin' able to plan anything, Willy. They're all too stupid. Low, I'd call 'em. Assholes. Things aren't like they used to be. There was a time when people had some respect. When a man could expect certain things," and so forth. Well, I've got to be careful who I talk to. I talk to Baggie because there isn't anybody else. But Christ, I find myself missing Cheerful Men. It was always half a joke, our little men's club. Now I daydream about it. The eight of us around a corner table at Le Cygne or The Four Seasons . . . The food, the wine, the camaraderie. The good male friendship. The ease and pride of being on top. I wonder if they still talk about me or if I've been replaced by a dozen more interesting things—and I don't want to know the answer to that.

I'm in the woods where the ackee grows. I finally shook Asshole Baggie on the English Town road, where he's sitting on a rock with a bottle of Mount Gay singing "God Save the Queen." I'd rather have the bugs and the snakes and the land crabs than the sound of his voice. At least I'm alone, trying to think straight about what happened this evening.

Nurse Geraldine with the big tits and her fag boyfriend invited the Bag and me for dinner. Probably Dinah told her to keep an eye on me, or she thought I needed deliverance from the kids.

It's hard to be with them. Jason's used to me; he knows when to leave me alone. But the others are full of Yale-and-Smith bullshit and bright chatter. Questions about my book, which nobody sees. Little glances and murmurs and nudges. It all gets under my skin, and I've been spending more and more time alone in my study.

I've been feeling like shit lately. Willy's computer hasn't been singing along the way it used to. Once it was responsive and flexible and did my bidding smooth as silk. Now sometimes it's balky just like any ordinary appliance that breaks down, and how the hell do you get it fixed; who do you call; did you ever send in the guarantee? It stalled like a car just as I'm getting into the real revelations in the central part of the book. I try to forget it for a while, thinking maybe when I go back it'll run again. Sometimes it does, sometimes not. I've been stuck all day and what the hell, dinner next door sounds better than the many other social options of our glorious island. When I tell the kids I'm going, they look relieved and ecstatic and take off for English Town on their motorbikes.

Geraldine's gone to a lot of trouble, and I guess it was around then I began to wonder. The maids are serving drinks and fancy hors d'oeuvres.

"Dr. Wakefield, I hope you don't hold what happened against Jerry," Geraldine whispers when he's out of the room. "He's an extremely physical person and sometimes not too good at judging character."

"No problem," I tell her. Maybe I'm wrong about her. She's not a very good nurse but Christ, she works like hell. "And Geraldine, it's Willy, for God's sake."

"Well . . . Willy. Though I don't feel right saying it. There's another guest coming. I didn't want you and Dr. Bagnold to be bored; I know you're both used to the very best society."

I'm just sinking into a nice cold martini when one of the

girls opens the door and in comes Wertzheimer. I swear to
God I almost fainted. Baggie's staring out of the good eye
and the glass eye, both sunk in little folds and pillows of
pink flesh, mumbling, "I say," his mantra for puzzling
situations.

The minute this bird appears, looking as grungy as always in his old shiny wool suit, Willy's computer stands up
and sparkles. Everything starts zinging around, clickety-
click. Like always, whenever it's going like sixty, I'm on
my toes. No demons and no slopping around telling lousy
jokes. I watch Wertzheimer like a hawk as he hunches into
the room on stiff legs. When I catch his eye, the bastard
looks startled.

"I think we've met in passing," he says. Not a trace
of an accent. They must have worked on him to get rid of
it.

"I think we have," I say, never taking my eyes off him.
He's mostly bald except for a few dark little pieces of frizz
here and there, and his dim little eyes peer through thick
lenses. Everything about him looks dirty, as though he's
been hanging in the back of a Manhattan closet for about
twenty years. His lips separate to reveal a row of small
yellow teeth. He's smiling. He's talking about walking his
dog and the ticks on the dog or some other damn thing.
Geraldine's recommending tick remedies, shooting nervous
glances at me and Baggie in apology for the inferior guest
list.

I read once that all these bastards have swastikas on their
dicks and that's how you can tell. It was in some medical
journal. But I don't have to look. This guy has guilt coming
out of every pore. He apologizes for everything—sorry this,
sorry that. We're all drinking like fish. The maid's running
back and forth with martinis. Everybody's apologizing all
over the place. Baggie gets playful—his worst mood. He's
winking at me, which fortunately only I can detect, being
familiar with the movements of his little pink pouches. He's

grinning and saying to Wertzheimer, "I say, old chap, do you happen to be European?"

Wertzheimer looks uncomfortable. "No, American. Why do you say that?"

"You look Continental, sir. I know you've said you're American, but there's a look about you, I can't actually say wot, that I've seen on the Continent. A sort of . . . Continental look. Wot, Willy?" I get up and move to another chair. I want to observe. The build is similar to the flimflam guy. Could they be relatives? I assume Dinah's fucking this one too, but I'm stunned by her lousy taste. She might be doing it under orders, to keep him happy.

"I say, Rolfe, where did you say you're from?"

"Pittsburgh," Rolfe chokes, looking miserable and downing half a drink in one slug.

"Oh, Pittsburgh. I once knew a chap from there, very big in the steel business. But see here, if I had to guess I'd say, hum . . . let me see . . . German! The Rhineland!"

Pittsburgh must be a code. This bird is in charge, and deadly clever because he doesn't look like he's in charge of getting through dinner. But I know clear as day he's a highly respected member of the KGB.

Geraldine tries to get us to the dinner table, not so easy because when the Bag gets going on one of his one-note jokes not even the Holocaust could stop him.

"Ever been married, old chap?" He settles down next to him.

"Er, er, er . . ."

"Oh, for God's sake, man. She couldn't have been that bad." Rolfe pales. Baggie's two big front teeth are smiling merrily. "I mean, had she a name?"

Rolfe is miserable. "Dottie."

"Dot-tie! Oh, I say! Are you divorced?"

Geraldine's serving plates at the top of her lungs. "I hope everybody likes flying fish. Carmena makes a superb onion sauce and—"

"Listen, Rolfie. I've been divorced for ten years, best thing I ever did. She was screwing everybody in sight. Was that Dottie's habit too?"

Then Jerry kind of swells up. "Now listen, Doc. I don't think Rolfe here feels like answering all these questions."

"Balderdash." Wertzheimer looks like he couldn't talk if he wanted to. My heart isn't exactly breaking. His moldy complexion kind of shakes and he stares at his food. Dinner is flying fish and chochos and yams and the usual local stuff, plus a few bottles of some South American white wine. He glances at me a couple of times, the shifty bastard. He's one hell of an actor. He picks at his fish. By now the rest of us are having the usual conversation about how rotten life is in the States—crime, pollution, noise, high prices, greed, and lack of values—to prove how lucky we are to be living on a sandbar. Rolfie looks like he's going to die. He still hasn't eaten a bite. Is he sick? I've tapped him in. I know everything about the guy from the little village near Heidelberg on up. He looks at me from time to time. I don't flinch! But I've got to be careful; I'm walking a thin line. When I check out I'll do it in my own way. It's all in the book. I'm still planning the hows and wheres of publication, and how to coordinate it with the grand roundup by the FBI and the CIA.

We're all gabbling away and suddenly Rolfe says in dire tones, "My ex-wife lives in Pittsburgh. We were divorced twenty years ago and I can't even remember why. I came here to get away from the alimony and child support, and I never went back."

Dead silence. "I say!" exclaims Baggie.

Geraldine pats his sleeve and says, "Now you don't have to talk about these things, Rolfe. You have a right to your privacy just like the rest of us."

Rolfe says, "No, I want to talk. I never talk. I'm a lousy, lonely, mean bastard. The girls are twenty-five and twenty-seven, and I haven't seen them in all this time."

More silence. Actually I'm amused. What a story! Every-body's staring at him, Baggie included. Geraldine says ten-tatively, "Well, Rolfe, have you considered going back to see them?"

"I'm too ashamed," Wertzheimer whispers. "I've waited too long. I've been angry for twenty years, and I'm afraid to leave the island." A tear comes out of his eye. What a performer. I glance at the Bag, and his mouth is hanging open like a startled rabbit's. "I can't face them. I'm paying the price."

A depressed drunk. Well, maybe it's partly true. So what? He could have a Dottie in Pittsburgh. I'm watching him warily, with the tiniest of smiles I hope only he will see. But what's this little charade about? Then I feel an uncomfortable stab. He must realize I know. He's telling me something. I've got to play dumb, so I look sympathetic like everybody else.

Then there's a lot of maundering and sympathy and I-say-it's-not-too-late. He needs his daughters and they need him. There could be grandchildren! Then Wertzheimer says he's sorry to unload all this and he never has in twenty years but now he's drunk and we're all friendly and he feels like shit.

Baggie keeps winking. The stupid bastard, grinning away. I begin to feel uncomfortable. He believes all this, and Baggie was the one who spotted him in the first place.

Then Geraldine asks Wertzheimer why he's spilling all this now, and he turns to me and says, "Because of you and your family, Doctor." Looking me straight in the face with his little eyes like snails in the shells.

"I'm afraid I don't understand."

Then, God help me, he tells me that somehow we'd gone straight to his heart—especially after he heard that the two older kids were Dinah's stepchildren. We all seemed so happy together. He watched her and the kids on the beach or down at the market in the square or walking along the

road, laughing and talking. And he thought of Dottie probably remarried and how some other guy was father to his
two little girls, now possibly married with their own families. And he pulls out some old moth-eaten snapshots and
there he is with Dottie, who has a beehive, and two blurry
kids.

Baggie roars and slaps me on the shoulder. "Hey, old
chap, we were a bit off base, wot?" To the others he says,
"Willy and I thought—"

I kicked him. "Shut up, you fucking fool."

Baggie's stunned. "Hey, old chap, no offense."

By this time Wertzheimer's confessing and crying and
telling his life story, how he was born in Minnesota of
German extraction and hitchhiked to Florida and worked
his way through school and went into the real estate business. I begin to get the chills. I didn't know KGB members
were good enough for three Academy Awards. I run around
in my computer room pushing buttons, but I can't figure
out why all this is happening. I just keep turning up no-
entry.

I feel like shit. We all leave the table and have coffee and
brandy on the terrace. Everybody is telling Rolfe he should
go home and the girls will forgive him and maybe even
Dottie and it will be better than never seeing them. Do
they really think? They do. Occasional grateful glances at
me. After an hour and a couple of brandies he's ready to
phone the airport. He looks at me.

"I'll always thank you for this, Dr. Wakefield. And your
wonderful family."

I have to get out of there. Either the beach or the road. I
decide on the road. The room is spinning around. I choke
out a thank-you to the hostess and the Bag follows me as I
flee and they all stare and make worried noises. Jesus, are
Bagnold and I drunk. There's three roads; for all I know
we're running in circles. He's trotting along with his two
Bugs Bunny teeth shining in the darkness.

"I say, Willy, wot a dash."

"Wertzheimer's a Nazi, I know he is."

He's surprised. Somehow we're half sober for a couple of seconds. "Oh now, Willy, you can't not believe the poor chap's story. I mean good Lord, he was crying like a baby."

"I've never seen such an act and all of you fell for it."

"See here, old chap, you're dead wrong. He came in with a urinary infection and he most decidedly doesn't have a swastika on his pecker. In fact I recall seeing a small American flag."

Dinah

———

Penny was in the nursery, giving her doll a bath. She was almost two now, and the more I looked at her, the more I thought she looked like me. The morning light came in and touched the dark straight hair that curved into the nape of her small neck, and her eyes were blue like George's. But she didn't know me, and I sat down on the floor and devoted an hour to winning her heart, bestowing some presents from St. Pet's—a carved dog, a funny patchwork pillow, some colored beads.

Rosie, watching us, said, "I thought you'd forgotten us."

"You can be sure I'll never do that." She'd cut her hair and neatened up her appearance, and Penny wore bright yellow rompers. There was something about the lift of that little chin that I was sure looked a lot like mine.

Rosie told me that the literal translation of the word *ashram* is "towards exhaustion." I'd expected bare feet and sitar music and a lot of kids strung out on dope. Instead I found a large, pleasant suburban frame house occupied by half a dozen single mothers and their babies. All the young women were gainfully employed. Nor were most of them, like Rosie, caught. Several had chosen to have their babies

without fathers. Some had used the Harvard sperm bank.
This way they could bring up their children without inter-
ference. There was a running argument about whether or
not men were necessary. They were delighted when I offered
to move in for a couple of weeks to cook and help out with
the children. George turned up often and took me to dinner
a couple of times—once with Rosie and once without. But
it was tricky because of Jackie.

"She understands that I want to see Rosie alone from
time to time, but I can't stay, Dinah. I mean I don't want
to start some big brouhaha for nothing when you seem to
be staying married to Willy."

"I can't hit him when he's down," I said. Nothing had
changed. I was very glad to see him. He was a little balder,
his pot a little bigger. But just as good-natured.

Something funny was starting to go on in my head, but
this time it didn't seem to be the loas. I began having some
of those déjà-vu experiences I'd had right after I came to.
Penny's breakfast egg in a little blue dish, George's purple
tie . . . where had I seen them before? In the yard one day
I stared so fixedly at a passing helicopter that Rosie asked
me what the matter was. Did I remember something? Did
I remember *her?* Her expression told me how much she
wanted me to, though being Rosie, she'd never admit it.

No, but . . . there'd been a helicopter outside the hospital window that I'd stared at just as fixedly. It had been
silver with red markings. I'd pondered its wonderful ability
to rise straight up, then swing gracefully off on its course
like a dancer in a hoop skirt. I thought of the ambulance
helicopters in MASH and the traffic helicopters that hovered
noisily over parkways . . . I thought frantically of whatever
I knew about helicopters, which wasn't much. And only
now did I remember Mike Portoff's voice in the hospital
room: "Did you hear me, Dinah? You had a child, it
showed in the physical. If you don't pay attention I can't be
responsible for . . ." I'd read that you could take a helicop-

ter to the airport or the beach . . . how perfect, to fly to
the beach! I promised myself to do it some time though it
certainly couldn't be cheap. But wasn't that what life was
about, setting goals and going after them? And now I was
free, wasn't I? Finally free!

I'd forgotten it all these years, till the helicopter flew
over the ashram. Now I know it was a sign of what happened a few days later. There was a clambake at a nearby
beach for the mommies, children, and friends. About sunset
we gathered at a wide, lovely beach where the kids were
filling a huge pit with seaweed. Some had brought guitars
and bongo drums, and something about the sound and the
salty fresh smell of the northern sea caught at me like a tug
on an old cobwebby door. George came, Jackie being mercifully out of town.

As dusk deepened, we drank beer and ate lobster and ears
of corn roasted among the coals and seaweed. The odd
collection of instruments made fetching music that echoed
out over the dark waters, so different from our bright,
sparkling southern ocean. Some began to dance, and I
watched Rosie in her white shorts swinging and swaying in
the firelight, a young girl of twenty who had found herself
with a baby, as I had, too young. I hoped this boyfriend
was better than the last one.

She was more real now, a lot more mine. We'd talked
and argued a lot about some of the same things I'd argued
about with the other kids. Men, sex, child care, female
identity, war, peace, God, and Mammon. I could hear my
voice behind my voice, like those old double-voiced records
of Patti Page. We were both right, we were both wrong.
Our two selves overlapped. I was claiming her for my
daughter; we were marking each other for life. Now her
face was not just the face of that sad waif who'd turned up
at the door or the angry girl meeting the mother who'd left
her; now it was the face of my kid. And I saw a face behind
her face, like the voice behind the voice.

They were haunting, those echoes—and a couple of beers couldn't explain the transported feeling I had as George and I danced in the firelight. But I felt drunk, and wild and happy as I hadn't in a long time. Here were my people—Rosie dancing, Penny half-asleep on a blanket with a couple of the other babies, and George, who might or might not have been necessary. The music pulsated louder and louder, and as George grasped my two hands to whirl me around he said, "Dinah." I knew what he wanted. George and I had never been much good at resisting each other and hadn't really bothered to try. I might have known it would happen. What I'd thought had faded to good-old-pals was as hot and urgent as ever. Would we ever outgrow it?

George took me by the hand, and we ran down the beach into a hollow full of beach grass, near a tidal pool. By now it was pitch-dark except for the flickering firelight we'd just left, and as we pulled at each other's various garments, we giggled and talked like the old friends we were.

"I don't know what it is about you, Dinah. I haven't even thought about you much, I mean in this way. I've lived without you all right."

"So have I, George. Very nicely, as a matter of fact."

"And it's not as though I'm really horny. I get it on with Jackie all the time."

By then we were more or less undressed and starting our slow, graceful wrestling. But the mention of her name made me burn with rage. God, he could make me jealous. I sank my fingernails into him. They were long, too—maybe I'd grown them for the purpose. I started to say, "I'll kill you for that," but by then I was helpless; he had me. Half sobbing, I said, "How could you say her name when you're making love to me?"

Said the bastard, "Because it makes you so excited."

And then, right as I was coming, so were the rest of the memories. Apparently all at once. Superimposed on this George was the young George I'd known before, saying,

"Because it makes you so excited." I heard him say it; the voice a shade higher, the body thinner and firmer and smoother. The erection almost indestructible, whereas this one was inclined to get weary from overwork.

I saw, at last, the little old house, the lumpy bed, the wardrobe where we hung our clothes. The little kitchen with the oilcloth-covered table, the pots and pans and cans of beer and jelly glasses and Tupperware, the candle stuck into the Chianti bottle for romantic dinners. The cheap Danish modern furniture with foam rubber cushions in avocado green, the gold shag rug on the floor.

In the corner of the bedroom was Rosie's crib, which we moved out for privacy when she got older. In the mornings she'd pull herself to her feet, hang on to the side of the crib and chirp, almost like a bird, "Mom-my, Mom-my." George sat up late at night over his books with a pot of coffee beside him at the kitchen table. The same glasses, but more hair. I'd ask, "Are you almost finished?" He'd say, "Dinah, stop it. Just give me fifteen minutes. I'll be right there." And I'd kiss his cheek, his nose, his ear. The back of his neck. He'd say, "How'll I ever pass the bar exams? Come on, I'm almost done." I'd slither onto his lap. "Hey, just let me finish this chapter." What a sweet struggle. If I were serious I'd pull down the top of my nightgown, and that was the end of the work. Or else we'd make love and then he'd go back to work again, while I drifted off to sleep. I remembered feeling love like the weather, everywhere around.

"George," I gasped, "I remember everything. I remember the house and us and Rosie and I even remember her being born. I remember the roses . . ." I felt his body all over mine in the dark, and it was though twenty years had peeled away. Each burst of the orgasm brought another burst of visions, like rockets that splinter into a hundred bright flowers. Rosie staggering across the lawn, falling onto all fours. Me working in the dime store, punching the keys of an old-fashioned cash register. A black-haired, flinty-eyed boss lady who didn't like me. Lunch at the coffee shop—a Coke and a BLT. Movies—Doris Day, Rock Hudson, Paul Newman. *Bikini Beach* and the Beatles . . .

Then there were bad days. I drank too much. I didn't clean the place up. I resented the baby, whining, pulling at me all the time, dropping cookies on the floor. I'd take her to the playground to meet my friends, Sadie and Megan. How bored we were, how trapped. How we longed for excitement, money, romance. Sometimes the three of us would go to one of our houses and get drunk while the kids played. And worse . . . oh, a lot worse. I got pregnant again. I didn't want the child. I didn't tell George. With Sadie's and Megan's counsel I jumped off chairs, took scalding hot baths, ran around the house. Then, desperate, we chose a night when George was out of town and I had a lot of gin and Megan took a knitting needle and . . .

"George, stop. Really stop." I didn't want to know any more. I was lucky I was alive. But the images kept exploding in my mind, darker and darker, more bloodstained now. I saw Rosie cowering against a door, heard my terrible voice yelling at her. She'd dropped something again. Spilled something. Another mess for me to clean up, the little bitch. I hit her and hit her, first on the bottom and then on the face. I saw the red welts rise and saw her small face contort with fear. I heard her scream, a scream that cut me to the heart. And not once but several times. Oh, those terrible long afternoons when the rest of the world was connected, only Rosie and I were alone. The pale sun on the bleached, dry lawn where I'd laid the clothes to dry. Rosie dirty, sweaty, covered with mud, and more mud in a plastic bucket. All over the clothes, very carefully. Then beating them with her muddy stick in a rage, like me. I grabbed her and shook her till her head snapped back. *"Don't . . . you . . . ever . . . dare . . . do . . . that . . . again!"* I shrieked. "Look at the clothes—*look at them!"* She

was as fragile in my hands as a little doll. "Now I have to
do them all over again! *All over again!*" I heard my own
crazy voice shrieking to the white sky. Then I wept; surely
I was losing my mind. I grabbed Rosie to me and the two
of us lay together on the bristly grass. "Mom-my, it hurts.
You hurt me." Oh, God. No wonder I had forgotten.

George and I lay together while I wept in the darkness.

"George, I can't bear it."

"It was our life, that's all."

"But I was awful . . . awful."

He said, "Oh, stop it. I did my part. I teased you with
Jackie." And the rage rose again. I saw him come in late
after I was in bed and not quite look at me. He looked
different, somehow. Smelled different. I was like an animal:
he was mine and nobody else's. I went for his throat and
tried to strangle him. He pulled himself free. "You're crazy,
Dinah. You're imagining things." Then funny phone calls
and secrecy. The evasive look, the small lie. I felt food stick
in my throat, felt my stomach turn over. I asked for the
truth and he denied it—then confessed. "Why not, Dinah?
You've turned into a shrew. If I go to another woman, it's
because I'm starved and you're not feeding me." I yelled,
"Why is it my job to make you happy? Why don't you
make me happy?" Then he left, taking a small suitcase. I
chased him down and found him with Jackie, a secretary at
the law school. Burst in and made a big scene. I might lose
him but I wouldn't make it easy. I went for her—hit her
and slapped her. George plunged between us and tried to
tear us apart. He finally grabbed me and took me home. I
had Jackie's slap on my cheek and I was laughing crazily.
"I won," I said. He was furious till I put my hands on his
pants very gently, and there it was waiting. He almost
cried. "I can't live like this. I can't get any work done. I'm
losing my mind." I said, "Then get rid of her."

We were on and off, he was in and out. Back and forth
between us. As I was back and forth with Rosie—loving

one minute, a maniac the next. Then guilty and buying her
things we couldn't afford. Trying to explain things: "Daddy's gone away for a while, but maybe he'll be back."
"When?" she'd ask. "I don't know. Soon. Let's lie down
together and read a story." We'd curl up together like the
two lost children we were, safe under covers. How clean
and sweet she was, how forgiving. I was all she had; she
had to trust me. I'd murmur the story, full of good resolutions. At least I had a vestige of conscience. "Rosie, I'm so
sorry I get mad at you. I act so terrible, I don't know why.
I'll never hit you again. I promise." And I'd cry.

We got up and washed off in the tidal pool before putting
our clothes back on. The figures were still dancing in the
firelight. I didn't know if we'd been here ten minutes or
two hours, but the drums had stopped. George asked, "Do
you remember the last evening?"

I remembered another fight, a bad one. Tears and shouts,
rage and threats. I tried to beat him up. Finally he hit me
—the only time he ever did. But this was something about
Rosie. I thought he loved her better than me, which by this
time was probably true. I shouted that they could both go
to hell and ran out to the car.

How angry I'd been, bursting with hate and revenge. I
could have killed them; my arm trembled to set fire to the
house, pull a trigger, push a knife into flesh. But though I
could feel the rage now all over again, I didn't know what
would have satisfied it. It seemed bottomless, insatiable.
Rosie and George just happened to be there. I kicked the
car, slammed the door. Turned the radio on high. I wanted
to weep with this endless anger which was like a curse on
my life. I must have always had it; it had come in with my
blood. Or perhaps with Troy and the dark house and my
mother slumped in a chair with the shades down. Or with
the car crash that killed them and left me nowhere. Flirting
at the roadhouse, fucking in the cars. I was lucky I'd met
George, as he'd pointed out. I still didn't know why he'd

wanted me. I knew nothing, only the red smoke. I slammed down the accelerator and the car tore down the road, faster and faster. Down toward town, past the station. In and out through the crooked streets at fifty, screeching around corners. They'd be sorry if something happened to me. I'd do it right—get on the parkway and really go fast. Fast as it would go, right down to the floor. Something was bound to happen that would stop the anger forever.

George held on to me as we walked back toward the bonfire. I was exhausted, as though I'd run a long, hard race.

By the time they found Willy, in a grove up above the house, it was too late. All they could do was take him to the clinic to be pronounced dead, then call and give me the news.

Baggie, I'm told, was magnificent, disaster being his métier. He was the one who diagnosed it, having had another case the day before at the clinic.

"He's eaten ackee," he told Conrad. He shook his head, his long, pouchy face puzzled. "Can't think why he'd do a thing like that, poor chap. Didn't he know about the bloody stuff?"

"Such a brilliant man," Geraldine said through her tears, "such a fine, distinguished doctor. Why does it happen to somebody like him?"

"Well, he was very unhappy," Con said miserably.

"Well, he did seem a bit pecky last night. We'd all had an awful lot to drink."

"Dinah was in the States with that woman and her baby and that man she's having the affair with," said Jessie. "She should have been here watching him."

This was the moral climate when I arrived, a day later. I was rigid with unknown fears, sweaty with terrible anticipation of I knew not what. It had started after the beach

party. Better if it had been grief, if I'd been able to cry.
Instead I was dumb and frozen, hardly able to take in what
was going on.

"You don't even cry," Jessie said, rubbing her puffy red
eyes. "What's the matter with you?"

"I don't know. People react in different ways."

"God. Fourteen years of marriage and you don't even
cry." Like Willy she's the kind of person who has a lot of
rules about the way things ought to be, and whose entire
life process consists of watching them be broken, one after
another. Poor Conrad felt the same way but pretended he
didn't. The man of the family now, he was the only one to
meet me at the airport. His hug was first tentative and then
desperate.

There were issues that had to be addressed quickly because Willy had already been dead over forty-eight hours,
and St. Pet's of course has complex funerary laws. If it was
suicide, the constabulary, the governor's office, the medical
board, and the diocese of St. Sylvie had to know. There was
a law against suicide in St. Petin, in violation of which
certain penalties were exacted. Notices had to be posted in
the public square, and the ombudsman would summon a
group of seventeen concerned citizens to rule on the nature
of the death and decide whether to allow burial in the
hallowed ground of St. Sylvie Cemetery. If permission was
granted, the tombstone would have to be made of wood,
not stone, and the inscription would be limited to ten
words, and only three ritual masses would be performed.
The grave had to be one man's length from the shadow of
the breadfruit tree, and a white oleander had to be planted
nearby if one was not already there, etc.

"It would be simpler to ship him to New York," said
Jason.

"No, they tell us what to do. It keeps everybody busy.
It's good really." Though the last thing made me pause—a
houngan had to touch his forehead three times at the grave.

Just to be on the safe side. Of course if it wasn't a suicide, it was no less complicated, just less colorful.

It appeared accidental, because Willy had not changed his will or made any financial moves. Nor had he stated what he wanted done with his remains. I don't think he expected to die. Others might, but surely there would be an exception for him. Doctors don't die.

So the question was why, for God's sake, had he eaten unripe ackee, which everybody knew was a deadly poison? We all looked at each other. Did he know? He never went shopping, never went to the market. He hadn't much concern or interest in food, except that it be delicious; how it got that way was somebody else's concern. Had nobody told him about ackee? And even if nobody had, why would he have done something so dumb as to just pick something off a tree and put it in his mouth?

I said, "Willy was always putting dangerous things into his mouth."

Jessie stormed, "It's not fair to bring up that ugly stuff when my father's not even in the grave."

"It might not be fair, but it's true." We always ended up talking about what was fair and what was true, and usually found that they were mutually exclusive. The kids were always on the side of fair. They forgot everything that had happened, and Willy became a flawless man tragically wronged by me because I hadn't sat him down and told him about ackee poisoning. Or Jessie and Con forgot, and Jason just got quieter and more miserable.

When Liz arrived, along with everybody else, the day of the funeral, she said to them, "You will not blame Dinah for Willy's death."

"I'll do what I want," Jessie said. "You can't tell me what to think." I tried reasoning with her, and she said, "You drove him crazy, you and your black magic." And I thought, Well, maybe she's right. Maybe I did. Emerelda was there by then, and she pressed my hand silently.

The seventeen concerned citizens decided that Willy had taken his own life, because it was inconceivable that anybody could live on St. Petin's and not know about ackee. So we had to have the fancier ceremony—St. Sylvie's, three extra hymns, and a different route to the grave, the one that went past the banana grove. There had to be a bamboo cross on the coffin, which would make it all right for Willy to lie in state on the altar, a local custom, so we could all kiss him good-bye as though he were a Mafia boss. There were of course certain local obeisances to the spirits.

At this Jessie said she wouldn't have any black magic in her father's funeral, and Conrad said it was a violation of the separation of church and state and he intended to raise hell with the constabulary and the diocese—until he was reminded that he was not in the United States.

Emerelda said, "Jessie, you got to do right by your daddy."

Liz said, "Jesus Christ, am I sick of all this. Let's just bury him." To me, "Well, Dinah, I hope we don't have to dance to the drums on Willy's grave."

I found the whole conversation very painful, as though I were being torn apart. I wasn't functioning very well anyway. I felt blocked off, surrounded by dimming screens— one paralyzing fear, one hopeless darkness. A few strange streaks of bright, pointless hope. If I didn't quite hear voices, certainly a lot of strange thoughts were coming into my head, and sometimes I seemed to hear a great confused clamor and chatter, like children playing in a schoolyard. Other times I was underwater, near the reef, but instead of fish there were spirits swimming around—hundreds of them, bright and beautiful and crazy, all pulling me in different directions. It was an effort to think straight.

"Go with the loas," I said.

There was a dreadful pause. Then Liz said carefully, "Dinah, you're being irrational."

I said, "You don't have anything to say about it."

Liz and I stared at each other in surprise. It had just popped out. She said, "Technically you're right. It's just that we've always . . . Never mind."

I sat with my face buried in my hands while the rest of them quarreled with Emerelda. I had never fought with Liz. She was my sister, my other half. I knew other families that split when someone died, but I'd never thought this would happen to us.

The morning of the funeral there was a flash thunderstorm, and by the time we'd gathered at the church, everything was bright and clean. Local law required us to wear black, and so clad we went into the plain, whitewashed church up on the grassy hill and filed inside where wooden chairs were set up.

Willy lay in state on the altar, his coffin banked with oleander and hibiscus, gardenias and passionflowers. He was dressed in a three-piece gray suit of tropical worsted and Gucci loafers; his wedding ring was on his left hand, in his right, a tiny applicator of Willy's glue. The slanted rays of the sun shone on his white shirt, along with the tiniest sprinkle of certain magic herbs (sneaked into the casket by Emerelda) and the tiny head of the silver "heart pin," which ensured his death and removed any possibility of live burial, zombification, etc.

The service was part Catholic, part Anglican, and part voodoo, and the sermon by the deacon, Brother Billy Pineapple, had a touch of Southern Baptist with philosophical overtones. Referring to Willy's death, he spoke of the danger of eating strange foods and how the mouth must be respected and only "excellent things" put in it. "But somehow St. Petin failed this fine man," said Brother Billy. "He gave us everything, and we could not give back enough to make him want to live." St. Petin would never forget his great medical skills, his tireless devotion to the poor and sick, his patience, sympathy, and wisdom. At that I really began to choke up.

All our neighbors were in the church, and when we, the family, filed up one at a time to kiss Willy good-bye, Geraldine came too. Then as we went outside and formed the funeral procession, who came creeping up but the Auschwitz killer. I didn't want him along with us, but there was nothing I could do about it.

I'd asked Mac Valpey, Baggie, Rickie, and Danny to be pallbearers with, of course, Con and Phil. Now they picked up the casket and led the way down the grassy hill toward the town, along King's Road to the main street of English Town for the one-mile walk to St. Sylvie's Cemetery. I was amazed at how many of us there were in that long line. Besides Liz and me, and Jessie and Jason, and Eureka pushing Charlotte in her wheelchair, and little Bornean Ping and Emerelda, there was the French family, the strange drunken couple, the three Dutch women, Herr Auschwitz, and Jerry and Geraldine, who was weeping visibly. There were the people from the clinic in their white coats, and Winnie, Christophena, Regine, and Lionel, a few town officials with red satin chest-ribbons, Bilge, the bartender from The Parrot Fish, and a whole lot of other people who, I guess, just felt like joining us. I'll never forget that procession—marching slowly along to the beat of the drums, like the sound of our hearts. They had started at dawn and would not cease until Willy was underground. As we went along the main street, all the kids and shop-keepers and sailors and fishermen and hookers—everybody lined up by the side of the road and threw flowers at the casket, and Willy seemed to be loved in death as he never was when he was alive. There was something magnificent about this ornate and somber ritual taking place against that spare and simple background.

The cemetery was in a grove of trees near the beach, so that Willy would be forever within sight of the blue, spar-kling Caribbean. We gathered around the plot and Brother Billy Pineapple did some more mumbo jumbo. There was

one bad moment. Emerelda and the houngan came popping
out to toss a string of red beads and a few dried flowers on
the coffin (to appease the cemetery loa, Baron Samedi), and
as soon as they did, Jessie actually jumped up and grabbed
the string of beads from Emerelda's hand and threw it into
the bushes. There was a scuffle while the houngan ran to
retrieve it, the drummer kept beating, and the earth shov-
eler stood waiting with his shovelful of earth, or rather
sand.

Emerelda said to Jessie, "I brought you up from when
you were a baby, Jessie. Please don't pay no disrespect to
your daddy." Jessie only folded her arms and said we should
go on without the beads, and when Brother Billy looked at
me, I only shrugged. Emerelda shook her head and dropped
her eyes, and Liz, standing next to Jessie, avoided my eye.

After the burial and a few more prayers and hymns,
everyone returned to our house for the customary lavish
spread for the whole neighborhood. Everyone had brought
something, and our girls had laid out an enormous buffet
of roast goat, cold fish with mayonnaise, bowls of pawpaws
and guavas and "pears," fried bananas, fried flying fish, red
beans and rice, roasted yams, sliced mangoes, lime chicken,
and more—with lots of rum and beer to wash it down. It
was a tribute to Willy. Half the island was there, many of
the mourners his grateful patients.

I felt very strange and disoriented. I'd sometimes imagined Willy's funeral, which I knew I'd be at someday, but
I'd thought it would take place in Episcopal Hospital somehow, surrounded by doctors in green scrub suits and Corfam
shoes. Willy would be laid out on an operating table draped
in a sheet while we all moved past him in face masks,
murmuring farewells. What were we doing in this strange
place, with all this delicious but peculiar food with drums
beating in the distance, and a definitely spiritual atmosphere?

Mac Valpey said, "You know, Dinah, to me he died

before, the day he screwed up the fingers. This is just some kind of finalization."

It was true. St. Pet's had never been his world; some other half-mad Willy had come here with me. My Willy hadn't been around in a long time. For the first time the tears came, and I felt a lot better.

Then Geraldine came over to me. "He was a wonderful doctor, Dinah. I never saw him impatient with a child or a sick person, or anybody unless they bullshitted him. He was never snotty to the nurses, not once, and he did more cleaning up and dirty work than any doctor I ever saw. He had a way of laying his hand on a sick child's head or a person's shoulder that seemed to make them better just from the touch. He said he got more satisfaction from the clinic here than he ever did from his famous operation," and so on till we were both crying.

Then I hugged Jason—he actually let me hug him, he was so sad—and Jessie smiled and said, "I feel better now. I thought you weren't human or something."

So we all cried and talked about Willy and how wonderful he'd been—only exaggerating a little. Even Liz dug back into that failed marriage and found a few happy moments and sniffled a little herself. Phil sat playing strange songs on his little square guitar all about his brother and how he'd loved him, and it didn't really matter that it wasn't true. And old Charlotte smiled and said it was a good thing God took Uncle Earl because the poor old man was getting quite disgusting. Now she had only me, and I resolved to keep her with me wherever I was—which was the next thing I had to think about. I was a widow not yet forty—though comfortably fixed, and with a lover. Things could be a lot worse.

Except that every once in a while I shuddered as though a ghost had walked right through me; my stomach churned with nameless fears and unspeakable horrors. I hardly ate anything and rum didn't help.

After a while I left the reception and went back to the bedroom Willy had turned into a study. I'd only been in it a couple of times, since he had kept it padlocked. It was very neat and very strange. It reminded me of something . . . the bareness, the locked metal file, the locked desk. It made me think of those rooms in movies about nameless Third World countries where they torture people. Except for the bookcases he'd had made and the telephone and the computer. Everything except the telephone was locked.

I went into our bedroom and went through everything of Willy's I could find and finally discovered a small key buried in a bottle of aspirin. Then later, after the good-byes, when everybody was asleep, Liz and I went back into the study. In our black dresses and bare feet, we looked like a couple of witches, unlocking his heart at last. The key opened one desk drawer, which contained directions to find the next key. Then the file drawers, the other desk drawers, the bookcases, and finally the computer. Liz knew how to work it, and she found something called GRAND PLAN stored in it. Then more of the scavenger hunt. The bookcases were full of books about World War II, the Nazis, Stalin, and so forth.

I'd been so relieved when Willy started his literary project that I'd hardly thought, or cared, what it might be about. I'd assumed it was about his epoxy, or maybe an exposé of the New York medical establishment, or maybe something psychoanalytical. But he'd insisted on complete secrecy for his "investigative" process.

Finally we found a little map leading to a certain spot in the sand near the sea grape, where we found, not too deeply buried, a metal box containing a manuscript. Liz gave me a funny look as we went back to the verandah and turned on a lamp.

"Shall I look first?"

I knew before I read a word that it would be pretty bad. Liz looked at it and put it down, saying, "Oh, poor Willy."

It was called *Auschwitz Lives,* and after I'd read two pages

I closed it and gave it back to her. It was all here. He'd
died on page 249, leaving his life work unfinished. And
nobody had known about it.

Baggie had told me how drunk and distraught Willy had
been after the disastrous dinner party at Geraldine's and
how upset he'd been to learn about poor old Rolfe Wertzheimer. They'd organized a search party and found him
("From the looks of things, Dinah, I'd say the poor chap
didn't have an easy time"), and they'd fixed the time of his
death at 11:22 P.M. For the first time I began to really put
it together. Willy had died at the same time that I was at
the beach party *fucking George and getting my memories back*. I
went over it again and again (Liz was chortling over *Auschwitz Lives*), but the information was relentless.

"Dinah, a passionate affair with a Nazi, you naughty
girl."

"I killed him," I whispered.

"What?" She turned the page. "Lord, poor Willy. Look,
he's got me fucking the whole Kremlin."

I got up and ran off the verandah, back down onto the
beach. How could I have left him? I should have stayed
here . . . And those precious, long-hidden memories were
only torture. I wished I could give them back. I couldn't
stop thinking about George, and feeling all the anger, and
remembering how I'd treated poor little Rosie. I'd feel the
rage, see her little, white, frightened face, feel my hands go
up in the air . . . I wanted to scream or tear out my eyes,
even walk straight out to sea and not come back. They were
too fresh, too raw. I'd had no time to get used to them,
soften them somehow and persuade myself I wasn't so bad.
Maybe I never would. I might have to live with them
forever, red-hot pokers in my brain. How lucky I'd been
before I remembered a single thing, during the early years
with Willy. He'd been right.

"We're starting from right here, Dinah," I remembered
him saying. "Today is square one."

It had been a beautiful idea, but it hadn't worked. Both

of our pasts trickled down like rain from a leaky roof. The people who refused to disappear—Sally, Liz, Rosie and George, Phil and Ping. They just kept turning up. And I loved Liz; I couldn't dispense with her as he'd wanted. A beautiful, stupid idea. A little island of foolish peace in life's troubled waters.

Then Liz was next to me, her arms around me. Like the rest of the world, she thought I was grief-stricken.

"It's not what you think. It's the memories. They're driving me crazy."

"Well, now you're like the rest of us. You'll get used to them; they kind of settle down and get covered by other things." She gave me a hug—brisk, businesslike Liz. "Come on, I think you need a jolt of rum, and let's see if there's any of that food left." She whispered, "Time, Dinah. Every day will be a little better."

"There's another thing," I said slowly. "Every single thing the loas have said has come true."

She looked at me with exasperation, bemusement, then a sort of phony tolerance. "Is that so?"

"It's true. The rest of my memories came back at exactly the moment Willy died."

"Really. Remarkable. Dinah, listen. I know it's soon to make plans and nobody's forcing you. But FK has a great therapist, Lucia Lilt, and I think it would be a good idea if you—"

"You know I'm telling the truth. Don't tell me you don't remember what we talked about in the jail cell that night. And the things I understood about when you were crazy. You know something strange has been going on. In fact I'm not so sure you were crazy at all. It was more like we had a memory pool that made you and everybody else think you were crazy, and Emerelda thinks—"

"Oh, shit." Her arm dropped. "All right, everything Emerelda said the spooks said can be construed by a great deal of twisting around to have vaguely to do with things that happened—sometimes. Spooks will not solve your problems."

"You didn't answer me."

In the moonlight, Liz looked very stern with her golden hair pulled back into a knot. "All I know is what my memories have taught me. I have to keep working and earning money till I drop in my tracks. Anything else scares me. That's my strength, not jumping around the magic fire." She frowned. "And you'd better learn it too."

"You'd better know," I said, "that those damn spirits have affected every single thing that's happened to us."

Liz ran back toward the verandah. "My butt!" she flung over her shoulder. "My God. You were both crazy!"

That's the last thing I remember that made any sense. I must have passed out, but I felt as though I'd been hit on the head or butted by an angry bull. I staggered, then fell over—and after that I had no more control over what was in my head. I was like a stage for a lot of crazy actors whose lines made no sense, but I couldn't get rid of them. I wanted to pull my head off, dash my brains against a wall. I dimly heard Liz calling my name in some alarm. For a brief period things came in focus, though through some otherworldly lens. I was a raging boar, I think; I galloped up onto the terrace, where I picked up a wine glass and bit into it. Not the wine—the glass. No pain. No blood. I enjoyed it. Chewed it up and swallowed it.

Then they put me to bed, and a great peace descended. What strange dreams I had. My head was filled with the loas. The drums kept up their slow, incessant beat. I hardly knew if I was asleep or awake for most of that strange night. Through the billowing white tent of mosquito netting I saw faces, flickering lights, long shafts of shadow that seemed to pass over me like still chords of organ music.

Sometimes I'd hear voices.

Liz's—"I'm worried about her. I've never seen her like this."

Jessie's—"Well, no wonder. She has no identity, and
now that Dad's dead, she's coming apart. She needs to find
meaningful work."

And Jason's—"Oh, shit. She's just sad, that's all."

More murmurs and speculations about what to do with
me. Then Emerelda said, "I will care for her. I understand
this malady."

Was I sick? Time seemed to stretch out, loop back, and
compress again. I could see its very shape; I could have
drawn a picture of it. I could see love as a river, and memories like islands in it . . . and I was on a high cliff, able
to see everything.

I saw Baggie's glass eye and two front teeth shining as he
handed me a couple of pills and a glass of water.

"I say, Dinah, I want you to take this." I knocked it out
of his hand. "Oh, you are naughty. Don't you want to get
better?"

Something about getting the psychiatrist from San Juan.
Christophena brought trays of food I didn't touch, then
Liz's face loomed close.

"Listen, Dinah. I don't know what's the matter with you,
but I'm taking the three kids back to New York. Jason
wants to go back to Dalton. I'll take care of everything."
She put her hand on my forehead. "Come back soon. It's
not good for you here."

I seemed to be functioning on two levels: the world as
I'd always known it and some dark, trackless region where
I descended from time to time, usually against my will.
Here the drums beat and the hounsi danced; here the gods
appeared in their primitive forms—the cigar-smoking
Baron Samedi, the shy bride, the wise old man, the snake.
All walked before me as though in introduction. The drums
beat, the chords of shadow passed over me as though I were
walking down some ancient pergola past a long row of
columns. Then I'd hear the houngan's bells and his rattle
and the tiny, myriad clicking of his beads and snake bones.
Sometimes, in the night, I'd see Emerelda muttering over

some potion or fragrant dust of dried plants which she'd
sprinkle on me, chanting incomprehensibly. Sometimes I'd
come to.

"Emerelda, what the hell's going on?"

"You are passing over into a state of high wisdom, Mistress."

"Am I going crazy?"

"Oh, no." She put her little dark hand on my arm and
her black eyes shone. "Just the opposite. You have been
chosen. But you must try to understand and try to open
yourself."

My nights were voodoo Valhallas on All Souls' Night.
Through my room sailed snakes, vampires, winged devils,
dogs with goats' horns, goats with dogs' feet, Sally with her
penis, Ada Grace in her galoshes. Women with black hats
and faces chalked white moved silently by my bed. On my
walls were vévés, those curly white voodoo pictures. Zom-
bies marched; souls flew in and out of bodies, in and out of
bottles, back into coffins. The tremendous amount of information began to fall into some order. There were good souls
and bad ones. Certain things could happen to them . . . I
tried to grasp it all. It was like an exhausting, speeded-up
cram course in civilization.

One night Willy came. He appeared in the room as I lay
in bed, pushed the mosquito netting aside, and sat down
. . . but then we seemed to be back in our old bedroom in
New York. It was like the old days. I could even hear the
traffic on Columbus Avenue. What a relief! Was it a dream;
had none of it ever happened? I longed for it to be that
happier time when Jason was young. In a moment I'd hear
his infant cry from the next room. Willy was wearing his
green scrub suit, mask dangling, scalpel in hand; he
smelled of formaldehyde.

"Now Dinah, I want you to listen carefully. I know it
seems like a stupid thing to do, but I was just tired of being
crazy."

"What, Willy?" I sat up.

"We'd had a lot to drink—plus a few little pinks and blues. Oh, I know, I know. Baggie and I shared some secrets. But Lord, after hearing poor Wertzheimer . . . I didn't think I could get through another day. I needed you badly and you weren't there."

"Oh, Willy." Tears came into my eyes.

"I knew about ackee. For the first time I had the nerve to just . . . do it. I was too drunk to really think about it. I'd lost you and I'd lost the Revelation. I had nothing. God, it was terrible. I got back to the house and banged on the door, but they were all asleep or still out. So I went back to the woods and died very unpleasantly. Shall I describe it to you?"

"No!" I grabbed his arm, but he pulled away.

"I don't have long. Tell me, Dinah, are you happy?"

"No, I'm miserable. I think I'm going crazy."

"I wanted to be close to you. I was jealous as hell of the guy in Boston. At one point in my muddled head I thought if I ate it, I could get rid of him. I sat there and said, 'Die, George. Die, die!' "

"You can't play with magic, Willy. You have to know how to use it."

"I know about medication, for Christ's sake!"

But there was something wrong with his hand; he kept hiding it. "Willy, get in bed. Let's make love." Then I saw that his hand was missing two fingers, and to my horror, they were stuck in his breast pocket with the ballpoint pens.

"I can't, Dinah. I have a killing schedule. I haven't even had time to stick my fingers on. Lord, it's as bad as Episcopal and just as much shit goes on. Though this practice is . . . very peculiar." Then he kissed me. "Good-bye, Dinah. I always loved you."

Poof!

Emerelda seemed to think it was just a dream. Well, it probably was. "You must learn, Mistress Doc. You must believe. They will strike again if you don't. Now the memories are part of you. You must hold them in your heart. You know how dangerous they are; you know Mister Wakefield died for them. Now you have been chosen."

"But I'm not sure I want to be chosen."

She sprinkled some dried hibiscus petals on me. "That makes no difference." She leaned close to me. "Please," she whispered, "you know the happiness is there. You must allow it in."

I can't document the next few weeks . . . or was it months? It's too complicated. I was on, then off. I believed, then I didn't. The dream about Willy got me out of bed, at least; it was the first thing that seemed even partly real. But once up, I reminded myself that it hadn't been real at all and that Willy was dead; so fevered and confused was my mind that the real and the unreal shifted back and forth like images on a screen—dark, light, daguerreotype brown, sizzling reds and blues like heat-sensitive photographs.

I had to get sane enough to go back to New York and see the kids and deal with Willy's estate, the house, and everything else. Now it was I who pushed toward health. It was probably a good thing, because I soon was able to detect a certain rough logic about what was wrong with me. Whenever I accepted the loas as perfectly natural and reasonable entities, like a tribe of rather peculiar relatives, I was contented and even cheerful. The minute skepticism or rationality triumphed, I was miserable—depressed, panicky, old as Methuselah, crawling with fears and imaginary ailments. Then I knew it was all there was—there was no point in living any longer. I began to think about killing myself.

I'd go back to bed to be pummeled by Baron Samedi and the guedés again, along with my own damn memories, like a brain fever; again and again I'd go over the night I'd followed George to Jackie's, or the scene in the yard with

Rosie. And it was Rosie I thought about most. The memories, the guilt, and the loas got all mixed up. I'd see a chicken with Rosie's head, watch myself bite it off . . . See a snake eat Penny while the loas all laughed and cheered. And speaking of snakes, one night I was raped by one, the snake Damballa, and so sick and depraved was I that I actually enjoyed it—more than I like to admit.

If the loas won, I'd wake up and think, Oh, what the hell? I'll go with them. I can't take it. They're stronger. And then I'd feel a jolt of happy confidence. Wave cheerfully at Geraldine as she rode off on her motorbike. Eat a big breakfast served by a beaming Regine, for I'd lost fifteen pounds. I'd write letters, make phone calls, start making plans to go back, find an apartment, put my life together. I felt optimistic and indestructible. The usual fears—disease, disaster, horrors of all kinds—shriveled up to near-invisibility. I had my people, my mysterious world, my closed curtain again. Not entirely closed, but half-closed, blowing open, beckoning and teasing.

Whenever so-called rationality overtook me, I'd look at myself in the mirror and say, "Oh, now really, this is ridiculous. You've just got island fever." Then—zonk! Rage, black depression, twanging, merciless, incapacitating anxiety. I'd stay in bed, brooding or crying, or sit on the beach trying to get the nerve to drown myself. I'd run into the sapphire water, swim out, put my head down . . . and then turn and swim back to shore. I'd tell Winnie I didn't like her cooking, take the car over Lionel's protests, and drive all over St. Pet's, which, save our corner of it, turned out to be barren, empty, almost ominous.

Occasionally Geraldine and I went out and got drunk at The Parrot Fish during one of Jerry's periodic disappearances. One night after three rum punches I told her I'd never loved Willy, we'd had a marriage of convenience. He'd stuck me with his house and his children and I'd gotten my revenge.

She was shocked. "You don't mean that."

"Oh, I do—every word."

"You're just upset over the terrible way he died."

"No, I wanted to get rid of him so I could go to my real lover in Boston, so I put a wanga on him."

First she believed me, then she remembered she was a member of a healing profession. "Really, Dinah. Then why don't you go to this lover? He must be waiting for you."

But I wasn't sure if I loved George either. If I went back there I might do it, break into his apartment as I'd done before and murder them both in bed. Worse, even if George got rid of Jackie, I wasn't sure if I wanted this ordinary, paunchy, balding, middle-aged man who was forever watching the Red Sox on television.

"I strongly suggest you make an appointment with Baggie. I think you're getting the Change."

I began to cry. "Fuck Baggie."

"Your husband's only been dead a month. You need more time. It probably doesn't seem real. You didn't mean all those things, I know."

But it had never seemed realer. That was the trouble. Where was that obedient, doe-eyed female picking up plastic toys and making popovers for dinner? How could I have been such a doormat, put up with people like Portoff, and Sally for God's sake, even Willy? Never angry, never resentful. How contented that bland creature had been, ordering groceries, working in the hospital gift shop. Dumb, blind—and lucky!

"This is where it ends, Geraldine. Two burned-out middle-aged broads getting drunk at a dumpy bar in the Caribbean. What do we have, anyway? I have a man who lives with somebody else, and you have one who treats you like shit."

"I seriously think you need estrogen therapy. I have my fulfilling work, and if you're smart you'll find something to do so you won't sit around feeling sorry for yourself."

I blew my nose. "I don't know what's the matter with me. I think I'm coming unwound."

Back home in bed, I'd pay. The loas would be all over the mosquito netting along with the bugs and come right through it. There was one nameless flying half-pig half-cat, which screeched and howled . . .

"I give up," I said finally. "You win." Not good enough —six headless white goats clung to the netting, tails, hooves, and zozos all sticking through, screeching and braying. "I believe in you, okay?" I had to get some sleep or I really would go mad.

As I said it, I knew they were perfectly real. It was absurd to suppose otherwise. Of course they were. Though uninvited, they were urgently, vividly in my mind. It was proof enough for me. I only doubted them out of the so-called rational thought I'd learned from Willy, and it certainly hadn't done him any good. I needed the mystery and haunting truth of the loas more. I'd gotten used to living with something that couldn't be explained.

After that I slept peacefully, blissfully, for the first time in weeks.

Dinah

___

I still live in the house on West Seventy-eighth Street, but I might sell it next year when Jason goes to college. I don't really need the space anymore. Old Charlotte died last year, and though Rosie and Penny were here for a while, now they've moved to Hoboken with Rosie's new boyfriend. He calls himself Krishna, and I just hope he's better than the last one. He and Rosie are running a Laundromat.

Jackie died last year. What a shame! Some mysterious thing just knocked her right off. Just as she was peeling the clothes off her middle-aged body one night, and George lay abed waiting for her. It must have been a terrible shock.

George cried for three whole days, then was right back on Amtrak. I must say he wasn't terribly devastated. Now, bit by bit, it comes out that they had all sorts of problems. Now he talks of making a change, of moving to New York. Do I want this paunchy, middle-aged man watching the Red Sox on TV? Well, yes. I think I do. We suit each other. And there's never enough time to reminisce. We're forever saying, "Remember the time when . . . ?" He doesn't make a lot of money, and he doesn't care—says he prefers the slow track.

He's perfectly at home with the loas and has even expressed an interest in coming along on one of my annual pilgrimages to Haiti. He's remarkably close to being ready. Maybe he could just slip into it without going through all the misery they put me through after Willy's death—now referred to by Liz and the older kids as "Dinah's breakdown." Of course it's easier if you don't fight it, and I fought hard because I learned to think from Willy. Jason didn't fight at all; he just slipped into his state of grace like a fish on the reef. I think he needed it pretty badly.

But I'm not so sure George does. You need a certain amount of anguish to want to embrace the spiritual life. George, out in the yard broiling a steak, singing in the shower, helping Penny with her homework, is a contented man. Damballa says there's no point in bothering with him. An occasional possession, but not the big serious stuff. Rosie's a good candidate; there's always been a darkness in her. But Penny is just like George—a cheerful, easygoing little girl with straight brown hair. She's in the first grade now, and she has the lead in the Christmas pageant!

Every so often George broods about Jackie. He should have married her, he says. It would have made her happy. I just shrug. And one night he said—staring at me as though the proverbial light bulb had just gone on over his head—"Dinah, you did it, didn't you?"

"Did what?" I was taking up a hem.

"Put some kind of hex on Jackie."

"How ridiculous." But I stuck my finger.

"You did, didn't you?"

"Of course not. I thought you didn't believe in black magic."

"I never said that." True, he hadn't. I'd just assumed he didn't. What kind of man was this, anyway? "I can't prove it, Dinah. But I have a very strong suspicion." His blue eyes were like spears from the sky. He shook his head. "You're guilty as sin, Dinah. How did you do it?"

"Come on, George. You're raving."

"Tell me," he whispered, running one hand down my blouse. "I want to know."

But I could never tell him, if he played with my left breast all night. I wanted to laugh. If I was guilty, so was he. He'd better not be. But the whole conversation was simply ridiculous. Jackie died of a pulmonary embolism, and George got in touch with her family and arranged the funeral.

Conrad is in medical school, no surprise to any of us. And Jessie has a small part in an off-Broadway play. For a long time it was hard for me to understand why they were so angry at me when Willy died, but now I do, and peace has been made. Now Jessie's in love and absolutely beautiful and as impossible as ever. There are more important things to her than the intricacies of her relationship with her step-mother. I pray that if she falls, she doesn't land too hard.

Jason is the only one who understands about the loas. He came to Haiti with me the last two times. Even the Gran Mait is amazed by his spiritual capacity, the distance he can go before tripping over "reason." My wonderful son! He's sixteen now and wants to study medicinal plant life in the Caribbean. He's hooked on life in the islands and will probably be spending a lot of time there.

I found very soon that I needed something to do. Just sitting around and chatting with invisible spirits was not enough. Erzilie tried to persuade me to be a sort of fashionable society mambo, conducting voodoo ceremonies for the rich and taking up prophecy very seriously. Or I could pretend to read the Tarot, and she'd whisper the things in my ear. But I don't trust her. She'd forget or find something better to do—and there I'd be with a blank future and an angry client. So I became an interviewer at Finders Keepers.

I've told Liz I have no interest in management. She asked, "Dinah, don't you long for power? Don't you want to make tons of money and push people around, like I do?"

I only laughed. I've tried to explain a couple of times, but it makes her very angry. "I can't believe you still think about that crazy stuff, particularly after all the trouble it caused," she says, as though spirituality is something I should have outgrown. But she merely scolds; she doesn't look grave or try to drag me off to Lucia Lilt. Somewhere in Liz is still a tiny spark, though she'd die rather than admit it. No mention of it at the office, period. Liz won't allow any religion or spirituality at all.

That's not always easy. The other day I interviewed a woman who appeared to have everything, personally and materially (or everything our society considers important), but she's tortured by the idea that there must be something else. She's adopted and thinks that if she found her real parents, she'd be happy. My job is to try to help her. But I know that even if we're successful, and if the parents turn out to be decent people happy to be reunited with their long-lost daughter, she'll still have that gnawing little worm of discontent. And it's true of the woman who wants to get married so badly, and the man desperate to "get into the loop" and make a lot of money. I could save them a lot of grief. But Liz says, "No loas, Dinah, or you're fired." Well, she's the boss, and she must be doing something right.

A large sign in the waiting room says, WE'RE NOT SELLING HAPPINESS—JUST FRIENDLY CONNECTIONS. Keep the expectations down, Liz is always saying. They're the purple poison! But how hard it is; everybody wants to drink. Oh, the faces that come through the big glass doors, the voices on the phone, lonely, frightened, desperate. You'd think we were selling the Holy Grail! "We supply the (friend, grandmother, perfect date, etc.), you supply the rest," we're supposed to say at the end of the interview. Then they get that look of desperate hope. Maybe this will do it. Maybe this time! Stop the pain; give me whatever-it-is. The therapy didn't work, the divorce, the remarriage, the baby, the new job. The emptiness is still there.

I remember a nice woman who reminded me a little of Mrs. Rappaport.

"I don't know what it is, Ms. Wakefield . . . Dinah. I just feel lonely . . . empty. Disappointed. My husband is very involved in his business; my children have grown up. We've moved a thousand miles from my hometown. I began to think, maybe I need a friend—another woman with similar tastes. Do you think . . . ?"

Easy! From the computer we plucked another fifty-seven-year-old affluent Manhattan WASP AvAt (as opposed to UnAt or VeAt) female interested in Impressionist art, Szechuan cooking, and French antiques. They met at the office with our blessing. Six months later she was back, looking slightly abashed.

"Oh, a complete success. Carol and I are very dear friends! It's just . . . well, we were both saying the other day—we had a few drinks with lunch—that we both have feelings of disappointment, as though we'd been promised things we never got." This from a woman in a mink coat, designer clothes, and diamond rings. "It seems so silly. We're both involved in charities, so it's not as though we don't *help*. I think it's because we don't have grandchildren. Our children are all so involved with their careers, and well, I don't dare hint anymore, my daughter gets so mad. But Carol and I were thinking, perhaps there are a couple of poor children we could watch after school till their mothers get home, something like that. Dark ones are perfectly acceptable, though we'd rather not catch anything, you understand. Do you think . . . ?"

No problem. These are the seekers who never seem to find. And there are more of them all the time, from every walk of life. Not just rich housewives, either. But stockbrokers, college kids, parking lot attendants, ballet dancers, people on crutches. Librarians, newspaper reporters, plumbers, insurance salesmen . . . But very few people of the cloth—ministers, rabbis, priests—and more women than men, and very few artists.

. . .

After my "breakdown" was over, and Emerelda was convinced that I'd accepted the loas in my heart, she and I went
to Haiti for the first time. I stayed at the Ollofson, a white
Victorian house that sits up on a hill overlooking Port-au-
Prince. (Emerelda always stays with her own people, and
now I do too.) The Ollofson is a gathering place for the
local elite—mostly *blancs,* who collect in the lounge every
day for rum and tonics. Duvalier was still in power, and I
didn't like what I'd read about the local politics. I stood in
my room by the window watching Emerelda walk down the
hill, scared to death, wondering what the hell I was doing
there. I could be shot dead in the town square and nobody
would know the difference.

Then, suddenly, they came—like fish on a reef. I
couldn't summon them or communicate with them the way
I can now, but in their peculiar fashion they were welcom-
ing me. I felt like a kid in a candy shop, watching them,
listening to their songs and nonsense, their schoolyard chatter, their dark serious tones like chords . . . I heard the
drums beating in the distance. When I went downstairs and
out onto the verandah, nervously glancing around for
bloodthirsty Tonton Macoutes, they all came with me and
swam around in the moonlight as I stood there, protecting
me. I'd never been so safe, and there might have been a
time when I was happier, but I can't remember when. It
was then that I learned that many of the terrible Tontons
are in fact houngans, the sacred priests, which was the
beginning of the knowledge that good and evil are the same,
opposite sides of the same thing, sometimes even the same
side. Among other things, it explains a lot about Willy.

I became a mambo at a special ceremony, deep in the
jungle. I'd pictured a kind of Disney forest, with talking
chipmunks and cute bluebirds. But it's a rough, hard place,
full of flies and snakes and mosquitoes and wild dogs and

spirits. Strange shrubs block the path, heavy vines hang overhead. There are screeching birds and peculiar lizards, poisonous toads, and graveyards and little altars everywhere, so that with all the loas and guedés flying around and an occasional zombie, you are actually *part of the dead.* In the jungle, it's perfectly, *ridiculously* obvious that there's very little difference between life and death and there are many states in between. And everybody who dies ends up a spirit of one sort or another, which has nothing to do with being so-called good or bad but is really much more *random,* which I already knew from the amnesia. But when Willy talked of noble doctors saving lives, I used to think, how wonderful, how important! And now I know it isn't that important at all.

We marched through the pitch-dark jungle by the light of seventeen candles borne by hounsi carrying red birds in cages. But I can't tell about the secret initiation ceremony, which took many days, and I'm bound to silence about many aspects of that strange world I'm privileged to enter once a year, though the loas are around all the time as they always were, enchanting as ever, pesky as ever! And I learned about the wangas that were on all of us, and how Legba chose me years ago to fulfill his "great and sacred purpose" of *saving the children.* He took my memories so I could save Liz's children, and then Liz started FK and saved *my* children, so to speak, all the lost people. And Liz and I had to learn the sacred concept of *caring* because we'd both been such horrible mothers. But the loas began fooling around with the memories as though they were toys, and it's a miracle Liz and I survived all this. And "all this" makes a lot more sense in the Haitian jungle than it does in New York.

I'm a little skeptical about this part, because I can't believe the loas are capable of carrying through such a complicated, long-term wanga involving a bunch of *blancs* thousands of miles from home. They'd like to think they could, but they're about as efficient as Penny. But no matter. I just know that I come back from Haiti every year renewed: cleaned, aired out, deeply at peace. Throughout the year, bit by bit, something dark and scratchy as city soot, silent as cancer, slowly builds up, so that by the fall, when we always go, I'm packed and ready and hounding Emerelda to leave a week or two early.

If only Liz remembered! But her mind has closed down. Even after a few glasses of wine, all she can say is, "Dinah, I don't know what pink dress with the buttons, for Christ's sake, or making out with who in cars? Jesus, you're weird." It's gone. She's embarrassed about the possessions and says she must have been drunk or stoned or something—though we both know she wasn't.

But she still has her antic sense of humor. The other day, with the blackest of grins, she brought a small, shy girl into my office. She couldn't have been more than twenty-one or twenty-two, and she'd come in bewildered, looking for help. Liz told her she had just the person for her to see.

Her name was Betty—or so she thought. She'd found herself in a limousine coming in from Kennedy. That was last Tuesday, and she can't remember a thing before that.